MEEK AND MILD

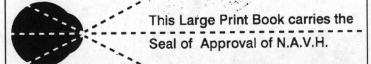

MEEK AND MILD

OLIVIA NEWPORT

THORNDIKE PRESS
A part of Gale, Cengage Learning

GALE
CENGAGE Learning·

Farmington Hills, Mich • San Francisco • New York • Waterville, Maine
Meriden, Conn • Mason, Ohio • Chicago

GALE
CENGAGE Learning®

LIBRARY OF CONGRESS CATALOGING-IN-PUBLICATION DATA

Newport, Olivia.
  Meek and mild / by Olivia Newport. — Large print edition.
    pages cm. — (Amish turns of time ; book 2) (Thorndike Press large print Christian romance)
  ISBN 978-1-4104-7640-1 (hardcover) — ISBN 1-4104-7640-5 (hardcover)
  1. Amish—Fiction. 2. Large type books. I. Title.
  PS3614.E686M44 2015
  813'.54—dc23   2014048604

Published in 2015 by arrangement with Barbour Publishing, Inc.

Printed in Mexico
2 3 4 5 6 7 19 18 17 16 15

MEEK AND MILD

PROLOGUE

Flag Run Meetinghouse
Niverton, Somerset County, Pennsylvania
1895

From the first scratch of sound to settle in her daughter's throat, Catherine Kuhn knew the coming squall would agitate a tempest in the entire row. Even as she tightened her grasp around the toddler and prepared to leave the worship service, Catherine looked across the aisle to catch her husband's eye. Hiram, the reddish hue of his beard distinguishing him in the third row of married men, kept his eyes forward. Probably he would not know she took the child out until Catherine told him later.

Clara's cry rose through her throat and burst across her lips. Catherine hastened her pace, easing herself outside the meetinghouse just before her daughter threw her head back and unfurled her distress into the unsympathetic empty air. Catherine carried

7

the writhing girl farther from the confines of the worship service. This was no simple task. Catherine was eight months along. The energy required for moving quickly enough to contain the disturbance sapped her breath. When she reached the grass at the edge of the clearing where the meetinghouse stood, she let Clara slide down her skirt to the ground.

Clara was tired and probably hungry. When she was rested and fed, she was a delightful child full of curiosity and fluid smiles. When she was tired, though, she seemed to require a primal eruption of temper before surrendering to sleep. Catherine squelched envy of the mothers whose children slumbered during church, content in the arms of their mothers or older sisters, with their mellow baby noises exuding comfort to anyone seated close enough to hear. Catherine had expected her own baby would be like this. She took the infant to church when she was only a few weeks old, believing it was best for the child to become accustomed at the earliest possible age to the routine of three-hour services on alternate Sunday mornings. But Clara, with her feathery light brown hair in wispy curls, had not been the sort of baby to fall asleep oblivious to surroundings.

Catherine was grateful to be part of an Amish district that met in meetinghouses rather than homes, alternating between two meetinghouses, both in the southern end of Somerset County, Pennsylvania. Catherine and Hiram had married three years ago in the Flag Run Meetinghouse, Catherine's favorite. It was silly to have a favorite, since the two were identical and two more just like them existed over the border in Maryland, but Catherine enjoyed this particular clearing around the unadorned frame structure.

The year after their wedding was when the trouble started. Bishop Witmer visited to help sort it out, but the results seemed dubious.

Clara settled in the grass, rubbing her cheek in its cool texture, and Catherine saw she had thwarted the tantrum. The child already had closed her eyes and slowed her breathing. Catherine's back ached, but even if she managed to get herself down to the ground, she wasn't sure she would be able to rise when the time came. About ten feet away was a fallen log of sufficient girth to keep her off the ground and give her a fighting chance to stand up again. The log had been there for years, and Catherine suspected it was going soft at the core, but it was her best option. Still catching her breath, Catherine lumbered to the log.

She didn't mind being alone. On most days she savored a few minutes to hold herself still and notice the signs of life around her, the green of the grass, the flutter of tree leaves, the insects crawling along a wooded path, the birds inspecting the ground with their perpetual optimism of finding sustenance. On this day, though, Catherine had hoped against hope that she would be able to remain in church and hear whether the rumors were true. From this distance, she could not discern what was happening inside the meetinghouse.

Twenty minutes later, the women's door opened, and the eldest Mrs. Stutzman emerged. She had five sons, all married with families of their own. Some of her grandsons had married as well, making "Mrs. Stutzman" an indefinite term. The youngest grandson, John, had only one year of schooling left before he would turn fourteen and join his father in the fields. Catherine had always thought he was the nicest of all the Stutzman children. Betty Stutzman now strode as purposefully as her age allowed toward the log where Catherine sat.

"Hello, Betty." Catherine reflexively laid a hand on her belly, where the baby had wakened to wriggle.

"You should go inside." Betty lowered herself beside Catherine and nudged her elbow.

A torrid burst fired up through Catherine's gut. "What's happening?" She glanced at Clara, who had thrown her arms above her head in her favorite sleeping position.

"Bishop Witmer should have stayed," Betty said. "How could he have thought this was settled?"

"Tell me what's going on." Catherine's gaze returned to the meetinghouse.

"Just go in." Betty nudged Catherine's elbow again, this time with more force.

Catherine rose. "But Clara —"

"She knows me," Betty said. "If she wakes, I'll bring her in."

Catherine was not sure Betty could lift Clara but supposed she could at least take her by the hand.

She wished her sister, Martha, were there. But Martha and Atlee were at the hub of the trouble, although they held in their characters nothing resembling maliciousness, and the decisions now stirring controversy were made nearly twenty years ago.

"What happened?" Catherine said, frustrated. "Everything's been fine for more than fifteen years. Why must we suddenly

11

quarrel?"

Betty smoothed her skirt and interlaced her fingers in her lap. "It was peaceful at the time. When some members considered a few small changes, it was a simple thing to use the state line to indicate the preferences."

"The ministers agreed, didn't they?"

Betty nodded. "People were free to worship where they were comfortable. No one held a grudge. We were still one church, and have been all this time."

Martha and Catherine were children when it happened, too young even to have memories of the event. They had grown to womanhood understanding that congregations meeting in Somerset County, Pennsylvania, held to the old ways, while those in Garrett County, Maryland, took a wider view. Still, the differences were small. Anyone looking in from the outside would not have perceived them.

"So why now?" Catherine said. "If the ministers have held their own opinions and yet served together all this time, why now?"

Betty held Catherine's eyes. "You're worried about Martha."

Catherine forced down the bulge in her throat. "It's just a class for children and a few new hymns."

Most of the members in Pennsylvania found the notion of Sunday school hideously of the world. The Amish had lived apart for centuries, so why should they now adopt a spiritual practice that began in Protestant churches? In Maryland, where Martha and Atlee decided to live after they married, church members saw no harm, and neither did Catherine.

"Go on in," Betty said. "The outcome will not change my life. It's different for you — and your little *boppli.*"

As quickly as she could, Catherine moved back toward the building and pulled the creaking door open. Inside, the congregation sat in stunned silence as Bishop Yoder spoke in the firm, full-throated manner the congregation had come to expect since he was ordained bishop earlier in the year.

"We will, of course, take a congregational vote," Bishop Yoder said. "But I will remind you that Bishop Witmer is well acquainted with the events that have occurred in our district in the last two years. Some of you met him while he visited to advise us on how we should proceed. I have presented to you the substance of his counsel to me as your bishop. Let us not respond to the division we have already suffered with more factions. I plead with you now for a unanimous

13

vote on this matter."

What matter? Catherine wished she could pull on Hiram's arm to find out what was happening and what his thoughts were.

A man's hand went up — one of Betty Stutzman's sons — and Bishop Yoder acknowledged it.

"Are we certain this is the counsel Bishop Witmer offers? Perhaps he does not realize the extent of our family relationships with the Marylanders."

Martha. Whatever had brought the conversation to this point, it was going to involve Martha. Heartburn spread across Catherine's chest, and she did not think it was because of the baby.

Bishop Yoder straightened his shoulders. "Jesus said, 'If any man will come after me, let him deny himself, and take up his cross, and follow me.' "

Deny. Bishop Yoder was talking about shunning the Maryland families, Catherine realized. *Meidung.* He wanted her to shun her sister. To not see Martha. To not speak to Martha. For her children not to know their *aunti.* Catherine stared at the back of Hiram's head, willing him to turn around and see her, but he didn't.

"After this date," Bishop Yoder said, "any families who join the fellowship of the

14

congregation in Maryland will no longer belong to our fellowship, and we will regard them as having abandoned the true faith."

Catherine twisted between relief that the shunning would only apply to future families who left the church and anxiety that shunning should occur at all.

Another hand went up and another man spoke. "In my conversations with Bishop Witmer, I did not find him so resolute."

Irritation flickered from Bishop Yoder's face. "I assure you that Bishop Witmer and I studied the Scriptures together. We also carefully considered the Discipline of 1837, which stresses the importance of a strict ban to maintain a vigorous church. I am sure we all want a vigorous church, do we not? When we neglect God's ordinance, the church falls away. Have we not already seen this in what happened with our former brethren in Maryland?"

Former brethren. The bishop had already cast aside Martha and Atlee Hostetler and the families who worshipped at the Maple Glen and Cherry Glade meetinghouses. How was it possible that the believers who labored side by side to build four meetinghouses should now see each other as former brethren? Catherine's body tensed. Her sister's heart had not fallen away from God.

15

If the bishop would visit the families in Maryland, he would see this for himself.

A few heads turned now, forming pockets of whisper around the congregation. Catherine watched husbands and wives leaning forward or backward around those among whom they sat to find the eyes of their spouses across the aisle. Hiram rotated at last and caught her gaze. Catherine felt the blood siphon out of her face.

"We must vote now," Yoder said, "and I again remind you that a unanimous vote is essential to protect us from further division. You are here at Flag Run in Niverton, and not at one of the meetinghouses only a few miles away in Garrett County, because you already realize the authority of the Word of God in this matter. You understand the spiritual benefits that flow into your lives when you submit to the church and the congregation is of one mind. Consider carefully whether you want to be responsible for causing a crack in our unity with a dissenting vote."

If there had been any honest discussion of the question, Catherine had missed it. The bishop now left members of the congregation with little choice but to vote as he wished.

"All baptized members may vote," Yoder

said. "I ask you to raise your hands with me if you uphold the Word of God and desire to be obedient to the teaching of the true church."

Catherine's throat thickened as she again looked at Hiram. Bishop Yoder had not asked whether people believed Sunday school violated the Word of God. He had not asked whether they agreed that the shunning was needful. He had framed his request in a way that marked anyone who disagreed with him as a heretic or an apostate.

Bishop Yoder lifted his right hand high in the air. Catherine, still standing at the back of the congregation, buried her hands in the folds of her skirt. Technically her sister had begun worshipping only on the Maryland side of the border before the ban the bishop now proposed. Catherine could still see her. Yet in her heart she was supposed to think of her as having fallen away. She could not make herself lift her hand.

Yet around the Flag Run Meetinghouse, one hand after another went up. Some lifted eagerly and some reluctantly, but the hands of baptized members present rose. Hiram's was one of the last, but he complied. Catherine knew her husband had no strong feeling on the matter of shunning those who

17

left to join other churches — even the Lutherans — but she understood that he did not want to be the source of friction in the congregation. Who among the church would accept that role? Hiram sat in a row of men who had already raised their hands. In front of him and behind him, the men watched each other. On the other side of the aisle, the women did the same. Only because Catherine stood in the back could she withhold her vote without notice.

When the bishop asked if anyone opposed, Catherine's heart pounded. But she said nothing. Perhaps with her silence she had voted in agreement after all.

Bishop Yoder smiled in pleasure. "We have a unanimous vote. God will be pleased that we have placed ourselves in His care and have chosen His will over our own. Let us do as the disciples did and sing a hymn as we depart."

One of the bishop's sons, Noah, began the hymn, and the congregation soon joined with German words their ancestors had been singing for two hundred years.

CHAPTER 1

Somerset County, Pennsylvania
June 1916

The pan lid clattered to the kitchen floor. Clara Kuhn scrambled to contain the noise by stepping on the lid and then picking it up to press against her chest while her heart rate slowed. Three-year-old Mari had gone down for her afternoon nap not six minutes earlier. Rhoda was likely to stick her head in the kitchen and scowl at her stepdaughter within the next seventeen seconds. Expelling her breath, Clara turned around and dunked the lid back into the sink of water to scrub it again. Once she had dried it and stowed it with its matching pot on a low shelf, she ran a damp rag across the kitchen table and declared the kitchen properly tidied after the midday meal.

Rhoda had not appeared.

Rhoda's propensity to scowl at Clara was a recent development in their relationship.

Clara didn't know what triggered it or what she could do to make it subside. She rinsed out the rag, hung it over the side of the sink, and drained the water. Mindful of where her skirts might catch or what her elbow might encounter, she moved out of the kitchen and into the hall leading to the front parlor. The voices were low, but with Josiah and Hannah in their last week of school and Mari napping, the house offered nothing to obscure the words. This was not a conversation Clara should walk into, accidentally or not. She halted her steps and held her breath.

"It's time Clara married," Rhoda said.

"She goes to the Singings," Hiram Kuhn said. "When she has something to tell us, she will."

"There must be any number of young men she could marry," Rhoda said. "Perhaps she's being particular."

"I was particular. After Catherine died trying to birth our child, I waited nine years to marry you even though I had a daughter who needed a *mamm*."

Rhoda's voice softened. "And I am blessed that you did. Your wait gave me time to grow up and meet you. I have done my best to love Clara as my own — I *do* love her as my own. I want what's best for her. She

20

needs a husband and her own house to run."

"I always thought she was a help to you after the children were born."

"She was. She is. But I can manage my children without help. Clara should be looking after her own *boppli.*"

Remaining still, Clara allowed herself to ease out her breath and cautiously fill her lungs again.

"Of course you can manage the children, but it's nice to have help, isn't it?"

"I won't have Clara thinking that I need her help," Rhoda said. "She must know that it's time to grow up. She's twenty-three."

"Hardly past the age of being marriageable," Hiram said.

"Very nearly. She could go to Maryland to stay with her mother's people," Rhoda said. "Perhaps she would meet someone to her liking in their church."

Clara visited her aunt Martha and her cousin Fannie often. Fannie had her own little girl now, and Clara adored Sadie. But Clara had never thought of joining their church. She certainly wouldn't look for someone to marry in the Mennonite-leaning congregation.

It was not for lack of possibilities that she had not yet married.

■ ■ ■

Andrew Raber liked going to the *English* hardware store. Whenever he had reason to do so, he allowed himself three times as long as his errand might legitimately require. If he needed a wrench he couldn't find in an Amish shop, he went to that aisle in the *English* store by way of the electric toasters. If he needed barbed-wire fence to keep horses in their pasture, he also marveled at the rolls of wire that could carry electricity. If he needed a new ax head, he first flipped through the brochures and catalogs of what could be sent for by special order. He could spend hours under the tin ceiling, walking the uneven wooden floor and investigating the overflowing shelves.

It was not that Andrew intended to purchase any of these things. It was only that he could not stifle his curiosity.

Today he was contemplating a new hoe and rake. Weeks of spring labor had made clear that handles on the cast-off overworked tools he received from his father years ago were ready for replacement. Andrew was fairly certain his grandfather had used those tools as well, and his faulty efforts to sand the long wooden handles back into service without risk of splinters in his hands had persuaded him new tools would not be an extravagance.

He would get to the tools, but right now he was looking at electric table lamps. Some were spare and efficient. Others had ornate bases and decorative glass globes. Some were sold as matched pairs and others billed as unique. Andrew had no doubt, though, that they were all wired alike. When they were plugged into a wall socket, electricity would flow through all the lamps in the same manner.

Andrew chose the lamp that appeared the least fragile and turned it upside down to see if the base might come off and give him a glimpse inside. If he had a screwdriver, he could pry it off, but the risk of damaging the lamp and then feeling obligated to purchase it was too much. He removed the shade and stared at the bare socket where a bulb would go, wishing he understood what he saw.

"Why are you looking at that?"

Andrew didn't have to look up to know whose mouth the words came from. "Hello, Yonnie."

"What are you doing?"

"I'm only looking." Andrew carefully replaced the shade and set the lamp back

23

on the shelf. His eyes flicked to a white globe with painted flowers on it.

"We have all the light we need to read by with our oil lamps," Yonnie said.

Andrew wondered if Yonnie Yoder even heard the perpetual stern streak that ran through nearly every sentence he ever uttered. Perhaps it was just the way he spoke, his own cadence of language. They'd been boys together, and Andrew learned to disregard Yonnie's tone years ago. Lately, though, it had begun to irritate him. He had always supposed Yonnie would grow into a more graceful way of speaking, but Andrew no longer thought he would.

"Why do you always fuss with the *English* things?" Yonnie said. "Our people do not use them."

"Maybe we will someday."

"You should not wish for something so worldly."

Andrew turned his back to the lamps. "I need a new rake."

Clara withdrew to the kitchen and then out the back door.

She was in the way. How had she not seen this years ago? It was one thing to be an eleven-year-old child whose father at last remarried and another to be twenty-three and thought to be without options.

Clara's own mother died when Clara was not yet two. Although Clara's birth was uneventful — at least that's what her father always told her — the boy her mother carried had taken too long to come. By the time he arrived — stillborn — Catherine Kuhn was exhausted. The bleeding that followed the birth quickly became uncontrollable, and within minutes Catherine was gone as well. Clara cocked her head, listening to the faraway sounds of that day. As always, she was unsure whether she remembered the screams and the rushing and the clattering of pans as she lay in her crib resisting a nap, or whether imagining the events had seared into her mind in the manner of memories.

Hiram was left with a small daughter and his grief. He was attentive and patient and sad.

When Clara was ten, Hiram met Rhoda, and the little girl saw the light in her father's eyes that she had longed for all her life.

But grief did not abandon the family with the marriage of Hiram and Rhoda. While Rhoda quickly became with child, one after another, three babies were born three and four months too early. Clara remembered the pall that fell over the house with each

25

loss and the nervousness that shrouded each succeeding pregnancy. Though daylight streamed through the home, weighty darkness pressed on Hiram and Rhoda. After each loss, Hiram withdrew into the shadows and Rhoda instigated a frenzy of "trying again." At the time, Clara understood little of the biological process that ushered in repeated, cumulative grief, and no one thought to explain it to her, but clearly marriage brought with it great risk of sadness and disappointment.

Finally Josiah safely arrived, and then Hannah, and then Mari. Rhoda was still young enough to have several more children, if God should choose to bless her.

When Clara was a child, before Rhoda, she used to visit her aunt and uncle in Maryland and their rambunctious household. After Fannie, only a year and a half older than Clara, Martha and Atlee produced a string of boys. At twelve, the youngest was scarcely four years older than Josiah. In the summers, when she did not have school, Clara stayed for weeks at a time with the Hostetlers. Sometimes she stared at Martha when no one was watching, wondering if Martha resembled Catherine. Could she look at her aunt and see her own mother's face? Clara couldn't imagine loving Martha more if she had been her mother.

But staying in Maryland now? Away from Andrew?

Clara was not without options, as her stepmother supposed. She could have married two years ago. She could marry in the next season if she wanted to. If Clara confided in her now, Rhoda would plant extra rows of celery in preparation for a wedding as soon as Andrew had his fall harvest in.

Clara did not want to leave Andrew. She did not want to go to a strange Singing and have a strange man ask if he might take her home in his strange buggy.

But neither could she marry Andrew Raber.

Clara glanced back at the house and decided it was time to go clean the *English* household. The banker's wife maintained a busy social schedule, and three giggly daughters felt no compunction to pick up after themselves. A woman who came in to cook the family's meals was adamant she would not clean beyond the kitchen, so the family depended on Clara to come twice a week and restore order. Later in the week she would go to the Widower Hershberger's house for her regular afternoon of housekeeping.

Rhoda's words rang in Clara's ears. Maybe it was time to find more housekeeping work.

Andrew bought his rake. He had come into town in Yonnie's buggy, and now they were headed back toward their farms — Andrew to the acreage where he grew up and now lived alone and Yonnie to his parents' home, where he lived while trying to save enough money to purchase his own land.

As the buggy jostled and Andrew's eyes soaked up the scenery, he wondered how his parents could have left this place for Lancaster County. No matter what the season, beauty spilled from every vantage point. The mixed green hues of early summer or the rich rust palette of autumn, the brilliance of summer sunlight or the heavy laden clouds of winter moisture — Andrew savored it all.

A glint of dark green caught Andrew's eyes. On its own, he might have thought it a believable June hue, but it bounced the sun's light in a way that vegetation didn't, and his eye quickly followed the shape to brassy lines.

"Stop!" Andrew said.

Yonnie glanced at Andrew but did not pull on the reins or reach to set the brake.

"Stop," Andrew repeated. He positioned himself to jump down off the buggy's bench whether or not Yonnie halted the forward motion. They were not moving so fast that he would hurt himself — at least not seriously.

The horse's hooves slowed. Andrew glanced gratefully at Yonnie and saw the skeptical expression on his face. Ignoring it, he dropped down to the ground and strode toward the object that had caught his eye at the side of the road, its rear positioned under the lowest branches of a spreading red maple tree.

"Andrew, no."

Andrew ignored the warning in Yonnie's voice. The worst that could happen was Yonnie would drive off and leave Andrew here, which was a risk worth taking.

The sign painted on a large wooden square and propped against the front of the object said FREE.

"Get back in the buggy," Yonnie said. "That's for the *English*. It's not our business."

Andrew moved the sign out of the way and felt the smile well up inside him.

"Andrew!" The sharpness of Yonnie's tone escalated.

"Relax," Andrew said. "Look at this. It's

beautiful." His eyes feasted. In town he always felt obliged to avert his eyes at such a sight, but out on a quiet road through an Amish district, his courage mounted.

"It's an automobile," Yonnie said.

Andrew grinned. It sure was. Shiny and clean and modern.

And free.

CHAPTER 2

A Model T.

Andrew pushed aside drooping branches and uncovered the upholstered seat with neat rows of tufted green diamonds. Hanging off the back of the seat were the neat, organized folds of the collapsed roof that left the seats open to the air. He felt the sun on his head and imagined wind in his face as the automobile rumbled at top speed. Andrew wasn't sure what the maximum speed was for a Model T, but it would be fun to discover it.

Behind him, Andrew felt Yonnie's silent judgment, but he ignored his friend's effort to bore into him with eyes of guilt. At the front of the car, brass-rimmed headlights were open eyes ready to stare fearlessly into the night. Andrew walked around the car, finding four perfectly round tires, two unbroken axles, and twin wide running boards — at least he thought that's what

31

they were called — which would make it far easier to step into the car than it was to get into a buggy. He opened the driver's door and climbed in.

"Andrew!"

"There's a note," Andrew said, taking a card tied to the center of the steering wheel.

"It can't possibly be for you," Yonnie said. "Get out of that *English* contraption before anyone sees you."

Andrew inhaled the alien smell of the vehicle as he unfolded the card and scanned the lines.

Congratulations. It's yours. I've come to the end of my wits with this thing. The ownership documents are in the box under the seat. Good luck getting it running.

Andrew allowed one side of his mouth to rise in pleasure. "Actually, it is for me. I just found a free car."

A squirrel darted across the road, and the dark gelding nickered.

"Let's go," Yonnie said. "I have chores to do and so do you."

Andrew glanced at the sky. Nothing on his farm mattered whether he did it today or tomorrow or next week. The horses had plenty of water and hay, and the two hens would lay eggs whether or not Andrew was there. He didn't keep a cow because he'd never liked milking schedules. Andrew's fingers fished for the handle again and he leaned into the weight of the door to open it, wondering how to open the cover over the engine. It could not be too complicated — a lever, a hook, a latch to displace. Andrew ran his hands lightly along the angled shape of the hood, feeling for possibilities. When he found the release latch, he paused before opening the motor's covering.

"Aren't you even curious?" Andrew gently lifted a green rectangle off one side of the motor.

"No, I am not." Yonnie's response was swift. "And you should not be, either."

"Curiosity is not a sin."

"If your curiosity takes you away from God's people, you'll have to reconsider that statement."

"Look at it, Yonnie. It's beautiful. Someone kept it in perfect condition. All I have to do is get it running."

"And what do you know about the motor of an *English* automobile?"

"Nothing. But I can learn."

Not everyone in the church spurned motor vehicles as instantly or vehemently as

Yonnie did. Although Yonnie was a third cousin to Andrew — neither of them was sure of the exact connection — his family's name was Yoder, and Yonnie never loosened his grip on the responsibility he felt in also being related to Bishop Yoder.

Yonnie was still on the buggy's bench.

"Just come down and look at it." Andrew poked a finger into a greasy connection in the motor and sniffed his blackened fingertip. Oil. He understood nothing about what he was looking at, but the thirst to learn compelled him. Wires. Cylinders. Rubber hoses. Parts he had no words to describe. Somehow all of this harnessed energy that could compete with the power of galloping horses.

To Andrew's surprise, Yonnie stood beside him now with his fists balled behind him. Andrew ran one hand along the sleek, polished rod that ran from behind the lights on the front of the car to a shield of glass in front of the steering wheel.

"It's a marvel," Andrew whispered. He saw cars on the road nearly every time he ventured beyond the ring of Amish farms, but never before had he enjoyed the freedom to touch and feel and explore.

"It's for the *English.*" Yonnie stepped back several feet.

"What are you afraid of, Yonnie?"

"I am not afraid." The edge in Yonnie's voice sharpened. "I take my baptismal vows seriously. I will live in submission to the church."

Andrew made up his mind. "I'm going to keep this car."

Back from the *English* house, where the electric lights and glittering trinkets held no allure for Clara, she climbed the steps to her room. Clara had slept in the same bedroom all her life. It was neither large nor especially comfortable. She supposed that if her mother had lived and her parents had more children, eventually she would have shared the room with a sister, but living alone with her father for most of her childhood allowed Clara the privilege of privacy. She was fifteen before Josiah was born and eighteen before she had a sister. By that time, no one expected her to share a room with an infant.

At twenty, Clara already had married friends with infants of their own the same ages as her little sisters Hannah and Mari. Her cousin Fannie, for instance, had a daughter barely a year younger than Hannah. Clara was certain Sadie and Hannah would like each other if they were ever al-

35

lowed to meet.

A dust mop stood propped in the corner of the room, reminding Clara she had intended to clean her own room before Rhoda's words drove her from the house. She ran the mop over the bare wood floor under her bed. She did this often enough that she did not expect to encounter serious accumulation of dust, but she took satisfaction in knowing her bedroom was company clean at any moment. Her mop bumped up against the one item she routinely stored under the bed, and Clara pulled out the small leather bag that once belonged to her mother. With a rag, she cleared the hint of dust that had begun to gather around the handle.

"I wish I had a bag like that."

Clara looked up to see Hannah enter the room and throw herself across Clara's bed. She kissed her sister. "I didn't realize you were home from school."

"Only two more days."

"You'll miss seeing Priscilla every day when school lets out."

Hannah giggled. "We've promised each other we will nag our mothers all summer to let us play together."

"Bensel." Silly child. Clara was certain both girls would fulfill this commitment.

Whether their mothers would cooperate in their response was another question.

"Can I use your bag?" Hannah rolled over and took the bag from Clara.

"What will you use it for?"

"Maybe I can go see Aunt Martha, like you do."

Clara had used this bag for overnight visits to Maryland since she was a little girl not much older than Hannah. As soon as her sister died, Martha insisted that Hiram Kuhn allow his daughter to know her mother's family. Hiram never objected. Because Martha and Atlee had joined the Conservative Amish Mennonites before the bishop's ban when Clara was a toddler, Clara broke no rules by seeing her aunt and cousins. The shunning was not strictly enforced anyway. Most of the families in the district traced to both churches at some point in the family trees, and those who were not related by blood were connected by friendships spanning generations. Amish business serving both congregations flourished on both sides of the border. Farms on both sides of the border supplied milk to an Amish dairy in Somerset County. Dairy drivers collected the milk on daily rounds, and the dairy sold milk, cream, butter, and cheese to the *English* as well as Amish families who wanted more than their own animals produced. No one stopped to ask what date a person had joined the Marylanders.

"I could ask *Mamm,*" Hannah said, "and maybe the next time you visit Aunt Martha, I can go with you. It's going to be summer. I won't miss any school. I could play with Sadie."

"We'll have to see." Clara did not want to make promises. Rhoda would be the first to point out that her children were not related to the Hostetlers in any way.

"That's what *Mamm* says when she hopes I'll forget about something." Hannah's lower lip trembled on the verge of a pout.

"She's your *mamm* and she loves you," Clara said.

"But you're my sister and you're a grown-up. You wouldn't let anything happen to me."

Footsteps sounded down the hall, and Hannah sat up in recognition of her mother's approach.

"Hannah!" Rhoda called.

"Go quickly." Clara nudged Hannah's thin form and was relieved when the child complied without arguing. The last thing Clara wanted to do right now was inflame her stepmother's mood. She would stay out of Rhoda's way, be as silently helpful as she could, and hope that the notion of sending her to live in Maryland would pass.

"Come on," Andrew said. "Help me."

"Help you do what?" Yonnie said.

"Move this car." Andrew picked up the FREE sign from the ground in front of the car and carried it to Yonnie's buggy.

"You've been making me do things like this our whole lives."

Andrew winked. "We've never moved a free car before."

Yonnie turned his head to look both directions down the road. "Where exactly are you planning to move it? We're still a long way from our farms."

"So you'll do it?"

"I didn't say that. I'm just pointing out reality."

Yonnie was especially good at pointing out reality. Even as a boy, he persistently hovered over what might go wrong or which rules they might break even accidentally in the course of ordinary childhood play. Perhaps that was why Andrew had long ago developed the ability to ignore Yonnie's lack of enthusiasm. He barely heard the protests anymore.

"There's a barn," Andrew said, "just over

a mile down the road. It's been empty for at least five years."

Yonnie cocked his head to think. "An *English* family named Johnson used to live there."

"That's the place. A fire took the house, and they didn't rebuild."

"If they were Amish, they would have. Everyone would have helped."

"Well, they weren't Amish and they were getting on in years. I heard they moved in with their son in Ohio."

"They must still own the land."

Andrew shrugged. "Probably. But they're not using the barn."

"It's more like a shed, as I recall," Yonnie said. "Three stalls at most. It might have served as a barn originally, before the Johnsons put up a more sufficient structure."

"Yes, I suppose so."

"But it would be a good place to hide a car."

"I'm not *hiding* it," Andrew said. "I only need a place to store it — a place big enough to work on it."

"How do you propose to get the car there?"

Andrew rolled his eyes. "You have a horse six feet away from you."

"I suppose he could pull it, but I'd have to unhitch my buggy."

Andrew waited. At this point in a conversation with Yonnie, he did not have to articulate his next argument. He only had to wait for Yonnie to catch up.

"I suppose the buggy would be safe here," Yonnie finally said. "Not many people have reason to come down this road, and no one could steal it without an extra horse and harness."

Andrew waited again.

"If we drag the buggy well off the road, it won't be in any danger. No harm has come to the car while it was parked here."

Now Andrew moved again. He had Yonnie right where he wanted him — persuaded that the job was possible and not, for the moment, entangled with his conscience.

"I'll get your rope," Andrew said, one hand already fumbling around under the buggy bench. He had no idea how to tie a rope to a car, but he supposed it could not be much different than dragging a buggy. The main thing was to not put too much stress on the axle, and he would have to figure out how to release any brake that might impede the tires' movements.

Common sense. That was the primary strategy to solving most problems. Despite

Yonnie's legalistic perspective on decisions, he was loyal. Right now, Andrew counted on Yonnie's loyalty toward him to run long and deep. As long as Andrew stayed one step ahead of himself and was patient enough to learn, he would have himself a car.

CHAPTER 3

Garrett County, Maryland

The vice gripping Fannie Esh's womb, all too familiar, meant only one thing.

The womb was empty. There was no child this month. Next would come the backache, and then the flow. Heartbreak would smash through hope once again.

Once she weaned Sadie more than four years ago, Fannie assumed another child would come as easily as Sadie had, another wash of luminous wonder into the household, another joyful pitch of a baby's giggle. She and Elam had never tried to avoid a child, but now all she had to do was catch his eye over his supper plate and he would know what the expression meant. Oblivious, Sadie would chatter through the silent exchange at their small wooden kitchen table. Elam would rise early the next day and be out in the fields before Fannie could fix him a proper breakfast. He would not come in for lunch nor eat more than a few bites at supper. They would not speak of it. What more was there to say after all this time, while their siblings and neighbors and fellow church members received child after child from God's hand? Sometimes the babes were not even a year apart.

"Sadie would like a little sister, wouldn't she?" Fannie's friends used to say.

"There's nothing as sweet as the smell of a baby's head."

"Have you seen the new Stutzman baby? She's their most beautiful child yet."

Now her friends had three or four children and somberly promised to pray for God's blessing to come to Fannie as well.

Fannie yearned for another child, but she was beginning to doubt whether the arrows in the quiver, as the Bible said, were truly a measure of God's blessing. Perhaps the psalmist meant something else entirely, something that would make Fannie feel less discomforted by her inability to bear another child.

She sat at the kitchen table, where in the past she would allow herself the release of tears when this moment arrived. Fannie had abandoned tears more than a year ago. Now she simply counted off ten slow, deep breaths and composed herself.

Sadie bounded in through the back door, her cheeks scrubbed fresh by the late spring air and her eyes lit with anticipation.

"It's today, right?" Sadie said. "Today we go to for supper with *Grossmuder, ya?*"

The desire to join her boisterous family for the evening meal could not have been further from Fannie's mood, but Sadie loved to go. Especially since Fannie's brother's son began to toddle, Sadie loved to take Thomas's hand and lead him around the house or yard.

And Elam would be waiting for them there. He walked over several hours early to help Atlee Hostetler put a new door on the outside entrance to the cellar. Perhaps it was just as well. Among her extended family it would be easier to avoid Elam's eye. He could have one more day of hope even if Fannie could not.

"Shall we fix your hair before we go?" Fannie said, taking her daughter's hand. "Your braids are coming loose."

"If we must," Sadie said, "but please hurry."

Fannie took in little of what Sadie said while they repaired her hair and rode in the buggy the two miles to the Hostetler farm. Most of it seemed to be about the words Sadie wanted to teach her young cousin,

45

though in Fannie's observation the boy showed little interest in expressing himself beyond the few simple sounds he already had mastered. There was plenty of time for that.

Fannie pulled her buggy in beside her brother's, and Sadie gripped the bench and looked at her mother for permission to get out. After Sadie once jumped out before the buggy stopped moving and nearly rolled under a wooden wheel, Fannie and Elam became stricter than their general natures about a rule that Sadie must not leave the buggy without explicit permission.

Fannie nodded. Sadie leaped down, and Fannie followed. They entered the back door together, and the little girl ran to embrace her *grossmuder,* flinging her arms around Martha's waist and laying her head against her abdomen.

"Grossmuder," Sadie said, "my arms don't reach around you anymore. Are you eating too much?"

"Sadie!" Fannie said sharply.

"Sorry." Sadie hung her head for a few seconds before looking up again brightly. "Where's the baby?"

Martha Hostetler laughed. "In the front room. But he's supposed to play on his blanket right now."

"I'll help him play." Sadie shot through the door.

"What can I help you with?" Fannie said.

Martha turned and removed a knife from a drawer. "I haven't done the vegetables yet."

"I'll do them." Fannie took the knife from her mother.

Amish dresses hid weight gain and shifting shapes, but in a startling moment Fannie saw what had sparked her daughter's impolite question. Her mother's bosom was heavier and her apron climbed a less defined waistline.

Martha was thickening.

"Clara!"

Clara jolted at the sound of Rhoda's voice. Whatever Rhoda needed, Clara would do — dishes, dusting, sweeping.

She stepped from her room into the hall. "Yes? What can I do for you?"

"Nothing," Rhoda said. "I only wanted to say that I'm going to walk the children up to the road and see them off to school."

"I'll take them," Clara said.

"No need. I can manage."

"Then leave Mari with me." The three-year-old would only slow down the others.

"I'll take her," Rhoda said. "I simply

wanted you to know I'll be out of the house for a while."

Clara glanced out the window. "It's a lovely morning to walk. Take your time. I'll start the laundry water to boil."

"I'll do that when I get back," Rhoda said. "If your father comes in, you can tell him I'll have coffee cake for him at midmorning."

"I'll mix it up," Clara said.

"I'm sure you have things to do," Rhoda said. "I know just how he likes it."

As if I don't, Clara thought as Rhoda herded her children out the front door. Clara followed them out and sat on the top step. Rhoda supported Mari on her hip with one hand while with the other she straightened the shoulders of Josiah's white shirt and smoothed his black suspenders. At the last minute, before they stepped out of the yard and onto the path to the road, Hannah turned and waved. Her expression was lost in the morning glare, but Clara was certain her mouth was a wide smile. It always was when she waved good-bye.

Clara blew out her breath and closed her eyes to focus on the sensation of the sun bleeding orange through her eyelids. The truth was, she had little to do since Rhoda had begun refusing her offers of help around the house, so she closed her eyes and raised her face to the sun. Each day was warmer than the one before, and the heat came earlier. Another week would bring unquestionable summer, vanishing the threat of retreating into the cool, damp days of spring. At least Josiah and Hannah would be out of school after tomorrow. Josiah would be eager and content to work alongside his father in the fields. Hannah would be the wriggly one. Hiram had never let Clara work in the fields, so she doubted his policy would change for Hannah. And Hannah wouldn't want to. She would prefer to flit in and out the back door doing whatever caught her fancy. Rhoda, on the other hand, would have a more structured method to keep Hannah occupied.

The approaching clatter of horses pulling a rickety wagon demanded Clara open her eyes.

Yonnie Yoder. Andrew brushed off Yonnie's mannerisms in amusement, but Clara was not so noble. Yonnie usually did the second collection route for the Amish dairy that employed him closer to midmorning, though occasionally he took a turn at the early-morning route. But what brought him to the Kuhn farm? The Kuhns did not keep extra cows. With six people in the house —

49

and Hiram's well-known affinity for cheese — they consumed most of what their two cows produced.

Clara descended the porch steps and paced out to meet Yonnie's wagon.

"Gut mariye," she said when he pulled to a stop. Who could complain about a morning greeting? For Andrew's sake, she injected an extra dose of friendliness into her words. "What brings you here this morning?"

"Your cousin was out at the road first thing this morning waving me down," Yonnie said.

"Fannie?"

"She sent a note."

"So early?" Clara took the envelope from Yonnie. "Thank you for coming out of your way to deliver it promptly."

"Are you suggesting sometimes I am not prompt?"

"No, of course not," Clara said, wondering how Andrew tolerated someone so inclined to be suspicious and snippy. She was not sure she would have the fortitude if one of her childhood friends had grown up to have Yonnie's temperament. "Thank you, Yonnie. I pray God blesses your day."

He turned the wagon in a wide circle around the yard and left. Clara tore off the end of the envelope and unfolded the single sheet inside.

Dear Clara,
Please come as soon as you can. My heart is heavy once again, and I have received stunning news which ought to make my heart glad but which instead weighs on my spirit. I can tell no one but you.

Your cousin,
Fannie

Clara read the words a second time but found no further meaning in them. An empty day stretched ahead of her. Why should she not go to Fannie now? She could walk and be there before the midday meal. Clara pivoted to scamper up the porch stairs and then to her second-story bedroom as she considered whether she ought to pack the overnight bag. When she heard movement downstairs, she expected Rhoda had returned from her errand to send the children off on their walk to school. Instead, the heavier footsteps ascending the stairs were her father's. Clara stepped into the hall.

"Hello, *Daed*. Rhoda asked me to tell you she will have a coffee cake ready by mid-morning."

51

"I hope she does not go to a lot of trouble. I'm not feeling well."

Clara looked at him more closely. When his head drooped at the breakfast table, she had supposed he hadn't slept well. Now she could see he was pale and his breath labored.

"You should lie down," she said.

"That is my intention," Hiram said, "but I must ask a favor of you."

"Of course."

"Take the buggy and go over to John Stutzman's farm. I promised I would go to help him with roofing repairs today. He will understand that I am ill, but I don't want him to think I have forgotten him."

Clara glanced into her bedroom at the bag on the bed. "Of course."

The Stutzmans lived on one of the most outlying of the Amish farms. They were near the Maryland border, but well west of the Kuhn land. A round-trip journey, with time for polite socializing or the meal John's wife was likely to offer, would take half the day. Clara was grateful, though, that Hiram had enough sense not to go up on a roof when he felt unsteady.

Fannie would have to understand.

Fannie tucked the lightweight quilt around

her daughter's shoulders and cracked the window to coax in cool air. Sadie bounced through her days with enough energy for three children. When bedtime came, she dropped into bed and often was asleep before Fannie finished murmuring soft prayers for her household. Tonight was no different.

Fannie sat on her daughter's bed and put out the lamp before listening for Sadie's even breath. She had hoped that Clara would come before the day's light petered out. Even without conversation, Clara's presence would have been a comfort.

Clara feared childbirth as deeply as Fannie longed for it. They knew each other's secrets more than anyone else. But this — who would have expected this? After five children, the youngest of them twelve years old? At Martha's age?

Elam sat in the front room studying papers about crop rotations. He knew Fannie's news now. But did he know Martha's?

CHAPTER 4

Clara lost the entire day. By the time she got home from the Stutzman farm, she'd missed the afternoon run of the milk wagon, her usual prospect for hitching a ride to a farm near Fannie's. Though she might still walk the six miles before darkness fell, she hesitated to leave without being sure her father was on the mend — or at least resting well — and Hannah was so full of after-school chatter that there was no place for Clara to break in and explain she was leaving. Clara recognized the precise moment she looked out the window and knew it was too late.

She barely slept.

On Friday morning, Clara paced before daylight the mile to the corner where she knew the milk wagon would pass. The words in Fannie's notes replayed in her mind. Though a stone dropped in her stomach when she realized the driver was Yonnie Yoder and not one of the two other — more pleasant — dairy drivers, Clara put a smile on her face and asked for a ride that went past the Maple Glen Meetinghouse the Marylanders used. At least she knew he would not require conversation beyond an initial greeting and departing pleasantries.

When he let her off, Clara ignored Yonnie's silent scowl and thanked him for obliging her with a ride. He no more approved of her visits to her Marylander relatives than he did his employer's choice to do business with the Marylanders.

None of that was Clara's concern. She only needed to see Fannie. When she knocked on the back door, Clara smelled the bacon and eggs Fannie cooked every day for Elam's breakfast. Her empty stomach gurgled in response.

Fannie fell into Clara's arms. Elam was gone to the fields or the barn, and Sadie stood on a chair with her skinny arms in the dishwater. Clara felt Fannie's tremble and squeezed her shoulders hard, while at the same time catching Sadie's grin. The girl was especially proud that she had lost three teeth and smiled wide to show her accomplishment.

Fannie composed herself and touched her daughter's shoulder. "Sadie, thank you for

55

helping with the dishes. We're going to go see *Grossmuder,* so please tidy your bed before we go."

Sadie pulled her hands out of the water, splashing droplets on Fannie and Clara. "I'm glad you're here," she said to Clara, pulling her lips wide again.

Clara smiled at Sadie and then turned to Fannie as soon as the girl was out of sight. "We're going to see your mother? Is she all right?"

Fannie pulled the last plate from the sink and rinsed it in clear water. "Yes. As far as I know. It seems she has not been confiding in me."

"But you're very close to your mother."

"You'll see," Fannie said. "Sadie!"

Fannie would reveal little in her daughter's presence, so Clara did not press. Instead, as they walked they talked about the state of Fannie's vegetable garden and whether the hens were laying enough eggs. Sadie circled around them in her bare feet, asking the names of sprouting vegetation and pointing out the birds swooping from their nests. On an ordinary day, Clara would have enjoyed the leisurely two-mile morning stroll. Today each step twisted her anxiety tighter.

Clara heard the aching breath Fannie drew as they approached Martha kneeling between the budding rows of flowers across the front of the house. Sadie raced ahead to greet her *grossmuder,* throwing her weight against Martha's back and disturbing her balance. Martha recovered quickly, but in the effort it took to stand up, Clara saw more than the strain of age.

Martha was not an old woman. She was only forty-four and actively managed her household.

Not *only* forty-four. Clara corrected herself mentally. A woman having a child at forty-four was not the same as a woman weeding her garden at forty-four. Already Martha's balance was off. Already her back arced slightly to compensate for the rising mound in the front.

Clara swallowed hard. Worry shot through her even as she reached out to put a hand on Fannie's arm.

"But your youngest brother is twelve," Clara whispered.

Fannie's response was a choked sob.

Even as Clara kissed her aunt's cheek, she felt the color drain from her face. Once, a woman in the church was pregnant at forty-six. Even the *English* doctor said it was dangerous.

Martha patted Sadie's head. "There's strudel in the kitchen. Why don't you go get a piece?"

Sadie's penchant for strudel propelled her into the house.

"You don't have to hide what you feel," Martha said softly to the two young women before her. "Clara, you're worried something will happen to me or the baby — or both of us. Fannie, you're heartbroken even though you want to be glad."

"*Aunti* Martha," Clara said — but she did not know how to finish her sentence.

Beside Clara, Fannie pushed her breath out slowly. "You didn't tell me. You waited until I could see it."

"I didn't know what to say," Martha said. "I know how much you want another child."

Clara moistened her lips and glanced at her cousin.

"*Gottes wille*," Martha said. God's will.

They went inside for strudel and coffee. Sitting on a stool, Sadie's face was already smeared with cherry filling. When Fannie took cups down from a shelf, clinking nearly obscured the toddler's cry.

"Thomas is here?" she said.

Martha nodded. "Lizzie asked me to keep him for a few hours this morning."

Sadie wiped her mouth on her sleeve. "I'll get him."

"Be gentle," Fannie called after the girl. "Hold his hand. Don't carry him."

Thomas, her brother's son, was a year and a half old. When Fannie heard the news that he was on the way to the newlywed couple, she was genuinely glad for them. But now another two years had passed. In all that time, Fannie had not had even one delayed cycle, not one morning of conflicted signals from her body, not one morning of hope that her faithful patience was rewarded at last. Lizzie and Abe likely soon would announce that they were expecting another *boppli,* and Fannie would once again have to kiss their cheeks in congratulation.

Sadie returned to the room with a crooked grin on her face and a sleepy boy wobbling on his feet.

A boy.

A son would please Elam. A stair-step row of sons, with another daughter or two along the way, would split his face in permanent joy. Fannie wanted to give Elam that vision. She wanted to hold that vision for herself.

But after more than five years since Sadie's birth?

Fannie looked at her mother heating coffee at the stove. Perhaps if she steeled herself with enough pastry, she could say she was glad for her mother.

She wouldn't *be* glad — not yet. But she would try very hard to say that she was.

Clara was grateful to be back at Fannie's house. Though the outing lasted barely three hours, it had exhausted Clara. It was not the miles they strode in lovely sunlight.

Her aunt was right. Clara was fearful, and Fannie was heartbroken.

At least in Fannie's home, neither of them had to pretend they felt differently. They only had to avoid speaking of the subject in Sadie's presence. As soon as Clara dropped into the davenport, Sadie snuggled against her and nudged her way under Clara's arm.

"Did you bring me a story?" Sadie looked up at Clara's face hopefully.

Clara stroked Sadie's hair. "No, I'm afraid I didn't think of it this time."

"Will you send me one in a letter, then?"

"I'll have to finish one," Clara said. "I'm in the middle of Joshua and the Battle of Jericho."

Sadie turned her head toward her mother across the room. "*Mamm,* do I know that story?"

"I don't know," Fannie said. "Do you?"

"You're being silly," Sadie said. "Just tell me if I know it."

Clara tickled Sadie's neck. "If you don't

60

remember, then I guess you don't know it."

"But you do, right?"

"Yes, I do."

"Then tell me from your head." Sadie scratched one bare foot. "You can send me the paper later."

"Well, let me see. Have you ever been surprised by a very big job? Something that seemed so hard that no one could do it? Maybe it made you afraid?"

"I remember when I was afraid of feeding the chickens."

"Bigger!" Clara said.

Sadie pushed her lips out, thinking. "I used to be afraid of carrying the milk bucket from the barn when it gets too full."

"Bigger!"

"I'm not afraid to pick up Thomas." Sadie giggled. "*Mamm* is afraid I'll drop him, but I'm not. And I'm not afraid to let the horse take an apple out of my hand."

"You're a brave little girl," Clara said. "But I'm sure if you think very hard, you'll remember something that seemed like a big, huge job, and when you do, you'll know just what Joshua felt like when God told him to lead the people in a walk around the city of Jericho. Joshua had to be brave enough to lead the people, but he also had to be brave enough to believe that when he obeyed

God, the very tall and very thick walls around Jericho would fall down. That's how the people would get inside the city."

Sadie's eyes were wide and bright. "Are you going to make sounds in this story? I like it when you make sounds."

"Now that you mention it," Clara said, "there are some very exciting sounds in this story. I'm going to need your help with them."

Sadie clapped.

"I'll make some lunch," Fannie said. "It should be ready by the time you get to the part about walking around the city seven times."

"We'll be hungry by then," Clara said. "Now Sadie, let's practice a trumpet sound."

Clara kept her voice cheerful for Sadie even as she watched the deepening droop in Fannie's shoulders.

After lunch, Sadie scampered outside with a promise that she would not stray far from the house. As soon as her daughter was out of earshot, Fannie turned her strained face toward her cousin. They stood at the front window watching Sadie run in circles.

"She's a gleeful child," Clara said. "I hope I didn't wind her up too much with all the marching and horn blowing."

Fannie gave a wan smile. "She'll never forget that story. She remembers all the Bible stories you tell her. And soon as she gets a letter, she makes me stop everything and read it."

"We'll have to work on teaching her to read them for herself."

"Thank you for coming." Fannie squeezed Clara's hand. "None of my friends here would understand. Everyone in the church will think it's such happy news."

It was happy news. Perhaps on another day Fannie would be able to make herself feel the gladness new life should bring.

"Have you decided whether to marry Andrew?" Fannie said.

Clara pulled her bottom lip down in a grimace. "What will I say if he asks me again?"

"Yes! You should say yes!"

"I know. I do care for him. Truly I do."

"Then don't try his patience any further. The wedding season will be here before you know it."

Fannie's mind flashed to what might happen by this time next year. Andrew and Clara could marry in the fall or early winter. By next summer, they could have a baby of their own on the way.

And it would be one more child wrenching at the grief in Fannie's heart, even though Clara would be terrified at the prospect of giving birth.

Martha's child — Fannie's own brother or sister — would be sitting up on a quilt in the sunshine, perhaps even rocking on hands and knees preparing to crawl.

Fannie swallowed the thickness of her throat. The world did not stop because God did not find her deserving of another child.

"Don't miss out on Andrew's love," Fannie said. "If there should be a child . . ."

"Let's not talk about that now," Clara murmured. "I should go."

Fannie nodded. If Clara didn't get to the Maple Glen Meetinghouse on time, she would miss the milk wagon going back across the border.

CHAPTER 5

The pressure in Clara's chest triggered tears in her eyes before she opened them the next morning. The dream had come again. Sadness trailed behind the vague shapes that never quite came into focus in those gray moments between disturbed sleep and opening day.

At least she had not wakened whimpering.

Clara hesitated to use the word *dream* for the unprovoked gloom that swam through her from time to time, as it had all her life. Nothing happened in these dreams, if that is what they were. She saw no faces, no landscape, no burning sun or swirling river water. The babies were gone before she heard their cries.

The babies. It was always the babies. Sometimes she thought she was the baby, but sometimes the baby was a boy.

Clara pushed her quilt away and swung

her feet over the side of the bed. She had not woken this way for months — long enough to hope that perhaps the misery she feared had dissipated and perhaps she could marry Andrew after all. Daylight had not yet broken through the window, but Clara would not sleep again. She never did when this happened. Her fingers knew where to find the matches on the corner of her night-stand, and she lit the lamp. She might as well finish writing Joshua's story for Sadie.

She didn't want to think about anybody's baby today.

This time Andrew did not linger over the electric table lamps or toasters.

On Saturday morning, he entered the hardware store with no list and no intended purchase. Instead, he sought space to won-der what he would do with the Model T. What he understood about the functioning of a motor — of any variety — was sparse enough that he could write it on the flap of an envelope. Andrew was fairly confident a hardware store was not the place to be schooled in the workings of an automobile engine. He would have to learn what the *English* meant when they said words like *piston* and *spark plugs* and *throttle.* For now he only wanted a place where he could look

66

thoughtful and occupied while acquiring a basic knowledge of what the store might offer in terms of supplies an automobile owner might require.

Andrew stood in front of a display of motor oil. How much did an engine use? Next to the oil was a rack of gloves made especially for driving. Were they essential? What about goggles? Andrew squeezed his eyes shut and then opened them again. He wouldn't need to worry about gloves or goggles unless he got the automobile running.

And since he did not know why it wasn't running already, he faced a conundrum.

"Andrew!"

At the sound of his name, Andrew snapped his gaze up. He let out his breath. It was only John Stutzman.

"Good morning, John."

"It is a good morning, isn't it?" John nodded his head in satisfaction.

Andrew had always liked John. The nine years' difference in their ages was enough that until not so long ago Andrew had called him a respectful "Mr. Stutzman," then "Smiling John" to distinguish him from his father, and finally simply "John." A husband and father of seven children, John was in a season of life Andrew hoped would arrive for him before long. The older Andrew got, the less marked the age disparity became. They were two farmers who went to church together and shared a way of life.

John stroked his beard and glanced at the display before Andrew.

He wouldn't ask. Andrew was sure of that. John Stutzman believed that a man's conscience was his own, which was just why Andrew felt no need to hide.

"I found something the other day," Andrew said.

John's eyebrows arched. "A horse that drinks oil?"

Andrew gave a half smile. "What if I said yes?"

"Then I'd say it was a horse that didn't eat hay."

"Not so far as I can figure, no."

"Not having to muck a stall would bring certain advantages."

Andrew laughed now. "Do you want to see it?"

"Do you mean to say you've taken possession of the remarkable beast?"

The remarkable beast. The description seemed apt, both for the automobile and for Andrew's rapidly growing affinity for it.

"I have indeed," Andrew said. "Free and clear."

"I will confess that does spark a certain degree of curiosity in me."

The fine lines at the corners of John's eyes creased, offering a faint suggestion of his age. For the first time, Andrew noticed wisps of faint gray in his friend's hair curling at the back of his neck.

"Then we shall have to arrange something," Andrew said.

With their heads tilted toward each other, Andrew revealed where the Model T was and the circumstances under which he acquired it. He'd poked and tugged at every loose edge inside and outside the automobile, looking for any evidence that the note and papers giving the Model T to whoever was willing to take it off the hands of its exasperated owner were not as straightforward as they seemed. Finding nothing, he took the papers home and stored them securely where even Yonnie would not know where to find them.

John laughed at Andrew's recounting. "You're hiding an automobile and you're worried someone will find the papers?"

Andrew shook his head. "I have no regret about taking the car. The possibility of being falsely accused of how I came to possess it enters my mind."

"What about Yonnie?"

"What about him?"

"Do you trust him?"

"He's my relative and my childhood friend."

"Yes. And do you trust him?"

John looked over Andrew's shoulder, and Andrew turned to follow his gaze. Yonnie stood at the end of the aisle.

Clara sometimes wondered what it would be like to court as the *English* did — always properly chaperoned, but without secrecy. Amish pairings were not always a surprise when engagements were published in church, but until that moment, no one could be certain a young man who offered to take a young woman home from the Singing where the unmarried gathered had true affection for her or whether she returned it. If a group took a buggy and food baskets for a picnic along the Casselman River, there might be a romantically aspiring couple among them or there might not be. Three minutes of conversation beyond the ears of anyone else could be casual insignificance or stolen, treasured words. Clara had her suspicions who might be announcing engagements as the harvest season approached this year — Ruth and Peter, for instance — but she made no claim to be certain of anything.

One thing Clara did know was that if she never left the Kuhn farm, she would never run into Andrew coincidentally — or not so coincidentally. After all, was there such a thing as a coincidence? Was not all that happened God's will?

So when Rhoda casually remarked on Saturday morning that she had forgotten to purchase green thread the last time she was in town and was now disappointed that she was not equipped for the mending in her basket, Clara cheerfully offered to go to the mercantile. To her surprise, Rhoda did not refuse the help and in fact gave Clara a list of several other small but needful items that would more than justify the excursion.

Taking just one horse with a small cart, Clara kept her eyes open for any sign of Andrew, who might come from a side road because he had been visiting a neighbor or who might come from the direction she was traveling. When Clara passed the turnoff to his farm, the urge to see if he was home tempted her, but she knew a daytime meeting would be much safer out where anyone might observe it and think nothing of it.

The thought that she *might* run into him, that it *might* be God's will for them to see each other today, was enough to stretch her neck in anticipation, but she chastised her own hope with determination not to lose her grip on her errand for Rhoda. If she wanted to prove herself useful, she could not disappoint Rhoda by tumbling into distraction and failing to come home with green thread and a few practical items.

Clara got all the way to Springs, where she drove around two small squares of shops looking for a place to leave the horse and cart. The shops still had hitching posts in front of them, but every time Clara came into Springs, there seemed to be more automobiles. Irritation pulsed through her good mood. The automobiles themselves did not bother her, but why did their owners have to leave them in front of the hitching posts?

The annoyance fled when the circuit around the blocks led to a sighting of a brown stallion with a stripe of white running down his long nose.

Andrew's horse — and room to share the hitching post. Clara eased her gentle spotted gray mare into the space and knotted the reins to the post before reaching under the bench in the cart for the sack of apples her father always kept there. She offered one to the mare and one to the stallion, tempted to feed them all the apples in the bag while she loitered with the thought that Andrew would have to return to this spot eventually.

Clara wiped her hands on her apron. Rhoda would wonder whether she truly meant to bring the thread. Clara pivoted to amble down to the mercantile.

At first she passed the hardware store. Then she idly turned. The store was Andrew's favorite. She opened the door and there he was, talking with John Stutzman. Clara contained the grin welling up inside her as she shuffled down the aisle.

And then she saw Yonnie with his dour features and set jaw. He stood with Andrew and John, only coming into Clara's view when John shifted his weight to one side. If Clara wanted to see Andrew, she would have to see Yonnie as well. At least John was there with his broad smile and eyes that twinkled for no apparent reason.

Andrew lifted his head and rotated his glance toward Clara. One corner of his mouth twitched in invitation, and she moved toward them.

John dipped his head toward Clara. "*Gut mariye,* Clara. My wife will be wondering what happened to me, so please excuse my departure."

"Of course." Clara gave John a small

73

smile. "Please greet your family for me."

Yonnie seemed to have planted his feet. Clara met his eyes with sufficient manners before fixing her gaze on Andrew's brown hair, with its ragged cut he insisted on giving himself, and the brown eyes that announced curiosity and pleasure as surely as if he spoke into a megaphone.

If only marriage did not mean bearing children.

Yonnie crossed his arms over his chest. If Andrew felt no shame for taking the abandoned car, then why should he mind if Clara Kuhn knew about it?

"Andrew was just telling John about the Model T," Yonnie said.

"The Model T?" Clara said. "It certainly has become popular among the *English.*"

"At least one *English* has lost interest," Yonnie muttered.

Clara creased her brow. "I'm afraid I'm not following your point, Yonnie."

Andrew put a thumb through one suspender. "He means the one I found."

Yonnie watched Clara's eyebrows rise. It was one thing for John Stutzman to show no concern that Andrew had taken possession of a valuable *English* machine — though Yonnie thought he should have.

74

Clara would be different. Her father was staunch in his convictions. He could have joined the Marylanders twenty years ago when the churches clustered around the border parted ways, but he chose the Old Order.

"You found a car?" Clara said to Andrew.

Andrew glanced around the store. *He says he's not ashamed,* Yonnie thought, *but he doesn't want everyone to hear.* Yonnie surveyed the store as well and saw no other Amish customers.

With soft tones, Andrew described the events of Wednesday afternoon. Yonnie was less interested in what Andrew said than in what he saw on Clara's face.

No alarm.

No shock.

Her blue eyes widened, but not in fear. It was more akin to inquisitiveness.

"Clara, what would your father think of Andrew's decision?" Yonnie asked.

She shrugged. "My father is not Andrew's conscience."

"What about you? What do you think?"

Clara smiled. "I'd like to see the automobile."

CHAPTER 6

Was it a sin to hope that Mose Beachy would be the minister selected to give the main sermon? Or to pray that this would be God's will?

Though she wouldn't speak it aloud, that was what Clara wondered during the final hymn before the sermons. In a moment, the bishop and three ministers who served the congregation would return from their private meeting and prayer, and one of them would begin to preach a short sermon. After another hymn, a second minister would bring the main sermon. Why could it not be Mose Beachy? Mose was a gentle, thoughtful man in conversation and in preaching.

But when the four men entered at the front of the meetinghouse, Clara could tell from Bishop Yoder's posture that the lot had fallen to him. Clara did not know much about lots and statistics, but it seemed to her that Bishop Yoder gave sermons more often than any of the others. She had been hearing them her entire life. He'd always been firm, but in the last couple of years, he had turned virulent. He wasn't ancient, but he was near seventy, so few men in the church exceeded his age. Lately, Clara observed, Bishop Yoder moved more slowly, as if his joints had stiffened and refused cooperation. His sons deferentially stood aside and held doors open with patience. Yet when Bishop Yoder stood to preach, his frailties seemed to leave him.

Bishop Yoder remained standing beside the preaching table, while his two sons, Joseph and Noah, took seats on either side of Mose Beachy on the ministers' bench facing the congregation. One of them would give a second sermon. Clara clung to the hope that she might yet hear Mose's words of wisdom today.

Clara settled in with her youngest sister on her lap. Mari had fallen asleep during the final hymn, and Clara doubted she would wake before the service ended. Beside them was Hannah and then Rhoda. Clara glanced across the aisle to the men's side, where Josiah recently had been permitted to sit with his father rather than among the women. He took the privilege seriously and sat somberly with his hands crossed in his lap and every muscle in his face under control. Clara nearly smiled in pride but caught herself just in time. Of all places, the worship service was the wrong place for pride.

In the row behind Hiram and Josiah, Andrew sat beside Yonnie with the unmarried men. Clara wished she could know what Andrew was thinking, but like all the worshippers, he wiped expression from his face. It pained Clara to think that even if she married Andrew, she could not sit beside him during church and feel him near.

Clara shook off all the trivial hopes and wishes that coursed through her. None of them mattered. She was here to worship and learn, though she did not have to wait for the bishop to announce his Scripture text to know what he would preach about.

Self-discipline. This seemed to be the only theme God had laid on the bishop's heart for the last two years.

Bishop Yoder began to preach.

Clara succeeded at remaining still and attentive, but under its outward form, her body ached to rise and pace across the back of the meetinghouse. Ironically, if she had a colicky baby on her hip instead of a sleeping sister in her lap, she could have done so.

She glanced at Andrew again.

At the sound of the benediction, Andrew's first thought was Clara. As she left the meetinghouse, she glanced over her shoulder at him and met his eyes. Outside, he meandered toward where she strolled without particular aim, making sure to greet several people along the way. Clara was doing the same, but Andrew knew she was waiting for their paths of greeting to cross just as he was.

"Gut mariye," he said when he reached her and they stood safely away from other members of the congregation — but not so far as to provoke speculation.

"Gut mariye," Clara answered. "The same as always, was it not?"

They had spoken of Bishop Yoder's sermons before.

"Please don't let him upset you," Andrew said.

"He is working up to something," Clara said. "I believe he can find the theme of discipline in any part of the Bible."

"He preaches what God puts on his heart."

"Does he? Does the Holy Ghost use such judgment?"

"Will you be at the Singing tonight?" Andrew would hear Clara out later, when they were alone, and then their conversation could move on to more personal matters.

Clara nodded. "You'd better go help with the benches."

Andrew's gaze held her eyes for a few more seconds before he turned away to his duties. A few men had already begun transforming benches into tables, and Andrew grabbed the free end of a bench and entered the process.

Beside him a conversation was under way, and it had nothing to do with benches and tables.

"He's doing it again," one man said.

"He never stopped," another responded.

"Almost thirty years of this, ever since he signed that letter in 1887."

"That's history."

"Is it? Bishop Yoder has never found peace with the decision to let the Maryland churches go their own way. That's why he preaches as he does."

With the approach of footsteps, the two men cut off their conversation and carried a bench out of the way. Someone took the other end of Andrew's bench and they moved it over several yards, where it would provide seating on one side of a table. Andrew's partner dropped his end of the bench with a careless thud.

"Are you all right?" Andrew walked along the length of the bench to stand beside the man, someone about ten years older than Andrew whom he did not know well.

The man looked around. Andrew followed his gaze across the room to Noah and Joseph Yoder.

"His sons are the same way, you know," the man said. "Mose Beachy is our only hope."

"Hope for what?" Andrew probed.

They picked up another bench, but the man clamped his lips closed.

"They are all following God the best way they know how," Andrew said.

"Then why does it feel so much like they want us to follow them?" The words, hardly more than a mutter, were the man's last contribution to the conversation. He turned on one heel and found another task in another part of the room.

Andrew straightened benches under tables, seeing in his mind instead of slats of wood the sleek green metal and brass of the Model T.

"It's 1905 all over again," Barbara Stutzman said.

Bishop Yoder had eaten and said his farewells, with Joseph and Noah at his elbows. Several other families had left as well. The women were clearing away the remaining food.

Clara remembered 1905. Rhoda had lost her first baby only weeks before the truth came out at church. At home, Clara's father cared much less about controversy swirling in the congregation than the fragile state of his young wife. Clara had not understood everything that happened at church or at home, but the silence of a child was expected in both places so she dared not ask questions. She muted her curiosity and kept a respectful distance from the grieving adults in her home.

"We were duped in 1895 and again ten years later," Barbara said. "It won't turn out that way this time."

Clara liked Barbara Stutzman as much as she liked her husband, John. But never had she heard Barbara speak out with such certainty. Duped? Surely that was a strong word for the decisions the congregation made.

Rhoda appeared beside Clara. "Are you riding home with us?"

Clara glanced at the group of men sorting out the last of the benches, arranging them in neat rows in readiness for the next time the congregation would gather in the Flag Run Meetinghouse.

"It's a nice day," Clara said. "Perhaps I'll take a walk."

"That's wise." Rhoda looked from Clara to a tangle of unmarried people forming at the meetinghouse door.

Hannah tugged on her mother's sleeve. "I want to walk with Clara."

"You'll ride with us." Rhoda's tone left no room for argument. Hannah knew better than to pout.

Clara squelched the urge to say she would be glad to have Hannah with her. She and Rhoda both knew the girl would tire and begin to whine before all the miles were accomplished, but Clara also saw in Rhoda's eyes the mandate to mingle with the young people who lingered. *"Find someone to marry."* Clara heard Rhoda's voice in her mind. *"Start your own life."*

"And you'll go to the Singing tonight?" Rhoda said.

Clara nodded.

"Good. Then I'm sure you have a full Sabbath ahead of you."

Clara kissed the foreheads of both of her

young half sisters and offered her step-mother a wan smile of assurance that she would not be underfoot in the Kuhn household today.

After a long service and a leisurely shared meal, the evening Singing was only a few hours away. Someone would suggest a group walk along Flag Run Creek or a sports game to pass the hours in friendship and laughter. Clara used to enjoy these afternoons more than she did now. Friends her own age had all paired off and married. She and Andrew were two of a diminishing number of people in their twenties who were not married.

And it was not Andrew who kept them in this state.

Clara reasoned that the socializing part of the day had begun and saw no reason not to join Andrew in his cluster of conversation. The circle widened slightly as Clara approached. She stood where she could see Andrew's round face. Whether to be beside him and feel him near or to be able to watch his expressions always was a choice she hated to make. But being seen beside him too often would spark speculation she was not prepared to confront. His eyes met hers but did not linger.

"Bishop Yoder has gone too far this time."

John Stutzman spoke with the same conviction Clara had heard in his wife a few minutes earlier. Had they already found a private moment to discuss their feelings about the sermon? Had they decided to speak out, or was it coincidence?

There was no such thing as coincidence, Clara reminded herself. *Gottes wille.* Everything that happened was God's will.

"He said nothing he has not said before." Mose Beachy gave Clara a welcome glance. She was glad to hear his voice, calm and peaceable.

"He's been proud of his power for years," John said.

"That is a serious accusation," Mose said.

Clara shifted her eyes to Yonnie, who stood silently listening.

"Are we not to speak the truth in love?" John said.

Mose reached under his beard to scratch his chin, as he often did during fragile conversations. Clara realized she was holding her breath. Andrew tilted his head toward Mose.

"You speak well," Mose said. "The Scriptures do admonish us to speak the truth in love. We do well if we remember the fine balance of the admonition. Neither truth nor love should obscure the other."

Clara exhaled softly. This was why she liked to hear Mose Beachy preach. These few sentences were more profound — and convicting — than anything Bishop Yoder said in nearly an hour of holding his big German Bible in his hands.

"Lucy is waiting," Mose said. "The little ones will need to go home for their naps." He stepped away.

"Little ones," Yonnie said. "With fourteen children, they've had little ones longer than anyone around here."

"They have a lovely family," John said. "But Mose sets a good example. My wife will be wondering what's become of me as well."

John crossed the room to find his family. The meetinghouse was nearly empty.

Yonnie looked from Andrew to Clara. "Will you be recreating with the others today?"

Clara looked to Andrew for the answer.

"Clara and I will take a walk," Andrew said. "Perhaps we'll join the games later."

Skepticism crossed Yonnie's face, but he moved away from them.

"A walk?" Clara said.

"Do you object?" Andrew gestured toward the door.

She twisted her smile to one side. "Actually, I was hoping to see your Model T."

CHAPTER 7

Andrew turned his buggy down a dark side road. He knew, and Clara knew, that choosing this route home from the Singing would add at least thirty minutes to the ride home. Andrew intended to add much more than that. He had always enjoyed Singings, though he went less often now. Unless Andrew was certain Clara would be there, his interest in the traditional social gathering faltered.

Two lanterns hung from the front of his buggy, lighting the dim, narrow road that divided fields of adjoining farms. Even without the lights, the nearly full moon and the canopy of stars hurled across the sky would have given them safe passage. Andrew knew the road well. No holes awaited the steps of his horse.

It was the stars that brought them out here tonight. Andrew slowed the stallion. The day had been beautiful — any day spent with Clara was beautiful — and he wanted this memory in his mind when he was alone on his farm tonight. Clara beside him. The sky vast above them. The sounds of evening restful around them. The night air cool and fluttering on their faces.

"Thank you for showing me the Model T." Clara's words came on a soft ripple.

The horse clip-clopped forward.

"It means a lot to me that you wanted to see it," Andrew said.

"I love your curious mind," Clara said.

"Even if I am curious about an automobile engine?"

"Would God have made you curious if He knew it would displease Him?"

Andrew turned and smiled at her in the moonlight and slowed the horse even more.

"Have you no doubt?" he asked.

"About the gift of curiosity? No."

"And about the Model T?"

"It was you who found it," she said, "not I."

"I care what you think."

"None of the ministers have preached against the automobile," Clara said. "Not even Bishop Yoder."

Andrew slowly eased the horse to the side of the road and gave the reins a final tug. "Bishop Yoder is too busy preaching about discipline in all its forms."

"Would he not think that owning an automobile is a lack of discipline in some form? Perhaps it has not occurred to him that anyone in the church would consider owning a device the *English* have taken such a liking to."

"Until it comes to a vote in the congregation, what harm will it be for me to learn something from it?" Andrew said. "Eventually the church will have to face the issue. Mr. Ford seems determined to make car ownership affordable."

"Perhaps affordable does not also mean desirable," Clara said.

"Do you find it undesirable?"

"No. Not precisely. I am only hearing in my head the arguments others will make."

"Automobiles could benefit the congregation," Andrew said. "It would be easier for families who live on the outskirts of the district to get to church. The dairy Yonnie works for could transport milk more easily and more quickly without risking spoilage. When someone falls ill, it would be faster to summon the doctor. Those who owned cars could be generous toward others who needed to travel."

"Those are all good points," Clara said. "I spent most of a day driving across the county to tell John Stutzman my father was ill and would not be able to help him with his roof after all."

The buggy creaked and settled. The horse snorted and stilled. Around them, a chorus of insects sprang up with sounds they had not heard above horse hooves falling rhythmically and the squeaking sway of the buggy.

Andrew stared into the jeweled darkness. " 'O Lord, our Lord, how excellent is thy name in all the earth! who hast set thy glory above the heavens,' " he murmured.

" 'When I consider thy heavens, the work of thy fingers,' " Clara said, " 'the moon and the stars, which thou hast ordained; what is man, that thou art mindful of him? and the son of man, that thou visitest him?' "

"I suppose I have told you that Psalm 8 is my favorite psalm," Andrew said.

"About as many times as there are stars in the sky." Clara's voice carried the smile Andrew could not see on her lips. "Whether in sunlight or moonlight, the sky is deep and mysterious. I can't help but think God made it that way so we would know how deep and mysterious He is."

"Do you think it grieves God when we try to make Him too simple?"

"He knows how frail we are," Clara said. "Perhaps our people should all stare at the stars together before we decide that any one of us knows better than another about the will of God."

Andrew twisted on the bench to face Clara. Moonlight threw its sheen over her blue eyes. "You are wise. I would go to your father tonight and ask his blessing on our union if only you would agree."

"I'm sure he would welcome you — though perhaps at a time when you would not be waking him."

"Ah, yes. More wisdom. I would not want to give him any reason to turn me down." He reached for her hand. "Tell me I should go to your father. Just say the word."

"Andrew." Clara withdrew her hand.

"Clara, what are we waiting for? We're ready, aren't we?"

Clara looked down at the hands in her lap. "You may think me wise, but you will not find me courageous."

"Why should it take courage to marry me?"

"No, not to marry you. It's . . . what comes next."

He was sure she was blushing. "We'll figure that out together, won't we?"

"But a child . . ."

"Don't you want to have a child — many children, if the Lord blesses?"

"Andrew, my mother died trying to birth a child. Rhoda lost three babes. Mrs. Wickey. Mrs. Eicher." She paused, and he heard her suck in breath. "The bleeding and the fever — childbirth terrifies me."

Andrew slid along the bench and put an arm around her shoulders. "I won't say it's not frightening. After all, I am not the one who would have to endure it."

She leaned her head against him. "I know. Women have babies all the time. The Beachys have fourteen children and nothing has ever gone wrong. Children *are* a blessing."

"But you're still frightened."

Andrew felt the reluctant nod of her head against his chest.

"Look up again," he said, and she did. "Can anything be more unknown than what lies beyond the planets? Yet you know God is there."

He listened to her breath, out and in, out and in.

"I promise to think more about it." Clara raised her face to him.

Andrew ducked his head down to meet her lips. She didn't pull away. He knew she wouldn't. The yielding welcome made him heady.

The clatter of a moving buggy pulled

Andrew out of the kiss. With Clara still in his arms, he leaned back into the shadow of his own buggy. When the buggy passed, they let out their breath together. Clara leaned away.

Clara woke the next morning, as she always did, to the sounds of Rhoda moving through the house and into the kitchen to prepare the family's breakfast. She rose to wash and dress with the efficiency of lifelong habit and reached the kitchen in time to see Rhoda whisking eggs in a bowl. The oven was heating.

"Good morning," Clara said. "Shall I make biscuits?"

"Good morning," Rhoda said. "Thank you, but no. We have corn bread left from yesterday."

Clara looked around the kitchen for something else she could do and settled on straightening the dish towel that hung from a hook. Surely Rhoda would allow that.

"Did you have a nice time at the Singing?" Rhoda poured the eggs into an oblong earthenware baking dish layered with cheese.

"Very nice."

"Who brought you home?"

"Andrew Raber."

"Oh? He's a nice man."

"Yes, he is."

"He's brought you home before, hasn't he?"

"Several times." *Every time,* Clara thought. *For two years.*

Rhoda slid the casserole dish into the oven. "I don't hear you speak of him."

Rhoda moved swiftly from the oven to the counter where the leftover corn bread was wrapped in a worn flour sack. She unwrapped it with one hand while reaching for a knife with the other and slicing the bread into thick chunks.

"I could do that," Clara said. "Are you planning to fry the bread?"

"I can manage." Rhoda wiped the knife clean, put it away, and arranged the bread on a platter. "Andrew Raber? Are the two of you . . . ?"

When Clara was younger, the time she spent with Rhoda in the kitchen before breakfast was an opportunity to talk about whatever might pass through her mind. It was one of the reasons Clara rose in the mornings as soon as she heard her stepmother's movements. Watching Rhoda now, Clara could not be certain if Rhoda asked about Andrew as she might have in their old rhythms or because she wished for Clara to find another home.

Words about Andrew would not form. Instead, Clara said, "I'll get Mari up and dressed in time for breakfast."

"I can do that," Rhoda said. She put the egg bowl in the sink, wiped her hands on her apron, and left the room.

Clara decided she could at least set the table and took six plates from the shelf. She looked up when she heard footsteps with a distinct shuffle that identified them as belonging to Hannah.

"*Mamm* told me to set the table for breakfast," Hannah said.

"I was just about to do it."

"*Mamm* said I was to do it."

"We'll do it together, then." Clara smiled.

Insistence grew in Hannah's tone. "But *Mamm* said I must do it."

Clara released her hold on the plates. The girl was simply trying to obey her mother. Whatever changes might come in Clara's relationship with Rhoda should have nothing to do with a six-year-old child.

After kissing the top of Hannah's head, Clara wandered into the dining room. Staying out of the way for a few minutes seemed a somber way to begin the morning, yet it seemed the sensible thing.

Breakfast was warm and hearty and

pinched Clara's heart. The scrubbed, earnest face of her brother, the tight, flawless braids of her sisters' hair and their bright blue eyes, the plain familiar practicality of the kitchen she had known all her life, her father's subdued, unflustered demeanor, the woman who had filled Clara's ache for a mother. Clara's appetite subsided, and for most of the meal she watched the others eat.

What had she done to make Rhoda so eager that Clara should leave?

Rhoda cleared the dishes and Hiram laid the family's thick German Bible on the table. That Bible had come from her mother's family, Clara knew. She had always supposed someday it would be hers. Now she wasn't certain. Hiram read with expression, even if he had chosen to lead the family through the book of Leviticus.

The family scattered to their chores after family devotions. Clara moved into the front room, wondering what might be a safe task to engage in. The mending basket sat at one end of the davenport. Clara remembered the green thread she brought home from the mercantile in Springs and decided to explore the basket. A dark green dress seemed to be the major item. Clara remembered that Hannah had worn it when she was smaller. Rhoda probably wanted to make it suitable for Mari. Lifting it with both hands and holding it out in front of her, Clara inspected the seams and hems and easily assessed what the garment required.

She finished restitching the main seam along one side of the dress just as Rhoda entered the room with Mari on her hip.

"I was planning to do that," Rhoda said.

"I know. I wanted to help." Clara ran the seam between her thumb and forefinger, feeling for any irregularities she had missed.

"Mari is an active child," Rhoda said. "I had in mind to double stitch."

"Certainly. I'll put in another row."

"Thank you, but I can do that later." Rhoda took the dress from Clara's lap, gave the seam a quick glance, and put the garment back in the basket.

Clara stood up, her eyes stinging. "I'm sure the henhouse could use a cleaning."

"That's Josiah's chore now," Rhoda said.

"I'm happy to help. I'll go find him."

"Your father and I are working on teaching Josiah responsibility. I would rather you didn't help him."

"Of course." Clara had always thought Josiah one of the most responsible children she had ever known. "What else can I help you with, then?"

"I can't think of a thing," Rhoda said.

"I can't think of a thing." That was ridiculous. On an Amish farm, there were always a hundred things to do, inside and out. Clara swallowed her objection to Rhoda's logic.

"I'll watch Mari for you," Clara offered.

"She's fine with me. Why don't you go for a walk?"

Rhoda smiled and her tone was perfectly pleasant, but Clara heard meaning beyond her words.

Rhoda did not need Clara's help.

Clara was too old to need Rhoda's help.

It was time for a change.

Clara should look for another arrangement.

CHAPTER 8

Andrew stood outside the shop for thirteen minutes before he found the resolve to go in. His horse and buggy certainly looked out of place in front of this particular establishment on the road out of Springs, and Andrew himself would look equally out of place inside. This was not the same as going into an *English* hardware store or the mercantile, or even visiting the *English* blacksmith if the Amish blacksmith was too busy and the need was immediate.

The sign over the door read HANSEN'S AUTOMOTIVE REPAIR.

Inside, Andrew scanned a small, unadorned space with two chairs and a large wooden desk. Beyond that was the large work area, with four automobiles lined up. Andrew already had noted five more outside.

A man was bent over an open engine.

Andrew cleared his throat.

The man looked up. "What can I do for you?"

Andrew hesitated over the ridiculous statement he was about to make. "I want to learn to do what you do."

The man stood up straight and looked Andrew in the eye.

"Are you Mr. Hansen?" Andrew asked.

"That's right."

"I have a Model T," Andrew said, "but it doesn't run. I want to learn to fix it."

Hansen picked up a rag and rubbed grease from his hands. "I'm not in the business of teaching. People pay me to fix."

"Couldn't I watch you for a while?"

Hansen scoffed. "I can tow your car in and fix it for you."

In the far corner a young man bent over a trash can and retched. Hansen expelled breath and tossed a wrench on a shelf.

"Sorry," the young man said, wiping his mouth.

"Go home," Hansen said. "You're no help to me in this condition. But clean up after yourself first."

Even across the large garage, the smell of the man's illness wafted as he picked up the trash can and stumbled toward a rear door.

"Let me help you today." Andrew pounced on the moment. "I'll scrub down anything the boy touched and hand you any tool you need. Just let me watch as you work."

Hansen rustled through a toolbox and came up with a tool Andrew had no name for.

"One hour," Hansen said. "If by then you've proven you're not an idiot, then you can stay the day."

"Thank you!" Andrew stepped into the work area.

"Hang up your hat," Hansen said. "It will only get in the way."

Andrew put a hand to the straw brim. He was not in the habit of doing without his hat. The Amish always wore their hats when they were out of their own homes. But he took it off his head and looked for a hook.

Six hours later, Andrew squinted into the daylight again. He and Jurgen Hansen had gotten along well, and Andrew now carried a small carton with several small parts and tools, along with a general idea that the problem with his Model T was that something was obstructing the fuel going into the engine.

Yonnie drove the milk wagon to the abandoned Johnson farm the next morning and guardedly turned into the lane that would lead to the outlying shed. It was the only place he could think to look for Andrew.

Living alone, Andrew had decided it was easier to buy milk, butter, and cheese from the dairy than to keep a cow. Yonnie checked a couple of times a week on what Andrew needed. When Andrew's milk box had no empty bottles in it that Tuesday morning, Yonnie had gone inside the house. Dishes in the sink had dried egg on them at least a day old. In Andrew's bedroom, the bed looked undisturbed. It took Yonnie a few minutes to sort out what else looked wrong, but finally it dawned on him.

Approaching the old Johnson barn, Yonnie knew he was right. Andrew's horse was tethered with a long lead that allowed it to nibble the ground freely, swish its tail, and shake its mane. Yonnie left the milk wagon and pushed open the shed door.

Andrew looked up. "Yonnie! How did you know where I was?"

Yonnie stepped inside. "I stopped at your house. When I realized every lantern you own was missing, I could think of only one reason. You've been here all night fooling with that automobile."

Andrew grinned. "And I think I've figured it out."

"Are you hoping I will congratulate you?" Yonnie counted nine lanterns burning, set on shelves, barrels, the roof of the car, and flat surfaces beside the engine.

"Think what you will," Andrew said. "I'm pleased."

"If you knock over even one of these lanterns, you could burn the place down."

"I'm not going to knock anything over," Andrew said. "Besides, I'm finished."

"You don't deny that you were here all night?" Yonnie put out the lamp that made him most nervous because of its proximity to the only bale of hay left in the barn.

"Since you're here," Andrew said, "it must be morning. So yes, I was here all night."

Yonnie watched the ruddy flush of pleasure in Andrew's face. Not many things would make Andrew stay up all night. He liked his sleep. That was one reason he decided not to keep a cow, gladly reducing his early-morning responsibilities.

"When was the last time you ate?" Yonnie asked.

"Are you planning to report to my mother in Lancaster County?" Andrew used a rag to polish a small hand tool that Yonnie did not recognize.

"Where did you get that?" Yonnie said. "And what is it?"

"I could answer you," Andrew said, "but

somehow I doubt the sincerity of your inquiry."

"You are getting in over your head, aren't you?"

Andrew flashed another grin. "Have you already forgotten that I said I fixed it? It was choking for fuel, and now it'll get what it needs for the engine to run."

"So now what?"

"We take it for a test ride."

"We?"

"Never mind. I know it would rattle your nerves to get in an automobile, so I won't ask it of you." Andrew bent down, found the opening, inserted the crank, and turned it. The Model T proposed no response.

Yonnie took a few steps closer, his brow furrowed. "Are you sure you know what you're doing?"

"Haven't you ever seen one of the *English* in town start a car?"

"Haven't you ever noticed how often they can't get them started?"

"Those are the older models," Andrew said. "This one is only a couple of years old." He abandoned the crank to check the levers inside the car.

"This is not wise," Yonnie said. "This automobile will consume your thoughts. You will neglect your fields at an important time in the growing season."

Andrew cocked his head. "My corn is growing just fine. All it needs right now is sun, rain, and time. I can't control any of those things."

"You're a farmer, not an automobile . . ." Yonnie was uncertain what to call a person who knew how to repair a car.

"Ah, yes," Andrew said. "I forgot this lever has to be up. Now I should feel the compression."

Andrew jumped back to the crank. He pulled up swiftly and the engine caught, its roar consuming the small barn.

"Are you sure that's how it's supposed to sound?" Yonnie shouted over the noise.

"It's running!" Andrew leaped onto the bench behind the steering wheel. "I'm going to take it out."

"Out where?"

"To the road, of course. Stand clear."

Yonnie did not move. How could Andrew not see that he would make an incriminating situation more serious if he took the car out of this barn?

"Out of the way," Andrew said. He looked down at his feet and moved the hand lever rising straight up out of the floor to the left of the steering wheel. A sound like the kick of a rifle startled them both.

Involuntarily, Yonnie jumped out of the way.

Andrew gripped the steering wheel with both hands as the Model T rolled out of the barn. He might have had a more accurate expectation of the sensation had he ever ridden in a car before. His instinct to pull on reins to control speed was no help, and instead of the brake pedal, his foot found the gear pedal and the car lurched forward.

Throttle, he reminded himself. What was it Mr. Hansen had said? Use the throttle lever to slow the engine and change gears smoothly.

The speed stabilized just as Andrew reached the farm's lane. He turned the steering wheel to the left, realized he had pulled it too far, and turned back toward the right slightly. The next turn would be better. The right front tire dipped into a rut in the road, and again Andrew tugged on the steering wheel with both fists to correct the forward motion.

"Whoa!" he said aloud, as he would to a horse. The Model T chugged forward. Andrew's eyes went from his hands to the levers as he tried to remember the notes he'd taken and what they meant. Mr. Hansen had spoken so quickly, as if Andrew understood all the terms he used. Andrew planted his feet on the floor, remembering that if he did not want to change from low gear to high or to slow the speed, his feet had nothing to do. That was not so different than driving a buggy. Looking through the glass shielding his eyes from the wind, he began to plan how to turn right onto the main road.

To his relief, no automobile, horse, or buggy was coming into his path. Without having to stop, he turned to the right, once again pulling too hard on the wheel and correcting as swiftly as he could. The Model T zigzagged across the road several times before he gained control of the trajectory.

He needed to slow down. Another driver could appear over the next rise, or a horse pulling a wagon, whether *English* or Amish.

Slow down. Find the gear pedal. Be ready with the brake pedal on the left. No, the brake is on the right. Yes, the right. Be careful not to press the reverse pedal.

While Andrew planned the series of motions, the car hit a bump. The entire automobile twitched to the left. Forgetting about the pedals, Andrew pulled the steering wheel to the right.

When he lifted his eyes again, a ditch was rapidly approaching. The front wheels dropped off the road. The car stopped abruptly, the engine died, and the right rear tire spun in the air.

Andrew let out his breath and then gulped fresh air, his heart pounding. He'd been doing so well. A horse didn't go off the road every time it hit a bump.

The soft spring earth had yielded graciously. Andrew was relieved to hear no thud or crash. He climbed out of the seat and inspected the Model T, ignoring the bump his knee had taken against the dashboard.

Yonnie slowed the milk wagon on the main road. Before his eyes lay the evidence that Andrew, in fact, did not know what he was doing. Andrew waved from beside the rear axle of the Model T, and Yonnie gave the reins a final tug.

"I'm going to need to borrow a rope again," Andrew said.

Yonnie eyed the precarious tilt of the car. "Perhaps this is the revelation of God's will for you."

"I doubt it." Andrew said. "Anyway, I can't just leave it here."

He certainly could, Yonnie believed. "I'm already late on my rounds."

"Dale won't begrudge you stopping to

109

help someone in need."

Yonnie sucked in his lips, thinking, *Even if your own sin brought you to your need?*

Andrew approached the wagon. "This is not the time to worry about rules, Yonnie."

"If you were concerned about rules, you wouldn't have this automobile." Yonnie reluctantly got out of the wagon and lifted a coil of thick rope from where it hung on the side. "Where is your allegiance to the faith of our fathers?"

"You can preach at me later," Andrew said. "Right now we have to figure out how to get out of the ditch without breaking the axle."

Yonnie tossed the rope to Andrew, sighing in disbelief that he agreed to have anything to do with this automobile. Even the *English* owner had the good sense to abandon it.

CHAPTER 9

The walk from the Kuhn farm to Springs was six and one-quarter miles.

But Clara found no reason not to walk.

Nothing pressing took her to town, either, but she had to get off the farm. In the last day and a half, she tried to polish Rhoda's cedar chest in the front room, wipe the dust from the kitchen cupboards, and mend the tiny weak spots she noticed in the good white tablecloth. Rhoda discouraged every indoor effort, so Clara moved into the June sunshine to sweep and mop the front porch, weed the vegetable garden, and scrub out the slop bucket. Even outdoors, though, Josiah or Hannah turned up with instructions from their mother to complete whatever task Clara began. They were small children. They could help and learn — even eagerly — but on their own they could not accomplish what Clara could do.

Rhoda did not raise her voice or express

impatience. She simply was firm and consistent. So Clara, who had only the cash from two housecleaning jobs to call her own and did not carry it around, walked to town and moved between the shops. Her father had accounts at a few of them. If Clara had a true need, she could make a purchase, but she knew she wouldn't. She only needed to be off the farm.

Clara stared at her reflection in the glass of the mercantile window. Down the street was an Amish furniture store, and farther down was a grocer who carried products from the Amish dairy. The bank in Springs held the mortgages on Amish farms. Clara could name many Amish families who rarely came off their farms and even more rarely transacted business with the *English,* but many others saw no harm.

The *English* and two Amish districts huddled around the border between Pennsylvania and Maryland. Most of the *English* could not tell the difference between the two types of Amish, though the Amish certainly recognized the subtle distinctions in clothing and hair coverings. Undoubtedly they knew who attended church in which meetinghouse on alternate Sundays.

When a clerk inside the mercantile looked out the window, Clara moved down the street. She had not brought even a few coins to buy a sandwich or a cup of coffee. She shuffled to the next shop window, an *English* dress shop. Realizing where she was, she didn't linger. It was better to keep moving even if all she did was walk around the block looking purposeful.

Maybe she should have walked to Niverton instead. She could at least sit on the old log outside the meetinghouse and feel less conspicuous.

Clara hadn't been to church with Fannie or any of the Hostetlers since she was a little girl, before her father married Rhoda and she used to spend long leisure weeks with her cousins. Then everything changed. Hiram became more firm that his daughter's visits over the border should conclude in time to have Clara home with her own family on Sundays when the congregation gathered at Summit Mills or Flag Run. In the last dozen years, Hiram did not explain his decision, but neither did he soften.

Would he really now allow Rhoda to dispatch Clara to Maryland to worship with her mother's family again? Or would he oppose Clara if she wanted to? Or would he insist Clara go if she did *not* want to?

Martha and Fannie and all the others would welcome Clara. They would welcome

113

Andrew if she married him, and he would go.

And why wouldn't he go? He was no more inclined toward Bishop Yoder's sermons than Clara was. His own parents had moved to Lancaster County. His married siblings were scattered over several districts in Pennsylvania and Ohio. Nothing held him to the Old Order Amish, as they became known after the 1895 split.

Clara wished she remembered more about that year.

Perhaps it would not feel so odd to join the Conservative Amish Mennonites — or at least to visit them.

"Clara Kuhn!"

Clara turned toward the voice. Sarah Tice strode toward her with a towheaded child attached to each hand.

"It seems like we never get a chance to talk anymore," Sarah said.

It was true. Clara had gone all the way through school with Sarah. After that they often found an excuse to visit one another. The distance between their farms had not been daunting. When Sarah married Jacob Tice, though, she moved farther out. Getting to her farm north of the Summit Mills Meetinghouse required more planning. Even at church, Sarah's attention was occupied with her little ones, and it was difficult to have a satisfying conversation.

Clara realized one child was missing. "Where's your little girl?"

"I insisted Jacob keep at least one of the children with him or I'd never get my shopping done."

One of the little boys raised his arms to be lifted up.

"Will he let me hold him?" Clara asked on impulse.

Sarah nodded, and Clara bent to lift the boy. Sarah had always wanted a houseful of children. It was no surprise that she had three within five years. Clara liked children — the wonder of them, the tiny completeness of them. It was the process of carrying and birthing children that simmered reluctance. As girls, whenever Sarah gushed about children, Clara changed the subject.

"Are you still cleaning houses?" Sarah asked.

Clara nodded. "Just two right now, Widower Hershberger and an *English* family."

"You might as well enjoy a bit of pocket money while you can. I heard Widower Hershberger is getting married. He's been corresponding with his late wife's cousin in Ohio. I imagine he won't need you much longer."

Clara determined that nothing should show on her face. Mr. Hershberger had said nothing to her. It was the sort of personal information Sarah always seemed to know before anyone else.

Clara stared into the dark eyes of Sarah's little boy, waiting to ache for her own.

"We should go," Sarah said. "But let's plan a proper visit. Can you borrow a buggy from your *daed* and come to our place?"

"Maybe," Clara said. She surrendered the boy to his mother.

"Please try. The children are down for naps right after lunch."

Sarah rearranged her grip on her sons' hands and resumed walking. Clara turned back to the mercantile window, though if anyone asked her later what she had seen, her answers would be vague.

A gleeful shriek behind Clara made her spin around to see a little *English* boy, older than Sarah's littlest son but younger than Mari, galloping down the walkway. The joy on the child's face evaporated in an instant when he stumbled. Clara reached out and caught him before his tender hands and face scraped the ground. Startled, the boy looked up at Clara with a trembling lower lip. Instinctively, Clara pulled the little one into her arms and whispered reassurance in his ear.

The child's anxious mother arrived a few steps later. "Thank you! He got away from me so quickly."

"He's fine." Clara released the boy into his mother's arms and watched them continue down the street.

Was this what her future held? Handing other people's children back to them because she was frightened to have her own?

Suddenly she wanted to see Andrew.

The wrench slipped out of Andrew's grip and knocked his kneecap before falling to the barn floor. With a short yelp, he hopped on one foot. This was the third time, and he hadn't successfully adjusted his grasp.

"Are you all right?"

Andrew refrained from rubbing his knee and looked up. "Clara! What are you doing here?"

She stepped inside, put her hands behind her slender waist, and leaned against the door frame. "I was out for a walk."

"On your way somewhere?" Andrew said. Clara was a fair distance from the Kuhn farm for a walk with no purpose.

She shook her head. "Just walking."

"Is everything all right?"

Clara pushed herself away from the wall. "How's the work on the car coming?"

"I can't seem to hold on to a wrench." He bent to pick up the tool. "Are you sure you're all right?"

Clara shrugged one shoulder. "I just needed some fresh air."

"Something on your mind?"

"Nothing important." She smiled, the gesture manufactured for Andrew's benefit. "Have you figured out what you're doing?"

Andrew tilted his head to consider her face and decided not to press. They hadn't seen each other since Sunday night. Anything could have happened in two days. When she was ready, she would talk to him. He'd waited two years for her already and did not plan to give up. If they never married, it would not be his decision bringing that result.

"I had it running yesterday," Andrew said.

She moved to stand beside him, her hands still behind her waist, and leaned over to peer at the engine. With another smile — genuine, this time — she looked at him out of the side of her eyes.

"You used the past tense," she said.

"I admit to an unplanned incident. But there were no witnesses to the actual circumstances, so I won't embarrass myself by divulging the details."

Clara burst out laughing. Andrew grinned.

She stepped back and examined the car. "It doesn't *look* broken."

"It's not broken. I fixed it."

She raised one eyebrow. "So you've put the . . . er, incident . . . behind you?"

"Let me offer you an irresistible bargain." Andrew closed the cover over the engine. "Come for a ride with me."

"A ride! Now?"

He fixed on her eyes and nodded.

Clara put her hands on the car and looked inside.

"Do you even know what to do with those pedals and levers?"

"Mostly."

She laughed again.

"You're a long way from home," he said. "Wouldn't you like to get off your feet?"

She gestured toward a misshapen bale of hay in one corner. "I could sit there."

"But it wouldn't be nearly as much fun." Andrew opened the automobile's door. "Here we have a tufted seat with a full back made of the finest leather."

"Well," she said, "it's true that while I've done a great deal of thinking today, I've had very little fun."

"We'll stay on the back roads," Andrew

said. After the detour into the ditch, he had found a balance between enthusiasm and caution.

Clara stepped up into the Model T. Before she had time to change her mind, Andrew reached in to set the levers, snatched the crank from under the seat, and sprinted around to the front of the automobile to insert it.

This time he got it started on the first attempt.

Clara gripped the bench with both hands, but she giggled as Andrew steered the Model T out of the barn.

"How did you learn to do this?" She raised her voice above the motor.

"After my . . . incident . . . I spent a good part of yesterday practicing." Andrew made a smooth turn onto a path barely wide enough for the Model T. After getting the Ford safely back to the barn, Yonnie had clucked his tongue in disapproval. Andrew, however, made a few adjustments that were surprisingly easy, considering his limited mechanical knowledge, and had the car running again before lunchtime. Then he gave himself some proper driving lessons around the abandoned farm.

"Today the back roads," he said to Clara. "Tomorrow, Springs."

Her eyes widened. "Would you really drive to Springs?"

"Why have an automobile if you don't plan to use it?"

"Why indeed?"

He gave her a half grin. "Well, maybe not tomorrow, but just wait. The day will come."

Gradually Clara relaxed her grip. She had imagined the sensation of riding in an automobile would feel faster, more like a constant gallop than a sedate trot. Before Sunday, when she saw the automobile for the first time, Clara had not been on the old Johnson farm. She was uncertain where the narrow road Andrew chose would take them.

"How fast can it go?" she asked.

"I'm not sure," Andrew said. "I haven't been in high gear yet."

"Are we going to try high gear?" The hopefulness in her own voice surprised Clara.

"If that's what you want."

She made no effort to contain her mischievous spirit.

"Let me find the gear pedal." Andrew let his knees fall open so he could see his feet, put his foot on a pedal, and moved the hand lever before opening the throttle. "Here we go!"

The car thrust forward. With the wind in her face, Clara noticed Andrew was not wearing his hat. She had never before seen the wave of brown hair in its entirety. Like all Amish men, Andrew was well trained to wear his hat, whether black felt in the winter or straw in the summer. Today it would not have mattered, because a hat would not have stayed on as the car picked up speed.

A clatter crumbled Clara's thoughts.

"What's that?" she asked.

Andrew's hands were busy adjusting levers. Despite his efforts, the engine sputtered and seized, and the Model T came to an abrupt halt.

"What happened?" she said.

Bracing himself and swinging his legs over the door without pausing to open it, Andrew leaped out of the car. "I'm beginning to understand why the previous owner was so eager to be finished with this car."

"But you're not giving up, are you?"

"Of course not." He flipped open the engine cover, releasing steam. "We might have to let it cool down, but it won't take long. We haven't been driving long enough for it to be too hot."

Clara found a lever that looked like it

might open the door. She got out and leaned against the car.

"That was the best four minutes I've had all day," Clara said.

Andrew joined her against the car, nudging her shoulder with his. "I had a feeling you weren't having a very good day."

The words swirling in Clara's mind were slow to find structure, but she knew Andrew would wait.

"You're a little older than I am," she said finally. "What do you remember about 1905?"

"A lot of things."

"I mean, in the church. Why would Barbara Stutzman say that last Sunday was like 1895 all over again? That the congregation had been duped then and again ten years later?"

Andrew sighed. "Bishop Yoder had just been ordained to the office in 1895. He had strong feelings about the Maryland churches separating."

"He still does. But the congregation voted, didn't they?"

"Yes. Officially. Ten years later the truth came out."

"What truth?"

"I remember eavesdropping while my parents talked," Andrew said, "although I didn't have to try very hard. They were upset. Their voices grew loud."

Clara moved away from the car to stand where she could look Andrew in the face. "What happened, Andrew?"

"When Bishop Yoder asked for the vote, he said he had consulted another bishop, Joseph Witmer. It's possible he sincerely misunderstood what Bishop Witmer meant to communicate, but my parents — and a lot of others — were convinced he knew exactly what he was doing. The congregation voted unanimously to do just the opposite of what Bishop Witmer had advised."

Andrew's soft words sank in.

"Bishop Yoder deceived the congregation?" Clara was stunned. "All these years — the sermons about shunning the Maryland believers."

"Hardly anyone really wanted to do that." Andrew picked up a pebble and tossed it into a field overgrown with weeds. "But the vote in 1895 was unanimous."

"And our people do not easily set aside such a vote." Clara pressed on her temples. "That explains why hardly anyone whose name is not Yoder obeys the ban."

"Bishop Yoder is getting old," Andrew said. "He won't be bishop forever."

"But his sons," Clara countered. "One of

them could be the next bishop."

"Or it could be Mose Beachy." Andrew paced back to the engine. "Let's not borrow trouble."

Chapter 10

"Please!"

Hannah tugged on Clara's sleeve two days later.

Clara dropped into the grass. She had wandered away from the house with a box of letter paper intending to finish a story to send to Sadie — and not knowing that Hannah followed. Clara glanced toward the house, wondering if Rhoda knew where her daughter was.

Hannah plopped down next to Clara. "I only want you to tell me about Sadie. I already know you like to visit her and she's your cousin."

"My cousin's daughter." Clara offered the gentle correction.

"That's still a cousin." Hannah rolled onto her stomach, planted her elbows, and propped up her chin with her hands. "What is she like?"

"Lively." Clara chuckled. "She likes running and doing cartwheels, and her *mamm* has to remind her about chores."

"Just like my *mamm* has to remind me."

"She's not old enough for school yet, but I think she's going to like it when she goes."

"Just like me. I like school!"

"And she loves cherry strudel," Clara said.

Hannah sat up. "I like apple strudel, but it's still strudel."

Clara's thumbs played with the corners of the box of letter paper. Intuition told her not to mention to Hannah the Bible stories that Clara sent to Sadie.

"Do you think Sadie and I could be friends?" Hannah crossed her legs and straightened her skirt around them.

"I'm sure you would like each other," Clara said. Why shouldn't they? Hannah and Sadie were two little Amish girls going to church and learning the ways their people had followed for more than two hundred years.

"I want to visit Sadie with you," Hannah said. "I want to very, very much."

Clara reached over and squeezed the girl's hand. "I know." The farm Sadie lived on was only five miles away, but it might as well have been the desolate settlement in Colorado that Clara read about in *The Budget.*

"Ask *Mamm* if you can take me," Hannah said. "I promise to be good and clean up after myself."

"We'll see," Clara said.

"Priscilla's dog is going to have puppies."

"Oh?" Clara was relieved at the change of subject.

"In about two more weeks. I'm going to start asking *Mamm* if I can go play with Priscilla every day. I want to be there when the babies are born so I can watch."

Clara winced. Her father had delivered the young of cows and horses over the years. It happened on every farm. But Clara never wanted to watch.

Their heads turned together toward the sound of Mari's crying. Rhoda approached, one hand tight around her youngest daughter's fingers.

"Hannah, you have chores to do in the barn," Rhoda said.

"See," Hannah said. "She reminds me, just like Sadie's *mamm* reminds her."

Clara nodded but did not speak.

"Ask her now," Hannah said. She scampered toward the barn.

"Ask me what?" Rhoda said.

"It's just something Hannah wants to do," Clara said.

"Why was she talking about Sadie?"

Clara stood up. This conversation would be difficult enough without having Rhoda towering over her.

"She wants to meet Sadie," Clara said. "We could go and come back on the same day."

"Meet Sadie? What on earth for?" Rhoda released Mari's hand, and the little girl stretched out in the grass.

"She's curious. That's all. I think they would get on well together."

"Absolutely not."

Clara took in a breath. "They're just little girls. I'm Hannah's sister and related to Sadie. It's not such a stretch, is it?"

"The Hostetlers are your mother's people. I have never suggested you should not see them if you wish. But Hannah is not related to them. I see no reason to confuse her about where she belongs."

Clara looked at Mari in the cool grass, her little fingers sliding up and down a single blade. Her eyes lifted to the barn in time to see Hannah disappear inside its cavernous door. Rhoda protected where Hannah belonged but plainly would feel no loss if Clara crossed the border. Clara was twenty-three and did not understand the false line represented by the state border. How would little children understand it? Hot disappointment seared through Clara.

Andrew wondered how many times he would have to bring a horse and buggy to Hansen's Automotive Repair. The Model T was safely back in the outlying barn on the Johnson land, but ever since he put it in high gear two days ago, it made a sound that unnerved Andrew.

Jurgen Hansen looked up from where he sat at a desk strewn with papers. "How's your Model T?"

"You were right about the carburetor." Andrew eyed the rack beside the door, hoping he would have another opportunity to hang his straw hat there. "The car is running now, but I don't believe it is as reliable as it ought to be."

"Automobiles are sensitive machines," Hansen said.

"I'm learning that," Andrew said. "I wonder if I might help you around the shop again today."

"I can't pay you," Hansen said.

"I would pay you if I could," Andrew said, "for teaching me."

"It's only a matter of some basic science about the combustion engine, and a little trial and error about your engine in particular."

"I suppose it's like getting to know the temperament of a horse," Andrew said.

Hansen laughed. "More like a small herd of horses."

Andrew licked his lips. "Will you help me tame my herd?"

The shop owner looked around. "If you clean up the two end bays, I'll let you watch while I work on the next two cars."

Andrew snatched his hat off his head and tossed it onto a hook. Outside the rear door was a water spigot, and he knew where the broom and mop were. While Andrew cleaned, Jurgen Hansen rummaged through tools and assorted small parts on three shelves. Inspecting the engine and undercarriage of his own automobile meant Andrew recognized some of the shapes, even if he did not know the names or functions for everything. Andrew attacked the clutter and dirt in a manner that would have made his *mamm* proud, determined to be ready to learn by the time Jurgen Hansen was ready to work. At one point, Andrew tilted his head back and followed with his eyes the path of the electric wiring that illumined the bays.

They worked for four hours. Andrew watched Jurgen's movements closely, asking as few questions as possible so he would not provoke impatience, but enough to undergird his growing understanding of the complex challenge of keeping an automobile running. The broom and a stack of clean rags were always within reach. Andrew kept the bays clean.

The afternoon yawned ahead of them. Finally, Jurgen went outside to the water spigot to scrub his hands clean and returned to his desk, where he pulled from a desk drawer a sandwich wrapped in waxed paper.

"Let's have lunch," Jurgen said, "and then I think I'd like to see your car."

Andrew accepted the half sandwich Jurgen offered. "I don't want to take up your time."

"Nonsense. The car I drive can go forty miles an hour." Jurgen winked. "Wouldn't you like to do that?"

Andrew glanced out the door at his horse. Despite being a large stallion, the animal had never been especially fast, even at a gallop — which Andrew rarely required of him. Forty miles an hour! And in a car that was not likely to cough and seize in the performance of its duties.

They finished the sandwich, and Jurgen tossed Andrew an apple before shuffling papers around to reveal a crank on his desk.

"Don't ever leave the crank in the automobile," Jurgen said. "That's all someone would need to take the car."

Andrew was so fixed on getting the Model T running that he had not thought how easily someone else might drive off with it. *Mine* surged through his mind, the intensity of possession surprising him. He offered his half-eaten apple to his horse, made certain the lead was secured to a tree, and then climbed into Jurgen Hansen's sleek, shiny automobile. Already Andrew could tell this Model T was one of the newest versions.

"Are those headlamps electric?" Andrew said in sudden realization. He had tested the lamps on his car and discovered they required oil to produce illumination.

"Yes sir!" Jurgen said. "The horn, too."

When Jurgen cranked, the car responded with a smooth compliance rather than the clatter Andrew expected. He had further to go than he realized in achieving the best his Model T could give.

Jurgen pulled on his driving gloves, adjusted his goggles, and put the car in gear. "Which way?"

Andrew pointed, and Jurgen took the automobile out on the road. The top was down on this sunny day, and the wind against his face reminded Andrew he had left his hat behind on the hook.

"Isn't it unusual for your people to own an automobile," Jurgen said, "even one that doesn't work very well?"

"Unusual, yes."

"It's not against the rules?"

Andrew paused before answering. "The automobile raises some questions that the church will consider with great thought."

Jurgen put the car into high gear, and Andrew felt the smile pushing against the corners of his lips as he judged the speed. Trot. Canter. Gallop. More than gallop. He could not see the speedometer, but surely they had reached forty miles an hour. Andrew squinted into the wind, understanding why the hardware store sold goggles among its automotive supplies.

This was how an automobile was meant to run.

Andrew gestured a couple of turns, and they arrived at the old Johnson barn. He pushed open the rickety door and Jurgen walked in.

After only a glance at the car, Jurgen laughed in rich, deep amusement.

"What is funny?" Andrew asked.

Jurgen pulled off his gloves. "I know this car. It has been in my shop many times."

Andrew's stomach soured. "Then it will never run the way yours does."

"Of course it will." Jurgen ran a hand along a front fender. "The owner often refused my advice. He didn't give it the care it required. I suspect your attitude will be different."

"I'll take all the advice you'll offer," Andrew said. "I want to learn everything about it."

"Once you get it running smoothly, it will be worth something," Jurgen said. "Don't give up."

The milk wagon rumbled onto the dairy grounds at the end of Yonnie's afternoon rounds. Twelve tall capped metal cans rattled in the wagon bed. Every day the temperatures crept up and Yonnie perspired more with the effort of lifting the cans from the springs where they cooled on Amish farms into the wagon to haul them to the dairy. Today Yonnie had worked in the dairy early in the morning, done a large unscheduled delivery, and then went directly into the afternoon loop to farms on both sides of the border. His muscles ached, and his lunch had long ago worn off.

Dale Borntrager stomped out of the main building, where workers bottled milk and churned butter.

"Yoder, where have you been?"

Yonnie gave the reins a final tug and jumped down from the bench. "On the rounds, of course."

"You disappeared early and didn't come back."

"I made the special delivery." Yonnie's stomach tightened. "An *English* order."

"On the wrong day!" Dale said.

Yonnie slumped against the wagon. "I saw the note in the office."

"For tomorrow." Dale glared.

"Tomorrow?"

"Nobody was expecting that delivery to-day."

Yonnie reached into the wagon. "But I got a signature."

"From a young woman who didn't know she could do anything else. She's not even out of *English* school yet and is just helping out for the summer. She closed up right after you left, thinking her boss must have known the milk was coming and would be there soon."

Yonnie closed his eyes. "He didn't come."

"Not for hours. The milk sat outside all that time."

"So it spoiled."

"You know better, Yonnie. You rushed and misread the note, then you rushed and left the order with that young woman. Your distraction cost me good money."

"I'm sorry. Take it out of my wages."

"Of course I will. When you make a mistake, you must be prepared to face the consequences."

CHAPTER 11

Clara wasn't sleeping, or even dozing. By midmorning on Monday, she had exhausted a brief series of small chores that could just as well have gone undone — which likely was why Rhoda offered no objection to Clara's efforts — and withdrew to her room and cleaned it unnecessarily. The floor was spotless, and her dresses and *kapps* hung neatly on their hooks. On the nightstand, her small collection of books was stacked according to size. Clara saw no reason not to stretch out on the quilt of red and brown diamonds and indulge in daydreaming about the next Bible story she would write for Sadie. Jesus' parable of the servant who received mercy yet refused to offer mercy came to mind.

Rhoda's steps clipped a firm rhythm on the bare wood of the upstairs hall. Clara sat up and snatched a book from the stack to look busy. Rhoda appeared in the doorway with Mari in her arms.

"When Hannah asked if she could stay the night with the Schrocks," Rhoda said, "I promised Mrs. Schrock I would fetch her before lunch. I'm going now."

Clara scooted to the edge of her bed. "Let me go. I haven't had my walk today."

"I can see you're reading."

Clara closed the book. "Just passing the time."

"*Danki,* but I can manage."

Mari put her open palms on her mother's chest and straightened her arms, pushing back. Rhoda compensated for the disturbance in balance by adjusting her grip.

"Mari!"

Rhoda's tone carried a warning Clara had first recognized years ago, but Mari ignored it. Instead, the little girl shifted her hips from side to side.

"I want down!" Mari said.

Rhoda gave the child a stern look, but she set her on her feet.

"It's a long way for Mari to walk," Clara said. "I would be happy to go."

"I'm going to take the cart," Rhoda said.

"I don't like the cart." Mari threw herself to the floor.

"Marianne Kuhn, you get up this minute." Rhoda planted her hands on her hips.

139

Mari had been a tempestuous toddler, and even now at three years old and with a more than adequate vocabulary, she still pitched fits. Rhoda responded by striking an implacable pose. Clara was never sure who would be more stubborn, mother or child.

"Get up!" Her hands still on her hips, Rhoda now widened her stance.

"No!" Mari flung her arms over her head.

"We're going to get Hannah."

"I don't like Hannah!"

"Hannah is your sister."

"No, Clara is my sister."

Clara averted her eyes, not wanting to witness the color that would flush through Rhoda's face at her daughter's declaration.

"Please," Clara said, "let me go for Hannah."

Rhoda huffed. "Under the circumstances, all right. But take the cart. Hannah will get halfway home and start complaining about having to walk."

Clara couldn't disagree with that assessment. Hannah was likely to stop in the middle of a field and insist that she couldn't walk another step.

Clara snatched a *kapp* off a hook and set it on her head before stepping around her youngest sister's tantrum.

"I want to go with Clara." Mari sat up.

"You most certainly will not." Rhoda glared.

Mari put a finger in her mouth and glared back.

Clara took the stairs quickly, whistled for the mare in the pasture, and hitched up the cart. The horse trotted cooperatively down the lane. As Clara arrived at the Schrocks' farmhouse, the front door opened and Mattie Schrock stood on the porch.

"I'm glad you're here," Mattie said. "I was just thinking I might have to bring Hannah home myself."

Clara got out of the cart. "I hope she hasn't been any trouble. She loves to play with Priscilla."

"They played together nicely," Mattie said. "But ever since breakfast, Hannah hasn't been feeling well."

"Hannah is sick?" Clara glanced past Mattie and into the house.

"She's up in the girls' room. I made the other children leave her alone to rest."

"May I go up?"

"Of course."

Upstairs, Clara touched the sleeping girl's forehead. Heat answered her inquiry. Hannah stirred.

"I'm here to take you home," Clara said softly.

"My throat hurts." Hannah's raspy reply gave evidence of her claim.

Next to the bed, a full glass of water appeared untouched. Clara picked it up. "Will you drink some water, please?"

Hannah shook her head. "It hurts to swallow."

"Just a sip?" Clara put the glass to Hannah's lips.

Hannah took a drink, grimacing at the effort.

Clara set the glass back on the side table and slid her arms around her sister's slight form, whispering a prayer of gratefulness for the cart.

At home on the Kuhn farm, Clara carried Hannah into the house and laid her on the davenport.

"What's going on?" Rhoda came in from the kitchen, Mari trailing behind her in an improved mood.

"Hannah is sick." Clara arranged a pillow under Hannah's head.

"I'll sit with her," Rhoda said.

Clara started to move away, but Hannah grabbed her wrist.

"I want Clara," Hannah whispered.

"Clara has taken good care of you to get you home," Rhoda said, "but your *mamm* is here now."

"I want Clara," Hannah repeated, tightening her grasp on Clara's arm.

Clara winced at the effort required for her sister to speak at all. She would gladly sit all day and night with the girl, but Hannah was Rhoda's child, and Rhoda wanted to care for her. Rhoda kissed Hannah's forehead and stroked her cheek. Hannah's fingers opened and her hand slid off Clara's wrist.

"We'll make ice cream," Rhoda said. "You'll like that on your throat, won't you?"

Hannah nodded.

Clara stepped away.

"Don't go," Hannah said.

"I'm here," Rhoda said, looking at Clara more than at her daughter. "Clara can go now."

After twelve days, the Model T looked at home in the rickety Johnson outbuilding. And Andrew felt at home with it. A few days of neglect required him to tend to the chores on his own farm — Yonnie was right about that. Andrew did need to take care of his crop. But now he left most of his lamps and lanterns with the automobile so that whenever he had a few hours to work on it, he could see clearly what he was doing. At home, alone in the big house where he grew up, Andrew could move one or two lights around as he needed them, but he spent most of his evenings with the Model T. Jurgen Hansen was generous with suggestions — and even spare parts. Though he spoke English, Andrew was not a fluid reader in the language. Still, he took home the papers Jurgen gave him to study, painstakingly sounding out words his German mind did not immediately recognize.

The moon was waning now. Andrew left the Johnson land, but rather than turning toward his own farm, he let the horse amble in the other direction — toward the Kuhn farm and a path running through Hiram Kuhn's fields. Experience in the last two years reinforced this inclination often enough that Andrew waited in the dark more frequently than anyone knew — even Clara. He waited for her. She would sometimes come out for a night walk, and he would "happen" to be staring at the stars when she did.

Andrew could hardly use that excuse tonight, though. The sky had clouded over while he adjusted the carburetor on the Model T. Dense humidity clung to the air, a portent of something more than an ordinary night in the middle of June.

Leaving the buggy, Andrew began to pace. The weight of the air deterred any real speed. Already the night's clamminess stuck his shirt to his skin. He would not wander more than an eighth of a mile in either direction. It would be foolish for Clara to come out tonight into the hovering storm, but if she did, she would come to this spot.

He paced a hundred yards before pausing to consider the sky. Lightning flashed in the distance, but no thunder answered — yet. Clouds obscured any starlight. Even the moon, though visible, seemed dim.

The rain started then, at first an uncertain drizzle and then finding a rhythm. The next lightning strike seemed closer. Andrew turned back to his buggy.

If Clara would marry him, he would not have to wait for her under heavy, damp sky.

The way she giggled when they rode in the automobile, and waited patiently while he got it running again, made him more resolute than ever. Many of the church members might think Bishop Yoder was going too far in his preaching about shunning, but few would consider an automobile as easily as Clara had.

The blackness brightened again, and in that split second Clara saw the shape of Andrew's buggy. She could turn around now, and he would never know she had been there. He would never have to see the stricken lines she felt in her own face.

But why else had she come if not with the hope that Andrew would be here?

"Andrew!" she called into the dark. Clara hastened her pace in a direct path to where the lightning had revealed the buggy to be.

"Clara!"

Though she could not see his form, his voice answered with an eager ring, and Clara moved faster. The rain was steady now, a falling river that drenched and chilled.

The afternoon had stretched endlessly, with Hannah whimpering in illness from the davenport and calling intermittently for Clara's comfort. Rhoda put Mari down for a nap and fully embraced her duties to nurse Hannah's sore throat and fever. Even while Hannah slept, Rhoda did not move more than six feet away. Clara hovered in the kitchen, in the dining room, on the front porch. When Mari woke, Rhoda was firm that Mari must keep away from Hannah but remain within sight. Eventually Rhoda gave Clara instructions to put out a cold supper of items from the icebox and allowed Clara to take Mari into the kitchen to eat with Hiram and Josiah.

But she did not relent in her determination that Clara should not tend to her sickened sister.

Hiram had carried Hannah to her bed, where Rhoda intended to spend the night, arguing that if Hannah needed her, the girl would have no voice to call out. With the rest of the family bedded down, Clara had eased out the back door. Even if she'd measured the threat of rain more accurately, she would have gone.

"I'm here," Andrew called.

Clara made out his form now, returning to his buggy. They reached it together, both drenched, his hat and her *kapp* askew.

"I'm glad you came," Clara said.

"Let's get in the buggy out of the rain." Andrew offered a hand to help her climb up.

Thunder now trailed lightning by only a few seconds. Clara shivered. Though the air was still warm, the moisture was damp and chilling.

Sheltered in the buggy, they watched the rain slide out of the sky in sheets. Clara felt sorry for Andrew's exposed horse, though the animal displayed no discontent. With one fist she began to squeeze the dampness out of her dress, but it seemed a futile effort.

"The rain is a blessing," Andrew murmured. "All the farmers will be pleased in the morning. After a soaking rain like this, we'll nearly be able to watch the crops spurt up inches by the day."

Clara nodded, but words knotted in her throat.

"What's wrong, Clara?" Andrew asked softly.

Clara sighed, making no effort to hide the current of air leaving her lungs.

"Tell me," he urged.

She couldn't tell him, though. If Andrew knew Rhoda thought Clara should make her own life in her own home, he would see the obvious solution. And she could not be wed to Andrew — or anyone — as long as she feared the blessing of children.

CHAPTER 12

It was odd for Hannah to be so still, and odd for her to be sitting in her mother's lap during family devotions after breakfast on Wednesday. Rhoda had moved Hannah from the davenport in the front room to her own bed and barely allowed Clara to go near the room. For two days Rhoda pampered Hannah, who had returned to the family table for breakfast that morning. The fever had lasted only a day, and with hot tea and freshly churned ice cream the sore throat was managed through the second day.

But here Hannah was at breakfast and morning devotions. Though she was in her mother's lap, she sat up straight with bright eyes. In Clara's consideration, Hannah seemed well, though Rhoda would want to be certain three times over before releasing the girl to resume her play and chores.

Standing beside them, Mari's lower lip protruded in a jealous unacknowledged pout as she leaned against her mother's arm. She wanted to be the girl in her *mamm*'s lap. Across the table, Josiah's feet gently and intermittently thumped the legs of his chair, as if in response to a thought that flitted through his mind.

Hiram Kuhn sat reading aloud from the big German Bible as he did every morning and evening. On many days, like this one, the sound droned. The older Hiram got — almost fifty now — the more he droned. The children were well trained to sit still and appear respectful, but Clara wondered whether they heard anything more than an undulating buzz.

Rhoda's countenance was as blandly perfect as it always was. Her eyes fixed on her husband as he read, her head nodding slightly at intervals. Outwardly, nothing about Rhoda had changed. If she suspected that Clara had overheard her say it was time for her to marry, she did not reveal it in her composure. Neither were her words unkind. An onlooker would suspect nothing.

Yet Clara twisted in confusion and frustration, her spirit wringing more tightly each day.

While her father's *Amen* still draped the room, the family scattered, Hiram and Josiah to outside chores and Rhoda and the girls to wash Hannah's hair. Clara sat alone for an instant.

Fannie. She would go see Fannie and Sadie. At least there she could do some good.

At the turn from the Kuhns' lane onto the road that led toward the border, a wagon clattered in the street. Clara stepped well to the side. The wagon slowed, and a milkman looked down from the bench.

"Looking for a ride?" he said. "I'm going over the border."

"Thanks, Reuben," Clara said, "but it's a lovely morning. I think I'll walk. Maybe on the way back this afternoon."

Reuben shook his head. "I'll be sorry to miss you. Yonnie has that run. Shall I tell him to look for you?"

Clara smiled and remained uncommitted. If she was at the Maple Glen Meetinghouse when Yonnie came by, she could face the question then whether she was in the mood to ride with him. The walk was only five miles in each direction. Clara had little else to do to pass the hours.

"I know where to catch him," she said to Reuben. "I pray God brings favor to your day."

Reuben clicked his tongue, and the horse moved ahead.

Clara doubted Rhoda would scowl even if Clara missed supper, although her siblings were sure to wonder where she was. Illness or essential overnight travel were the only reasons for missing the evening meal and devotions. In this expectation, the Kuhns were no different than any other Amish household — on either side of the border.

What did Andrew eat for supper? Clara occasionally wondered about this question. Did he cook or eat a cold plate? Did he accept invitations from families who pitied him after his parents moved to Lancaster — or who had a daughter of a marriageable age? Did the young women who eyed him at Singings turn up on his farm with casseroles or pies? Clara never asked Andrew these questions. If she would not say she would marry him, why should he not accept invitations?

Still, the thought that he might stung.

Yonnie Yoder had a younger sister who had trailed after the boys when they were children as much as she was allowed. In his telling of the stories, Andrew never seemed to mind that she was there digging worms with them or climbing the lower branches of a tree while the boys scrambled higher. She was old enough to wed now, and though Andrew's great-grandmother had been a Yoder, the relationship was distant enough to allow for a marriage.

Clara pushed the thought out of her mind. Andrew was waiting for her.

Andrew with his Model T.

Alone on the road, Clara smiled at the memory of riding in the automobile while Andrew drove. He was not afraid of the form that joy might take in his life.

Old Bishop Yoder might have other ideas.

"I can do it!" Sadie raised a shoulder to interfere with Fannie's movement. The girl knelt on a chair to stir the apples, brown sugar, and raisins for the *apfelstrudel.* Her tongue poked out one side of her mouth in concentration as her fist gripped the wooden spoon handle and she pushed through the mixture in swift, thorough circles.

Fannie returned to kneading the dough. In a few minutes Sadie would insist on helping to stretch the dough thin, and Fannie would let her. Sadie was only five, but she had a knack for baking already. She knew just what the dough should feel like as she pulled it into a rectangle to fill with the apple mixture.

As troublesome as it was to think that Sadie might be her only child, Fannie delighted in ordinary moments like this one.

Sadie would forget them. She would grow up with the automatic motions of making strudel, and dozens of other dishes, flowing from her fingers. One day she would prepare food in her own kitchen, perhaps with her own little girl.

But Fannie would store up these moments in her heart, the way she was sure Mary had stored up the moments of Jesus' childhood.

"Knock, knock." The voice came from the back door, which stood open to disperse the oven's heat.

"Clara!" Sadie dropped her wooden spoon and scrambled down from the chair to throw herself at the visitor.

"I didn't know you were coming." Fannie brushed flour between her palms and wiped her hands on her apron before embracing her cousin.

"Neither did I," Clara said. "I only decided after breakfast."

"We're having strudel for lunch," Sadie declared.

"Or," Fannie said gently, "dessert after supper."

"Or both!" Sadie's eyes glistened with optimism.

They stretched the dough, filled it, rolled it, and slid it into the hot oven.

"We have something to show you," Sadie

said once her hands were clean and dry. "A surprise."

"Oh?" Clara's glance moved from Sadie to Fannie.

"Can I go get it, *Mamm*?" Sadie was nearly jumping in excitement.

"Yes. Remember to take care." Fannie watched the marvel that was her daughter scamper down the hall. She gestured for Clara to move into the front room.

"Close your eyes!" Sadie called from down the hall, and Clara complied.

Fannie nodded encouragement for Sadie to lay the gift in Clara's lap.

Clara's eyes popped open. "What's this?"

"It's a Bible storybook!" Sadie's enthusiasm gushed out of her. "It's all the stories you've sent me in a scrapbook, and when you write more, we'll put those in, too. Hurry up and write more!"

Clara giggled, the same girlish giggle Fannie had heard through the secret moments of their childhood. Neither of them had a sister. They were sisters to each other.

"I can't read all the words yet," Sadie said. "Actually, I can only read a few. But I know them all by heart because *Mamm* reads me your stories every night before bed."

"They're not my stories," Clara said, "they're God's stories."

"I know that, silly. *Mamm* says you're helping me hide God's Word in my heart."

Fannie sat on the arm of a stuffed chair watching the pair of blond heads meeting temple to temple as Clara and Sadie turned the pages in the scrapbook with a plain green woven cover.

"It was Sadie's idea," Fannie said. "She saw the book in the mercantile in Grantsville and told me what she wanted to do."

"It's lovely." Clara closed the book and ran two fingers across the thick weave.

"Are you going to tell me a story today?" Sadie turned her face up, her eyes wide in hope.

Clara smiled. "As a matter of fact, I was going to mail you a story, but I decided to bring it myself." She reached under the bib of her apron and pulled out two sheets of paper.

Sadie jumped up. "I'll get the paste. Let's put it in the book right now and then you can read it to me."

"Perfect," Clara said.

"You have to visit to my Sunday school class." Sadie's voice trailed out of the room.

Clara glanced at Fannie. "Why would she suddenly ask me to visit?"

"You haven't been to church with us since we were very small," Fannie said. "You

156

really should come."

Clara watched the door slam behind Sadie as the child skipped out the kitchen door to play in the sunshine.

"You're very patient with her," Fannie said. "You didn't have to read so many stories. I'm trying to teach her to be grateful for small blessings and not demand the universe!"

Clara chuckled. "I get to go home. You're the one who will have to read more at bedtime."

Fannie cut a slice of *apfelstrudel,* still warm, and slid it onto a plate to hand to Clara. "Do you remember being five?"

"Not very well." Clara poured two cups of coffee and settled in a kitchen chair. "I remember more about visiting your family than being at home with my *daed.*"

Fannie sipped coffee. "Remember when we found the litter of seven kittens in the barn and didn't tell anyone for five days?"

"I was eight. We were afraid your *daed* would drown most of them. Nobody needs that many barn cats. By the time he caught us, we'd named them all."

"As soon as they were old enough to wean, he made us drag them around in a cart until we found homes for all but two."

"I'd do it again," Clara said. "Poor kitties."

Fannie nibbled strudel.

"What about when we were older?" Clara said.

"What do you mean?"

"When we were twelve or thirteen. You must remember something."

Fannie raised an eyebrow. "About what?"

Clara chose her words carefully. "There was new information in 1905 about the vote of the Pennsylvania congregation ten years before to shun the Maryland churches. Something about a misunderstanding."

They both looked out at Sadie, who was tossing a stick for the dog Elam had brought to the Esh marriage. The dog was aged and reluctant, though.

"Obviously my parents weren't at either meeting," Fannie said. "We heard rumors. Some boys who came down to an auction were rude to my brothers."

Clara vaguely remembered. For a while Rhoda had not wanted Clara to visit the Hostetlers, at least until things settled down again.

"What did your parents do?" she said.

Fannie shrugged. "What they always did. After family devotions one night, they told us what they thought we needed to know."

"Did we ever talk about this?" Clara asked, wondering why she couldn't remember.

Fannie shook her head. "*Mamm* took me aside and said there was no need to talk about it with you. It wouldn't change anything. You were always welcome to come, and she hoped you would still want to."

"But what did they say about the vote? About the shunning?"

"People voted against their conscience to please the bishop." Fannie took an indulgent sip of coffee. "They used to talk to us often about conscience. A sense of what's right doesn't come from pleasing a man, even a bishop. They wanted us to please God."

"But the bishop must have thought he was pleasing God."

"My parents also said some things we must leave to God." Fannie brushed crumbs off the table into her hand. "So much trouble over whether or not to have Sunday school for children — it seems ridiculous after nearly forty years."

Clara lost interest in her coffee. Forty years or not, the matter was not settled. Andrew might think change was coming, but Clara dreaded the impending rancor.

CHAPTER 13

The Maple Glen Meetinghouse easily could be mistaken for the one at Flag Run or even Summit Mills. They all dated to the same effort. Yonnie's father, uncle, and grandfathers all were among the men who built four meetinghouses clustered around the border that the two groups of Amish would share. As long as they used them on alternate Sundays, no conflict rose between the two groups, despite their differences over the Protestant notion of Sunday school. Another decade passed before ministers began clearing their throats, saying what they thought, and moving to serve on the side of the border where they would be among kindred hearts. Though unchanged in outward form, the meetinghouses became symbols of opinions and convictions.

Each time Yonnie drove the milk wagon past the Maple Glen Meetinghouse — nearly every day — he felts its sting. The people who worshipped there dallied among the world. Some of the canisters of milk in his wagon came from the cows of families who thought Yonnie's family did not understand the will of God.

Yonnie emptied his lungs and pushed the dilemma out of his mind. He was past the meetinghouse now. He needed to concentrate. Once again he mentally reviewed the movements of his day — the deliveries he made in the morning, the milk canisters he lifted into the wagon in the afternoon, the routes he took, the conversations he had, the notes he made. Another mistake could be costly.

Between the rhythm of his horse dropping hooves and the patterned sound of the creaking hitch, Yonnie heard his name from behind. He glanced over his shoulder and saw Clara Kuhn running along the side of the road waving one hand widely. Yonnie pulled on the reins. Stopped, he twisted in his seat and waited for Clara.

She was out of breath when she finally reached the wagon.

"Thank you for stopping." Clara gulped air. "I didn't realize how late it was. I should have been waiting for you at the meetinghouse."

From the wagon bench, Yonnie looked

161

down at her round face, her blond hair pulled tight away from expectant blue eyes.

"You are going back toward Niverton, aren't you?" Clara asked.

Yonnie nodded. "If you'd like a ride, get in."

Clara took the hand Yonnie offered and pulled herself up to the bench.

"Thank you," she said again.

Clara would not likely speak to him further, Yonnie knew, unless he found something to talk about. They had little in common. She was pleasantly polite, as she would be with anyone, but all she wanted from Yonnie was a ride home. For a man's companionship, she would go to Andrew.

"Have you seen the Model T?" Yonnie maintained a forward gaze.

"Andrew's?"

Did she really consider it to belong to Andrew?

"The one he found." That was how Yonnie preferred to think of the automobile.

"He has it running, you know."

"I pulled him out of a ditch."

"He told me. Thank you. But he's been practicing driving, and he's getting better."

Yonnie looked at her now. "Have you seen him driving?"

She didn't answer.

"You got in that machine with him, didn't you?"

Clara stuck her chin out. "Yes."

Yonnie drove for most of a mile without speaking. If Clara had been in the Model T, she was as reckless as Andrew.

"Do you think that's wise?" Yonnie said.

"The automobile? Is it so different from having a horse and buggy? It's a way to get from here to there."

"You know it's more than that."

"Do I?"

They returned to silence for another mile.

"Andrew has a curious mind," Clara said. "God gave him that mind."

"Andrew is a baptized member of the church," Yonnie countered.

"You don't have to preach at me."

"The Bible tells us to exhort one another," Yonnie said. "We all made the same promises to follow the teachings."

"And what does the Bible teach about automobiles?"

"We promised to follow the teachings of the church."

"Shouldn't the teachings of the church be the teachings of the Bible?"

Clara's challenge dropped an edge between them. Yonnie clicked his tongue to urge the horse faster. The sooner Clara

163

Kuhn was out of his wagon, the better off they would both be.

Andrew saw two forms in the approaching milk wagon. Yonnie must have picked up a passenger. As the two horses drew closer, a satisfied smile shaped itself on Andrew's face.

Clara.

Andrew pulled his buggy to the side of the road and waved an arm at Yonnie. By the time the two rigs were side by side, Andrew had caught Clara's eye. He expected to see a flicker in her eye that meant she was glad to see him even if she would not appear outwardly forward in the presence of Yonnie or anyone else. Instead, the light he saw was an ember of constrained fury.

"Hello, Yonnie," Andrew said, pulling his gaze from Clara to Yonnie. He nodded toward the load in Yonnie's wagon. "It looks like you have a good haul there, along with a pleasant passenger."

Yonnie shrugged. "The usual, I suppose."

"Maybe you'd like to go straight to the dairy," Andrew said. "I can take Clara home if you like."

Clara did not wait for Yonnie's response. "Thank you, Andrew. That would be a great kindness."

"Whatever you'd like." Yonnie's belated response was moot. Clara was already out of the wagon.

Andrew jumped down from his bench to offer assistance, but Clara barely touched the hand he presented. She'd been in and out of his buggy enough times to know where to step and how to shift her weight and pivot to sit. Still, Andrew was surprised at her fleet, unassisted movements.

"I hope your evening goes well," Andrew said to Yonnie.

Yonnie had already urged his horse forward. Andrew turned to watch him go before picking up his own reins again.

"Thank you." Clara's sigh was unmistakable.

Andrew held his horse to a speed barely above grazing in a pasture.

"We're going the wrong way now," Clara said.

She was grumpy. That much was clear.

"There's a wide spot in the road just ahead," Andrew said. "We'll get turned around."

Clara nodded, expelling breath again. Andrew recognized this tactic. She was trying to regain composure after being upset.

"We'll never get there at this rate," Clara said.

"Are you in a hurry?"

"I don't want to be late for supper. Rhoda —" Clara cut herself off.

"Rhoda what?"

"Never mind." She looked off to one side, her face twisted away from Andrew.

"You know you can talk to me," Andrew said.

"I know." Her breathing slowed, but she offered no further information.

Andrew reached the wide spot in the road and slowly turned the rig to head toward the Kuhn farm. He still had a mile and a quarter before the turnoff to their lane, and he didn't think Clara was in any danger of being late for supper, so he did nothing to speed the horse.

The unhurried swaying *clip-clop* seemed to soothe Clara. In his peripheral vision, Andrew saw her shoulders relax. He waited another three minutes.

"So," he said, "what happened?"

"Yonnie," she said quickly. "Yonnie happened. I just needed a ride, and he wanted to give me a sermon."

"And what was his topic?"

"He doesn't approve of the Model T."

Andrew laughed softly. "What *does* Yonnie approve of?"

"Baptismal vows, apparently. Utter submission to church leadership."

"Ah, yes."

"How can you put up with letting him think you're not as serious about the faith as he is?"

"We did all promise to live by the teachings of the church," Andrew said.

"And the church should live by the teachings of the Bible." Her retort was swift. "Isn't that what we hold each other accountable to? When did it become impossible for us to discuss what that might mean?"

Andrew spoke with deliberate quiet. "This is about more than Yonnie and the car, isn't it?"

A sob caught in Clara's throat, but Andrew heard it.

"We're young," Andrew said. "We will see change."

"Do you keep the car because you believe that?" Clara found her voice again. "The church hasn't said much at all about automobiles, but it may be like the telephone or electric lights. If other districts vote against it, ours will, too."

"Mose Beachy has a level head," Andrew said.

"Why are you so sure he'll be the next bishop?"

"I'm not. *Gottes wille.* But he is a minister, and I am confident he speaks his mind when he meets with the others."

"But if one of Bishop Yoder's sons gets the lot, you can't be sure what will happen."

"None of us can be sure of anything except that what happens will be God's will. But God's will for the congregation may not be God's will for everyone *in* the congregation."

He met her quizzical expression without further words. They arrived at the end of her lane.

"Shall I take you up to the house?" Andrew said.

She shook her head. "I'll walk."

He squeezed her hands as he helped her out of the buggy, wishing he didn't have to let go.

Josiah was the most studious child Clara knew. Morning and evening, he leaned forward over his knees, back flat and straight, as if he feared if he sat with his shoulders against the chair he would miss the key word that unfurled the meaning of the Bible passages their father read in somber tones. Though he was a well-trained

168

Amish child, Clara sometimes wondered if her brother — *half brother,* Rhoda would point out — couldn't wiggle at least a little and still be within the confines of worshipful manners. On more than one occasion, Josiah voiced his intention to learn to read the German Bible, and Clara had no doubt Josiah would become fluent in High German. Already he was a good reader in the English he learned at school, and Rhoda made sure her son was also learning to read Pennsylvania Dutch.

Clara's little sisters were another matter. Mari was too young to judge yet what kind of student she would be, but Hannah's lithe form embodied enough wiggles for all of Rhoda's children. It had from the day she mastered rolling onto her back and giggling in triumph at her success. Now, at six, Hannah had mastered sitting still during family devotions, but Clara suspected the intense focus required to accomplish this feat precluded absorbing any spiritual meaning from the words Hiram read.

The Bible should be more interesting to children.

Clara realized she was not listening any more than Hannah was. Hiram had never been one to consider what his children would be interested in. Even when Clara was the only other family member to hear his twice-daily readings, Hiram chose passages of interest to his personal Bible study. Clara, and then Rhoda, and the other children, were only listening in. Generally Hiram offered little in the way of explanation, preferring instead to observe a few minutes of quiet reflection.

Clara knew what went through her mind during these silences when she was a little girl, so imagining what Hannah and Mari were thinking did not require serious effort.

Like all boys, Josiah might someday be called upon to serve as a minister, or even a bishop, in the congregation. Perhaps this motivated his serious nature. The girls, on the other hand, could be sure they would never stand before a congregation and look into expectant faces awaiting God's message to come through their words.

That shouldn't matter, Clara thought as her father closed the Bible and announced the time of reflection. Were not the girls called to a life of faithfulness just as the boys were? Was it not reasonable that they should learn to love the Bible even as little children? To look forward to its stories and themes and exhortations?

Sadie loved Bible stories. She treasured them. Resentment burned through Clara in that moment of watching her sisters labor to control their wandering eyes and maintain appropriately dour angles in their faces.

Maybe Sadie was right. Maybe Clara should visit a Sunday school class in the Maryland congregation.

CHAPTER 14

Bishop Yoder's words on Sunday stunned Clara. She moistened her lips and tucked her tongue into one corner of her mouth as she concentrated, forcing herself to listen carefully. Her mind fell back on the tricks she had employed as a schoolgirl and mentally repeated each phrase.

Streng meidung. Strong shunning.

"It is my thinking," Bishop Yoder said, "that the ban and shunning were instituted by Jesus Christ, the Son of God, and His holy apostles. I recognize them as a teaching that shall not be changed by man. Already many have done much to reduce shunning far below the status given it by Jesus and His apostles."

The bishop paused and looked intently into the congregation. Clara couldn't resist looking across the aisle to the men, wishing she could know what Andrew was thinking — or her own father.

"Jesus' teaching is more enduring than heaven and earth." Reinvigorated, Bishop Yoder resumed. "In Matthew chapter eighteen and verse seventeen, we read that Jesus said, 'Let him be unto thee as an heathen man and a publican.' How long shall the transgressor be so regarded? Till he comes to the place of which the Son of God spoke to his disciples in Matthew eighteen and three: 'Verily, I say unto you, except ye be converted, and become as little children, ye shall not enter into the kingdom of heaven.' "

Although the room was not overly warm, perspiration seeped out of the pores along Clara's hairline. Tension thickened the rows of women around her. A couple of small children whimpered, but their mothers made no move to soothe them, instead keeping their eyes fixed on the bishop. This was not a sermon the Lord had laid on the bishop's heart that morning when he was selected — again — to preach. This was a sermon he had aimed at for months — or years.

"I believe also," he said, "that those who have in regular order been placed into the ban should be shunned, even if they join another church, so that they may indeed repent, regret, and sorrow with humble hearts and become reconciled with the church from which he or she left or was separated from. Paul wrote in 2 Thessalonians in the third chapter and the sixth verse, 'Now we command you, brethren, in the name of our Lord Jesus Christ, that ye withdraw yourselves from every brother that walketh disorderly, and not after the tradition which he received of us.' "

A rustle rose from the congregation, and Clara realized her own movements contributed. Bishop Yoder spoke over the disturbance.

"If we speak loosely about the ban and shunning, as we have done, we give a testimony that our principles can be violated in this part of Paul's teaching. But when it is received in the right way before God, so that the transgressor can be brought from death to life, the one who brings the transgressor out of darkness into light is worthy of honor."

Worthy of honor? Martha and Atlee. Fannie and her brothers. Elam and Sadie. Could Bishop Yoder truly be convinced that Clara would find honor in turning her back on her family simply because they had joined another branch of the Amish almost thirty years ago? Could he be serious in his expectation that shunning in this manner would woo any of the Marylanders back to the Old Order?

Clara's spirit rebelled. Because the vote in 1895 had been unanimous, even when the truth emerged ten years later that Bishop Yoder had pressed his own feelings upon the congregation, the vote could not easily be reversed.

And if anyone was inclined to suggest a new vote, Bishop Yoder seemed intent to prevent open discussion.

Clara swallowed hard.

Andrew cringed. Bishop Yoder's sermon sucked the air out of the room. He was asking for trouble in the congregation, and Andrew suspected that this time he was going to get it.

The bishop held his heavy Bible in front of him at the plain, unvarnished preaching table made of poplar wood. "We must heed the words of Paul in Romans, chapter sixteen, verse seventeen: 'Mark them which cause divisions and offences contrary to the doctrine which ye have learned; and avoid them.' This is now our insight on how the ban and shunning should be kept by all true disciples of Christ."

The congregation was not likely to tolerate this strict stance set out in such nonnegotiable terms. *Who was causing the division now?* Andrew mused. Mose Beachy would preach a doctrine of peace. Was that not the doctrine the church had learned forty years earlier when the Maryland and Pennsylvania churches amicably chose slightly different paths to express their shared faith?

And the differences *were* slight.

In the ten years after the peaceable division, families and ministers had realigned gradually with the groups that most closely shared their convictions. Andrew had heard the stories from his own grandparents. The groups had enough in common to build meetinghouses together and continue to share them. When consciences settled, each congregation had ministers and members sufficient to flourish and live harmoniously along the roads that crisscrossed the state border.

Andrew felt his head shaking ever so slightly in dread of the dissension this sermon was sure to stir up.

Bishop Yoder ministered in the Maryland district in those days. No one thought less of him when he decided he belonged among the Old Order. He had done the right thing to follow his conscience. But for two decades, since being ordained bishop, he had preached sermons meant to convict his new congregation of their participation in the sin of their Maryland families.

He knows what he's doing, Andrew thought. *Only a fool would not see that he lacks support for this hard line.* Andrew chastised himself for characterizing his spiritual leader as a fool, though he did not temper his opinion that the congregation would resist Yoder's indictment of their own consciences on this matter.

The sermon wound down. Stern faced, Bishop Yoder nodded toward his two sons, and one of them began a final grave hymn. Andrew drew in his breath and joined the singing, though he was certain that a hymn with twelve stanzas sung at a ponderous tempo would do nothing to quell the brewing disagreement.

At the final intonation of the benediction, Andrew turned to catch Clara's eye. Her head tilted nearly imperceptibly toward the door, and when Andrew freed himself from the entrapment he felt on the bench where he sat, he followed her outside. By the time he reached her, huddles of conversation had formed across the grass in the clearing.

"Surely he is not serious," Clara said. "Is he?"

"I'm afraid he is," Andrew said, "but he

has closed his eyes to the fallout."

"But no one wants the sort of *meidung* he is preaching about."

Andrew wished he could take her hand. "Everything will sort itself out. *Gottes wille.*"

Yonnie sidled toward Clara and Andrew. Clara's face alternately paled and reddened, but her eyes never left Andrew's face, and his were fixed on her.

They were standing too close together. It was improper.

With their gazes interlocked and strained, they wouldn't notice Yonnie creeping closer one slow step at a time. He circled slightly so he would come up behind Clara. Andrew was less likely to object to Yonnie's presence. If Clara saw him, her face would tighten as she clamped her mouth closed and stepped back. Yonnie could hear them now.

"I think God must be very sad," Clara said. "The bishop's mind is hardened against anyone who does not think as he does."

"He speaks from conviction," Andrew said. "He takes seriously his role as leader in the church."

"But all the families read the Bible in their homes," Clara countered. "Any of the men could have had the lot fall to them to become a minister. Why should Bishop Yoder think that others cannot also discern God's will?"

"The lot fell to him," Andrew said, "first to be a minister and then to be bishop. Don't you believe God reveals His will in the lot?"

Yonnie turned up one corner of his mouth. Perhaps Andrew was not as rebellious in spirit as he had judged him to be.

Clara crossed her arms over her chest. "I don't know what to believe."

Yonnie stepped forward, and now Andrew lifted his eyes from Clara's face.

"If you don't know what to believe," Yonnie said, "then God has shown you that you need the bishop's wisdom."

Clara spun around. Andrew's failed attempt to catch her elbow did not escape Yonnie's observation.

"Yonnie," Andrew said quickly, "Clara and I were speaking privately."

Yonnie swept a hand around the clearing. "This is a church gathering. Anyone might hear you."

Clara blanched. "Excuse me." She turned and left them without looking back.

"Yonnie," Andrew said, "why do you treat Clara as you do?"

"I don't treat her any differently than I do anyone else."

"Yes," Andrew murmured, "sadly, I think you are right. But if you could hear our words, then you know she is upset."

"She has no reason to be upset. The bishop's authority protects all of us. He is our spiritual shepherd."

"You know Clara has close relatives in the Maryland congregation." Andrew's tone heated. "Her own mother came from one of the Maryland families. Try to look at the question from her perspective."

"And if her relatives were thieves or fornicators, would you excuse that as well?" Yonnie widened his eyes and met Andrew's locked gaze.

"How can you compare such matters to this?"

"How can you draw a line between sin that should be confessed to the church and sin that should not be?"

"Yonnie, we've been friends for a long time. I hope that means as much to you as it does to me."

Andrew stepped back, pivoted, and strode through the clearing — not back toward the meetinghouse, but along the path Clara had taken.

■ ■ ■ ■

Fannie walked beside her husband and watched their daughter run ahead and then turn around and grin at her parents. Elam lifted a hand and waved a response to Sadie. This was not a church Sunday in the Maryland district. Instead of a shared meal at the meetinghouse, families and neighbors would form their own groups. The Eshes, as usual, would gather at the Hostetler table for the midday meal.

Fannie was not anxious to go. She suspected Elam also would have preferred to stay home. But what excuse would they give that would satisfy Sadie, and how would they send a message to Fannie's parents not to expect them? Logically, it seemed easier to go. The closer they got to the Hostetler farm, though, the slower Fannie's steps became until she finally called to Sadie not to get too far ahead.

Martha was halfway through her months of being with child. Perhaps if Fannie had learned earlier that the babe was coming, she might have accepted the news by now. But she had only learned her mother was expecting a couple of weeks ago. The wound was still fresh.

The wound.

Her mind told her no child was a wound, but her spirit sliced open afresh every time she thought of her mother receiving this blessing rather than Fannie. It was a wound that seemed to come straight from God and fester with disappointment, the puss of infected distrust multiplying every month.

Every week now. Every day.

Every day she felt the frailty of a body that could not — or would not — conceive a child because God had willed it so.

The wound oozed with the truth that Fannie did not want to see her mother right now. It was too hard. It was too hard to see Martha's thickening waistline and yet trust God that her own might also grow wider.

Sadie was becoming impatient, but Fannie would not make her feet move faster on the road toward her parents' farm. Even if she had willed it — which she did not — her feet would not have answered.

CHAPTER 15

"Did you hear?"

Fannie looked up from the mending in her lap at Elam, who poured himself a mid-morning cup of coffee.

"Hear what?" she said. Who would she hear news from on a Tuesday morning when she hadn't left the farm?

"Dale Borntrager was doing his own milk run this morning. He said Bishop Yoder came down hard on Sunday about the shunning."

"He's been doing that for twenty years." Fannie moistened the frayed end of a spool of black thread and pushed it through the eye of a needle.

"He means it this time." Elam stirred sugar into his cup.

"What's different about this time?"

"Dale said it sounded like an edict. The Old Order families are supposed to shun us without exception."

Fannie dropped her needle. "But Clara —"

"I know."

Fannie pushed the mending basket out of her lap. "I must go see Clara."

"I need the horses," Elam said.

"All of them?"

"The gelding needs to be shoed, so that only leaves me two. I've decided it's not too late to plow and seed another field, but I can't waste even a day."

Fannie sucked in her lips. "All right. I'll find my own way and be home to cook your supper."

If she left now and hurried across the back field, she could still catch Dale at the end of his route and ride to Clara's with him. Fannie bustled to the back door and called for her daughter.

"Sadie!"

A couple of chickens clucked in reply.

Fannie glanced at the clock on the kitchen wall and realized it had stopped. She didn't know how much time she had. If Dale skipped a stop or gained time, she would never catch him.

"Sadie!" Fannie began to march across the space between the house and the barn.

The girl appeared with a black streak across one cheek. Fannie grabbed her hand.

184

She would deal with the grime later. Right now she had to persuade Sadie to move steadily across the back field.

"Are we really going to see Clara?" Sadie asked when Fannie explained the hurry.

"Yes. We must catch Mr. Borntrager or we'll have to walk the whole way."

"Have I ever been to Clara's house? I don't remember it."

Fannie startled briefly at the truth that her daughter had never seen where Clara lived. Fannie herself had met Rhoda only once at one of the *English* shops in Springs, but that was years ago. Clara was in her first summer out of the eighth grade and Fannie a year older. Rhoda was vacantly pleasant when Clara introduced Fannie to her. That was before Josiah was born, before Rhoda began drawing distinctions between Clara and the Kuhn children who followed.

"Have I, *Mamm*?" Sadie tugged her mother's sleeve. "Have I been to Clara's house?"

"No," Fannie said. It was probably unwise to take Sadie there now, but the thought of not hearing from Clara herself about the events in the Old Order church propelled Fannie past the risk that she would not be welcome on the Kuhn farm. If she had to, she would linger down the lane, hidden among early-summer leafing until she found an opportunity to see Clara alone.

"You're walking too fast," Sadie whined.

Fannie slowed long enough only to grasp her child's hand and tug her forward. They crossed the field, emerged on the road, and followed its curve toward the Maple Glen Meetinghouse. When they reached it, Fannie stood still long enough to catch her breath before spitting on a corner of her apron and scrubbing the black streak from her daughter's cheek. Sadie squirmed and scrunched her face.

Dale Borntrager rumbled toward them in the milk wagon. Fannie raised a hand to flag him.

"Your husband must have told you the news," Dale said.

Fannie nodded and lifted Sadie up to the bench before scrambling in herself.

"What news, *Mamm*?" Sadie turned her face up.

"Just something I need to talk to Clara about." Fannie smoothed her daughter's hair, glancing over Sadie's head at Dale. Her mind burst with questions Dale would have answers for. What did Bishop Yoder preach? How were people in the congregation saying? Did he think people would defy or obey the ban? But Sadie sat between them on the bench. She was a five-year-old girl who did not deserve the fear that would strike her heart if she thought Clara would never come to see her again.

Andrew cranked the engine. It caught without hesitation. He smiled.

Every time Andrew worked on the Model T, he learned something. On some days, he learned that he should not have done what he did, and he spent tedious hours backtracking and trying another improvement. On other days, he successfully thought through where the sputter or rattle might originate and made small adjustments until he achieved the desired result. In his toolbox were multiple sheets of paper with small drawings of parts he observed as he lay on his back on the barn floor studying the undercarriage of the automobile. When he found corresponding drawings in the tattered publications Jurgen Hansen loaned him, he carefully labeled what he had identified with neat notes in Dutch about what the function of the part was. Where he had a question, he made a large *X* to remind him to ask Jurgen for further explanation.

Few possessions had ever given Andrew the pleasure the Model T provided. The thrill came not only from the promise of a well-running automobile but also from the process of discovering how the complex parts worked together. Andrew had been a mediocre student in the classroom. Learning to farm from his father, he had paid closer attention. Yet nothing had made his mind feel this alive. He did not have to ask deep questions about what made the *English* invent one new machine after another. What the machine might be capable of doing was only a small part of the triumph. Andrew imagined that it was the same for the *English* inventors. Understanding how and why the machine would perform drenched him in satisfaction.

He had so much to learn.

And while Andrew worked on the car, he pushed Bishop Yoder's words out of his mind. Yesterday's sermon preoccupied enough people. Andrew would not be one of them. He had disciplined himself not to labor on the Model T on the Sabbath, but Monday morning found him on the forsaken Johnson property wearing his oldest clothes so he was not distracted by where grease might splatter.

A form blocked a stripe of sunlight coming through the open barn door. Andrew looked up.

"Hello, Mr. Hansen."

"I told you to call me Jurgen." The garage

owner had both hands in deep pockets as he sauntered into the barn. "It sounds marvelous! Smooth and steady. That's what we want."

Grinning, Andrew reached inside the Model T and took the car out of gear. The engine silenced.

"I didn't know you were coming by," Andrew said.

"I can't get this car out of my mind." Jurgen walked around to the back of the car, stepped back, and examined the view. "Do you need more parts?"

They talked for a few minutes about what Andrew had done to the Model T in the days since Jurgen last saw it. Andrew had watched Jurgen work on seven vehicles. He knew that the repairs on the Model T had been minor compared to what could go wrong — and might still go wrong. If Andrew hoped to maintain the vehicle beyond the next few weeks, he would have to work alongside Jurgen for many more hours. Only because he was an unmarried man could Andrew juggle the responsibilities of his farm and the recreation of working on the Model T.

"It looks good, Andrew," Jurgen said. "You're doing very well."

"Thank you," Andrew said. "I respect your

opinion. I know you're familiar with this automobile."

"A Model T can last a long time if you take care of it," Jurgen said. "Ford Motor Company may like to make new automobiles affordable for everyone, but many people will prefer to purchase a used vehicle at an even more agreeable price."

"I know your services are valuable," Andrew said. "You are generous to give me your time and advice."

Jurgen sauntered around the far side of the car now. "I have an ulterior motive."

Andrew raised his eyebrows.

"I'd like to buy this car," Jurgen said. "I've always admired it. Every time it came into my shop, I thought of how nicely it would run if the owner would let me maintain it properly."

"Why didn't he sell it to you?"

"He didn't know I wanted it. I thought if he wanted to sell it, he would come to me. The idea that he would abandon it on the side of the road never entered my mind."

Andrew's throat went dry.

"I would give you a fair price," Jurgen said. "More than fair."

"You want to buy my Model T?" Andrew was still getting used to using a possessive pronoun in the same sentence with the name of an automobile.

"I do." Jurgen looked over the hood at Andrew. He named a price.

A response stalled in Andrew's throat. Words failed to form in his mind.

"Let me sweeten the offer." Jurgen named another figure.

Andrew licked his lips. "What about the original owner?" If he received money for the vehicle — especially the sum Jurgen suggested — shouldn't the funds to go the man who left the car on the road?

Jurgen shrugged. "He signed it away. And I heard he took a new position in Indiana. Maybe it was Illinois. Or it could have been Ohio. The point is, we wouldn't know how to find him anyway."

Learning from the automobile was one matter. Profiting from it was another in Andrew's mind. Enjoying the Model T fell somewhere in between.

"Will you think about it?" Jurgen tilted his head to one side to hold Andrew's gaze. "Promise that if you decide to sell you'll come to me first."

Clara left the meetinghouse on Sunday without eating and didn't notice until Monday that the Kuhn cupboard now contained two identical pie plates. This had happened before when Mattie Schrock and Rhoda both prepared pies to serve at the congregational meal. One or the other of them ended up with both plates. On Tuesday Clara rose early, before the house heated up with late June temperatures, and baked identical pies. Now she carried a still-warm pie down the lane to the Schrock farm.

Priscilla sat in the yard with her elbows on her knees and her face drooping between her hands. She jumped up, startled, when she saw Clara.

"I'm sorry," Priscilla said.

Clara pushed her eyebrows together. "Sorry about what?"

"Never mind. I'm sorry." Priscilla dug a bare toe into the dirt, her head hanging.

Clara balanced the pie in one hand and knelt to put herself at eye level with Priscilla. "Is everything all right?"

Tears clouded the girl's clear green eyes. "I'm afraid," she whispered.

"What are you afraid of?" Clara glanced around them.

"*Daed* says I must learn to slop the pigs by myself, but I don't like pigs! They're too big!"

Clara took one of Priscilla's hands.

"The mud is slippery," Priscilla said, her

voice catching, "and the noises the pigs make frighten me. And I'm afraid I'm going to drop the slop bucket, or even just spill it, and all the pigs will attack me."

The child's hand trembled in Clara's light grasp. "That reminds me of a story. Would you like to hear it?"

Priscilla nodded, her face scrunched with the effort of restraining tears.

"This is a story about Jesus," Clara said, "so you don't have to be frightened."

Priscilla looked unconvinced.

"One day, Jesus was very tired," Clara began. "He had been working very hard to tell people messages from God. When He got in a boat with His friends, He fell fast asleep."

"Did Jesus have a pillow?"

Clara pictured the words of the story in the family Bible. "Yes, He did!"

Priscilla's shoulders began to relax. Clara continued.

"A great big windstorm started blowing across the water, and the waves sloshed up over the sides of the boat. Jesus' friends started to think the boat was going to sink!"

"And did it?"

Clara smiled and shook her head. "They woke up Jesus and said, 'Don't you care what happens to us?' Jesus stood right up in the boat and He said to the wind, 'Peace, be still!' And the wind stopped. Everything was calm and peaceful again. And Jesus said to His friends, 'Why are you so afraid?' "

Priscilla looked at Clara, wide eyed. "Does it make Jesus angry if I'm afraid of the pigs?"

Clara squeezed the girl's hand. "We're all afraid of something. The story reminds us that even when we are most afraid, Jesus is right there with us."

Priscilla turned and looked toward the pigpen. "I'm still afraid."

"I know. Sometimes it feels like we're right in the middle of a terrible storm. But Jesus is there with us, and remembering that can help. Do you think you can remember that?"

Priscilla nodded.

The rattle of the approaching milk wagon pulled Clara's gaze up. She intended only to glance, but the two forms on the bench beside Dale Borntrager made her suck in her breath. Meeting Priscilla's eyes again, Clara smiled.

"Would you like to do a big job for me?" Clara said.

Priscilla nodded, and Clara held out the pie.

"Take this to your *mamm* and tell her to enjoy the pie!"

"I'm not afraid to do that." Priscilla arranged her hands around the rim of the pie plate with great deliberation.

"I know you'll do a good job." Clara watched as the child carefully measured her steps toward the house. She turned her own attention to the little girl leaning out of the clattering milk wagon and waving with vigor.

Fannie!

The wagon slowed. Fannie gripped Sadie's shoulder to keep her from leaping out of the wagon at the sight of Clara.

"Jump in, Clara," Dale said. "I'll take you all to your house."

"Yes!" Sadie clapped. "I can meet Hannah."

Clara's heart raced. How could she explain to Sadie that Rhoda's welcome would be insincere?

"Thank you, Dale, but I think we'll get out here." Fannie dropped her feet to the ground and turned to lift her daughter out of the wagon.

"But I want to see Hannah," Sadie protested.

"Not today."

Clara was grateful for the firm tone she heard in her cousin's voice. Sadie clamped her mouth closed. Dale waved and drove off.

"Do you see those rocks over there?" Fannie said. "Why don't you see what kind of bugs live under them?"

Sadie wandered away.

"I can't believe you came." Clara's embrace was tight.

"I only wish I could come to your house," Fannie said. "But we heard about your bishop's sermon. Rhoda has never invited us before. I don't imagine she'd be glad to see us now."

"No, not now," Clara said. Not with tension already scattered around the Kuhn house like hidden tree roots waiting to trip her. It was God's will for both pie plates to ride home with Rhoda and for Clara to carry a pie to the Schrocks only to discover Priscilla alone. If she had gone straight to Mattie's kitchen, she would have missed Fannie.

"Is it true?" Fannie said. "You're not supposed to see us?"

"You're still my family."

"Dale said there were no exceptions to the *meidung.*"

"It won't hold," Clara said.

"But if it does?"

"It won't. You were never in our church. How can Bishop Yoder place you in a ban? That would be like saying the Baptists or the Lutherans are under a ban. He's only talking about anyone who leaves the church now." Clara took a deep breath, a whole body prayer that what she said was a right understanding. She would not accept the alternative.

"So we'll still see you?"

"Of course. But I may have to be careful for a while." Clara glanced at Sadie, refusing to imagine the absence of this wondrous child from her life.

"We should go," Fannie said.

"Find some shade and wait. I'll come back with a cart and drive you home."

Fannie shook her head. "Sadie's a good walker. You're right to be careful."

Clara kissed Fannie's cheek. "I'll see you soon."

CHAPTER 16

With her form hidden under the loose-fitting folds of her dress covered with a cape and apron, Clara doubted anyone could see that she did not fill out the dress as much as she had just a few weeks ago. She spent long hours away from the farm now, most of it walking in a manner others would perceive as recreational. Clara knew the truth. The tension at home was less severe if Clara spent most of her day away. She was present for breakfast and supper and the family devotion times that followed, but even Hannah had stopped asking why Clara often was not home for lunch anymore. Even in rising summer temperatures, Clara walked to her housekeeping jobs, to shops where she spent little money, to the homes of childhood friends too busy with their own children for a leisure conversation. Clara could hardly tell them she had too much time and too little to do.

After days of restlessness, on Saturday Clara wandered along the property line between the Kuhn farm and the adjoining Schrock farm. The crop promised an abundant yield — as long as summer rains followed the pattern all the farmers were accustomed to. Clara's bare feet sank into pliant dark earth as she ambled through rows of corn rising above her knees. With the sun full in the sky, she was hopeful Andrew was finished with morning chores and might have time to talk to her. The first stop in her inquiry would be the weather-battered Johnson outbuilding. Even if Andrew was not there, Clara could take refuge from the midday heat in its shade.

When Clara heard giggling and rustling, she paused to judge the source. Three voices still thin in timbre exuded conspiracy.

"This can be our story place."

Clara recognized that voice. It belonged to Priscilla Schrock and evidenced none of her fear of slopping the pigs. Clara crept forward with stealth until she saw three sets of little-girl bonnets nodding in a close circle.

"This story is about Jesus," Priscilla said. "Whenever you're afraid, this story will help. You might still feel afraid, but you won't feel alone."

Clara stilled her breath and gathered her skirts in both fists to keep them from brushing cornstalks. Priscilla's rendition of Jesus stilling the storm on the Sea of Galilee was earnest and factual. What she added to Clara's version were the sounds of the roaring wind. The other girls joined her in expelling loud breath and swaying precipitously as if they were in a sinking boat. Suddenly Priscilla popped up, spread her arms wide, and declared, "Peace! Be still!"

That was the moment Clara met the girl's confident, clear, green eyes.

"It's Hannah's sister!"

At Priscilla's announcement, Naomi Brennerman and Lillian Yutzy broke their concentration and jumped up as well. Clara soaked up three eager gazes.

"This is God's will!" Priscilla pushed through the stalks.

"Careful," Clara said, "don't trample the corn."

Her warning did not slow the girls.

"Did God send you to tell us another story from the Bible?" Priscilla's eyes brimmed with expectation.

Clara glanced across the field, wondering where the girls' mothers were and if they knew how far from the house their daughters had wandered.

"Please," Priscilla said. "It doesn't have to be a long one."

Naomi gently fingered a silken cornstalk. "Are there any stories in the Bible about crops?"

Clara swallowed hard, barely believing what she was about to do. "Crops and fields and soil and barns and so many things that are part of our life."

"Tell us," Priscilla said.

Clara sat on the ground and tucked her skirt around her knees. "This story is about a farmer sowing seed." Clara dug her hand into the ground and let the black soil run through her fingers. "What difference do you think the soil makes?"

The girls all lived on Amish farms. Clara described four kinds of soil and four kinds of yields, watching their heads bob in understanding.

"What kind of soil are you?" she asked. "That's the question Jesus wants us to think about."

Thoughtful silence hung for a few seconds before a mother's calling voice shattered it. The girls jumped up.

"We have to go," Priscilla said. "When can we do this again?"

Clara hesitated. She loved their attentive faces and little-girl answers to the questions

201

she asked as she navigated through the story. But telling them they could meet like this again would be an unfair, false promise.

"You'd better go," she said. "Don't keep your mothers waiting."

The trio scampered down the row calling out to answer the summoning voice. Clara let the responses fade before she stood. It would only be a matter of time before one of the girls told an adult about the story — maybe even before suppertime that day. Most likely they would be admonished not to bother her, to tend to their chores, or to ask their questions about the Bible at home.

In this moment, though, Clara savored the flush of satisfaction.

Andrew turned a wrench and asked, "Why do you feel guilty?"

"I know it's silly," Clara said. "It's not as if I put up a sign to advertise. I found Priscilla frightened in her own yard, and I couldn't have known she would bring her friends to the field today at the same time I happened to walk through."

"Gottes wille." Andrew ducked into the engine again.

"That's what Priscilla said."

"She's an Amish child," Andrew said. "She probably learned to say 'God's will' before she learned to say her own name."

Clara chuckled.

"Did you tell them anything your father would not say?"

"My father is not much given to commentary. His method is Bible reading and silent reflection."

"There's a time and a place for that," Andrew said, rubbing his hands on a rag, "but you have a gift for communicating with children that your *daed* might not share."

"All I've done is tell a couple of stories about Jesus. Why do I feel so guilty?"

"I don't know. Why do you?" Andrew caught Clara's gaze.

She picked at a fingernail. "Perhaps because their parents don't know."

"Did you make the girls promise not to tell their parents?"

"No, of course not."

Andrew turned a palm up as if his point were self-evident.

"No one but my father ever told me a Bible story, and he sticks to his favorites," Clara said. "I didn't understand most of the sermons at church. I had to learn to read High German before I could read the Bible for myself. I still have many, many questions about what everything means."

"You don't have to persuade me," Andrew

said, "but you're making a pretty good argument that what you did will help those girls."

"I suppose it does not feel very much like submission." Clara studied the back of her hand. "No women in the church are teachers."

"Mothers teach their children." Andrew tossed his rag over a headlamp and stepped closer to Clara.

"That's different. They have husbands to help guide them."

"You could have a husband," Andrew said. "And to remove all doubt, let me say that I believe you would do a wonderful job with our children and anyone else's."

She blushed. "Andrew —"

He held up a hand. "I know. You're not ready. I'm not rushing you."

Clara laid a hand on the Model T. "Do you ever feel guilty about the automobile?"

"Not especially."

"Yonnie doesn't think you are in submission, either."

"I'm not worried about Yonnie."

"He might tell the wrong person you have a car," Clara said, "just like the girls might tell the wrong person about my stories. Bishop Yoder could make us both stand up and confess before the entire congregation."

What Clara said was true — and if someone happened upon them together in this remote barn, the list of their transgressions would likely lengthen. But Andrew found fear an unlikely basis for a faithful life.

"If someone asks you not to speak to their children," he said, "I am sure you would respect their wishes. And as for Yonnie? I will not borrow tomorrow's trouble. The Bible tells us each day has enough trouble of its own, right?"

Clara nodded. She raised her eyes and looked beyond him. "You have a visitor."

Andrew pivoted and saw Jurgen Hansen striding into the barn. He'd been so intent on listening to Clara that he hadn't heard the sound of the vehicle Jurgen must have driven.

"Am I interrupting something?" Jurgen said.

"You're always welcome," Andrew said. "This is my friend Clara Kuhn. Clara, this is the garage owner I told you about."

"Are you also interested in Model Ts?" Jurgen offered a hand to Clara, who shook it awkwardly and glanced at Andrew.

"She's interested in *my* Model T," Andrew said.

"I hope she's not too attached," Jurgen said, "because I'm here to renew my offer."

"It's only been a few days," Andrew said. "I thought I had more time to consider the question."

"I realize I may be rushing you," Jurgen said. "I have a customer who wants to buy the car I drive. I'd sell it to him if I knew I could have yours."

"But your automobile runs far better than this one."

Jurgen ran a hand along a shiny polished fender. "I've been enamored of this machine since the first time it came into my shop. Have you thought about my offer at all?"

"I have," Andrew said. "How could I not after the number you named? But I'm afraid I'll have to decline. I'm quite enamored with this Model T myself."

Jurgen swung one foot and kicked up a small flurry of dust from the barn floor. "I don't blame you, but I thought it was worth asking. Consider it a standing offer."

"Thank you, Jurgen, but I don't plan to sell the automobile."

Jurgen made polite farewells. Andrew and Clara stood still as they listened to him crank the engine of his own Ford outside the barn.

"You're really going to keep the Model T," Clara said.

"I am."

"And if you're disciplined?"

"Mose Beachy will stand with me."

"And will that be enough?"

"Others will be glad to stand with Mose."

Clara's candle burned long after the rest of the Kuhn household was shrouded in rest. She resisted the urge to light an oil lamp for brighter illumination. Her father and Rhoda were just across the hall. If one of them happened to rise in the night, the yellow gleam under her door would launch a battery of questions about what would keep her up when morning was nearer than last evening's nightfall.

Andrew's modern thinking emboldened her. A box tucked deep under her bed held the scribbled first drafts of the stories she copied over and sent to Sadie. Clara had lifted the pages one by one and made a list of all the Bible stories she'd written in words Sadie would understand — or Priscilla or Naomi or Lillian. One day perhaps she could even tell them to Hannah and Mari.

Until now, Clara had written the stories stirring her own heart. Now she considered where the gaps were. Had she written enough about the history of Israel and the good kings and the bad kings? What about the prophets? Elijah's and Elisha's lives were full of miracles to encourage faith. Had she balanced the miracles and parables of Jesus? What about the book of Acts? She hadn't begun to try to put the letters of Paul into language for children.

Clara didn't know if she would see Priscilla and her friends again for a story, but if she did — *Gottes wille* — she wanted something ready in her head and heart. Sadie would always be eager for a new story. Clara resolved to copy afresh all the stories she had written up until then, and from now on to make one clean copy to send to Sadie and a second to keep for herself.

Someday she might also want these stories for her own children — if she could bring herself to marry.

She thought of the image of little Priscilla standing in the field and announcing, "Peace! Be still!"

Clara's own heart craved the assurance she had declared to Priscilla.

CHAPTER 17

For a week Dale Borntrager did both the morning and afternoon milk runs himself, leaving Yonnie with the dairy employees who bottled milk, kept the butter churns moving, checked on the process of the cheeses, and sorted orders for delivery. In the winter, everyone preferred the indoor work. At this time of year, though, Yonnie relished sitting on the uncovered wagon bench and watching summer's splendid settling in.

His exile to bottling had ended, but the route was shorter now. On Monday morning, Yonnie returned to the dairy with about two-thirds of the canisters he would have collected only nine or ten days ago. He steered the wagon tight up against the platform where he and others would unload.

Dale Borntrager scowled. "Where are the rest?"

"This is everything." Yonnie heaved a

canister out of the wagon and onto the platform.

"Cows do not suddenly stop producing milk," Dale said. "This can't be right."

"There are fewer stops now." Yonnie puzzled at explaining the obvious.

Realization broke over Dale's face. "Do you mean that you didn't pick up from the Marylander farms?"

"Of course not."

Dale grabbed a canister so forcefully that milk sloshed around the edges of the closed top. "Get these unloaded. Then go back and get the rest before it's too late."

Yonnie's feet froze. "But the bishop — the ban. He was quite clear."

"The bishop has a nice, quiet farm. He's not running a business," Dale said. "The Marylander families supply thirty percent of our milk, and they buy from us as well."

"Didn't you explain to them when you made the rounds yourself?"

"I made those visits to make sure they know where I stand." Dale hefted another canister. "It seems you are the one who doesn't."

Yonnie's feet finally moved, and he gripped the handles of a milk canister. He had assumed Dale would cull his lists.

"The ministers might call on you to

explain your actions." Yonnie spoke respect-
fully. "I did not want to put you in the position of facing discipline."

"I'll decide that," Dale said. "Your job is
to do what I ask you to do."

Yonnie hesitated. He did not want to face
discipline, either. Bishop Yoder's sermon last
week made clear that lax shunning would
no longer go unnoticed. Church members
would be accountable for their interactions
with the Maryland church members.

Dale straightened back, hands on his hips.
"Yonnie?"

Yonnie met his employer's eye.

"You've worked for me for a long time,"
Dale said. "But if you're not in agreement
with my business policies, I can find somebody else to drive the wagon. I'll understand
if you quit, but as long as you're on the
payroll, you'll pick up the Marylander milk
right alongside the Old Order milk."

Yonnie needed his job. He would always
be welcome in his parents' home, but he
had too many brothers. The farm would not
be enough when they all began to have
families. His father had given Yonnie a slice
of land he had never considered tillable, full
of stumps and boulders. Even if Yonnie
cleared it, one backbreaking step at a time,
the acreage was not large enough to plant

profitably. If he had any hope of his own farm someday, he needed the income that came from the dairy.

"Are we of one mind on this matter?" Dale said.

Yonnie swallowed and nodded.

Clara took to morning walks that began shortly after family devotions. Each day the radius of her path widened, keeping her occupied a few minutes longer before she wondered, out of eight years of habit, what the children were doing or whether Rhoda needed help in the kitchen with the day's meals.

When Clara caught herself pacing back toward the front of the house on Monday morning, she halted. Her breath lodged in her throat, neither inhaling nor exhaling, as she wondered what might happen if she spoke her mind to Rhoda or picked up Mari and carried her out of a room over Rhoda's protests. Pressure in her chest forced a gasp, and Clara's shoulders rose and dropped three times. Stinging tears clouded her gaze, and Clara backed away, turning instead to circle around the perimeter of the yard around the house. Familiarity led her to the path to the vegetable garden. What harm could she do inspecting the burgeoning yield that would find its way to the family's table through the summer and into canning jars that would see them through the winter? She had not seen the garden closely in weeks, knowing that Rhoda kept the girls near during her daily visits for weeding and thinning.

The sight of the new section of earth her father had turned a few weeks ago buckled Clara's knees.

Celery. Rows and rows of celery.

Clara did a quick calculation and arrived at nearly four hundred plants. No one grew that much celery unless the family expected a wedding in the fall. The plants were fledgling, and not all of them would survive, but the bounty would be ample for the traditional decorations and dishes of a wedding. Any neighbor or church family who saw the rows would presume, and Clara would be the recipient of sly glances during church. Clara knelt in the dirt and raised her eyes to the clear sky, muttering halting thanks that the Kuhn garden was set back from the house, not in the front in view from the road.

Rhoda could not force Clara to marry.

Rhoda could not force her will. It was God's will Clara awaited.

Clara marched toward the house, around

the barn, past the henhouse, through the back door, and straight up the back stairs to her room. She pulled out her sheaf of papers, the result of one late night after another pouring her heart out before the Lord the way she knew best.

Page after page, she had copied marked-up stories onto fresh paper in tiny script to conserve space. With her heart's ears and eyes open, she added what she saw and heard. She didn't change the stories — she would never change a jot or tittle of God's Word — but she sought what a child might see and hear in the story. Clara remembered the places where Sadie had tugged on her sleeve to pause and ask questions. She heard again Sadie's pleas to hear her favorite stories again and again.

They weren't perfect. God's Word was the only perfect book. The stories weren't even a book, just a stack of papers tied together with string to keep them from scattering in the wind as Clara walked. She doubted anyone noticed when she left the house after lunch and aimed toward the main road. A few months ago, she would have supposed Andrew was too busy on his farm to bother him — and she wouldn't have been brazen enough to seek him out there. The Model T changed Andrew's rhythms, though, and the dilapidated structure where he worked on the automobile was a more reasonable walking distance. Clara had been there several times in the last ten days, and with each visit the refuge of the old barn deepened and sharpened, whether or not Andrew was present.

Clara judged the sun carefully when she pushed open the barn door and discovered only the automobile and not its mechanic. She could wait several hours for Andrew and still be home for supper. She missed Josiah and Hannah and Mari. Hiram Kuhn discouraged chatter at the dinner table, and Rhoda hustled the children off after meals before Clara could do much more than catch their eyes and offer a smile instead of the words spoiling on her tongue. If she could not be useful with the chores or helpful with the children, what harm was there in finding refuge on the Johnson farm? Sagging and broken slats allowed nearly as much air inside the old barn as outside, and if she wanted more illumination than what filtered in jagged stripes, Clara could always light one of Andrew's lanterns. Leaning into the stubborn barn door, she closed it far enough that its disturbed state would not cause a confirming glance to anyone who passed by on the road.

She walked around the Model T twice before reaching for the latch and opening the door to climb into the comfortable upholstered seat behind the steering wheel. Clara knew how to drive a buggy or an open cart, and for the first time she wondered if she might learn to drive a car as well. Closing her eyes, she felt again the wind tickling her cheeks the day Andrew took her for a ride, leaving her rosy and glowing.

Such an unabashed sensation, one that she had never known to crave before that day.

Andrew would take her out again if she asked.

Andrew stood for a moment in the reduced opening and wondered what Clara was thinking about. He was not unhappy to see her sitting in the automobile — quite the opposite. With her hands on the wheel, she was without reticence or guile, and he was grateful to see her in such a state. Clara had made no suggestion that he should have accepted Jurgen Hansen's offer to buy the Model T. Her trust in his judgment had evoked a tenderness he had not thought possible.

He stepped into the barn. "Would you like a driving lesson?"

Her head turned with a grace that stirred him.

"I would hate to cause a breakdown," she said.

A half-dozen strides was all it took to take him to her side. She scooted over on the bench, and only then did Andrew see the papers in her lap.

"What have you brought?" He climbed in beside her.

Her nerves made her swallow with such force that Andrew heard the spongy thump.

"Stories," she said. "Bible stories. I write them for Sadie."

He raised both eyebrows. "I had no idea."

"No one in our congregation does." Clara lifted the stack of pages. "I want you to read them and tell me if they are a good that will honor God, or if they are a sinful, selfish pride that will undo me."

He took the papers but did not move his gaze from her eyes. "You know the answer to that."

She pulled a loose end of string and the knot came loose. "I know that I would be getting a man with an automobile. I want you to know what you would be getting."

Andrew gave in to a half smile. "So you're thinking about it."

Clara blushed and glanced away. "Just

217

read some."

"Right now?"

"I'll get one of the lamps if you need it." She started to get out of the Model T, but he put a hand on her arm to stop her. He wanted her near.

Andrew dropped one shoulder to clear the shadow over the top page, adjusted his eyes to the light, and began to read silently. Beside him, Clara was unnaturally still. He hardly heard her breathe. One by one he slid the pages to the bottom of the pile.

"These are very good," he said when he was halfway through.

"Keep reading," she prodded.

Andrew smiled and chuckled and nodded and put his finger under favorite parts. When he came again to the page where he had begun, he was tempted to keep reading. Instead, he looked at her eager eyes.

"How long have you been working on these?"

"A few months. I've written a lot in the last few days."

"You have a wonderful imagination."

"Some of our people would caution me on that matter."

"Not me," Andrew said. "Never in our home."

She blushed again, but this time she did

not look away.

Behind them, the door creaked open. Andrew hoped for Jurgen but saw Yonnie.

"What are you doing?" Yonnie said.

Andrew stifled a sigh and did not answer. Even he was losing patience with the tone he heard in Yonnie's voice the last few weeks, a cross between false authority and trepidation.

"I wanted to talk to you," Yonnie said, "but I see this is not a convenient time for you."

Andrew sensed Clara was going to rise and put out a hand to cover hers, away from Yonnie's view. He didn't want her to go. Clara could hear whatever was on Yonnie's mind or Yonnie could find Andrew again later.

"What can I help you with?" Andrew said.

Yonnie pressed his lips together, not in sternness but in uncertainty. When they were boys, his chin would have been drooping in a moment like this one. As an adolescent, Yonnie had learned to clamp his jaw closed when he didn't know what to say. Andrew waited.

"It's about the bishop's sermon," Yonnie said.

Andrew tightened his grip on Clara's hand. "Each man will have to seek his own conscience."

"Yes. We can talk another time." Yonnie's eyes went from Andrew's to Clara's. "I also wanted to be sure you both knew about the barn raising on Thursday."

"Mose Beachy reminded me," Andrew said.

"Then I'll see you there."

Yonnie turned to go, and Andrew released Clara's hand.

She tied the string around her pages again. "He has more on his mind than a barn raising."

"You go," Fannie said to Elam.

"What will I tell your mother?" Elam poured water into his hands and splashed his face over the kitchen sink, rinsing the day's labor from his skin.

"The truth. I'm under the weather and need to rest." Fannie ached to lie down. "That's no reason for Sadie to be disappointed, and you'll get a much better meal at my mother's than I could offer you tonight."

Elam rubbed a towel over his face. "If you're sure."

"I am."

"She'll want to send some food home for you."

"I'm not hungry."

Fannie's teeth grated through the next twenty minutes of getting Sadie into a clean dress and Elam out the door with their daughter. She forced herself to stand upright long enough to return her daughter's farewell wave.

Then she went into the bedroom, climbed into the bed fully clothed, and put a pillow over her face to block the still-streaming summer sunlight.

All she wanted was to be alone in a dark, quiet space.

At church the day before, her mother's condition had become the news of the day, followed by the announcements that two other women were also expecting new *boppli.* Fannie had choked back her own grief and mustered congratulations to two women only a few years older than she was. They were still in their childbearing years. As disappointment gave way to envy in the pit of her stomach, Fannie knew she could not avoid women in their twenties or thirties having more children. It was only natural that they would.

But her own mother? At forty-four? It was too hard. Fannie craved only release from that vision. She closed her eyes and relinquished her mind to the shadows.

CHAPTER 18

Yonnie's eyes popped open and his breath caught. The room sprang into vivid focus, down to the miniscule white dust particles riding on light streaming through the shutterless window.

"Are you coming or not?" His mother's voice echoed up the stairwell. "I can't keep your breakfast hot forever."

The two beds on either side of Yonnie's were empty, though on most mornings his brothers' forms rolled and moaned at his movements no matter how quiet he tried to be. Only moments ago he was awake — at least that's what it felt like. The strength of the sunlight betrayed the true hour. Yonnie had fallen back into the deepest sleep of his night and slumbered through the morning household commotion. Even his brothers would be at their farm chores by now.

Twice during the night Yonnie got up for a drink of water, which did nothing to soothe his spirit.

By the time he finished wrestling with his thoughts, he felt like Jacob, lame from the touch of God on his hip.

When sleep surrendered its reluctance and eased its way into his body, Yonnie knew he had at best two hours before he would rise and prepare for his day's labor. It was no wonder he had examined the shadows of the room and allowed himself another ten minutes.

That was hours ago.

Yonnie's heart pounded. A milkman never had the luxury of beginning the day so long after sunrise. He did not have to consult a clock to know that by now a scowl twisted Dale Borntrager's face. On the way to the hook where his trousers hung, Yonnie paused at the water basin long enough to plunge his face into liquid that was neither hot nor cold. In one swift gesture, he snapped his suspenders into place and dropped his hands to fasten his work boots before thundering down the stairs.

His mother stood at the stove with a spatula in one hand.

"I'm sorry, *Mamm*." He whizzed past her, bending to aim a kiss at her cheek, knowing it would not land. "I don't know what happened."

Despite the allure of scrambled eggs and fried ham, Yonnie could not allow himself the indulgence of breakfast when he was so late. Maybe there would at least be coffee in the pot at the dairy.

Outside the house, Yonnie groaned in realization that his father and brothers had taken all the horses into the fields already. As late as he was, he had no alternative to racing on foot to the dairy.

His night of grappling with the bishop's message had yielded fruit in those final exhausting moments. *"Each man will have to seek his own conscience,"* Andrew had said, and he was right. Yonnie suspected Andrew meant the words as a defense of his own choice, but as they rolled through the night watches of Yonnie's mind, he heard in them the obedience of his own conscience.

The right course was to bring to Bishop Yoder's attention that one of his flock owned an automobile. The clarity that illumined Yonnie's spirit during the watches of the night now made him wonder why he had tussled so long — weeks — with the decision. In his baptism, he vowed to submit to the authority of the church. It was God's will that Yonnie had witnessed the spurious circumstances under which Andrew had allowed his commitment to falter. The strength of the church mattered more than Yonnie's personal fondness for his child-hood friend.

And it mattered more than Yonnie's job. He would have to look for work that would not require him to silence his own conscience for mere financial gain. Not everyone in the congregation dismissed the bishop's leadership with the indifference of Dale or Andrew or John Stutzman. As his father liked to say, "If you are true to your faith, there are things you give up."

Yonnie barreled into the dairy without the extravagance of catching his breath. In the office, he scanned the order sheets for anything out of the ordinary. The clock confirmed the degree of his tardiness, but Yonnie pushed through the distraction and mentally calculated how he could economize his movement and trim a substantial margin off the lost time. Cheese, milk, cream, butter. He could pack three crates at a time instead of one and put more in each crate so he could make fewer trips to load the wagon. In the main room, where everything was kept cold, Yonnie moved into action.

Eventually, though, he felt Dale's glare on the back of his neck. He moistened his lips and turned to face his employer.

"I'm sorry to be so late. I overslept," Yonnie said. If Dale were in a fair frame of mind, he would acknowledge that Yonnie had never succumbed to this malady before. One incidence had no resemblance to a habit.

"And will you tell that to the customers who expected fresh cream with their morning coffee?"

"I will make every apology necessary," Yonnie said quickly. "I will ask forgiveness and make clear that the lateness of the rounds is no fault of yours."

Dale glowered. "First you spoiled an entire order of milk. Then you took the liberty to remove milk suppliers from your rounds. Now you're intolerably late."

Yonnie's gut burned. He had worked for Dale for years and knew the dairy's operation better than any of the other employees. It should not be so hard for Dale to recognize these truths.

Demut, Yonnie reminded himself. Humility.

"I will make up the time," he said. "You will find no more dissatisfaction in my work at day's end."

He would have to make inquiries soon about other work — before Dale had opportunity to spread an opinion that disparaged Yonnie. Several Amish farms were large enough that he might be able to hire himself out as a field hand. Most likely, he would not receive any salary until after the harvest and the work might be temporary, but it would be a start. Or the Amish furniture store in Springs might need help in its workshop at the edge of town. Yonnie was not much of a carpenter, but he could clean up and make deliveries.

By the time the milk wagon clattered out of the dairy, Yonnie was formulating the precise wording of his inquiries. He would have to be certain a new employer planned to properly respect Bishop Yoder's authority.

Sweat tickled Fannie's ear along a fine line from the roots of her hair down to the side of her neck, and she raised a shoulder to swipe at the irritation. Lifting a hand from her task would have been a vain effort. Tenacious humidity overpowered the air. Fannie had no thermometer, but she had lived through enough Julys not to put false hope in the notion that the weather would break into a stream of tolerable temperatures. If anything, the sweltering days would grow more intense before the turn of the earth yielded relief. Systematically, Fannie pushed a dust rag across the neglected wood surfaces of her front room. She did not much care whether the dust piled up. She only knew that keeping herself in constant motion was the most likely cure for the profound urge to go back to bed that had trailed through the hours since breakfast. Perhaps if her house was tidier, her mind would feel less cluttered as well.

At the dining room table, Sadie banged her heels against the legs of the chair and the pencil in her hand against the tabletop.

"Have you finished copying your letters?" Fannie asked, though she had only given Sadie the task to keep her from pulling items out of drawers and cupboards faster than Fannie could put them away.

"I don't want to copy letters." Sadie leaned her chin into one hand. "I'm not old enough for school yet."

"You will be soon. You can at least learn to write your name."

"I want to play. That's what I'm good at."

Fannie cocked her head and surprised herself with a smile. "Yes, playing has always been your special talent."

"Then why can't I go out and play?"

"You heard *Daed* at lunch. It's going to rain."

"But it's not raining now." Sadie's eyes rounded into solemn pleas.

228

Fannie tossed the dust rag on a side table. "All right. We'll both go outside." At least outdoors a breeze might flutter and divide the damp air into a small space of relief.

They went into the front yard, where Elam had dug the vegetable plot wider and longer this year. Fannie could keep her hands busy weeding and inspecting produce.

Sadie immediately threw herself into a patch of grass and rolled one direction and then the other.

"Watch me!" she called.

"I'm watching." Fannie wondered if Sadie was old enough to recognize when the expression on her mother's face was not quite sincere, though she did observe the girl's glee and remembered how cool grass close to the earth could refresh a day with little other promise. The caution that formed in Fannie's mind went unspoken. She should have reminded Sadie to take care with her dress and to roll only in the grass and not in dirt, but she lacked energy to enforce a warning so she supposed there was no point in voicing one. Needle and thread and a cool bath would remedy any damage. Fannie turned to the garden, kneeling in the loamy soil and wishing she had thought to pick up the basket on the front porch. She glanced at the sky and judged that they would not be outside for long. Elam was right. Rain seemed inevitable, and Fannie would have to persuade Sadie to go back inside.

Sadie popped up. "Look! It's *Grossmuder.*"

Stone formed in Fannie's stomach. Her mother struggled for a moment with the latch at the gate.

Pull it up, Fannie thought. Martha always seemed to try twice to open the latch by pulling it down before resorting to the opposite motion. Why didn't her mother bring a buggy? She should not have walked in this heat in her condition.

Her condition.

Martha had a definite sway now. Her waistline had seemed to explode in the last few weeks, making it impossible for Fannie to avoid thinking about the child in her womb.

Fannie might be able to hide her feelings from a five-year-old, but her mother would be a steeper challenge. She stood and smiled.

"Hello, *Mamm.*" Not since Fannie had begun going to Singings on her own had she wished this hard that her mother would go away.

"Are you feeling better?" Martha said,

dabbing an apron corner at the sweat on her forehead.

Fannie had no desire to lie to her mother. Neither could she tell the truth.

Sadie tugged at Martha's hand. "Do you want strudel? We have a lot."

"Yes," Fannie said quickly, "why don't you go get *Grossmuder* a piece of strudel? Wrap it in a napkin and don't squeeze it."

Sadie skipped toward the house. Fannie felt the first widely spaced drops of rain as she turned to face her mother.

"I know why you didn't come to supper last night," Martha said softly.

Fannie said nothing.

"I prayed for years that God would give you another child," her mother said. "I still do. I never asked for this for myself. I have a house and a heart full of children, and after twelve years I was content to think that the days of new babes were over for me."

"I know." Fannie forced out the reply. She *did* know. Other than her husband, her mother was the one to soak up Fannie's heartache month after month as if it were her own.

The rain spattered with sudden force, and thunder rumbled. Sadie stood on the porch cradling a napkin, unsure what to do.

"Stay there!" Fannie called to Sadie.

Raindrops splotched her apron, coming faster and harder like a certain birth.

"This child will be your brother or sister." Martha raised her pitch above the thrumming shower. "I hope you will love it as much as you do the others."

Fannie nodded, if only to bring the conversation to a close. She could not keep her mother standing out in the rain, and neither could she expect Martha to begin the walk home in a thunderstorm. She would have to invite her inside. Sadie, at least, would be delighted.

"I'll find you a cold drink to have with your strudel."

CHAPTER 19

The remains of a barn that stood for fifty years had been removed. Melvin Mast had been talking about a new barn, with more and bigger cow stalls, for close to ten years. Now, instead of a rickety weathered structure, the space beside the Mast house featured precise stacks of beams, joists, rafters, siding, and shingles. The foundation, laid last week, was already covered with floorboards. Clara could see the clear shape of the barn.

"I understand Young Dave is the boss of the raising today." Hiram Kuhn guided the family buggy to a clear spot along a pasture fence and pulled on the reins.

"His first time," Rhoda said. "I'm sure he has learned well from his father."

Clara got out and then raised her hands for little Mari. Hannah would insist she could get down on her own. Josiah was already helping Hiram unhitch the horse, and Rhoda gripped the handles of two baskets of food. Clara welcomed Mari into her arms, giving the three-year-old a quick hug and a kiss on the top of her head without looking at Rhoda.

"I want to really help this time." Josiah straightened his eight-year-old height. "I'm old enough."

"We'll see," Hiram said.

"I don't want to go with the *kinner.*" Josiah's face set with his mother's determination. "I want to learn to build a barn."

Clara watched the glance that passed between Hiram and Rhoda.

"Come with me," Hiram said, "but you must obey carefully today." They walked away.

Mari tugged Clara's skirt. "Is this a frolic?"

"Yes, it is," Clara said. A hundred people or more would turn out. Glancing around, she could see most of the church families were already present.

"I like frolics, don't I?" Mari, standing beside the buggy, looked up at Clara for confirmation.

Clara smiled. "You are the best frolicker I know."

Rhoda cleared her throat. "Please don't fill her head with pride."

Clara cupped her hand around the back of Mari's head but said nothing.

"Come along, Mari," Rhoda said. "You, too, Hannah. Let's let Clara enjoy her day."

"I'll keep the girls," Clara said, gesturing at the baskets Rhoda carried. "You have other things to do."

"Thank you," Rhoda said, "but I've already spoken with Hannah. It's time she took on more responsibility. She's old enough to keep Mari occupied."

Once Rhoda turned her back, leading the girls away, Clara let out her sigh. Clara would have enjoyed her day very well with her little sisters in tow. Even when her father first married Rhoda, Clara knew she had a determined personality. Her penchant for order served the household well after Hiram's years of limited cooking skills and uncertainty about what a little girl needed. But now, the way Rhoda drew lines around her stepdaughter without ever being rude — this was something Clara would not have predicted.

Clara turned her eyes to the bustling scene. Men clustered around supplies, women unwrapped food at a series of tables, and children scooted off to find friends and have the run of the farm. Young people old enough to go to Singings would eye each other.

She would enjoy the day. As a motherless little girl, she loved any sort of frolic that brought her into the arms and attention of the church. No one today would have reason to think anything was wrong between Clara and Rhoda. She could be with people she had known all her life, doing something no one would disagree about.

Clara caught Andrew's eye across the farmyard cleared for the day of the chickens that normally occupied it. He would be working hard. She had seen Andrew's contribution to a barn raising before. He let older men lean into the poles that would raise the first bent to an upright position, while nearly two dozen others held it with ropes from falling over. As soon as the second bent was raised, Andrew would lead the scramble of agile young men up to jiggle and fit the crossbeams into place and drive in the locking pins. He had never been afraid of heights or of standing on surfaces more narrow than his boots. The men were already arranging themselves, awaiting Young Dave's call to begin raising the skeleton.

Clara decided to be useful by helping to set up a water station. It was already after eight o'clock, and in the middle of July, temperatures would soar by midmorning. A large dispenser was positioned on a table, no doubt well chilled in spring water. Clara pulled out one of several crates under the table and found glasses, which she began to set out in rows.

"Clara!"

The voice came from behind her. Clara pivoted to see Priscilla Schrock a few feet away.

"I was hoping you would be here." Priscilla bounced on her heels.

"And here I am," Clara said.

"I'm going to tell Naomi and Lillian you're here. We can have a story class."

"Priscilla, I don't think —"

The girl was already in motion, unhearing of Clara's gentle protest. As she looked round, Clara wondered if she appeared as furtive as she felt.

Young Dave strode past her, positioned himself in a central location among the supplies, and gave the first call.

Yonnie joined the crew framing doorways and windows. Uncomfortable with climbing the rising form of a barn, he was consistent in his choice of tasks that kept both feet on the ground with little risk that any sudden movement would endanger his balance. Now he wished he had paid more attention over the years to the details. If he had learned to frame a window rather than simply hand tools to the carpenter, he might have a skill to offer a new employer.

Mose Beachy turned a palm up, and Yonnie laid a tiny awl in it. At least he knew which tool was needed, even if he hadn't learned to use it himself. He watched carefully, though. The barn would have several doors and a bank of windows letting in daylight.

Bending his wide girth, Mose finished an adjustment and signaled that Yonnie should help him lift the window frame into the space left for it in the side of the barn. Outside the barn, older men marked with chalk where siding boards would cross a beam before handing the boards off to others who carried them, three at a time, and passed them to younger men stationed among the framing. The sound of swinging hammers striking nails would not abate for hours as siding boards went onto the frame in a rolling wave.

Younger boys, old enough to help but not yet trusted with tools or heights, moved around the barn and yard collecting waste wood to pile out of the way. One of them trailed Mose and Yonnie now. It was the Kuhn boy, Yonnie thought, though he never could remember the boy's name. Joshua. Jeremiah. Something like that.

Mose worked with few words. Suddenly he shouted over Yonnie's shoulder. "Watch out."

A thud launched a clatter, followed by a yelp.

"Put the window down." Mose swiftly lowered his end to the barn floor. Yonnie set his end down carefully and balanced the frame against an interior post, irritated that Mose had left him with the weight of the fragile window.

Mose knelt beside the boy, who had fallen and dropped the waste wood balanced in his arms.

"Josiah, are you all right?"

Josiah. That was the Kuhn boy's name. His eyes were closed, and he made no sound.

"Josiah?" Mose said again.

"My head hurts." Josiah raised a hand to one temple, his eyes still closed.

"It's all right. You can open your eyes." Mose pulled out a shirttail and gently wiped sawdust from the boy's face. "It's only a small cut."

"Is it bleeding?" Josiah's eyes popped wide open.

Yonnie rolled his gaze at the boy's fright. "You should have been more careful."

The boy's face crumpled.

Mose looked up through the unfinished slope of the rear portion of the barn. Yonnie followed his view and saw Andrew peering down.

"Anybody hurt?" Andrew said. "A board got away from somebody up here."

Mose looked at Josiah. The boy was startled and on the brink of tears.

"We're fine," Yonnie told Andrew.

"I think Josiah will want to go find his mother." Mose helped the boy to his feet.

"You should have been paying more attention," Yonnie said. "It's dangerous to have children in the way of the men while they're working."

"I'm helping," Josiah said.

"Look at the mess you've made." Yonnie pointed to the strewn waste wood.

"I'll pick it up again." Josiah's voice trembled.

Mose put a hand on the boy's shoulder. "The important thing is you're safe. But maybe you'd like some water or a pastry before you get back to work."

Josiah nodded.

When the boy had left the barn, Mose began picking up the spilled wood and stacking it against the wall. "You were harsh with the boy. It wasn't his fault one of the men above dropped a board."

"If fathers want to let their sons work," Yonnie said, "they should supervise more closely."

"I have fourteen children," Mose said. "Not a one of them would fail to look around and see what needs doing when the church community is together. They want to belong. Your parents taught you the same way. I can remember when you were a boy picking up waste wood."

"He has to be aware of what's happening around him." Yonnie mumbled now. "He could have been hurt."

"And if he had been, we would have taken care of him. That's what we do. Jesus teaches us to do unto others as we would have them do unto us."

The admonishment, though delivered with gentleness, stung.

Yonnie returned to the window frame. "Let's get back to work."

The men ate lunch in two shifts, selecting food from the women's offerings and find-ings seats at tables inside the Mast house or in the shade of trees in the yard. After the men were fed, the women and children would eat. Women shuttled around refilling water glasses and clearing plates to wash quickly for the next wave of diners. Finishing his meal with the second shift, Andrew watched Clara amble back toward the water table where she had spent most of the day so far. Stopping to greet others who spoke to him, Andrew followed Clara in a vague way. On a day like this, a working man could always use another glass of water.

On the verge of speaking, Andrew held his words when Hannah Kuhn whizzed past him and grinned at her big sister.

"I thought you were watching Mari," he heard Clara say.

"Nap time!" Hannah answered. "*Mamm* said I could go play."

"Then you should go find your friends."

"Priscilla said I should come here."

"She did?"

"Yes. She has a surprise for me!"

Priscilla, Naomi, and Lillian arrived in tangled unison.

"I told you she was here," Priscilla announced. She turned to Clara. "You don't have to stay here every minute, do you?"

Andrew's soft steps took him closer, still behind Clara. His curiosity piqued.

"No," Clara said. "I don't suppose so."

"Grown-ups can get their own water," Naomi said. "But they won't tell us a story like you will."

Andrew saw Clara's frame stiffen. Pride rose through his chest, though he did not allow it to form on his lips.

"A story?" Hannah said.

"That's the surprise," Priscilla said.

Clara's nervous glance swept the farm-yard. "I'm not sure that's a good idea right now."

"It is! It is!" Lillian said. "We've been waiting all day for Mari to go to sleep so Hannah could come, too."

Andrew recognized the shift in her posture as Clara embraced the notion. His mind's eye saw again lines jumping from her sheaf of papers. He glanced at the barn, where the side boarding continued on one end and the roofing began on the other. He judged there were enough young men willing to scale the heights and do the work, and he might not have another opportunity to hear Clara tell a story.

She could not know he was there, though, or she might get shy. And he did not want his presence to inhibit the enthusiasm he witnessed in the little girls. Andrew gave Clara and the girls a head start, the girls tugging at her hands and skirts as they walked down the tree-lined lane. He could easily keep them in sight, see where they settled, and lean against a tree out of sight but within earshot.

Andrew wished he could watch her face as she arranged a circle with four little girls to tell the story of one little boy who offered his lunch — everything he had — to Jesus.

CHAPTER 20

Fannie drowsed on her bed with the door ajar. If the rhythm of Sadie's play in the other room rumbled or heightened, Fannie would hear it and judge the need for intervention. On Tuesday afternoon her efforts to stay awake and interested in her daughter's chatter had succumbed to the weight stifling her spirit as much as to the heat and humidity that tortured her relentlessly more than any summer she could remember. It was past time to start supper. Elam would come in from his work in the far field both deserving and expecting a nourishing meal, and Sadie should eat. Behind her closed eyes, Fannie thought how unfair it seemed that the person least interested in meals should be responsible for the nourishment of the small household. She mentally inventoried the cupboards and icebox, trying to come up with a meal that would not leave Elam wondering what she had done all afternoon.

"Mamm," Sadie called.

Fannie meant to answer, but after a few seconds realized she lacked the energy to speak aloud.

"Mamm!" Sadie's tone grew insistent.

Fannie forced open her eyes to see Sadie standing in the doorway — with Clara beside her.

Clara stepped into the room. "Are you all right?"

What did *all right* mean? Fannie was not certain she would ever be all right again.

"Fannie," Clara said.

Fannie heaved herself upright. "Clara, what are you doing here?" Clara usually came in the morning. It wasn't morning, was it? Fannie glanced out the window and saw that the light had shifted toward its evening arc. Panic subsided.

"Are you all right?" Clara repeated, approaching the bed.

Fannie waved her off. "I only meant to rest a few minutes. The heat." Her eyes focused on the patches of perspiration dampening Clara's clothes. Had she walked five miles while Fannie did not even sit up in bed? Fannie regretted blaming the heat.

"Sadie," Clara said, "I think your *mamm* could use a glass of cold water. Can you fetch it?"

Sadie scampered out of the room. Fannie let her bare feet touch the floor, wishing to find it cool as in winter but encountering a layer of humidity even there.

"It's not just the heat, is it?" Clara picked up a cloth from the washstand and dipped it in water to put against Fannie's face.

Fannie knew it would be tepid, not refreshing, but she let Clara wipe the cloth across her face. "No," she said. "I'm trying, but the week has been difficult. My mother is getting big so fast that you'd think she's expecting triplets."

"I felt the heaviness of your spirit all the way in Somerset County." Clara sat on the bed beside Fannie.

"Did you walk? It's so hot."

"I'm all right."

"Sadie should get you a glass of water, too."

"I'll get one in a few minutes. I'm worried about you."

Fannie plumped the pillow her head had just vacated. "I should be grateful. I have a husband, a child, a home, a farm. There is so much to do, but all I want is to lie on my bed."

Clara put an arm around Fannie's shoulder, and Fannie laid her head against her,

her own chest exploding with ache.

"Let's go sit under your oak tree," Clara said. "It will have good shade at this time of day. Then I'll make supper."

"I can make supper," Fannie said.

"I know. But I'd like to."

"Doesn't Rhoda need you?" Even in Fannie's foggy state, she did not miss Clara's hesitation.

Sadie arrived with a glass brimming with water. "I didn't spill a single drop!"

Fannie smiled and sipped. "Sadie, Clara's been walking a long way."

The girl brightened. "I should get her some water, too!"

Fannie turned to Clara again. "It's not too late to catch the milk wagon back to Somerset to help Rhoda."

Clara shrugged. "There's no hurry."

Fannie fished around her mind for what Clara wasn't telling her but could not frame the thought. She tried to recall the last time Clara said anything to her about Rhoda or any of the Kuhn children. Something was wrong. Fannie ought to care, ought to probe. She took a long gulp of water, unconvinced it would help but determined to try.

The back screen door creaked open and slammed closed. Elam's heavy footsteps crossed the kitchen linoleum. He said something to Sadie that Fannie couldn't make out, and the girl's voice lilted in laughter.

"Good," Clara said. "You can sit with Elam in the shade while I prepare the meal. You'll have some extra time together with Sadie."

Time with Elam would not heal what pierced Fannie, but at least the diversion might prevent Sadie from innocently telling her father where her mother had spent the afternoon.

Dale Borntrager would never say he was punishing Yonnie with an unscheduled delivery into Garrett County to one of the Marylander households. If Yonnie had challenged him, Dale would have said it was a last-minute order and he only got the message long after the regular afternoon run was finished. Other employees at the dairy made offhand remarks that suggested this was true. Four generations of two families that had married into each other several times were gathering to celebrate the birthday of a great-grandmother and the birth of the latest great-grandson. They wanted abundant provisions for their evening festivities. Extra milk to churn into ice cream, extra butter for favorite dishes, extra cheese, extra cream. Extra everything.

So Yonnie had put the order together and turned the wagon around. Was it not enough that he swallowed his indignity in serving the Marylander families at all? No matter how many people believed that *meidung* did not apply to business dealings, Yonnie was certain the bishop intended that his congregation should have nothing to do with the Marylanders. Yet here he was, submitting to his employer rather than to his bishop.

He was in no hurry to get back to the dairy. The other employees would have gone home to their families long ago. If sending Yonnie with the extra delivery was not outright punishment for his convictions, Dale's explanation likely would have been that Yonnie had no wife and children waiting for him to come home. His parents, sister, and brothers would eat supper without him, though his parents would scowl at the notion that Dale should keep anyone from the evening meal and family devotions. And they had a point. Dale could have sent word that it was too late in the day to fill an order in Garrett County. The Marylanders would have scooped out smaller portions of ice cream and consumed their coffee black. There was no need to intrude on anyone else's family evening. But it was a large order, and Dale had made the sort of business decision an *English* would have made. The thought stirred further indignation in Yonnie.

Now the sky had grayed, descending deeper each moment toward the release of this day's troubles. Burning Amish lamps would soon be put out as families set the last of the clean supper dishes in the cupboard, closed their German Bibles, finished reading the news from *The Sugarcreek Budget,* and inspected their children's fingernails to see if the dirt had been scrubbed out. Daylight came early at this time of year; with most of their work outdoors, few Amish farmers stayed up more than an hour after darkness fell.

Yonnie let the horse set its own pace. His own gelding was grazing in Dale's pasture beside the dairy. At this hour, what did it matter if he returned Dale's horse and retrieved his own thirty minutes sooner or thirty minutes later?

In the beam of the lantern hanging from the front of the buggy, Yonnie saw a slender, dark-clad figure walking along the other side of the road. He peered more closely and saw it was an Amish woman.

What was an Amish woman doing out on

this road by herself at this hour?

Clara Kuhn.

Yonnie pulled on the reins to slow the horse even further. Clara should not be out. If she had the audacity to visit her Marylander relatives in defiance of Bishop Yoder's sermons, she ought to have the good sense to get herself home for supper. If he stayed behind her for a few more minutes, she would walk past the next turnoff, and he could divert his route and leave her to the consequences of her own foolishness.

She paused then and turned around, lifting one hand to flag his attention.

Clara could not have imagined she would feel such relief at the sight of Yonnie Yoder, of all people. Whatever his reason for still being out in the milk wagon did not matter. Clara was not so proud that she would fail to recognize God's provision when it trotted toward her.

She did, however, think that it could trot more briskly. Yonnie was holding the horse back on purpose. Finally he pulled alongside her.

"I thank God you're here," she said. "I need a ride. Would you be able to take me all the way home?"

A flood of questions flushed through his

face. No one ever had to wonder what Yonnie was thinking. Humiliation suffused her gratitude.

"Yes, I was at my cousin's," Clara said. "I felt God leading me to visit her today."

She had said the same thing to Fannie, and it was true. Still, she hoped a spiritual response would have some influence on Yonnie's sense of compassion.

"Why didn't you ride the wagon home hours ago?" he said.

"That turned out not to be possible." Clara awaited Yonnie's permission to board the wagon.

"You do it all the time," he said, disapproval ringing in his tone.

"Today's circumstances were unusual."

"Your cousin has a husband. Why would he send you into the night alone?"

"Conditions were complicated." Clara was not going to tell Yonnie Fannie's private business. He didn't even know Fannie, other than picking up milk from the Esh farm. "My father expected me back hours ago, I'm sure."

"Then you should have gone home hours ago."

"Yonnie, please. It's dark, and it's still very warm to be walking so far."

He stared at Clara in silence, as if to say

253

she had not begged with enough sincerity. Fury roiled, tempting her to withdraw her request and march on. When she left Elam and Fannie, she was prepared to walk the full distance, refusing Elam's offer of a ride out of conviction that Fannie should not be on her own tonight. She would have stayed the night, but she was due at the banker's home right after breakfast. Clara met Yonnie's unsympathetic expression with an unspoken threat to mention his refusal to the bishop. Yonnie would not want to risk the bishop's judgment of his lack of Christian compassion. But Clara could not count on the bishop not to defend Yonnie's choice to separate himself from church members who had been cavorting with the Marylanders.

"Yonnie, it's late," she said, trying to keep desperation out of her voice. "I ask only for a simple act of charity." *Don't make me beg.*

"I, too, am very late getting home." His response was unyielding.

"Then you understand that circumstances arise that we cannot control." If an appeal to compassion meant nothing to Yonnie, perhaps simple logic would.

Yonnie tilted his chin up and examined her beneath lowered eyelids.

Clara swept back the strand of hair that

had escaped the pins in her coiled braids and adjusted her *kapp.*

"Yonnie, please," she said, humiliation burning through her.

He lifted the reins, and the horse took a few steps forward.

"Yonnie!"

He paused again before finally nodding his head toward the empty space beside him on the bench.

Anger poured another layer of perspiration through her clothing while Clara sat as far away from Yonnie as she could.

Chapter 21

Andrew raced his wagon to the dairy just before lunch the next day. Dale sat at a desk in the office with an account book open.

"I need to see Yonnie," Andrew said.

"He's working." Dale didn't glance up. "I'll tell him you were looking for him. He'll find you later."

"Thank you, but I'll find him now." Andrew pivoted on one heel and charged into the main bottling room. The rhythmic thud of his work boots made every head lift and turn toward the sound.

Yonnie capped off a pint of cream and stiffened.

Good, Andrew thought. *He should be nervous.*

Aloud, he said, "How dare you?"

Hands stilled around them.

Yonnie picked up an empty bottle, moved it six inches, and set it down again. "Maybe we should go outside — when I get a break."

"I can speak my mind here." Andrew planted his feet.

Behind Andrew, Dale spoke. "Your break just started, Yonnie. Whatever this is about, take it out of my dairy."

Yonnie led the way through the back door. Aggravated by Yonnie's sluggish pace, Andrew nearly stepped on his heels. They moved ten yards away from the building. Three sets of curious eyes peering out a window did not deter Andrew.

"You humiliated Clara."

"How is it she has spoken to you privately already?"

"Don't," Andrew said. "Don't think you can escape this by accusing Clara or me of wrongdoing."

Yonnie ground one boot heel into the dirt. "You said it yourself. Each of us has to follow our own conscience. My conscience says to obey the bishop."

"And leave a member of your own church stranded on the side of the road?"

"Clara was hardly stranded. She walks that road often."

"Not alone in the dark."

"She would have gotten home eventually. I was following Bishop Yoder's instructions to separate ourselves from those who have joined the Marylanders."

"Clara has not joined the Marylanders."

"But she was visiting them. She didn't deny that she had been to see her cousin."

"Did you think she would somehow contaminate you?" Andrew exhaled laden fury. "Is that what you would have said to the man on the Jericho road? You are like the religious leaders who walked past the man who had been beaten nearly to death because they didn't want to become unclean."

"It's not the same at all."

"Isn't it?" Andrew said. "Or maybe you were ready to punish Clara in your own way."

"If I can show her the way of obedience more clearly —"

Andrew cut him off. "Shall I remind you it was a Samaritan who showed compassion, not a stuffy, self-righteous man of religion?"

Yonnie stared. "You bear false testimony toward me. It is daring of you to use the words of Jesus to do so."

"I've been fond of you for more than twenty years." Andrew shook a finger. "I've defended you. I've understood you. Now you go too far."

"If Clara were your wife," Yonnie said, "I might understand this show of defense. But she is not your wife. You don't owe her this, at the peril of your own soul."

"I've heard every sermon you've ever heard," Andrew said. "Don't preach at me. And don't come around my farm."

Andrew turned and strode along the side of the dairy to find his wagon.

Yonnie shifted his weight from one foot to the other and back again, hoping the movement would disguise the tremble that overtook him.

Before he slept the night before, he prayed for God's forgiveness for his weakness. Perhaps God could commend his mercy in driving Clara all the way to the Kuhn farm instead of returning directly to the dairy. Perhaps God would strengthen him to be righteous in the days ahead while church people, like Dale and Andrew and Clara, would choose their own path instead of God's.

The rear door of the dairy opened, and Dale stepped out. Yonnie moved his feet forward, determined not to falter or appear reluctant. He stopped in front of Dale.

"This isn't the place for your personal business," Dale said. "After all the mistakes you've made lately, I would have thought you would know better than to allow this to happen."

"I didn't ask Andrew to come here." Under the shame Yonnie felt at yet another scolding from Dale, defensiveness surged.

"Straighten up," Dale said. "I can't give you endless warnings if I don't see that you are at least attempting to improve your performance."

Yonnie swallowed. "I understand."

"Now get back inside. We still have dozens of bottles to fill. This display has distracted everyone."

Yonnie followed Dale back inside and returned to his tasks without meeting any gazes around him. If anyone spoke to him, he would pray for strength to resist the taunting.

When he drove the dairy wagon, he did not owe Clara or anyone else a ride. He was being paid to pick up milk and make deliveries, not to run a taxi service. Even Dale did not benefit by as much as a penny from the presumptuous way travelers on both sides of the border waited for rides. Yonnie could say no, especially if his own holiness was endangered.

He owed his allegiance to Bishop Yoder and to the decision the congregation made in 1895. Yonnie had once seen the written record of the meeting with his own eyes. The vote had been unanimous. In ignoring their own decision for the last twenty years, the congregation had only brought harm to themselves. They could have had a clean, fresh start with the *meidung.* In separation, their witness would have drawn their relatives and friends back to the true fold of God. Now twenty years of disregarding God's law, in spite of the consistent voice of Bishop Yoder and his sons, made people unwilling — or unable — to recognize their own sin.

Yonnie moved faster, knowing Dale's eyes were on him, to make up for the time he lost with Andrew's distraction. He would be a faithful worker who served God, even if his employer was spiritually lax.

"Please, *Mamm,* please?" Sadie's entire body seemed to beg with expectancy. "It's a good day to go see *Grossmuder,* isn't it? We can make some pound cake and open a jar of blueberries. *Grossmuder* would like that. I know she would."

"*Grossmuder* is busy." Fannie dried the last of the lunch dishes and added it to the stack on the kitchen counter.

"She's never too busy for *me.* I'm her only granddaughter."

"You must learn not to take advantage of her." Fannie swiped a damp rag across the

261

table, pausing at the place where Sadie usually sat to scrub at a spot of spilled milk.

"Because I'm getting big?" Sadie said. "Or because she's going to have another *boppli*?"

"Both. Besides, we have a lot to do around here."

"*Grossmuder* says the new babe will be my *aunti* or *onkel*. That doesn't make sense. How can a baby be an *aunti* or *onkel*?"

"I'll explain it when you're a little older. I want you to clean your room today, please."

"Are you going to help me?"

"You're old enough to do it yourself."

"After that can we go see *Grossmuder*?"

"By then I'll need to start supper."

Sadie's shoulders slumped. "Maybe tomorrow?"

"I have to beat the rugs tomorrow." Fannie handed Sadie a dust rag and a broom whose handle was twice as tall as the girl. "Do a good job, please."

Sadie shuffled out of the room. Fannie ached to feel the soft comfort of her bed under her weary back. Maybe she would pull a quilt over her head if she could stand the heat. She wouldn't sleep, just rest where she could easily hear Sadie.

No.

She would not go lie down. Two nights in

a row Elam had asked if she felt well. There was always a chance he would come back to the house in the middle of the afternoon, and why shouldn't he? Fannie used to hope that he would.

Now, though, she did not want him to.

She did not want to speak to Elam or anyone — especially not her mother.

Resisting the urge to find her bed, Fannie instead went into the front room and sat on the davenport. She would not stretch out. She would only put her head back and pull the first quilt she ever made off the end of the davenport and into her lap.

Her guilty spirit weighed heavy. Guilt for sending her five-year-old off so she could be alone. Guilt for hoping her husband would not come in from the fields early. Guilt for not rejoicing in the new life her mother carried. Guilt for holding Sadie back from delighting her *grossmuder* with her presence. Guilt for not wanting to cook supper. Guilt for wishing she could be blessedly asleep.

At least, Fannie knew she *ought* to feel guilty about those things. The truth, though, was that she had left guilt behind days ago. Her limbs were too heavy to lift, and her lungs too weary to inflate, but no longer from guilt. Leaning back on the davenport, she closed her eyes.

Unburdening herself to Andrew on Wednesday morning had allowed Clara to breathe evenly again. For that she had no regrets. When she heard on Thursday that he had confronted Yonnie, though, doubt skulked into her peace of mind. Stirring dissension between the two of them was not her intent. By Friday, Clara wondered if the dissent had only risen to the surface as it was meant to do, as it was inevitably going to do. And by Saturday, she dreaded seeing Yonnie again at church the next day. She knew the row where he preferred to sit and could make sure to sit well behind him on the women's side of the aisle.

Clara now sat in the Schrocks' living room with a length of black fabric in her lap. She could practically make a new apron with her eyes watching evening fireflies instead of her stitches under a lamp, but cutting one out in the company of other women would pass the morning pleasantly. Their chatter would be about recipes and children and laying hens and the new threads at the mercantile. Clara would not have to think about Yonnie or the *meidung.*

Worry for Fannie scoffed her optimism, though. Never had she seen her cousin this way. The *English* would have a word for the condition, Clara supposed. Melancholy? Was that it? It was not a raging illness, but a gentle sadness that threatened to clot and scar Fannie's future.

The next time Clara visited, she would make sure to arrange with her father to take a horse and cart — or at least a horse. She could not rely on Yonnie, and perhaps not on any of the milk wagon drivers.

A small presence blew breath across Clara's cheek, and she turned slightly toward it. Priscilla Schrock leaned in and whispered in Clara's ear.

"Another story, please."

The request was not unexpected, but Clara found it daring. It was one thing to wander away during a busy barn raising. It was another for the child to make this request in her own home, under her mother's watchfulness. Clara glanced down the hall and saw three more sets of eyes leaning around a corner in anticipation. Lillian's and Naomi's mothers were present, and of course Rhoda had brought Hannah to the sewing frolic.

Clara knew just the story she would tell. The wise Abigail knew how to help the great King David to control his temper and do the right thing. The girls could learn that a true friend helped others understand how to please God, even someone who was great and powerful.

It was only a matter of time, Clara realized. Four girls knew she told Bible stories, and one of them was her own sister and shared her home. One of them would innocently drop a reference to a story into conversation with a parent over farm chores or evening prayers. Clara almost wished that Hannah was not among the girls who would be tangled in confusion when the mothers began to speak to each other. But why would she hold back God's Word from her own sister?

She wouldn't.

Priscilla had scampered away after seeing Clara's slight nod. Now Clara excused herself, slipped out the back door of the Schrock house, and quickly rounded the corner of the barn.

There they were, seated in the grass and waiting.

CHAPTER 22

Clara jammed a fist against her mouth, stopping the scream rising through her sleep but helpless to thwart the wail flashing through time.

This version of the dream had faces.

Fannie's. Sadie's. Martha's. Atlee's. Hiram's.

Drawn. Pale. Stunned. Tormented. Lost.

A baby's cry faded. Martha collapsed.

Clara gasped and sat up. The morning breeze through the window, still cool in advance of the sun, blew across her suddenly sweat-drenched nightgown. Chilled, she scrambled out of bed, stepped to the washing bowl, and splashed tepid liquid on her face repeatedly until her breathing slowed.

Martha's baby. How would any of them recover if this dream proved true?

Clara sat on the bed. The vague sadness that startled her every few months now growled full terror.

From down the hall, Mari's cry sounded. Rhoda's footsteps responded.

Clara released pent-up breath. Perhaps her little sister crying in her sleep was all that triggered the dream. She should have been used to the sound. It was not unusual for Mari to cry out for her *mamm* without waking and remember nothing in the morning.

Little-girl dreams easily soothed with a mother's touch.

Clara had no *mamm* to call for when she was little. Would dreams of sadness have followed her for years if her mother had been there to stroke her forehead and hum a soothing tune? She would never know.

An early walk, before the bustle of breakfast and readying for church, would release her burning muscles and relieve her of the image of Martha's empty arms. Clara pulled on a dress and shoes. When she returned an hour later, the household had wakened. Hiram and Josiah were milking the cows, and Rhoda was braiding the girls' hair.

A normal morning. Everyone was safe.

After breakfast, Clara went to her room to freshen up. She tucked the last pin in her hair and checked her reflection in the dull glass that hung beside her bedroom door to be sure she had taken captive every rebellious strand. On this first church Sunday in August, filled with worship and socializing, she would have little opportunity for repairs.

She did not hear the footsteps coming down the hall. Bare feet in summer slapped the wooden planks more kindly than winter shoes. Instead, the swish of skirts, which the seasons did not alter, alerted Clara. It was not enough fullness of yardage to be Rhoda. She supposed Hannah, and in a moment her guess was confirmed.

"*Mamm* wants to know if you're ready," Hannah said, standing in the doorway.

"Nearly." Clara looked around for what she had done with her prayer *kapp*.

"Are you going to tell us a story today?" As it always did when she was excited, Hannah's voice rose in pitch and volume.

Clara sucked in her breath, grabbed Hannah to pull her into the room, and closed the door.

"No," Clara said softly, "we won't have a story today. It's a worship service. We'll hear sermons."

"Sermons make me sleepy," Hannah said. "I don't understand them."

"You will soon."

"We could have a story after the service."

"I don't think so."

269

"But it's been weeks and weeks." Hannah's pout accelerated.

"It only seems that way," Clara said. It had been just over two weeks, but to a six-year-old that must have felt like half the summer.

"But Priscilla will be there, and Lillian and Naomi. And lots of other girls."

Clara had worried the girls would speak to their parents about the Bible stories, but they had only to speak to their friends. Priscilla, after all, had initiated Lillian and Naomi by retelling a story. Another innocent child would ask her mother if she could hear the stories, too. Before she knew it, Clara would be standing in front of Bishop Yoder with his demand that she explain herself pounding in her ears.

"We might not be able to have any more stories," she said. "At least not for a while."

"But we like them." Hannah pushed out her lower lip another half inch.

"I know." Clara straightened her sister's *kapp* and knotted the strings beneath her chin.

"I won't tell anyone if you don't want me to." Hannah's eyelashes blinked over her blue eyes in wide simplicity.

Clara ran her tongue behind her top lip. Hannah was no secret keeper. She wasn't a tattletale motivated by self-righteousness or maliciousness, but when she got excited, words gushed out when she didn't mean them to. It was a wonder Hannah hadn't already told her mother about the stories. Arranging her own *kapp*, Clara puzzled over why Hannah hadn't said anything yet. She would never tell the girls to withhold truth from their parents. A secret was too close to a lie. To a child, condoning one would be to condone the other. A six-year-old should not be responsible for discerning the difference, nor burdened with conflicting loyalties should a choice come down to the secret or a lie.

Clara blew out a soft breath. She knelt and put her hands on Hannah's elbows, trying to form a response that would neither ask the child to keep a secret nor send her running to divulge one.

The footsteps in the hall now were firm, quick, and evident of shoes.

"Where is everybody?" Rhoda's voice rang out. "It's time to go."

"Never mind," Clara said to Hannah. She pushed up out of the crouch, opened the door, and took her sister's hand to lead her down the stairs.

In the family buggy, Rhoda sat in the front bench beside her husband with Mari on her lap. In the second bench, Clara sat between Josiah and Hannah. All three of them folded their hands in their laps as they had been taught to do as a reminder to keep themselves still and not cause danger in the buggy. Clara could still remember Hiram setting her on the bench beside him and folding her little hands when it was just the two of them, with a stern warning that she must obey or she would fall out of the buggy. By the time she was old enough to be trusted not to move suddenly, the habit was long instilled.

Clara regarded the posture as fitting for preparing for worship. It quieted the body for the long service and encouraged a calming of the spirit as well. She wanted a clean heart for worship.

Her posture came from outward effort, however, while her heart rebelled against every notion she'd ever learned of being ready for church.

She did not feel guilty about telling Bible stories to little girls, but neither did she want to confuse them about right or wrong.

She did not feel guilty for knowing about Andrew's car, nor for her lack of judgment over his ownership of it.

She did not feel guilty for her intention to see her relatives in Maryland no matter what the bishop said.

No matter how tightly she wound and pinned braids against the sides of her head or how perfectly her *kapp* sat on her hair, Clara knew what was in her own heart.

At the Summit Mills Meetinghouse, Clara lingered outside while Rhoda ushered the girls inside and her father and brother took their places in the men's processional. At the last minute, before the men began to march in, she slipped into the bench at the back of the women's section where she could watch Andrew in the mass of black suits and hats. His defense of her to Yonnie had poured cleansing love over her spirit, washing away the humiliation of a dark night. But at what price? While Clara had never felt personal warmth toward Yonnie, Andrew did. Now because of her a chasm ran through their friendship — if it could still be called a friendship.

And the chasm was one more truth that did not spawn guilt.

Was it possible to feel guilty about not feeling guilty?

Andrew's urge was to cross his arms against his chest in doubt that Joseph Yoder's sermon would speak to Andrew's heart. His brother Noah certainly hadn't in the first sermon, although his point had been clear. How would the transgressors who strayed from the church turn to repentance without shunning?

Joseph now announced that his theme would look at two Josephs in the Bible. Andrew's skepticism notched up.

"Where did the brothers of Joseph need to go to become reconciled with him after they behaved so unmercifully toward him? They needed to take the distant trip to Egypt. One might say they went to Egypt only to get grain during the famine, but I believe they were sent of God, since this Joseph is an example of the heavenly Joseph, Jesus Christ. In Egypt they bowed before Joseph and acknowledged their trespasses against him. All hardened transgressors must come to Jesus in the same spirit. Joseph's brothers came in a spirit of undoneness and brokenness. So long as a transgressor has not come to that place, the status of a child of God is not applicable."

Andrew did cross his arms now.

"And let us move to the greatest Joseph of the New Testament. Mary and Joseph left the child Jesus, naturally speaking, and could not find him until they returned to where they left him," Joseph Yoder continued. "This is a lesson for us. If anyone loses a child, spiritually speaking, he should search again at the place where he lost it. Those who have been placed into the ban should be shunned, even if they join another church, so that they may indeed repent, regret, and sorrow with humble hearts and with a demonstration of a sincere lifestyle become reconciled with the church from which they left. The ban can only be lifted if the wanderer renews his commitment with God and the church on bended knees and by seeking the peace where he lost it."

Joseph Yoder's eyes panned the congregation in dramatic silence. "By holding fast to the ban, you will be an instrument of God's will, drawing the transgressor back to true peace. If we do not do so, the transgressor may draw away the entire church. Would such a disturbance of the peace please God? I do not believe so. I call upon each of you to bring to the attention of your ministers and bishop any knowledge you have of individuals who have lost their peace and threaten the peace of the church with their transgressions. Though the ban may seem difficult, we bear the cross Christ calls us to that we may pray for the transgressor's return to peace before we all share in the disturbance of our mutual peace."

Joseph paused again, letting his words sink in.

If there were a third sermon, Andrew wondered, and Mose Beachy were to stand with his Bible open, what would he say? The peace was already disturbed. Bishop Yoder disturbed it himself when he insisted on a strong *meidung* against people whose only transgression was to form a slightly different kind of Amish congregation a generation ago — two generations ago. It was sermons like these that could leave a young woman humiliated on the side of the road. Andrew saw no peace in that.

Andrew glanced at John Stutzman and then at Caleb Schrock. They held their posture better than Andrew did, but he knew their straight spines did not express their thoughts. He would seek them out even before helping to turn benches into tables for the shared meal.

Yonnie nodded his head. He was right. Dale and Clara and Andrew — and so many others — had turned their hearts from obedience to Christ. Hadn't the minister just said so?

Yonnie shifted his head slightly to glance at Dale, whose expression gave away nothing. Perhaps he had closed his heart to the truth so long ago that he would not hear the Holy Ghost knocking even through two sermons that spoke plain truth. Both sermons made clear the responsibility that had stirred Yonnie's heart for weeks, ever since the day he helped Andrew tow the Model T to the abandoned barn. He had been weak, too much under the daring influence of his childhood friend. When he later pulled the car out of the ditch, he was no better. But at last he grasped hold of the fortitude God offered when he rightly interpreted that Dale should avoid contact with the Marylander families out of loyalty to Christ. Clara was a woman. Since she had no husband, she would need the guidance of her father to find strength to shun her cousin, but Hiram Kuhn had been lax for so long that Yonnie almost counted him among those who needed to seek peace where they had lost it.

Clara was not Yonnie's responsibility, but Dale and Andrew were fellow men. Any of them could be called upon to be a minister in the future. Dale was already married, and Yonnie and Andrew would be eligible themselves once they wed. The day might come when someone would nominate one of them to be a minister and they would face the lot — a slip of paper tucked in a hymnal that would indicate God's choice.

In a flush of vindication, Yonnie resolved to seek out the bishop immediately after the close of worship to make an appointment to speak privately.

CHAPTER 23

Sarah Tice had proved right on that June day when Clara ran into her friend in Springs. The Widower Hershberger did go to Ohio to marry. A younger couple would have waited for the fall harvest season to pass, but Mr. Hershberger rode the train, married, and returned all within the space of four days. Clara's housekeeping work diminished. At least the *English* banker's family still depended on her services.

Clara spent most of her days in the far corners of the farm. Crouching among the rising corn to clear weeds always was an option, and her innate industriousness was not so far spent that she turned her nose up at the chore. At first she avoided the places where her father worked with Josiah under his wing. Gradually she began to work beside them, briefly at first, as if she had some more important responsibility at the house, and then for increasingly longer stretches. Hiram never asked why she was not occupied with more feminine labor.

Between sermons that grew more stern each time the congregation gathered and her determination not to rely on the milk wagon for transportation as long as Yonnie was driving the route, Clara hesitated to leave Kuhn property. Three days had passed since Noah and Joseph Yoder rained the latest scoldings on the congregation. She hadn't seen Fannie in three weeks — not since Yonnie would have gloated to leave her on the side of the road — and while Andrew was always glad to see her, Clara did not want to aggravate whatever trouble might be brewing for him because of the Model T. The expression on Andrew's face when he drove the automobile was adorable, and Clara loved the sensation of the car in motion, but if anyone saw her with Andrew and the car, she couldn't be sure of the consequence. Automobiles were *English* machines. Driving one had not yet faced the practical test of defiance that visiting relatives in Maryland had withstood, and certainly not a congregational vote. Clara was fairly certain who agreed or disagreed with the Yoders on the shunning. She was far less sure how members of the congregation would divide on the question of an automobile.

In the end, Andrew would be all right. It was Fannie who worried Clara with her melancholy. She had not been the same since discovering Martha was expecting a child, and Clara suspected Elam did not realize how deep his wife's emotions had plummeted.

At midafternoon on Wednesday, Clara wandered back to the house, too warm and too thirsty. She was barely in the back door when Hannah barreled at her from across the kitchen.

"You got a letter!" Hannah waved the envelope.

Rhoda rapped her knuckles on the kitchen table. "Hannah, that doesn't belong to you."

"Clara doesn't mind." Hannah looked at Clara. "Right?"

Clara glanced at Rhoda. She would not take sides between mother and daughter.

"Why don't I have a look?" Clara took the envelope from Hannah.

"It's from Sadie, isn't it?" Hannah wiggled in anticipation of the answer.

"Don't be silly." Rhoda sealed the lid on a jar of fat. "Sadie is younger than you are. She doesn't know how to write a letter."

Clara wished she could scoop Hannah into her arms the way she could have done

281

a few months ago.

"It's from her mother," she said. "But you and Sadie will both be big enough to write letters before you know it."

"When I am, I will write to Sadie," Hannah said.

Clara resisted the urge to glance at Rhoda again. "One thing at a time."

"Hannah," Rhoda said, "let's go outside and get the laundry from the line."

Hannah constrained the pout that flashed through her lips and followed her mother. Rhoda paused at the back door, turning toward Clara.

"This is your turn to clean the Flag Run Meetinghouse, is it not?"

Clara nodded. "I'm going soon."

"You can take the cart if you like."

"Thank you."

"I want to help clean the meetinghouse," Hannah said.

"You're going to help me with the laundry." Rhoda's tone left no room for negotiation.

Clara took her letter upstairs to her room, opening it only when she was certain she wouldn't be interrupted.

Dear Clara,

Do you remember how we used to

282

write letters over the winter when our parents did not want to take the buggies through the snow? At least I understood that excuse. The news we hear from your congregation is almost unbearable. And you do not fool me. I know you are not happy at home.

I must apologize for being such an inadequate hostess when you last visited. Whatever weighs in my heart, I should have welcomed you more ably. Sadie asks every day when you will come again, and I don't know what to tell her.

Why don't you come to stay for as long as you like? Come to the Maryland district. You would be much at home here. You can stay with Elam and me. Sadie would be thrilled — I don't have to tell you that.

I know you are fond of many people in your own congregation, but the thought that they would even consider keeping you from us casts a new light on the question of your visits.

You must come. You must.

Love,
Fannie

Clara had no doubt of Sadie's abounding glee if she were to go to sleep with Clara in the house and wake to discover she was still there. And Clara's presence might cheer Fannie — or at least keep the household running until Fannie could cheer herself. Clara prayed every night for the news that her cousin was with child.

But Sadie was Sadie. She wasn't Hannah or Mari or Josiah. Or Hiram. Or even Rhoda as she had been until recently. If Clara went to Maryland for an indefinite stay — especially if she visited the church there — her own family would be required to shun her. The silent division running through the household would widen into permanence.

Clara couldn't bear the thought.

Neither could she imagine not seeing Fannie and Sadie and Martha and all the Hostetlers.

She pushed her fingertips into her closed eyelids. How was it that the Yoders saw a clear straight line between right and wrong, and Clara saw only the wiggle of uncertainty?

Clara tucked the letter back into its envelope and slid it under the winter nightgown lying in a drawer. The meetinghouse was waiting to be tidied and swept. Bishop Yoder had already announced that the next service of the congregation would be at Flag

Run. Clara loaded a bucket with rags, filled two large jugs with well water, chose a broom, and arranged everything in the small open cart before hitching a horse.

When Clara drove past the adjoining Schrock farm, she waved at Mattie Schrock, who strolled along the road with a small basket of apples braced against one hip.

Clara slowed the horse. "Good afternoon. I hope everything is well with the Schrock household."

"We are well." Hesitation wafted through Mattie's face. "May I have a word with you?"

"Of course."

"Our breakfast conversation this morning was unusual." Mattie steadied herself against the side of the cart.

"Oh?" Clara's mouth dried out in an instant.

"Priscilla asked when she was going to get to hear another Bible story from you."

Clara tightened her grip on the reins. So it had begun.

"Of course her *daed* and I did not know what she was talking about. Imagine our surprise when she explained."

Clara steeled herself to withstand Mattie's gaze. "The stories are in the Bible. I'm sure she has heard them before and will again."

"Yes, I suppose that's true. You know that we are not overly strict in our interpretation of the church's teachings about these matters."

While the words might have carried encouragement if they appeared on paper, the tone with which Mattie delivered them made Clara's breathing grow shallow.

"It is not so much that we disapprove of children hearing Bible stories," Mattie said. "Rather, it is that such instruction is the role of parents — or at least should have the approval of parents."

"I meant no disrespect. I am sure you teach your children well."

"Others might protest more than Priscilla's father and I do." Mattie shifted the fruit basket to the other hip. "I'm sure your own father would be happy to see you married and settled with children. Then you could use your gift under submission to your husband, as the Bible teaches."

Clara swallowed, coughing to cover the gag in her throat. "Thank you for telling me how you feel. You will have no reason for further concern."

"I was sure you would understand."

Clara raised the reins, and the horse trotted forward. She blinked back stinging, indignant tears for the next four miles before letting herself into the meetinghouse. With the door propped open to capture whatever breeze might stir the sweltering afternoon, Clara swept the floor before launching into a furious scrub of the windowsills and benches. The water in the bucket grayed rapidly. It was impossible to keep summer dust out of the structure. Clara hefted the bucket outside to dump it in the clearing. Above the splash of water, horse hooves clattered. She looked up to see Yonnie drive past in his own open buggy, not the milk wagon. He slowed slightly, his eyes meeting hers, before his rig disappeared behind a grove of trees. Clara rotated, expecting to see him come out the opposite edge of the cluster. When he didn't emerge, she stilled her hands and breath to listen, certain Yonnie had seen her. If he were passing on the road, he should have appeared by now. Clara glanced at the open meetinghouse door and at her own cart, pondering where her steps should take her.

The rattle in the bushes sent her scurrying toward her horse. She ran straight into the clasp of a man's hands.

"What's going on?" Andrew gripped Clara's trembling shoulders, preventing her from turning away from him.

"Nothing," she said.

Something had spooked her. "Did I frighten you?"

She turned her head and looked through the trees. "I wasn't expecting you."

"I know. But we haven't spoken in a long time. I remembered you would be cleaning today and hoped I could catch you."

She stepped away from him. "I'm glad you're here."

"What happened, Clara?" Andrew followed her line of sight to the road.

She exhaled. "Yonnie just went by. I saw him approaching, but he never came out on the other side of the trees."

Andrew paced toward the road, peering through the dense foliage. "Maybe you just couldn't see him."

"The noise stopped," Clara said. "I should have heard him coming past."

He looked at her white face. "He won't hurt you."

She said nothing, not convinced.

Realization struck. "The bishop," Andrew said.

"What about the bishop?" Clara said.

"If Yonnie turned off to go south to the bishop's house, you wouldn't have seen or heard him go past."

Clara groaned.

"I'm not worried," Andrew said.

"Maybe you should be."

"Each day has enough worries of its own," Andrew said.

"What will he say?"

Andrew shrugged. "The Model T, your visit to Fannie, my temper. Who knows?"

"He could hurt you."

Andrew shook his head. "I could tell my side of things, and Yonnie would not look innocent, either."

"No!" Clara said. "That would just stir up trouble for everyone."

"It won't matter. Despite what Yonnie thinks, Bishop Yoder is not as powerful as he once was. Someone will step forward to say the congregation must vote."

"But who? Who would stand up to the bishop?"

Andrew was unsure. "He's getting old to be an active bishop."

"Sixty-nine is not ancient."

"He's been leading a long time. We're due for a change."

"You can't know that."

Andrew looked again through the silent trees. "Mose Beachy will be our greatest hope."

This was not the first time Yonnie visited

the bishop's house. Even though the congregation worshipped in meetinghouses rather than homes, every household in the district found ample reason to extend hospitality to other families. And Yonnie was a Yoder, just like the bishop. Once a year, everyone descended from the Yoders who first came to Somerset County a hundred years ago gathered for an afternoon frolic. Yonnie knew the farm from a lifetime of reunions.

This was the first time Yonnie had come with a purpose as serious as the one on his mind now. Three days of patient waiting for the appointed time had not deterred him. In fact, the time had nailed in his determination. Today Bishop Yoder would know exactly what Andrew Raber was up to. And Dale. And Clara.

Maybe not Clara. And maybe not Dale, at least not until Yonnie found other work.

But nothing held him back from telling the bishop that Andrew had an automobile.

He arranged his stance on the Yoder front step and knocked firmly.

Caroline Yoder answered the door with a dish towel hanging from one shoulder. "Hello, Yonnie. What brings you out here?"

"On Sunday I made an appointment with the bishop for today," Yonnie said.

"Oh, I'm sorry you've come all this way

for nothing," Caroline said. "My husband was called away a few minutes ago. He's not anywhere on the farm."

"But I made an appointment."

She shrugged. "Appointment or not, he's still gone. Emergencies happen."

"When will he return?"

"I don't have the mind of God, Yonnie."

"Perhaps I should wait."

She shook her head. "I have a feeling it would be a long wait. I'm sure you have other things to do. The bishop will be happy to speak to you. Please come by again another time."

Back in his buggy, Yonnie considered his options. He was finished for the day at the dairy. Dale had sent Reuben on the afternoon route, which happened more and more often. Dale seemed to prefer keeping Yonnie where he could see him.

Yonnie picked up the reins. Perhaps God had given him this unscheduled afternoon for a purpose. Perhaps this would be the day his inquiries about other employment would bring a favorable answer.

If they did not, Yonnie would double the time he spent praying for discernment and trust. If he gave Dale his notice, surely God would provide.

CHAPTER 24

Clara wondered if anyone would notice if she did not attend worship. It would be just once. From time to time, everyone had a reason to be absent — illness in the house, a cow birthing on a Sunday morning, a journey to visit relatives in another district. Clara had none of those reasons, though. She could hardly tell Rhoda and Hiram that she was staying home because she could not bear the thought of another sermon by the Yoder ministers.

She hadn't seen Fannie and Sadie in over a month, and she hadn't visited Martha in almost two months. By now everyone in the Maryland church must know her aunt was with child.

And Clara stayed home, on the farm, waiting for whatever was going to happen.

No more, she thought. She only needed to plan more carefully — walk the miles to Fannie's farm early in the day, before the heat bore down, or arrange with her father to have a horse and cart. He would not turn her down if she asked ahead of time.

A congregational meeting was scheduled to follow the worship service. Clara was of a mixed mind whether she wanted to be present.

But Andrew. If she excused herself from church on a pretense, she wouldn't see Andrew. Clara braced herself, already planning to mentally work on a story for Sadie during the sermons, and rode with her family to church.

Noah Yoder preached, and Clara spent the time visualizing the words on the pages of the family Bible about Jesus healing Jairus's daughter and then trying out phrases and cadence in the retelling of it.

When Mose Beachy stood to give the second sermon, though, Clara's wordplay tumbled out of her mind. For weeks she had prayed it would be God's will for Mose to preach.

The text God laid on his heart, Mose said, was Romans 12:18. "If it be possible, as much as lieth in you, live peaceably with all men."

Mose recited the verse twice, looking with deliberation around the congregation.

"This verse falls naturally into three parts,

which we must fully consider with our hearts and minds," Mose said. "First, 'if it be possible.' Second, 'as much as lieth in you.' And third, 'live peaceably with all men.' "

Clara gave her rapt attention. Mose preached not only with his words, but also his demeanor. When he gazed at the congregation, he had none of the sternness of the Yoders. He did not brace his stance to exude authority but rather leaned over his Bible as if to bind his heart to those of his listeners. Clara wished she could write down everything he said.

Fifty minutes later, he concluded. "I ask you to consider three questions. If you answer them well, you will know you have this portion of God's Word in your heart. Is it possible for you to live in such a way to bring peace? In what ways does peace depend on you? And finally, who is the *all* with whom God wants you to live in peace?"

Andrew was right. If the lot to become bishop fell to Mose Beachy, things would change. Clara resolved to pray every day that this would be God's will.

Yonnie scowled, unsure what to make of Mose Beachy's sermon.

Who could disagree with a sermon about

peace? But surely there was much room for misinterpretation. The bishop wanted unity of mind, and this would bring peace to the congregation. Mose spoke of a different peace. He made no mention of discipline or obedience to the church's teaching.

Yonnie stood for the brief break between the end of the worship service and the beginning of the congregational meeting. Women took children outside to let them run for a few minutes. Men clustered in conversation or rearranged furniture for the meeting. Yonnie stood still as Andrew approached, forming in his mind what he might say if Andrew asked forgiveness for his actions on the day he came to the dairy and embarrassed Yonnie. Familiar proverbs would serve well. *Let your life story be for God's glory.* Or, *A heart at peace gives life to the body.*

But Andrew did not stop.

He did not even catch Yonnie's eye.

Instead, he walked past as if he were shunning Yonnie and joined John Stutzman and several other men only a few feet away.

A shaft of heat burned up through Yonnie's torso and lodged in his throat. Andrew's behavior only proved the necessity of the decision Yonnie had made. Regret billowed. He should never have let another ten days pass before trying again to see the bishop privately.

Mose called the congregational meeting to order. Beside him at the front of the meetinghouse sat Joseph Yoder.

"We are meeting today," Mose said, "at the request of some of our members to consider a clarified understanding of recent teaching in our church. Specifically, members have raised questions about the *meidung* that the bishop called for a few weeks ago."

Joseph Yoder cleared his throat and glanced at his father's stiff pose. "May I remind everyone that the *meidung* is not new. My father merely asks us to be obedient to the unanimous congregational vote taken many years ago."

Caleb Schrock stood up. "I believe our brother refers to the vote taken in 1895, when many of us were children or just beginning our own families. The congregation has seen many changes since then."

Does truth change? Yonnie thought. *Does the Bible's teaching change with the generation? No.*

Yonnie watched the bishop, waiting for him to speak. Slowly, Yonnie nodded in understanding. This was a time for the Yoder sons to show the strength of their own leadership. Bishop Yoder was training his sons for their calling.

Now John Stutzman stood. "Our brother Mose brought us the Word of God today. I believe God gave Mose words that we need to fully consider. What does it mean to live peaceably? Did not the church members who peacefully divided the Old Order from the Conservative Amish Mennonites live peaceably? There was no rancor in the separation of the two districts, and people were free to go where their consciences led them. The broken peace comes only with the insistence of *meidung*."

John sat down.

Noah Yoder stood. "We must not misunderstand the *meidung* as an instrument of punishment. It is an instrument of reconciliation."

That's right, Yonnie thought. He had heard this message from Bishop Yoder all his life.

The Yoders read from the Bible the command to separate from the heathen.

Mose had just finished preaching the Bible's command to live peaceably with all.

Yonnie was looking for the line that would connect these two commands. How was it possible to obey both?

As Bishop Yoder intoned a solemn closing

prayer, Andrew was uncertain what the meeting had accomplished. Nothing that was said would lead anyone to a change of mind about the need for shunning friends and relatives who worshipped on the Maryland side of the border, and no one suggested a new formal congregational vote on the question. Neither those who spoke nor those who kept silent surprised Andrew.

Nothing had changed.

People milled between the benches, exchanging news and opinions. Andrew doubted anyone would forgo the shared meal. Amish farms were spread widely enough that many families did not see each other except on church Sundays or organized frolics. The fellowship was as essential as the worship or a congregational meeting.

Andrew drifted toward John Stutzman, who was restoring order to the furniture at the front of the meetinghouse.

"Thank you for speaking up," Andrew said. "Many in the congregation agree with you."

"More should speak up," John said. "The ministers should know what is on our minds."

"They know." Andrew's fingers thrummed the high back of a chair. "They've known for years." The fall communion was coming. No one would want to defy the bishop and imperil communion for everyone.

"Mose gave a good sermon."

Andrew nodded. "It's puzzling why he does not have more opportunity to preach. With four ministers, he should be preaching one sermon out of four."

"The lot only means that each Sunday Mose has a one in four chance he will be called on. What happens one week has nothing to do with the next."

It seemed to Andrew that over time the odds should even out more than they did. "Folks might find greater appreciation for the sermons if Mose preached more often."

"Gottes wille." John gestured to shift Andrew's attention. "Here comes someone you might like to hear from."

"Good morning, Clara." Andrew hoped his smile was sincere without revealing too much.

"Good morning," Clara said. "I hope you are both well."

The two men nodded. Andrew considered Clara's features and coloring. The same strain that distracted her in this place the week before — when he helped clean up her bucket, rags, and broom — gripped her now. He knew her well enough to know when the smile on her face was an intentional arrangement of muscles and not a spontaneous response to what her eyes saw.

Clara glanced around. "I haven't seen any of the Brennermans today."

"I heard there was illness in the house," John said.

"Not little Naomi, I hope."

"Her mother, I believe," John said. "She's been poorly for several days."

"She must be very ill for the whole family to stay home," Clara said.

"Perhaps several of them are afflicted now," John said.

John made reasonable statements. He could not know that Clara would be particularly concerned for Naomi.

Fannie washed supper dishes while Elam sat at the kitchen table with paper and pencil in front of him. This was his Sunday evening ritual. After observing the Sabbath all day, whether or not it was a church Sunday, after the evening meal his mind invariably turned to the week ahead — what attention the crops needed, signs of ill health in the animals, the horseshoes requiring replacing, the repair of a buggy wheel.

Fannie did not mind. Elam was working hard to care for the family, as small as it was, and Fannie had her own thoughts to manage.

"I miss Clara," she murmured.

"Mmm?" Elam did not look up.

"Clara is the sister I never had," Fannie said. In the old days she would have told Elam her every thought. Lately she said little to him other than matters of the household. But Clara was important. She sat at the table across from her husband, and he finally lifted his eyes to her.

"Has she written?" Elam said.

Fannie waved a hand. "A silly letter about how the summer is passing so fast and she hopes Sadie is well."

"What is silly about that?"

"It's not the kind of letter Clara writes. Something's wrong."

"So write to her."

"I have. I invited her to come here and stay."

"You know she's always welcome."

Elam had not a bone of jealousy about his wife's affection for her cousin, something that always had endeared him to Fannie.

"We must persuade her," Fannie said. "It's not like her to be silent." She gave no voice to the abandonment she felt. Her disconnection from her own family was her doing, but she could think of nothing she had done to cut herself off from Clara.

"So write to her again." Elam shifted papers in front of him.

"She should think about joining the Marylanders. Surely Andrew would agree. His own family is in Lancaster County. He's on his own with that farm, and he's not a strict man. He would do anything to make Clara happy."

At this point, Elam put down his pencil and gave full attention to the conversation. "Just what do you know about Andrew Raber and Clara?"

"Clara speaks of him from time to time." Clara had confided Andrew's multiple proposals, but Fannie saw no reason to reveal details. She was thinking aloud when she spoke of Andrew, falling into the old habit of telling Elam everything as if they shared one mind. Fannie surprised herself. In the restraint of the last few months, the lack of a baby hung in the middle of every conversation between them, and it had become easier not to talk.

Elam raised his eyebrows.

"Never mind Andrew," Fannie said. "Clara should make her own decision about which church God wants her to be in. If she comes to visit, we will give her every reason to visit our congregation."

Elam half smiled. "Just give Sadie permission to nag."

Fannie surprised herself again and laughed softly as she returned to the dishes.

CHAPTER 25

Clara cooked on Monday — not for her family but for the Brennermans. When Rhoda took the children with her into Springs for some shopping, Clara took over the kitchen. By the time Rhoda returned, Clara had a pot of chicken soup, a casserole laden with garden vegetables — but no celery — and bread with sliced cheese. If one dish did not appeal, surely another would. It would all bring nourishment, even if only a bite or two at a time. Clara wrapped everything in towels to hold in the warmth and arranged the items carefully in a milk crate to put in the cart. Rhoda had her arms full of a fussy, overtired three-year-old and offered no objection to Clara's departure with the horse and cart.

Having a purpose invigorated Clara. After a summer of aimless wandering and finding her friends busy with their own young families, she relished the thought of easing

Mrs. Brennerman's day. She sat up straight on the cart's bench and insisted the horse oblige with a brisk pace for the entire six miles.

The Brennerman yard was quiet, and Clara's alarm heightened. The family had seven children. Someone ought to be outside playing or weeding the vegetable garden or beating rugs. Two chickens clucked and fluttered from their positions on the front steps as Clara carried her crate to the door and knocked.

Clara hoped the only reason the windows were closed and shuttered was a defense against August heat pressing in. Finally she heard shuffling from within, and the front door opened. Mrs. Brennerman, beleaguered and pale, stood before her.

"We have sickness," Mrs. Brennerman said. "You ought not to come in."

"I only came to help." Clara gestured to the crate. "I brought some food."

"Thank you, but no."

A series of flabbergasted sounds passed Clara's throat, but none of them were words. She cocked her head.

"Naomi told me all about your stories," Mrs. Brennerman said.

"I see." The crate suddenly weighed heavy in Clara's arms. She set it on the porch.

"How many of you are feeling poorly? I thought it might be helpful if you didn't have to fix food."

"Are you going to confess your sin to the congregation?"

For a woman with a houseful of illness, Mrs. Brennerman was stubborn. Clara chose her words with deliberation.

"How can stories from the Bible be sin?" she said.

"If that's how you feel, then you won't mind if the bishop knows."

Clara's spine tingled as it straightened. First Mrs. Schrock — whose rebuke at least had been gentle — and now Mrs. Brennerman. Lillian's mother would be next, and the trail from there to Rhoda would be short. Clara could not take back the stories she had told, nor did she want to. This was the moment in which the realization took full form. No, she would not mind if Bishop Yoder heard about the stories. Living in fear was no way to receive a gift from God's hand.

"Do what your conscience tells you is right," Clara said, "but my food will bring only good to your children. I hope it will offer you a moment of needed rest."

She turned and strode toward her cart without looking back.

■ ■ ■ ■

The decision to see the bishop on Tuesday afternoon was an impulse. Andrew allowed that it might even be the prodding of the Holy Ghost. He paused only briefly at the intersection before taking the turn toward the Yoder farm. If the Bishop Yoder was not there, Andrew would only have lost an hour of his afternoon. *Gottes wille.* He murmured a prayer for a kind and merciful conversation.

The bishop opened the door himself. "Scrappy Andy."

The nickname had fallen away once Andrew's parents moved to Lancaster County and he no longer shared his father's full name in the same congregation. The bishop's use of it unsettled Andrew.

"I wonder if you have time to talk," Andrew said.

"I will heat up the *kaffi.*"

"Please don't go to any trouble."

Bishop Yoder had already turned to lead the way through the house to the kitchen at the back. He lit the stove. Andrew wondered if the coffee had been in the pot since breakfast.

"What has God put on your heart to speak

to me about?" Bishop Yoder pulled a chair from the table for Andrew to sit in.

He was breathing heavily, it seemed to Andrew.

"If you are unwell," he said, "I can come to talk another time."

"I'm not as young as I used to be," Bishop Yoder said, "but it's nothing a cup of *kaffi* won't help mend."

The coffee turned out to be lukewarm and bitter, which did not seem to bother the bishop. Andrew took a few polite sips before abandoning the effort.

"What brings you here?" The bishop raised an eyebrow.

"The congregational meeting has been on my mind."

"The lessons are not buried so deeply. They will find them."

"Perhaps," Andrew said, "a middle way?"

"The pages of the Bible are one."

Andrew inspected the bishop's reddening face. "Help me understand your meaning."

"We look into a glass darkly. Thus saith the Lord." Bishop Yoder stared into his cup before abruptly lifting it to swallow its contents in one gulp.

"The congregation," Andrew said.

"The ninety-nine and the one. The word of the Lord is irrefutable."

Andrew had found little to agree with in the bishop's recent sermons, but at least their meaning had been clear. These riddles befuddled Andrew — if that is what they were.

The back door opened. Mrs. Yoder entered with a basket of vegetables over her arm, black earth still clinging in clumps to blotches of green and orange.

"Am I interrupting?" she said.

"Scrappy Andy had a question, which I have just finished answering," her husband said.

Andrew stood, puzzling how he might ask Mrs. Yoder if her husband had fallen ill in the last two days. Though the bishop had been quiet during Sunday's service and the meeting that followed, no one had remarked that he seemed unwell.

"You ought to stick to your appointments." Mrs. Yoder touched her husband's shoulder before setting the basket on the counter and glancing at Andrew. "The bishop has always preferred to give careful thought to how to respond to a spiritual matter."

Illumination washed over Andrew. She was protecting her husband.

"The lessons are not buried so deeply. They will find them."

"The pages of the Bible are one."

"We look into a glass darkly. Thus saith the Lord."

"The ninety-nine and the one. The word of the Lord is irrefutable."

Caroline Yoder, Andrew realized, was not surprised that her husband might not make sense.

"Is it today?" Sadie asked.

"Is what today?" Fannie leaned forward in the glider and reached for a foot to rub. Lately her feet were not happy in shoes and not happy barefoot.

"The quilts. The ones that aren't finished yet."

"The quilting bee?"

"Yes. That's what I mean. This is Wednesday, isn't it?"

"I'm afraid we missed it," Fannie said.

"The whole thing? It's supposed to last all day, isn't it?"

Sometimes Fannie wished that Sadie did not listen quite so carefully to the adult conversations around her. She wasn't sure where Sadie gathered her information, but she'd absorbed it correctly. This was indeed Wednesday, and indeed quilting bees lasted most of the day.

"It's too late to go now," Fannie said.

"Can't we still go?"

Fannie sucked in a breath in the hope that the exhale would bring patience.

"It just didn't work out for us this time," she said. "There will be another bee."

"And we'll go?" Sadie came close and widened her eyes to stare into her mother's.

"We'll see." Fannie kissed Sadie's forehead. "Do you think you could go pick some beans for supper all by yourself?"

Sadie dashed off for a basket as Fannie knew she would. Her daughter thrived on opportunities to prove her independence.

Her mother was going to the quilting bee. Plain and simple, that was the reason Fannie could not muster enthusiasm for the event.

Fannie missed Martha — at least, the balance between them as Fannie waited for a second child. She missed confiding monthly disappointment to her mother. She missed knowing that Martha stood with her in prayer for a child. She missed being in and out of each other's homes several times each week.

Martha's pregnancy changed everything. Fannie could not look at her mother without resentment. And no matter how guilty she might feel about the attitude, she couldn't change it. Every day that passed, she cared less about it.

She cared less about everything.

Fannie leaned back in the glider and pushed it into motion. She was upright, not napping in the middle of the day. In a few minutes she would engage in a needed task. But the effort or normalcy exhausted her.

The screen door thwacked. The footsteps crossing the kitchen were Elam's. He came through to the front room.

"I'll get your lunch," Fannie said, though her muscles did not respond to the thought with movement.

"I expected I would be on my own," he said. "Isn't this the quilting bee day?"

"A bee is a long day," Fannie said. "If anyone tries to leave early, the others make a fuss. It's better to stay home if you don't feel well."

Elam did not speak. Fannie met his gaze for as long as she could bear it. Now she insisted that her feet find their place and support her weight. When she walked past him, he reached to catch her hand but she pulled it from him.

At the sound of the *English* motor roaring toward him from behind, Yonnie took his horse and open buggy as close to the edge of the road as he could without risking the ditch. Traffic on the farm roads was less threatening in the days before Henry Ford decided that every household in the country should have an automobile. Fewer and fewer of the English used horses to move around the county, and along with their former habit they had dispensed with a sense of the speed at which horse and buggies traversed safely.

Yonnie glanced over his shoulder at the approaching car, a green Model T with the roof down stirring up a cloud of dust. With an irritated groan, Yonnie pulled the horse into the middle of the road and slowed almost to a stop. If Andrew insisted on driving an *English* machine, then let him be the one to drive along the ditch.

Andrew honked his horn. Yonnie ignored it, refusing to turn his head again. The automobile crept along behind the buggy.

"Yonnie, move over!" Andrew shouted.

Yonnie hunched his shoulders but gave no command to the horse, instead maintaining his position in the center of the road at a near crawl for more than a mile. Andrew should not take lessons in impatience from the *English.*

At the widening of an intersection, Andrew accelerated past the buggy. What Yonnie had not expected was that Andrew would swing his car around to block the road, forcing Yonnie to stop. Andrew got out of the car and leaned against it.

"You can't block the road," Yonnie said.

"You did," Andrew shot back over the idling engine.

Yonnie rearranged the reins in his hands. "You could use your knowledge of machinery in other ways to serve the community. You don't have to be like the *English*."

"I have not abandoned the community," Andrew said. "It is you who presumes to know what is in my heart on the matter."

"You have no family to keep you here. What is to stop you from one day driving away from the church?"

"Do you think an automobile has more power over my actions than my own conscience?"

"You put yourself at risk."

"Do I? Or do you push me toward that edge by thinking you know what a man-made machine means to me?"

"You cannot serve both God and mammon, Andrew."

Andrew glared at Yonnie. The horse nickered. Andrew got back behind the wheel and sped off, leave Yonnie to cough in the dust.

CHAPTER 26

Clara pushed the wheelbarrow through the barn, pausing at each stall to throw in a layer of fresh straw and assess how soon mucking would be required. Rhoda thought of the barn as her husband's purview and rarely entered. Helping in the barn now, with Josiah wrangling a wide broom behind her, transported Clara's mind back to the days when she was the child trailing Hiram. Those years held their grief, but the framework of life had been simple and predictable. The line between Hiram and Clara had been straight and clear.

When had life in a family become so complicated?

Clara threw her brother a smile, and his grin soothed her.

"Are you going to help me muck when it's time?" Josiah said.

"Of course." Cleaning animal stalls was Clara's least favorite chore, but if it meant she could spend time with Josiah without wondering when Rhoda would snatch him away, Clara would do it gladly.

She pushed the wheelbarrow out into the bright daylight. In a couple of weeks, summer's furnace would cease its blasts. The harvest would swallow up every free moment for farmers and their families. Hiram had already struck his deals for selling the portion of the Kuhn crop that he did not need for feeding his family and animals through the winter.

A buggy turned off the main road and progressed down the lane toward the house. Clara released the wheelbarrow handles and pulled a sleeve across her forehead before brushing off her apron.

"*Gut mariye,* Mrs. Brennerman," Clara said, surprised that the visitor who emerged was the woman who rejected her offering a week ago.

"I've brought Rhoda's pots back," Mrs. Brennerman said.

"I trust everyone is well."

"Well enough. Is Rhoda home?"

"Yes," Clara said. "Please come to the house."

Clara took the dishes from Mrs. Brennerman, hoping that that food had nourished the family after all and had not been thrown

316

straight to the pigs. She led the way across the yard, up the front steps, and into the house.

Inside, Rhoda offered coffee to Mrs. Brennerman — not to Clara — and the two of them withdrew to the kitchen. Clara took quiet steps across the wood floor and stopped outside the kitchen, to one side of the open door. This could be the moment Rhoda learned of the stories. Clara wanted to hear Mrs. Brennerman's account for herself.

"Have you heard about the bishop?" Mrs. Brennerman said to Rhoda. "He's fallen ill — quite ill, I believe."

"We must remember to pray for him," Rhoda said.

"His wife has him in seclusion. She believes he needs complete rest. No one is to try to speak to him."

"We do have three other ministers," Rhoda said. Clara heard the cups in her hand clink.

"There are some who would take advantage of Bishop Yoder's illness."

"He will recover."

"He is quite ill," Mrs. Brennerman repeated.

Clara stepped away. Of course she would pray for the bishop's recovery to full strength.

But what if he did not recover?

Andrew had expected only to buy a box of nails while he was in town, not to hear that Bishop Yoder was too ill to see anyone. The news did not surprise him. He let pass the speculation that the illness was likely the same one that had infected other households. In a few days the bishop's appetite would return. He would be back to preaching by Sunday.

Andrew was certain that was not true.

He didn't take his buggy home to his own farm. Instead, he unhitched his horse behind the old Johnson barn with the confidence that the animal would not wander far. John Stutzman was the man Andrew wanted to talk to, and he lived on the other side of the district. The Model T was running well these days, and Andrew had practiced enough to believe he was not a menace on the road. This would be a useful demonstration of the time the automobile would save. Andrew pushed open the barn door, cranked the engine to life, and drove onto the main road.

Andrew was relieved to find John in one of his fields with none of his sons in sight. He had been prepared to park the Model T out of sight and walk the last half mile to avoid the gawking eyes of John's family. Instead, he had only to cross the road to speak privately.

"I saw for myself," Andrew said after reporting the bishop's illness. "I was there Tuesday. He was clearly unwell. Chicken soup will not heal his ailment."

John glanced across the road at the automobile. "Thank you for coming all this way to tell me."

"Even if he recovers physical strength," Andrew said, "the question is not far off whether he is fit to continue as bishop."

They ambled up the space between rows of grain ready for harvest.

"Until he steps aside, he is the bishop," John said. "We should make sure his crop gets in."

"I'm happy to help," Andrew said. All the farmers would help each other with the harvest, moving from one farm to another during the critical weeks. "It's the church I'm worried about."

"Why should you worry?" John stopped walking and faced Andrew.

"*Worry* is the wrong word." The Bible said, "Worry not," and for the most part Andrew enjoyed the freedom that came with the command. "Surely, though, you can see there will be some commotion in the congregation if the bishop does step aside."

John shook his head. "God's will. We can do nothing to change that, nor should we try."

"But perhaps we can find a way to help each other live in peace, no matter what happens."

"Each of us must follow our own conscience."

Andrew examined his friend's face. While John did not look away, his eyes carried a cloud Andrew was unaccustomed to seeing.

John gestured to the Model T at the side of the field. "So it's running well?"

His words softly closed the door on conversation about the bishop.

Hours later, Andrew stood on the side of a road admiring the sky. Whether black against starlit brilliance or incomprehensible behind hanging low clouds, Andrew loved the night sky.

So much transcendent possibility. So much wonder beyond farm fields and milking schedules. So much assurance beyond the mysterious lots of God's will.

Andrew wished he could simply knock on the Kuhn door and say he had come to call on Clara, the way the *English* courted. Instead he leaned against his buggy wondering if she would decide to take an evening stroll and come this way. If they should meet on any night, this was that night.

He stared into the deep, wondering what was beyond the beyond.

Andrew almost did not hear her arrive, turning at the crunch of a step to find her near and breathless.

"You've heard," he said.

Clara nodded. "I can't get it off my mind."

"I saw him last week," Andrew said. "He spoke gibberish as if it were chapter and verse from the Bible."

"Everyone will pray for him." Clara fiddled with the cuffs of her long sleeves.

"We should."

"I'm afraid selfishness will be like an illness in my prayers."

"Selfishness?"

She raised her eyes to his. "At least two mothers know about my Bible stories with the girls. As long as the bishop is ill, no one can tell him."

"Someone might tell one of the other ministers."

Clara shook her head. "Everyone knows Noah and Joseph Yoder don't do anything without first talking to their father."

"And they know Mose Beachy does not have much sympathy for tattletales." Andrew slipped a palm under Clara's fingers. "So you're safe."

"And safe is selfish. It's hard to pray for the bishop to get well."

"Don't be ashamed, Clara. And don't fear the gift God put in your heart."

She sighed. "What about your car? Don't you feel relief that at least for now, Yonnie can't draw attention to it?"

Andrew patted the side of the buggy. "I still use this most of the time. But I am not afraid."

"And if the ministers tell you that you must get rid of the automobile, what will you do?"

"One day at a time." Andrew grazed her face with one hand, setting his fingers under her jaw. "I do not worry what will happen to me, and if you were my wife, I would not have to worry what will happen to you, either."

She turned her head to his palm and laid her cheek in his hand. "Andrew, you know how much I care for you."

"You don't tell me what's bothering you at home," Andrew said, "but I know something is. I have a farm. We could make our own home together, and I would do my best not to fill it with anything that bothers you."

Clara laughed softly. "Even you are not

that perfect."

"Tell me you're thinking about it."

"Every day."

"Whatever frightens you, we'll face it together." Andrew leaned in to kiss Clara, tasting the tart lemon pie she must have eaten after supper.

"Ruth Kaufman asked me to be an attendant at her wedding," Clara said after she broke the kiss with reluctance that pleased Andrew.

He laughed. "She is marrying Peter Troyer, *ya?*"

"Ya."

"He asked me to be in the wedding party."

Clara laughed softly. "If they knew we were —"

"I know," Andrew said. "They are not supposed to ask two people who are thinking of marrying."

"Should we tell them?"

He raised an eyebrow. "Have you decided?"

She ducked her head away from his gaze.

As far as Sadie knew, they were headed to her *grossmuder*'s house. Fannie was not anxious to arrive. She had not actually agreed to a midmorning visit to her mother's, only to go for an exploring walk with her daughter. It was Sadie who assumed a destination. Fannie examined the sun's position, judging how long they had before it would rise to a height that ushered in a wilting heat. In a few more minutes, she would speak the words that would make her daughter pout and they would start the circle taking them to their own home, rather than to Martha's.

For now, Fannie inhaled deeply the fragrance of the end of summer. Late-blooming lilacs, sweet apple trees, pungent cows — the humid air swirled it all together and trailed the result in unexpected wafts. Fannie ached to savor these bits of life as she had every other summer. She yearned for them to call her back from the precarious edge of her days.

The milk wagon rattled toward them in a medley of clanging milk cans, horse hooves, and creaking wheels. Fannie reached for Sadie's hand and at the same time eyed the spot where they would turn away from her mother's house.

Sadie waved, and from the bench of his wagon Dale Borntrager returned the morning greeting and slowed the rig.

"I suppose you've heard about Bishop Yoder," Dale said.

"No," Fannie said. "What news?"

"Very ill. Some say he won't be well enough to lead again."

Fannie's pulse fluttered. "Will you have a new bishop, then?"

Dale chuckled. "We might at least have some more peaceful preaching. The lot to preach will have to fall to Mose Beachy more often."

Fannie knew she ought to say she would pray for the bishop, but she prayed little these days. Why should she pray when God was stubbornly silent?

Sadie pulled against Fannie's grip and spoke with patient politeness. "It's nice to see you, Mr. Borntrager, but my *grossmuder* is waiting."

"I'm headed there now," he said. "Why don't I give you a ride?"

"Danki!"

"No, thank you," Fannie tightened her hold on Sadie.

Fannie ignored Sadie's protests as the milk wagon pulled away. The bishop might get well, and everything would be as it had been for decades. Even if he stepped aside, one of his sons would likely become bishop. And if the lot fell to Mose Beachy, the Pennsylvania congregation would be unsettled. Clara had so much to gain if she simply came to the Maryland congregation, with or without Andrew. Fannie would write as many letters as it took to persuade her.

"Come on, Sadie. We have to get home."

"What about *Grossmuder*?"

"Another day."

"But I miss her!"

So do I. "We're going home, Sadie. Don't argue with me."

CHAPTER 27

Andrew followed John Stutzman, who followed Mose Beachy through Mose's field of alfalfa mown and standing in windrows.

"Two more days of drying," Mose said. "Then we'll thresh."

"With three teams, the work goes well," Andrew said. Mose tried to cut hay three times a year. Andrew, John, and Mose had developed an efficient rhythm for cutting and later threshing.

"My older boys can handle the grapple fork and getting the hay into the loft," Mose said. "One of the girls can lead the horse when it's time to pull."

They paced to the end of the field, across a path, and toward the Beachy barn.

"I need to put a new chain on the grapple fork," Mose said, "but I'll have that ready by the time you come back."

"Saturday morning, then," John said.

"Danki." Mose paused in the middle of the

barnyard and scratched under his beard. "I imagine you both would like to know how the bishop is."

Andrew nodded but said nothing. Three days had passed with no further news about Bishop Yoder's illness.

"Noah and Joseph were here yesterday," Mose said. "They seem to think their father needs an extended rest."

"He should take all the time he needs to heal," John said. "And if I know Caroline, she'll see to it."

"She was a bishop's daughter before she was a bishop's wife," Mose said. "She knows the demands."

"And Lucy?" Andrew said. "Would Lucy know the demands if the lot fell to you to be the next bishop?"

"It's too soon to say the lot will fall to anyone," Mose said.

"Eventually we will have a new bishop," Andrew said. "Do you not ever think about the question?"

"If I am called upon, I will serve as best as I am able, by God's grace. If God does not choose me, I will continue as a minister. In the meantime, I gain nothing from wondering what might be. God will make clear His will."

Andrew found sincere acceptance in his

friend's face.

Lucy Beachy appeared on the porch and called out her husband's name.

"I must go," Mose said. "I promised to fix the stair railing today before one of the children gets hurt. Thank you again for your help with the hay."

Andrew and John watched Mose walk toward the house and then moved toward their own buggies.

"Do you think it may be God's will to disturb His people?" Andrew said.

"With the new bishop?" John swung his gaze around to Andrew.

"Of course we all pray for Bishop Yoder's recovery," Andrew said. "But many in the congregation disagree with him. I find myself wondering how the church can thrive while he leads."

"Most likely one of his sons will follow," John said.

Andrew nodded. "Wouldn't you say that many find that thought disturbing?"

"And if the lot falls to Mose Beachy? Won't others be disturbed?"

"You see my point," Andrew said, stroking his horse's long brown nose. "No matter who is bishop, the church harbors unhappiness. If this is so, should we conclude that God wills for us to be unsettled?"

"God has His purposes. His ways are not our ways."

John was giving the right answers, cautious words with which no one could find fault.

"John," Andrew said, "we are true friends, are we not?"

John nodded. "For many years."

"Then please speak freely."

John scraped a boot through the dirt. "The *meidung* will not bring unity to the church. I will not shun, no matter what the rule."

Andrew took in a long breath through his nose, waiting for the rest.

"The Yoders refuse to regard the Maryland congregations as true Amish churches," John said. "They also refuse the truth that some in our midst are prepared to join the Marylanders if they continue to push the question of shunning families and neighbors."

"I see," Andrew said. "You are considering this."

"Have you not?" John met Andrew's gaze. "You are the one with an *English* automobile."

"It is only a matter of time before the church must consider the question of automobiles," Andrew said. "I do not presume to know what the answer will be."

"And if the congregation votes that we must not follow the *English* way in the matter, will you sell your car?"

Andrew worked his lips from side to side but did not answer.

Yonnie straightened his spine against Noah Yoder's barn so tightly that he felt the seams between the slats of wood. Next to him, the window was open.

"Have you been to see *Mamm*?" Noah asked his brother. "How is *Daed* today?"

"He sleeps all day," Joseph said.

"Has the doctor been in?"

"She won't have an *English* doctor. Mrs. Weaver came by with some herbs."

A fly buzzed around Yonnie's left ear. He waved a hand. The fly circled and swooped in again, this time settling on the window ledge. Yonnie stared at it while he listened.

"I pray he recovers soon," Noah said. "I am beginning to hear talk among the church families."

"He must recover," Joseph said. "If Mose Beachy becomes bishop now, the church will lose its way."

"The lot would more likely fall to you or me. As long as we stand together, God's truth will prevail."

The fly twitched and lifted, making a straight line toward Yonnie's face. He blinked and swatted. Unthinking, he moved his left foot to rebalance.

He had not seen the slop bucket earlier. Now it clattered against the side of the barn before spilling its swill across his boot.

"Who's out there?" Joseph's voice boomed through the open window.

Yonnie held his breath, hoping blame for the disturbance would fall to an unseen stray dog or a clumsy barn cat. He dragged the side of his boot through the dirt in an attempt to dislodge food scraps. When he looked up, Noah was coming around the corner of the barn.

"What are you doing here, Yonnie?"

Now Joseph's face popped through the window. "Didn't you find our milk in the spring?"

"Ya," Yonnie said. "I found it."

The brothers waited.

"I'm sorry about the bucket," Yonnie said.

"Have you come to visit, then?" Noah raised his eyebrows.

Yonnie shifted his weight. "I wonder if you might be looking for a hired hand."

"I would think you'd be plenty busy," Joseph said. "Between your job at the dairy and working on your *daed*'s farm, you must wear yourself thin."

"My brothers are a big help on the farm now," Yonnie said, "and it may be time for me to find other work. I am not proud. I would do whatever you ask of me, on either of your farms — or your father's."

"I thought you wanted your own farm." Joseph leaned both arms across the window ledge.

"I do. I'm still saving for a down payment."

"What's brought this on?" Noah asked. "You've been with Dale Borntrager for a long time."

Yonnie looked from one brother to another. "I find myself unsettled there of late."

"It's a solid business," Joseph said. "Steady employment."

"In my spirit, I discern that working for someone else would keep me obedient."

"I see," Joseph said. "So you feel it is the will of the Lord to seek other employment?"

"I do. If I were to work for the bishop's sons, both ministers of good conscience, my own position would be more clear."

"Is there something you want to tell us about Dale?" Noah said. "Perhaps the Holy Ghost has convicted you to come forward."

Yonnie swallowed. The fly buzzed at the back of his neck. "I only seek to safeguard my submission to the church."

"You have chosen wisely," Noah said. "You can be certain of our calling to protect and pass on the faith of our fathers."

"Thank you for bringing Dale Borntrager to our attention," Joseph said. "We will be sure to pay him a call."

Yonnie toyed with regret. If the Yoder brothers confronted Dale, he hoped they would not mention his name — at least not unless they offered him work. Any of Dale's employees might have gone to the ministers, he realized. They all knew Dale continued to do business with people the bishop placed under the ban. Still, Dale's suspicions would settle on Yonnie soon enough.

"Might you have work for me?" Yonnie asked again.

"We'll need to consider the question." Noah glanced at his brother. "We still have time before the harvest. Why don't we speak again in a week or two."

A scowl settled on Yonnie's face. Everything could change in a week or two. The bishop might or might not recover. The congregation might or might not have a new bishop. The Yoders might or might not confront Dale, who might or might not decide Yonnie deserved no further warnings.

"Thank you for your time," Yonnie said. He banished the word *might* from his mind. Yes, anything could happen, but God's will was certain — and how could he regret God's will?

CHAPTER 28

"I don't see them." Rhoda lifted Mari from the buggy and set her on the ground outside the Flag Run Meetinghouse.

"It's still early," Hiram said.

"I don't care if he is the bishop," Rhoda said, "his wife is not going to let him come to church if he's been ill all week."

Clara was the last to exit the buggy and dallied as her family walked ahead. She spied Wanda Eicher wrestling with her toddlers. With a child on her hip and another swelling her belly, Wanda might have stood there all morning pleading for the recalcitrant boy's cooperation. Clara strode over, lifted the stunned child, and set him on his feet.

"Thank you," Wanda said. "He insists on independent thinking every moment of the day now."

"He doesn't seem the worse for wear." Clara brushed off the boy's trousers and held his hand tightly. "I'll sit in the back with you, if you like."

"Everybody wants to know about the bishop," Wanda said. They started to walk. "It's not as if he's never been ill before."

"They say it's very bad this time."

"Whoever *they* are," Wanda said. "The illness gets more severe with every telling."

Clara nodded. What Wanda said was true. In the absence of facts about the bishop's illness, rumors had crisscrossed the district all week.

They settled in the rear of the meetinghouse, each of them holding a child in her lap. The men marched in, a hymn began, and the ministers withdrew to determine who would preach. After twelve stanzas, the hymn faded and prayerful silence descended while the congregation waited for one of the men to feel moved to begin another.

When Clara heard the tenor strains, she knew the voice immediately.

Andrew.

"To be like Christ we love one another, through everything, here on this earth," he sang.

Clara was one of the first to join. "We love one another, not just with words but in deeds."

The hymn mounted gently with admonition. "If we have of this world's goods (no matter how much or how little) and see that our brother has a need, but do not share with him what we have freely received? How can we say that we would be ready to give our lives for him if necessary?"

Clara watched the door through which the ministers would return. If only there were a way for Mose Beachy to preach both sermons. The rhythms of the hymn rose and fell with its centuries-old tune and High German words. Clara, who knew the words by heart, chided herself to heed their message.

"The one who is not faithful in the smallest thing, and who still seeks his own good which his heart desires, how can he be trusted with a charge over heavenly things? Let us keep our eyes on love!"

Faithful in the smallest thing.

Clara's lips stilled as she paused to absorb the challenge. All of her life felt small.

Let us keep our eyes on love!

The next worship Sunday would be the day of preparation, the final worship service before the fall communion the next time the congregation gathered. The hymn's message was a fit one for the occasion, giving everyone something to meditate on in the coming weeks. Clara stroked the drowsy

338

head of the child in her lap while she sang and prayed that the words would sink into her own heart.

When the ministers returned, the postures of Noah and Joseph Yoder announced that the lot had fallen to both of them to preach. Clara clung to the words she had just sung as disappointment seeped through her spirit.

Lord, let me hear Your truth. Clara took the first of many deep breaths that would see her through the service. Despite the inner peace Clara cultivated for the next two hours, the end of the sermons had the effect on the congregation that became more predictable on each Sunday the church gathered.

Relief.

Clara could think of no other word to describe the aggregate sensation as she heard the rolling wave of sighs.

"Well, that's that," Wanda said after the final hymn, "at least for another two weeks."

"The singing was nice," Clara said. *Let us keep our eyes on love! Eyes and words and hearts,* Clara thought.

The boy in her arms slept soundly, a condition that overtook him at the midpoint of the first sermon. Awake, his sister squirmed in Wanda's arms.

"Let me take him," Wanda said.

Clara shook her head. She rather liked the sensation of the child limp in surrender, his mouth opening and closing in shallow breaths. "I'll just sit with him a few more minutes," she said.

Wanda winced and put a hand on her belly. Her daughter took advantage of the moment to escape Wanda's lap.

Clara's heart thudded as she caught the little girl's hand to keep her from wandering off. "Are you all right, Wanda?"

Wanda's shoulders rose and fell three times with her breath before she replied. "That was rather a sharp pain."

"How close is your time?"

"Not close enough for this." Wanda's face tightened again.

Clara looked around. "I'll find your husband."

Wanda put a hand on Clara's arm. "No. You have no idea the fuss that would stir up."

"If you are unwell, he should stir up a fuss."

"It's easing up." Wanda leaned back on the bench. "I'm all right."

The little girl tugged against Clara's grasp. "I want my *daed.*"

Clara wondered if the child was capable of finding her father and bringing him back into the meetinghouse.

"We'll go together," Wanda said. She braced herself to stand up.

"Wanda —"

"I'm all right."

"Tell somebody."

"It's nothing, Clara." Wanda steadied herself on her feet. "Odd things happen when a woman is with child. Someday you'll understand. Not every twinge means something is wrong."

That was more than a twinge, Clara thought. It *might* mean something was wrong.

Clara offered no further argument aloud, though she noticed Wanda was not walking as easily as she had a few hours ago.

The benches gradually emptied and conversations clustered and spattered the meetinghouse.

"We need another vote," a woman whispered behind Clara, who did not try to turn and see the speaker lest the boy wake. Clara had enough experience with small children to respect the final vestiges of a nap.

"If we change the vote, they will have to stop preaching these sermons."

"Undoing a unanimous vote that has stood for more than twenty years will not be easy." The second voice carried caution.

"My husband and I have given up talking about it, but I think it's time we began again. Surely some of the older men can do something."

The women drifted away with their hushed conversation. Clara caught Andrew's eye as he moved past in conversation with John Stutzman. Later, when they were alone, she would have to remember to thank him for choosing the hymn that had kept her calm.

Wanda's son lifted his head and rubbed his eyes. "Where's my *mamm*?"

Clara rearranged his shirt and straightened his suspenders, as she had done for Josiah when he was this age. With three young half siblings, she knew she could care for a child — or a half dozen. Mrs. Schrock was right. In her own home, Clara could tell as many Bible stories as she wished.

If only the thought of birthing a child did not terrify her.

The boy slid off Clara's lap, and she trailed him outside to be sure he found his mother.

During lunch, Clara moved between tables, sometimes listening to the conversation before her but just as often catching snippets of interchanges behind her or down the table.

342

"The bishop's sons will make sure nothing changes."

"Now is the time to ask for reasonable consideration."

"Pray for the bishop. Protect your heart from thinking ill."

"Mose Beachy should speak out more. It's his duty."

For the most part, Clara did not have to look around to know how opinions lined up. Those with a family relationship to the Yoders close enough to inspire loyalty tended more and more to band together. A few other families, headed by men who had known the bishop for decades, took their plates and sat with the Yoders and those who had married into the Yoders. The much larger group were church members with family scattered over the border between the Pennsylvania and Maryland districts.

Clara was grateful Andrew's connection to the Yoders was distant enough that he felt free to think for himself. She sponged up the last of the gravy on her plate with a final bite of biscuit and peeked at Rhoda. Mari was refusing to eat, Rhoda had barely touched her own food, and Hannah was nowhere in sight. All of this left Clara with the conclusion she had time for some fresh air before the Kuhns would be ready to depart and she would have to decide whether to go with them.

She was barely out of the clearing when two small forms popped out from behind a tree.

Clara gasped. "You startled me."

"We've been waiting and waiting," Priscilla Schrock said.

"We want a story," Lillian said.

A few yards farther away, Hannah and Naomi appeared.

"It doesn't have to be a long one like the sermons in church." Priscilla's features settled in the most earnest expression Clara had ever seen on a six-year-old. "God can speak to us in a short story."

Clara sighed. "I'm afraid we can't have a story today."

"I told you she would say that," Hannah said. "Next time you should believe me."

"Hannah's right," Clara said. "But you can have a lovely time playing together and enjoying your Sabbath."

Clara ignored the ring of dramatic scowls and hastened her stride. At the sound of steps crunching behind her, she turned to reiterate that there would be no story. But the girls were scampering in the other direction.

"Yonnie," Clara said.

"What did they mean about stories?" Yonnie's blocky form continued toward her.

"Never mind," she said. "It's nothing."

"It didn't sound like nothing."

Clara resumed walking. Yonnie kept pace. The last thing she needed was for Yonnie to get wind of the Bible stories she told the girls.

"You know the imagination children that age have." Clara rummaged around her mind for a change of subject. If she could manage something kind, perhaps the rift between Andrew and Yonnie would not seem as impassable as it had the last few weeks. "I heard talk that your father's crop is plentiful this year. I'm sure you had something to do with that. Everyone says you understand the soil."

"Our family works together," Yonnie said.

"We would all do well to follow your example."

"Better our example than others'."

Clara stifled a sigh. She pitied Yonnie Yoder. He had no notion of how smug he sounded.

"Andrew has too much joy in his automobile," Yonnie said. "It will be trouble."

"It doesn't have to be," Clara shot back, already chastising herself for being unable to sustain her good intention for more than eight seconds.

"No, it doesn't — if Andrew makes the right choice."

"What does that mean?"

"The bishop will not be in seclusion forever. If you are true to your faith, there are things you give up." Yonnie pivoted abruptly and reversed his direction.

Clara had always detested that particular Amish proverb. She balled her fists to keep herself from scooping up a handful of pebbles to throw at the back of Yonnie's head.

Her urge for a few minutes of fresh air matured into the resolution for a good long walk. If she did not turn up at the Kuhn buggy when Rhoda and Hiram were ready to leave, they would assume she had decided to go to the Singing and would find a way home later. Clara wanted to bolt for the meetinghouse, collect Andrew, and disappear with him. Instead, she bided her time by taking that long walk and ending up at the appointed barn for the Singing. Dutifully, she sat among the unmarried women and watched Andrew from across the barn. He sang with enthusiasm, his tenor piercing the gathering with its irresistible precise pitch.

The hymns passed, the evening ended,

and the moment Clara awaited all day arrived. She was alone with Andrew in his buggy.

"The hymn you started this morning convicted me," she said.

Let us keep our eyes on love!

How quickly she had failed her resolve that afternoon.

"It was for my own admonition," Andrew said. "Whatever others do, I hope I will remember its message better than I have. I owe Yonnie an apology."

"I talked to him today," Clara said. "I'm not sure he's of a mind to receive an apology."

"He always was the tattletale who would go running to our mothers before anyone could be properly sorry. As the saying goes, 'Some people are like buttons, popping off at the wrong time.' "

Two proverbs in one day, Clara thought. No matter how clever, traditional proverbs would not smooth the rough edges in the congregation.

Clara said, "In this case I think he's only waiting for the bishop to recover."

For a few moments, only the sluggish drop of horse hooves punctuated the silence.

"Don't worry about what Yonnie does," Andrew said. "I don't."

"He infuriates me."

"I know."

"Where can I find love in a puddle of infuriation?"

"Love must be the pond that swallows up the puddle. I'm going to apologize to Yonnie for my anger."

"It won't change his mind."

"That is not my purpose." Andrew took Clara's hand. "Let's talk about something else. I saw you with Wanda's boy today."

"I'm worried about Wanda. She had some pains. It's too soon for that."

"She's had two children already. She'll know if something's wrong."

"What if she realizes it too late?"

"What if nothing is wrong at all?" Andrew countered.

Clara sighed. "I always think the worst, don't I?"

"Not always. Only when it comes to babies."

"The heartbreak would be too much to bear," Clara whispered.

"Joy cometh in the morning," Andrew said. "You'll be a wonderful mother."

"If I ever find the courage."

"You will. When you do, I'll be right here."

She squeezed his hand but could not form a response.

"Why don't you go stay with Fannie for a few days?" he said. "It's been weeks since you saw her, which seems ridiculous for the sake of five miles."

"I don't know," Clara said. "I don't want to stir up trouble."

"You told me Fannie was discouraged."

"She is." The words of Fannie's letters flowed through Clara's mind. She read between the lines that Fannie's doldrums were not abating.

"I'll take you, and you can send a message when you want to come back," Andrew said.

"I'll think about it."

"Why wait?"

"I don't want you to get in trouble."

"I won't."

Clara rubbed the cuff of her sleeve between thumb and forefinger. "Perhaps, but I want to be back for the day of preparation."

"Of course."

She wouldn't even write to say she was coming. A surprise visit would cheer both Fannie and Sadie. And while she was gone, tensions in her own district might settle down.

"Can you take me on Saturday?"

Andrew squeezed her hand. "Keep your eyes on love."

CHAPTER 29

"The bishop is not seeing anyone."

Caroline Yoder did not raise her voice, but Yonnie had heard this tone before. He broadened his smile.

"I come with the prayers and good wishes of my entire family," Yonnie said, sliding one foot closer to the threshold Mrs. Yoder occupied.

She did not budge.

"Surely his withdrawal from appointments does not apply to visits from extended family." Yonnie did not budge, either.

"It applies to whomever I choose."

"Should not the bishop choose?"

"The bishop requires complete rest. When he is feeling better, I'm sure word will get around the district quickly enough and he will welcome visitors."

"Might I not come in and say a prayer for him?"

"God will hear you from your buggy."

At that moment, Yonnie was grateful he was related to the bishop — even if only distantly — and not to this woman who failed to even offer him a cup of coffee. He supposed that if he traced the family lines far enough back, he would find a connection to everyone in the district, but the Yoder name is what mattered.

"Everyone missed you both in church last Sunday," Yonnie said. The service was six days old now, yet there was no word of the bishop's improvement. "You'll be glad to hear your sons preached faithfully."

"That is their way." Mrs. Yoder wiped her hands on her apron. "If you will excuse me, I have a long list of tasks to fill the day."

Although Yonnie did not step back, Caroline closed the door firmly, barely clearing the end of his nose. Yonnie stood on the porch and shook his head. He could think of no one in the district who would not at least have offered a bit of refreshment to a visitor, even while holding firm on the matter of seclusion.

After waiting this long, a few more days would not matter.

Andrew's attempt at an apology had not changed Yonnie's mind. Andrew might be sorry that he lost his temper and embarrassed Yonnie at the dairy — as well he should be — but he showed no remorse about possessing the Model T. It was only a matter of time before the bishop would call on Andrew to confess his sin.

"I'm going to take Thomas outside to play," Sadie announced.

"Sadie, I don't think —" Fannie began.

Her sister-in-law broke in. "That's a lovely idea, Sadie. He loves to roll in the grass."

"We have *lots* of grass." Sadie took the hand of her toddler cousin.

"Perfect." Lizzie smiled at Sadie and then at Fannie. "Your mother and I will be right here in the kitchen if you need us."

Against her better judgment, Fannie resigned her opposition. "I'll pour the *kaffi.*"

"Thank you. The children will be fine."

"Sadie is only five." Fannie set out two cups. She glanced out into the yard, but already Sadie had taken the boy out of her line of sight.

"She has always been careful with him," Lizzie said. "It's your *mamm* I'm worried about today."

Fannie brought her gaze back indoors and fixed it on her brother's wife. "Is she unwell?"

"She'll never admit it," Lizzie said. "But I don't think she's well at all."

Fannie moved to the stove, turning her back as she gripped the coffeepot. "She's with child. It's not unusual to feel unwell. More rest would help, would it not?"

"She works too hard. There is no question of that. She claims she never let expecting a child interfere with her work before and that she's nowhere near her time."

Fannie poured the coffee, but she had already dismissed the idea of drinking any.

"She's right," Fannie said. "I never saw her slow down a day with any of the boys."

"She's not as young this time around," Lizzie said. "She won't listen to any of us. You must come and talk sense into her."

"What makes you think she would pay heed to me?" Fannie's stomach clenched.

"You're her only daughter."

"She couldn't be any more fond of you if she had birthed you. You are a true daughter." Fannie had heard Martha say this dozens of times since Abe married Lizzie.

"It's not the same." Lizzie leaned across the table and put a hand on Fannie's arm. "Outside of church, you haven't seen her for weeks. Elam comes to suppers without you. You don't bring Sadie for strudel in the mornings. Martha's heart is heavy for you."

Fannie's throat thickened.

"Why don't you come?" Lizzie said softly.

"You have always been close. She's your *mamm.*"

Escalating giggles outside the back door made Fannie turn her head. She was grateful for a fleeting excuse to glance away from Lizzie. Any month now Lizzie would break the news that Thomas was going to become a big brother, and Fannie wouldn't be able to look her brother's wife in the eye any more than she could look at her mother.

She moved to the sink and dumped her untouched coffee. "I'll try to go."

"Don't wait too long."

"I won't." Fannie gripped the edge of the sink in determination to believe her own words.

Lizzie stood. "I'd better get Thomas home for his nap. I could drop you off on my way."

"No," Fannie said. She gave a smile she did not mean. "There's no need to trouble yourself. I will come."

Fannie walked outside with Lizzie. Sadie protested being separated from Thomas so soon, and Fannie took her daughter's hand as a reminder of the behavior she expected. The girl's shoulders slumped but her objections ceased, and they watched Lizzie put Thomas in the buggy and signal the horse into motion.

"Can I stay outside to play?" Sadie asked.

355

Fannie inhaled and sighed. "Yes, I suppose so."

"Will you play with me?"

"I don't feel very playful just now."

"Then watch me play. Please?"

Fannie glanced toward an outdoor chair Elam had made for her during the summer she was expecting Sadie.

"All right," she said, "for a little while."

Sadie tumbled into the grass again. Fannie sat in the chair and lifted her face to the sun. In mid-September, the days were still full of summer but with the edge shaved off the heat.

"*Mamm,* you're not watching!"

Sadie's thin voice scolded, and Fannie opened her eyes. She would have anyway, because behind closed eyelids she saw her mother, heavy with child and refusing to slow down. Lizzie had put the image in the place where Fannie closed off her pain. If she could not retreat there, then where?

Sadie squealed and began to run along the side of the house. Fannie gasped and popped out of her chair.

Clara was walking toward them — with her small brown suitcase. Sadie took it from her, gripping the handle with both hands and leaning to one side to keep the bag from dragging in the dirt. In a moment, Clara's arms were around Fannie, and Fannie resolved that on this visit her cousin would not find her in the bed — or anywhere — unable to get up and make a meal.

Clara could not have ridden the milk wagon. The time wasn't right.

"You didn't walk, did you?" Fannie said.

Clara hesitated and then smiled. "Andrew Raber left me at the top of the lane. He'll be back Friday."

Six days together. Something soothed and brightened within Fannie. The smile creeping across her face took her by surprise.

"Andrew Raber," Fannie murmured. "He could have come down to the house for some refreshment."

Clara's face flushed.

"Sadie," Fannie said, "take Clara's bag to the spare bedroom. She's going to stay awhile."

"Good!" Sadie said. "She can visit my Sunday school class tomorrow."

Sadie lugged the suitcase into the house.

"You should visit the class," Fannie said. "Sadie loves it."

"I know it's a church Sunday for you," Clara said, "but I thought I would pass a quiet Sabbath on my own."

Fannie held the screen door open for Clara. "You haven't been to church here

357

since we were little. You might enjoy the changes. The new hymns have lovely four-part harmonies, and the stanzas are much shorter than you're used to."

Clara did not respond as she pulled a chair away from the table to sit down.

"I have a feeling we have a great deal to catch up on," Fannie said. "Your letters have not said much."

"Let me settle in," Clara said. "And Sadie will want some attention."

"Have you brought her any new stories?" Fannie took a plate of cookies from a cupboard and set it on the table.

Clara nodded. "I can't stop myself from writing them."

"And why should you?"

Clara sucked in her breath but said nothing.

"Sadie is going to insist you visit the class," Fannie said. "She'll pester you all night."

One side of Clara's mouth turned up. "I admit I'm curious what it would be like to see what a teacher does with a class of children talking about Bible stories."

"Then come to church. The Sunday school class is right after the shared meal, before everyone goes home."

"Maybe just for the class," Clara said.

"We won't bite."

"It might . . . complicate things."

Fannie munched a cookie. The class was a start. Clara could see for herself how well she would fit in with the Maryland church. Maybe on her next visit, she would come to worship.

Clara walked to the Maple Glen Meetinghouse the next afternoon, carefully calculating her arrival to coincide with the close of the meal. As soon as the last of the food was stowed away, Fannie had explained, classes for children met around the tables on one side of the meetinghouse, while adults quietly continued their visiting on the other side. Clara stepped inside the building — identical to the meetinghouses where she was accustomed to worship — and looked around.

"There's my cousin Clara." Sadie's voice rang out, and she wiggled off the bench where she sat with a cluster of little girls. Some were even younger than Sadie, but others were older.

The teacher followed Sadie toward Clara. "I'm Ellen Benton. I'm so glad you could visit our class."

"I won't be any disturbance," Clara said. "I only wanted to see what it is like."

Ellen grinned. "You help make my job quite pleasant."

"Me?"

"Your stories, silly," Sadie said. "I showed her the scrapbook."

"Oh!"

"The girls love them," Ellen said. "They bring the Bible to life in just the right ways. And what an inspiration! I've even begun to try my hand at it, although I have not the skill you have. We teach the boys separately from the girls, of course, but even the boys' teachers enjoy your stories."

Clara did not know what to say. She knew Sadie went to Sunday school, but it never crossed her mind that Sadie — or Fannie — would share Clara's stories with anyone else. Surely the teachers had their own plans or instructions from the ministers.

"We tell the stories so the children can understand them," Ellen said. "Then we work on learning High German so they can learn to read the Bible for themselves someday. The little ones practice picking out letters."

"I'll just have a seat over here and watch," Clara said.

"Wouldn't you like to tell a story?" Ellen said. "I was planning on Daniel and the lions' den."

Clara had first told a story to Priscilla, then to two girls, then to four. Thirteen heads now bobbed around the table. Daniel and the lions' den was one of the stories in the scrapbook. Clara had written and rewritten the words a half-dozen times before she was satisfied. The taste of them saturated her tongue.

"O taste and see that the Lord is good."

"Thank you for asking," Clara said, "but I'll watch and listen and learn right along with the girls."

She sat down on a bench a few feet away, where she could hear and see clearly. A moment later Fannie slid in next to her.

"Next time visit church," Fannie said. "You'll see."

"See what?" Clara said.

"You'll see."

CHAPTER 30

"I want to go see *Grossmuder!*"

Clara watched Sadie's bare foot lift and stomp, though her slight weight made little sound on the polished wood floor.

"We'll have to go another day," Fannie said, her eyes fixed on the mending in her lap.

"You always say that, but we never go. Isn't that a lie?"

Fannie looked up now. "Sadie Esh, you mind your tongue."

"Sorry," Sadie muttered. "But I still want to go see *Grossmuder.*"

"Let me take her," Clara said. "I've been here three days and haven't seen my favorite aunt."

Fannie poked a needle through a seam in one of Elam's shirts.

"I know it's not a good time for you to go." Clara chose her words with care. Sadie was standing right there. "But I want to see

362

Martha anyway. Sadie may as well come with me."

Fannie didn't look up. "All right."

Sadie shot out the front door. Clara nearly had to trot to keep up with her. Martha had strudel ready, as she had for as long as Clara could remember. When she was Sadie's age, she relished a visit to Martha's kitchen as much as Sadie did now.

"Where are my uncles?" Sadie swiped crumbs off her lips with the back of one hand.

"Doing barn chores," Martha said.

"I think they want some strudel," Sadie said.

"I think you may be right." Martha laid two pieces of strudel in a dish towel cut from a flour sack. Clara remembered when her aunt had stitched the blue-and-yellow border on it.

Sadie carried her offering carefully out the back door. Clara watched Martha's movements around the kitchen as she wrapped the remaining strudel in a flour sack and tucked it away in a cupboard. Her rosy complexion was absent, and she occasionally flinched with the movement of her left leg. They moved into the front room.

"I am so glad you came." Martha finally allowed herself to sit. "When we heard about the kinds of sermons your ministers have been preaching, we wondered what would happen. For a few days, it was like what happened to your mother all over again."

"What do you mean?" Clara leaned forward in her chair.

"You were little — about Thomas's age — when Bishop Yoder first became stern about the ban. Catherine and I were determined to see each other. She didn't vote for the *meidung,* you know."

"But it was a unanimous vote."

"Not exactly." Martha put a hand on her back and winced.

"Are you all right?" Clara thought Martha looked inordinately tired even for a woman with child.

"I'll be all right." Martha blew breath slowly. "Catherine was close to her time. I was her sister. Of course she wanted me to come. As soon as the message arrived that she was laboring, I went."

Clara swallowed. She had been too little to remember the night her mother birthed a baby who never drew breath.

"She held my hand the whole time." Martha's gaze found a distant point out the window. "The baby took too long. Catherine was exhausted, but she never let go of my

364

hand. Not until . . ."

Clara's breath stilled against her will. She knew the story. Martha had told it more than once. Catherine bled too much too fast. The baby was gone and then Catherine as well. That was the moment when her grip on Martha's hand slackened. Story and vague memories of a toddler swirled in Clara's mind, leaving her once again uncertain of the difference between what she remembered from that day and the bits of information she had acquired over the years.

Martha's breathing sounded heavy to Clara.

"Are you sure you feel all right?" she asked.

"Perfectly fit. I'm just having a baby, and I miss my sister at a time like this." Martha sighed. "And my daughter."

They dawdled through lunch, which Clara insisted on helping to prepare. The three Hostetler sons still living on their parents' farm alternated between teasing and adoring Sadie. When the meal was over, Sadie announced she was going to help wash dishes and pushed a kitchen chair up to the sink. Clara and Martha worked on either side of the girl, both encouraging and inspecting her efforts.

"Time to go, Sadie." Clara hung the damp

dish towel over the back of a chair.

"Not yet!"

"Your *grossmuder* needs to rest." Clara glanced at her aunt over Sadie's head and was relieved to see no resistance in Martha's features.

"Come give me a kiss," Martha said to Sadie.

Sadie leaned into her grandmother. "The *boppli* is getting big!"

Martha took Sadie's hand and laid it on her belly.

A few seconds later Sadie gasped. "What is that?"

"The babe is kicking."

"Is it trying to get out?"

"Not just yet."

"Wait until I tell *Mamm* the baby kicked me."

Clara pressed her lips together to keep from grimacing. Sadie chattering about the active baby would do nothing for Fannie's fallen spirits.

"Let's go, then," Clara said. She kissed Martha good-bye and promised not to wait so long before visiting again.

Sadie, who had practically run the entire distance that morning, now dragged her feet about going home. Clara kept up a brisk pace, pausing periodically for Sadie to catch up. She would see the child home, but she would not so much as drink a glass of water before setting out again.

"Aren't you coming in?" Fannie asked when Clara nudged Sadie through the front door.

"I have an errand," Clara said. "Does the midwife still live on the other side of the pond?"

"Midwife?" Fannie startled. "Surely not yet."

"How often is your mother seeing the midwife?"

"She's weeks away from her time."

"Fannie, your *mamm* is having a harder go than she admits."

"That's what Lizzie said." Fannie glanced at Sadie, who picked up her faceless rag doll from the chair she insisted was the doll's bed. "She scolded me for not visiting more."

"I can see her point."

"Not you, too, Clara!"

Clara pulled on one *kapp* string. "I know it's difficult for you."

"No one understands," Fannie said. "I don't know a single other woman who is watching her mother have the baby that should have been hers. Only me!"

They stood on either side of the threshold, matching eyes inherited from their mothers fixed on each other. Clara's heart thudded against her ribs. Only a few months ago she could not have imagined anything would separate Martha and Fannie. Their intimacy had always made her miss the mother she did not know — it still did. Clara never expected to stand between them aching for them both.

"She misses you," Clara whispered finally.

"I know." Fannie looked down at her skirt, her voice viscous and constrained. "But I can't help her right now. I just can't."

Clara nodded, a knot rising in her throat. "I'll go see the midwife."

Fannie stepped back and closed the door, pressing it softly into its frame while Clara exhaled grief.

Clara visited Martha again before she went home on the following Friday and had a word with her cousins. The boys were twelve, fifteen, and seventeen — old enough not to take their mother for granted, old enough to notice how tired she was, old enough to take over some of Martha's chores without being asked.

Now more than two weeks had passed. Every day that no urgent message came from Garrett County allowed Clara to breathe another day's relief that her aunt was probably fine. She wished she could know for sure that the midwife had been to see Martha.

Sitting in the Flag Run Meetinghouse in Somerset County for the first service in October, Clara pondered the fine line between calling and regret. Her reason for not going to the worship service with Fannie's family at the Maple Glen Meetinghouse in Garrett County was that the repercussions might usher in regret. The decision was hardly an act of submission to the church. Keeping herself from a progressive church service might qualify as outward obedience — which was what people like Yonnie concerned themselves with — but it certainly was not a humble offering of her spirit to God.

The Maryland congregation would have no worship service today, but many of them would restore their souls with Sabbath visiting. Fannie *ought* to visit her mother, but *ought* and *could* were not the same thing. Clara prayed Fannie would not be mired in regret so impenetrable that turning back would be as impossible as flying to the moon.

For the first time in her life, Clara wished she could pick up an *English* telephone and tell the operator she wanted to talk to her aunt.

None of this had anything to do with the Sunday morning church service of the Pennsylvania congregation. Clara readjusted her posture, laid her clasped hands in her lap, and gave her attention to the sermon.

Clara saw no sign of Bishop or Mrs. Yoder, though one of their sons who lived in Missouri was present. She had not seen him in years. If he was home because of his father's illness, it must be serious. Joseph Yoder concluded his sermon and suggested a hymn. Noah stood for his sermon. Sometimes Clara wondered if Mose Beachy even participated in casting lots for the sermon. What else would explain why it so seldom fell to him?

After the final hymn, Noah stepped forward again.

"We have the glad news of publishing several engagements," he said.

Clara glanced at Andrew. Noah named three couples, including Ruth Kaufman and Peter Troyer. As one by one, the brides' fathers stood and issued invitations for the congregation to attend the weddings, Clara kept her eyes in her lap. She did not want to know how many eyes might be on her — including Rhoda's — wondering if yet another harvest season would pass with no wedding celebration at the Kuhn home. While she plotted how to politely slip from the meetinghouse, at least long enough for immediate stares to wear off, Joseph stood again beside the preacher's unvarnished table. At the sound of his shuffling feet, Clara tilted her head to one side, a necessity rising from her recent habit of sitting in the rear of the meetinghouse.

Joseph unfolded a sheet of paper. "I have a letter from my father to read to you."

A wave of shifting posture rolled through the meetinghouse.

" 'My beloved church,' " Joseph read. " 'As you know I have been unwell for some time. While I have faith in our Lord for my recovery, I know I am becoming older. My family encourages me to ease my load. Serving as your humble bishop all these years has brought me great joy. Now it is time that I find a new service. In obedience to God, I resign as your bishop effective October 1. May we continue together in our devotion to Jesus Christ. Humbly yours, Moses Yoder.' "

October 1. Today!

Joseph folded the paper. "The hymnals have been prepared by my father himself. Following communion this afternoon, the ministers will prayerfully choose a hymnal and discover the slip of paper that reveals the will of God."

Andrew ate little, just a slice of bread and a few beets. He watched Clara make the rounds pouring black coffee, but he did not see her sit down to eat.

Andrew's mind jumped back and forth between the careful words of the letter Joseph read and his own conversation with the bishop in the Yoder kitchen. The bishop could not have written that letter on his own. Caroline had probably insisted on the resignation.

The meal lacked the usual leisurely socializing. A baby wailed. Andrew didn't turn his head to see whose it was, instead watching the ministers. After eating together, they now stood, a signal that benches should once again be arranged for a worship service.

The fall communion service began. As the bread and wine were served, guilt pinged Andrew. This was a solemn ritual that occurred only twice a year, yet his mind was fixed on the procedure that would follow. He could read nothing on the faces of the three ministers. When his turn came, Andrew knelt to eat the bread and drink the wine and prayed that Christ's love would find a home in his heart. Though the congregation took communion seriously, it seemed to Andrew that the stillness and attentiveness around him was due to more than the somber service.

Finally the ministers returned to their bench in the front, facing the congregation. On the preacher's table were three hymnals. Each one showed the tattered wear of decades of service to the congregation. All were tied with identical string, making it impossible to discern which one held a slip of paper with a verse written on it.

Joseph Yoder was first to select a hymnal. Noah laid a hand on one of the remaining two and then changed his mind and picked up the other. Mose's task was simple. He had only to lift the last hymnal from the table.

Andrew still saw nothing in their expressions. No eagerness. No anxiety. The work of a bishop was consuming. Andrew did not envy any of them the task. *Gottes wille.* God would choose the next bishop.

One by one the ministers began untying the strings. Then together they flipped the pages of the hymnals in search of the slip of paper. Joseph reached the end of his hymnal and began shuffling pages in the other direction, consternation creeping across his face.

Andrew's heart rate kicked up, and involuntarily he peeled himself away from the back of the bench.

Noah was slower, more methodical. But he found no paper, either. The brothers maintained solemn expressions but audibly shifted their weight on the bench.

Andrew watched Mose Beachy's face and saw the instant Mose moved his eyes to the spot where his wife sat with their daughters.

A fraction of a second later, Lucy Beachy failed to contain the cry rising through her throat.

The lot had fallen to her mild-mannered, peace-loving husband. Mose laid the hymnal open across his knees and lifted the slip of paper tucked against the binding at the center of the volume.

Andrew gripped the back of the bench in front of him. Mose stood up beside the preacher's table.

"God has chosen me for your new bishop."

Chapter 31

Seventeen days.

For seventeen days the district buzzed with speculation. Everywhere Clara turned — in Niverton or Springs for the shops, walking through the farms as harvesting teams rolled from one to the other, visiting neighbors on the Sabbath between services or after the worship services — conversation turned to how Mose Beachy would be a different sort of bishop than Moses Yoder had been.

Reports circulated that Bishop Yoder was not as ill as he had been, but he still did not leave his farm. His sons and grandsons were bringing in his harvest. His wife, accounts said, would not allow him to return to church before he was fully recovered.

"I'm not sure he will recover," Andrew said when Clara recounted a conversation.

"Are you a doctor now?" Clara teased.

Andrew polished a headlight on the

Model T. "Mrs. Yoder was right to make him step down."

"That's what you think happened?"

Andrew shrugged.

"How is it you're not working the harvest today?"

"Mose is generous with his thresher. He's loaned it out. When he gets it back, we'll help John Stutzman for the next few days, and then it's my turn."

"That's just like Mose. What would everyone do without his thresher?"

"He's skilled enough with the machinery to keep it operating."

"Like you." Clara met Andrew's eyes and smiled.

"Shall we go for a ride?" Andrew's eyes twinkled.

Clara grinned. "Are you feeling more daring now that Mose Beachy is bishop?"

He tilted his head and opened the door for her. "She's running beautifully these days."

"Is Jurgen Hansen still offering to buy?"

"Every time I see him — which is not as often now that she's fixed up."

They drove into the sunshine, still warm enough to keep the top down. Clara wondered whether being inside a car with the top up would feel much different than riding enclosed in a buggy. For now she closed her eyes and leaned her head back against the diamond tufted upholstery, relishing the breeze prickling her face as the car rumbled along a back road that had become Andrew's favorite.

She sat up abruptly. "What was that noise?"

"The knocking?" Andrew said. "She just needs a slight adjustment." He pulled over, and they stepped out into a vibrant medley of autumn hues.

"It's glorious here," Clara said, stretching out her arms and spinning in a slow circle. "They're the same trees any of the farms around here have, but somehow I never notice them at home."

"No fields to interrupt them." Andrew took a wrench out of a small toolbox he kept in the automobile now and opened the hood. "No one pays attention to this road. The Amish don't come out here."

"Do you really think Mose will change things?" Clara said.

"If he doesn't, things will change themselves." Andrew leaned over the engine and made a quick adjustment before handing the tool to Clara.

"What am I supposed to do with this?"

He grinned. "Think of me while you hold it."

Clara thought of Andrew most of the time, but she couldn't say so aloud. He would only propose again, and she had no answer for him — at least not the one he wanted. Her aunt's pale face drifted into her mind, brooding in shadow. Clara wondered again whether the midwife was watching Martha closely enough. She pushed away the thought of what might happen to Martha or the baby — or Fannie, who would never forgive herself for not reconciling with her mother if the worst came to be. Clara squeezed her eyes closed, trying to picture Martha, rosy and healthy, with a baby in her arms and swathed in lemony dawn light. But the colors collided. Rather than airy and illuminating, they were gray and dense and spinning in a certainty Clara wanted to scream against. If loss struck the Hostetler house, Clara was not certain she could ever bring herself to consider marriage again. She could never be as brave as Martha.

Clara blew out her breath.

"What's wrong?" Andrew said, taking the wrench.

"I need to visit Fannie again."

"We could take the car."

"Perhaps that is *too* daring — at least until

we know what Mose would say."

"There is nothing in *Ordnung* about automobiles," he reminded her.

Whatever adjustment Andrew made cured the rattle. He needed both hands to drive, but Clara slipped a palm into the crook of his elbow.

Later, she wandered home drenched in contentment. The sight of a visiting buggy parked along the fence piqued her curiosity. Striding up the lane, she realized the horse belonged to the Schrocks. Inside the house, Clara found Rhoda setting a plate of cookies on the dining room table, where the Schrocks and her father sat. Hannah and Priscilla snatched cookies and scampered out of the room, tugging Mari by the hands.

"The Schrocks have some news," Hiram said. "Since we're their closest neighbors, they have come to us first."

Rhoda's jaw was set and her eyes more interested in the stitching of the tablecloth than her guests' faces.

"Is everything all right?" Clara said.

Caleb Schrock cleared his throat. "We've decided to join the Marylanders."

Heat raced through Clara's chest. "That *is* news."

"It seems that it is partly because of you." Rhoda's voice snapped.

379

"Me?" Clara fingered a *kapp* string.

"I explained how you comforted Priscilla with a Bible story," Mattie Schrock said.

Clara felt her skull squeezing. "She was frightened."

"You gave her a new attitude about her chore to feed the pigs. We can't believe the difference. I was wrong when I said you shouldn't be telling Bible stories to someone else's child."

Clara looked into her neighbor's eyes and found there assurance that she had said nothing about the other stories, or the fact that Rhoda's daughter was part of the group who heard them.

"Of course we read the Bible in our family devotions," Caleb said. "I try to explain things in a way the children can understand, but they need to hear more."

"We've talked about this a great deal," Mattie said. "This is not a hasty decision. A farm came up for sale in Maryland a few weeks ago, and recently we decided to buy it. We just signed the papers."

"But there is a Marylander church in Springs," Clara said. "Why do you not join that congregation?" Although the Pennsylvania district primarily was Old Order, there were Marylanders on this side of the border. Selling one farm and moving to another only a few miles away seemed like an extreme measure to Clara.

"We're moving for the children," Caleb said. "If we live in the Conservative Amish Mennonite district, it will be less confusing for them as they grow up."

"When?" Clara asked, a knot forming in her throat.

"Tomorrow."

"We think the Sunday school in the Amish Mennonite Church will be good for Priscilla," Mattie said. "She can go to Sunday school with your Sadie now."

Clara drew in a deep breath to offset the gasp she heard from Rhoda.

"Hannah talks about Sadie," Mattie said.

"They've never met," Rhoda said.

"Still, Priscilla is curious," Mattie said. "Whether Old Order or Amish Mennonite, we are all Amish."

"But the *meidung*," Clara said.

Mattie laced her fingers together and set her hands on the table. "We understand that some will feel they must shun us. That is another reason why it will be better for the children if we live in Maryland, among the people we will worship with."

Clara wanted to scream in objection. Instead she looked at her father and Rhoda, unsure what stance they would take. They had no family connection to the Schrocks, no intermingling business, no reason to justify continuing social contact with them.

"The new bishop will have something to say, will he not?" Clara said.

"Mose Beachy is a good man," Caleb said. "I admire him a great deal. He seeks peace, and I pray it will come. But we feel we must be true to our conscience in the way we express our faith."

Clara could hardly try to argue the Schrocks out of the decision. They had already purchased the new farm.

"Does Priscilla know?" Clara said.

"She is excited about Sunday school." Mattie's smile was tentative.

What about Hannah? Clara thought. Would Rhoda set aside the ban for the sake of her daughter's friendship?

Seventeen days since Mose became bishop. Andrew was right. No matter what Mose did or did not do, the church would change.

Relieved, Fannie let herself in the back door. The invitation for Sadie to play on the next farm over could not have been more welcome. Elam was sorting out the fields after harvesting the corn and would not be anywhere near the house for several hours.

Fannie moved through the rooms shuttering the daylight out before crawling onto the davenport and cradling a throw pillow against her waist. If only a child would grow there. If only her waist would thicken with new hope.

Fannie closed her eyes. With enough practice over the last few months, she required fewer and fewer minutes to successfully retreat into sleep, her only escape.

When her eyes popped open, it was at the prodding of an insistent voice standing over her.

"You can pretend you're not here," Martha said, "but you'll also have to be like the *English* and lock your doors."

"I didn't hear you," Fannie said truthfully, pushing herself upright. "I must have dropped off."

"I stood on the porch knocking for a long time," her mother said. "I've never known you to sleep through the kind of ruckus I was making."

"I'm sorry." Fannie stared into her mother's midsection. How was it possible she was this large?

"Do you feel unwell?" One hand on her belly, Martha lowered herself beside her daughter.

Fannie scooted over a few inches, uncertain how to answer her mother's question. She had no headache, no stomachache, no dizziness, no nausea, no fever.

But no, she did not feel well.

"Do you want *kaffi*?" Fannie stood up, her eyes fixed on her mother, who seemed to have gained more weight than she had with her last three babes put together. Perhaps she had miscalculated and was closer to her time than any of them realized.

"No, thank you," Martha said.

"Something cold, then?" Fannie's brain refused to clear. She glanced at the clock. Barely thirty minutes had passed since she fell asleep, yet her body felt like a millstone dropping in a river. Even in the presence of her mother — or especially so — sleep beckoned.

"Fannie, I have not come to be entertained. I want to talk."

"I have a dozen things to do. I don't get much time without Sadie underfoot."

"You were sound asleep," Martha pointed out.

"I didn't mean to be." It was a half truth.

"It's not like you."

"Are you sure you don't want *kaffi*? I'm going to have some."

Martha grabbed Fannie's hand, pulling

her back. "I had no idea things were this bad."

"What do you mean?"

"I don't see you except at church. Lizzie said you didn't look well. Then Clara came to visit without you."

"She was anxious to see how you were doing."

"And you weren't."

Fannie reclaimed her hand. "I really need some *kaffi.*"

"You only drink it to be polite."

"Lately I've taken it up with more enthusiasm."

Martha braced her arms behind her and pushed herself up, abdomen first. "Then I'll come with you."

"You must have better things to do than watch me drink *kaffi.*"

Martha touched her daughter's face. "I have nothing better to do than talk to you. I didn't know Sadie wouldn't be here, but perhaps it is God's will that we have this time without interruption."

Fannie took a step back.

"You're avoiding me," Martha said. "You won't come to me, so I've come to you. I want my daughter back."

Fannie said nothing.

"We've never had anything between us,"

Martha said. "Why must this baby separate us?"

"The baby is innocent," Fannie said.

"Then I am to blame?" Martha said. "How can you think I would want to hurt you?"

Fannie swallowed. "You wouldn't."

"Then whose fault is it that I conceived and you did not?"

If her mother said *Gottes wille,* Fannie thought she might scream. What good was prayer if God's will made no sense?

"This child deserves love," Martha said.

"Love will not be lacking," Fannie said.

"This child deserves *your* love, just as much as any of your brothers did. Sadie is excited about a baby *aunti* or *onkel.* She needs to see you excited, too."

"I'm Sadie's mother. I will decide what she needs."

Never had Fannie spoken to her mother with stinging words, but she could not stop herself.

"This is *your* baby sister or brother," Martha said. "I will decide what my child needs, and my child needs *you.* "

Fannie turned away, not under the guise of making coffee but only to escape her mother's scrutiny.

Martha lumbered around Fannie and

grabbed her by both shoulders, pulling her in and wrapping arms around her. "And *you* are my child. I will not watch your pain and do nothing."

Fannie tried to lean away, but Martha did not let go. Her embrace tightened the same way it used to when Fannie was young and tempestuous, annoyed by one of her little brothers or wounded by a friend's remark. Her mother would hold on indefinitely.

Fannie felt the child physically between them, her mother's womb firm and round. Martha stroked the back of Fannie's head. A sob welled up and burst out of Fannie's throat.

CHAPTER 32

Andrew walked up the path to his mailbox and extracted the stack. The latest issue of *The Sugarcreek Budget* came to him courtesy of the subscription his mother launched years ago when she lived at this address, and for which she still paid the annual fee. An advertisement for seeds and farm equipment came simply because the Rabers were farmers, not because either Andrew or his father had ever purchased from the company. Sandwiched between these two items was the envelope Andrew was genuinely interested in, a letter from his mother. Tucking the larger items under one arm, Andrew broke the seal on the flap and removed the familiar folded pages in his mother's meticulous handwriting and began to read as he walked.

Dear Andrew,

We've heard the news about your new bishop, though we are eager to hear your perspective on what this means for the church in Somerset County. Several here in Lancaster have received letters from family and friends in Somerset. I'm sure I don't need to tell you that a coin has two sides. Some write to applaud Mose Beachy because they are certain that he will at long last set aside rules that, in their opinion, have done nothing but cause unclarity and division for all the years that Bishop Yoder was in office. Others, naturally, write with downcast hearts that one of the Yoder boys was not selected. But of course who can dispute the will of God? If God selected Mose Beachy, He must have a plan for the church.

I hope that in all the fracas you will see your way clear to let your conscience guide you. In circumstances like these, your father and I have always recognized how simple it is to do what causes the least disturbance. That is, in fact, the reason we moved to Lancaster once your brothers and sisters were married and settled.

You are old enough to remember

389

something of 1895, or at least 1905, though perhaps you did not perceive the depth of people's confusion. Whether he intended to or not, Bishop Yoder misled the congregation in the original vote about the *meidung.* When the truth came out ten years later, no one was certain how to correct the matter. Someone would have had to state before a communion service that they did not agree with the teaching regarding shunning, and of course to do so would mean that communion would not occur. Who among us wants to be responsible for withholding the body and blood of Christ from the rest of the congregation?

To this end, your father and I decided we would rather move to Lancaster. After all, we have family here. If we could not submit to the bishop, it seemed best to remove ourselves. We had no desire to be a stumbling block to anyone else. Perhaps if someone — even we — had mustered the courage to bring the issue to a new vote, the harm could have been undone long ago and Somerset would not be in crisis now. Alas, we did not. I hope we have not contributed to any discomfort you may be experiencing now.

Mose has never agreed with the shunning. Of this I am certain. But he believed that if the congregation endured all these years, then let it continue to do so. If the letters arriving in Lancaster are any indication, I doubt he can sustain this position much longer. Hearing the news across the miles, it seems to me that Somerset is going to split after all, and perhaps this would not be an entirely unwelcome event.

My prayers are with you, my son. If I had spoken plainly before moving away, I doubt it would have made a difference. You were so eager to have a go at running the farm on your own! And your father had every confidence that your temperament would both bring you success and allow you a peaceable existence in the church where you grew up.

I trust your harvest was satisfactory and will prove profitable. Do let us know the results once your crops have come in and the funds have been sorted out.

With love,
Your mamm

Andrew read the letter again once he was inside the house and in a comfortable chair. When his parents moved away and left him to run the farm, he did not ask more than a few questions.

"Are you sure?"

"Wouldn't you rather sell the farm to someone who can pay what it's worth?"

The truth was, he was eager to run the farm. Now, he realized, the advantage blinded him. And now the congregation had once again been complicit in upholding the ban. Though many disagreed, no one would speak up. No one would be the dissenting voice that deprived the congregation of communion.

Andrew moved to the desk his father had crafted twenty years ago and took a sheet of paper from the drawer.

Dear *Mamm,*

Thank you for speaking with directness about what prompted you to withdraw to Lancaster. Someday, when we have a good visit, perhaps you will tell me more.

I think you are right about Mose Beachy's position. It seems to me that people have gone along with the rule for these twenty years out of respect for the office Bishop Yoder held and the conviction that God chooses the bishop. But if this is true, would it not also be so for

Bishop Beachy? Perhaps God has raised our brother up for such a time as this.

I do feel that since Bishop Yoder has resigned, people may feel less obligated to defer to his opinions without discussion. If the question of officially removing the ban were put to a vote, I would be surprised if it failed, though there may be some who support it because of tradition more than conviction. Of course Noah and Joseph Yoder would argue for sustaining the ban. The Yoders are nothing if not loyal.

I know that Mose Beachy's father was in favor of the ban, but Mose has a mind of his own. I suppose we will see if he has the strength to express it. You may be right about a split. I pray that it would be as amicable as the decision in 1877 was meant to be when this journey began.

Yours,
Andrew

If Joseph or Noah had become bishop, Yonnie would have known what to do. Even if the *Ordnung* by which church members lived their daily lives did not mention automobiles, everyone knew how the Yoders felt about the *English* contraptions. If

Andrew's owning the Model T was not already against the rules, the Yoders would have made an example of Andrew and the resulting rule would be clear. Joseph and Noah were still ministers. They were not without influence, and the two of them would stand together.

But Mose Beachy? Who could say how he would respond?

Yonnie chewed on this conundrum as he made his dairy rounds on Thursday.

Passing Mose's farm — not one of his stops because as a family of sixteen the Beachys consumed everything their cows produced — Yonnie recognized the distinctive white stripe in a horse's tail waving like a flag. It was Noah's horse.

If Noah was at Mose's home, Joseph likely was as well. The three of them would have many subjects to discuss. Ministers had meetings all the time.

Yonnie slowed the wagon, stopped for a moment, and then pulled to the side of the road where he could tie his own horse to a tree. He scanned the farmstead, with the house and barn dominating the assortment of outbuildings. Would the ministers meet in the new bishop's home, with his wife and children within earshot, or would they look for a more private spot? Yonnie decided to aim for Noah's rig.

As he moved alongside the house with its covered front porch, Yonnie heard voices, a blend of children too young to attend Crossroads School vying for their mother's attention. A young man, probably fourteen and in his first year out of school, intoned caution, and the rumpus subsided. Lucy Beachy's calm assurance was muffled, but the children seemed satisfied. Yonnie saw no one outside and paced toward the enormous barn.

Noah's horse turned his head and swished his flag of a tail in acknowledgment of Yonnie's presence, but he made no sound. To one side, a half-dozen hogs snorted and rummaged, oblivious to the impending fall slaughter. A hen fluttered her wings and brushed past Yonnie, whose ears focused on the drifting sound of male voices. Glancing over his shoulder again, Yonnie approached the equipment shed.

"Would you not agree," Noah Yoder said, "that it is important for all the ministers to be of one mind?"

Yonnie paused outside the open door, out of sight.

"I have been bishop less than three weeks," Mose said. "I pray each day for God's will to be clear to me."

"We cannot continue preaching our message but turning our heads from the violations we are certain of." Joseph's pitch raised in emphasis.

No one spoke for a few moments. Yonnie heard the clink of metal against metal. Mose must have been adjusting the thresher so many of the Amish farms depended on.

"Perhaps," Mose finally said, "we should agree to a period of time during which we will open our hearts to the Lord for this new season in the church."

"A church does not have a new season," Noah said. "Our responsibility is to preserve the faith as it was given to us."

Joseph spoke. "Your own father was in agreement with ours. They both signed a letter objecting to the lax enforcement of shunning."

"That was a long time ago," Mose said. "We were all boys. Now we need to examine our own consciences. The original separation of the Marylanders was peaceful. Why do we continue to fight against peace?"

"Would you have all our people join the Marylanders?"

"I would have them follow their consciences."

"They have vowed to be obedient to the church."

"And Christ is the head of the church," Mose said.

"We have *Ordnung* for our own good," Noah said. "We protect the salvation of the church members when we hold them accountable."

"Jesus said the Sabbath was made for man," Mose retorted, "and not man for the Sabbath."

"I suppose you would claim freedom to drive cars or use telephones like the *English* in the name of conscience."

Yonnie stilled his breath for the response.

"It seems to me," Mose said, "that it has always been our way for the congregation to consider such questions together. All the members may vote. Perhaps we should also vote on the *meidung* again."

Joseph's sigh could have filled a milk jug. "I see that we will need many conversations."

"That may be so. Right now, I have promised to take my thresher out to the Troyer farm so he will have it first thing in the morning."

Yonnie moved around the side of the shed and watched as the Yoders, reluctantly, climbed into Noah's buggy and turned the horse toward the road.

"Yonnie, you can come out now," Mose said.

Yonnie pressed himself against the structure.

"I know you're there. I can still see your shadow."

Yonnie exhaled and stepped into view.

"Did you get the answer you were seeking?" Mose asked.

"I don't know what you mean," Yonnie said.

"Do not cultivate dishonesty."

Yonnie licked his lips but said nothing.

"I did not ask to become bishop," Mose said. "God chose me, and I will serve faithfully as God gives me strength. I know people are watching me and wondering if there will be change. But you have come to my farm and hidden yourself for your own purposes. That is deceit, is it not?"

Embarrassment flowed in Yonnie's blood.

"Did you want to speak openly to me about a matter?" Mose said.

After what he'd overheard, Yonnie would say nothing to Mose about Andrew's car or Dale and Clara's interaction with the Marylanders.

"I must finish my rounds," Yonnie said.

Mose nodded. "That's a good idea."

CHAPTER 33

From the barn at midday on Saturday, Clara heard Rhoda instructing the girls just outside the door as they selected the chicken that would be the center of the evening meal. She unlatched the stall where one of the Kuhn milk cows stood. At the end of October, the nights were cool and the days no longer steamy and dripping with humidity, but there was no reason to keep the animals indoors. One cow was already in the pasture, and Clara slipped a rope around a second's neck and led it out into the daylight. This particular cow had never moved quickly a day in her life. Clara had long ago resigned herself to letting the animal set the pace when they went back and forth between barn and pasture.

She removed the lead, knowing the cow would immediately begin to nuzzle the ground. Clara draped the rope around a fence post and turned around to see a buggy approaching. The horse was unfamiliar, and she shaded her eyes to more clearly see who was driving.

An arm waved out one side, and a second later a face leaned out.

Andrew's face. Clara walked across the farmyard to greet the visitors. John Stutzman halted the buggy.

"Feel like an outing?" Andrew asked.

"What do you have in mind?" Clara said, though she was likely to agree to whatever Andrew suggested.

John leaned forward to look past Andrew and catch Clara's eye. "We're going to see the Schrocks' new farm. Then we could stop at your cousin's, if you like."

"I would love to," Clara said.

Andrew dropped off the bench to properly assist Clara into the buggy.

"Do you need to let someone know you're leaving?" John glanced toward the house.

"Will I be home for supper?" Clara said. Rhoda and the girls had retreated into the house with the unlucky hen.

"Long before, I would imagine."

"Then no need." Clara settled between John and Andrew.

John took the horse at an enthusiastic clip. Clara watched the landmarks of the familiar route go past — the half-painted barn, the oak tree split by lightning years ago, the trim *English* flower garden that always made her wish she could wander in and lean over to smell the fragrance of every kind of flower in sight.

Another buggy came toward them.

"That's Noah Yoder's rig," Andrew said. "The horse's tail gives him away."

"We'll wave and go on by," John said.

But Noah gradually moved his buggy toward the center of the road, making it impossible to go past unimpeded.

"Good afternoon." Joseph Yoder sat beside his brother.

"Good afternoon," John said.

"Nice day for a drive." Joseph eyed the trio.

"That it is," Andrew said.

Clara intended to say nothing.

"Heading south, I see," Noah said.

"That's right," John said.

"Be careful your horse doesn't step in the pothole about a quarter of a mile down."

"Danki."

"Are you visiting one of the Old Order families in Maryland?" Joseph said.

Clara moistened her lips.

"Friends," Andrew said. There was no untruth in the response.

Joseph settled his gaze on Andrew for a

long silence.

"May God bless your day," John said. "If you might take your horse to the side, we'll be on our way."

Noah made no move to signal the horse. "Perhaps we could add our greetings to the ones you carry," he said. "May I ask which friends you are visiting?"

"We will be sure to let them know you said hello." John eyed the road. Clara could see him calculating whether there was enough room to bypass the Yoder buggy after all.

Still Noah held the center of the road. Only when John's buggy came within inches of Noah's horse, causing the animal to snort and try to back up, did Noah lift the reins. John navigated past and let his mare have her head for a few yards.

Clara gripped the bench with both hands. "Surely it has not come to this."

Andrew's jaw set. "Don't let them bother you."

"It's as if they think themselves the *English* police trying to catch a criminal," Clara said. "We are not criminals. We should tell Mose."

"Tell him what?" John said. "That the Yoders greeted us in the road to remark that it was a nice day and warn us of a pothole?"

"They did more than that," Clara said.

"They said nothing objectionable."

"My objection is not to their words."

Andrew covered her hand with his. "Don't let it spoil the day."

"I hear the Schrocks have more tillable acres on their new farm," John said.

"And it's closer to the river," Andrew said.

Clara saw what they meant to do. They could make cheerful distracting comments for the next five miles and it would not change the fact that the Yoders thought themselves superior. Did they disagree with God's choice of Mose Beachy for bishop? Maybe the Schrocks were right to join the Marylanders and even to move away from their former district.

Andrew squeezed her hand, and she squeezed back.

Eventually John slowed, looking for a road. "Does this seem right?"

Andrew craned his neck from side to side. "Three oaks on the corner. That's what he said."

They took the turn and traveled another quiet mile. When the farm came into view, Clara smiled. It was a beautiful setting, the house painted white and trimmed in dark green with a bright red barn and a rolling front yard. The Schrock children chased each other through the grass, their gleeful shrieks ringing across the farm.

Priscilla stopped and watched the buggy lumber toward the house. Finally a smile of recognition cracked her face, and Clara could not help but grin back.

Fannie had not withdrawn to the darkness of sleep for two days. She doubted anyone could understand the triumph, so she kept her self-congratulations silent. Melancholy was not wholly unfamiliar. Fannie had read about the subject and had known a person or two she might have described as having the melancholy, but she never expected to see its drab gray walls from the inside of her own mind or to watch the hands creep around the clock until it was legitimately time to bring the bedding up to her neck and sink into black release.

Elam was in the brightest mood Fannie had observed in months. His harvest was in. Neither insects nor weather had caused great harm this season, and the price the broker quoted would carry them nicely through the winter and into the spring planting.

Fannie, too, had reason to feel grateful. The family's vegetable garden had nurtured them well through the summer and fall, with bounty enough also for canning and stocking the cellar. Though Fannie didn't actually *feel* grateful, at least she recognized that God had provided for the household, and perhaps with enough time she would be able to express thanks.

Sitting outside in the weakened autumn sunshine, she watched Elam playing with Sadie. They balanced open cans along the top of the fence and tossed pebbles. Neither of them managed to get many into the cans, but the sound of their laughter in the effort occasionally brought a feeble smile to Fannie's lips.

When the buggy rolled onto their property, Fannie folded her arms across her abdomen. She was unprepared for her mother to return so soon. Fannie had promised to go to supper at her parents' house on the Sabbath, a visit that required Fannie to dig deep in her spirit's soil for strength. The digging was not finished.

But it was not her mother, Fannie realized. The horse was a strange one, as were the two men who emerged on either side of Clara.

Clara. They had very nearly quarreled the last time Clara was here. Fannie had been uncertain she would want to return. Six weeks had passed with only the skimpiest letters from her cousin. Tepid relief eased out on Fannie's breath. Elam paused the rock-throwing game, and Sadie hurtled herself into Clara's arms. Fannie rose and walked toward them.

"This is Andrew Raber," Clara said.

Ah. This was Andrew. On Clara's last visit he had dropped her off and picked her up out on the main road. One corner of Fannie's lips turned up. "Welcome," she said.

Andrew and Elam shook hands.

"And this is our friend John Stutzman," Clara said.

"I'm pleased to meet you," Fannie said.

"We were visiting our friends, the Schrocks," Clara said. "They recently moved to a farm a few miles south of here."

"It's lovely to have you here." Fannie very nearly believed her words. "Please come in and let me offer you some refreshment."

"Strudel?" Sadie slid out of Clara's arms.

Fannie nodded. "We have strudel, of course."

She took her daughter's hand and they led the entourage up to the house. Behind her, the three men fell easily into a conversation about crops and harvests, the topic on every farmer's mind at this time of year.

"Are you sure it's all right that you came?" Fannie said to Clara once Sadie scampered ahead of them.

"I won't ever not come," Clara answered. "I know it's been a few weeks, but I will always come."

Fannie sucked in her lips to suppress the sob that lived in her throat these days.

They gathered at the dining room table, with berry strudel, coffee, and apple slices. Sadie guzzled a glass of milk with her pastry before losing interest in the adult conversation and going to look for the dog. Fannie listened carefully to Clara's account of her former neighbors' decision to move to the Maryland side of the border.

"Have you always been Marylanders?" John asked.

Elam nodded. "Our families embraced the new music and Sunday school long ago."

John glanced around. "Your home looks no different from any in the Old Order district."

"We are Amish," Elam said simply.

"I hear some of your people own cars."

"This is true," Elam said, "though of course an automobile is expensive, and we rarely go farther than a horse can easily take us."

"I have seven children," John said. "I have a feeling they would enjoy a Sunday school class."

"You should visit sometime," Fannie said.

"My wife and I seem to discuss that idea every time we drive past the Mennonite church in Springs, where we do our shopping. We're becoming more serious about it, I think."

Fannie watched Clara, whose glance had snapped up sharply at John's admission.

"We had a good visit with the Schrocks this afternoon," John said. "I'm sure my wife will be interested to hear how they are settling in. I don't think we would sell our farm, as the Schrocks did, but what is there to keep us from visiting to see if the Marylanders might be where God leads us?"

Clara's coffee cup rattled on the way from her lips to the saucer. Andrew's arm twitched, and Fannie realized he was resisting the urge to reach out to Clara. She hoped Andrew and Clara were listening carefully to their friend. It was only a matter of time before John Stutzman would turn up in one of the Marylander meetinghouses with his wife and seven children.

First the Schrocks.

Then the Stutzmans.

What was there to hold back Andrew and Clara?

Hope flickered within Fannie.

CHAPTER 34

After church the next day, Clara pivoted at the sound of her name. Wanda paced through the narrow aisle formed by two tables. Clara could not help but notice how large Wanda was now. Each time Clara saw Wanda, relief oozed through her that her friend and her child were still well. The worry would not fully abate until news came that Wanda was safely delivered.

"I heard the bishop is looking for you," Wanda said.

"The bishop? Why would he be asking for me?" Clara set down the pitcher of water she had been pouring from.

"I think he's in the anteroom."

Clara smoothed her skirts. "Then I'll go find him."

She threaded her way between tables and benches to the front of the Flag Run Meetinghouse. Bishop Beachy had preached wonderfully that morning — finally. When-

409

ever Clara heard one of his sermons, which she hoped would become less rare, encouragement gushed into her like refreshing spring water. So many people ignored the ban, but she hoped to see it lifted. Beyond that, it seemed to her that Mose found uplifting themes in the New Testament that made her feel that God was eager to work in her life.

Still, she had no idea why Mose Beachy would summon her on a Sunday morning. She knocked softly on the door. Someone on the other side turned the knob and opened the door.

She stared into the eyes of Noah Yoder.

"I'm sorry," she said. "I got a message that the bishop asked to see me."

"Yes, he does. Please come in." Noah stepped aside.

Clara crossed the threshold. The dim room with sparse but heavy furniture gradually came into focus. Behind a table sat Bishop Yoder. To one side of him was his son Joseph. In straight-back chairs facing the table were Andrew and John with an empty chair between them.

"Please be seated." Noah gestured to the vacant seat and then sat on the other side of his father.

"I don't understand," Clara muttered.

"Just sit down." Noah's voice was a razor.

Clara looked at Andrew, who nodded slightly, and took her place.

"Are you well, Bishop?" she said. Clara had not noticed Bishop Yoder's presence during the worship service. Perhaps her habit of sitting in the rear was catching up with her — or perhaps he had not been present. Surely she would have noticed him enter with the men, and surely conversation would have buzzed with the news of his recovery if others had seen him.

"My father is much improved," Joseph said. "Thank you for your kind inquiry."

Clara's stomach clenched, and she was glad she had not yet eaten her meal.

"Will Bishop Beachy be joining us?" she asked.

"I don't believe we need to trouble him with this," Noah said. "We can speak to you in our authority as ministers."

What was *this*? Clara could only assume the Yoders had assembled this meeting because of yesterday's encounter on the road. She wished she could reach for Andrew's hand.

"I'm sure you all realize why you're here," Joseph said.

Andrew bit back his response, determined

411

to remain nonchalant for Clara's sake if nothing else.

"Clara," Joseph said, "it is well known that you visit your mother's family even though they no longer belong to the Old Order."

"I don't deny it," Clara said. "They left the Old Order before I was born."

Bishop Yoder shuffled his feet under the table. "You must stop. They are under the ban."

Until that moment, Andrew had not been certain Bishop Yoder would speak at all, supposing his presence was merely a ruse so his sons could mislead him and the others with a message that the bishop was asking for them. But the bishop did seem much recovered. His eyes were clear and his gaze focused when he spoke. Beside Andrew, Clara crossed her ankles.

"Andrew," Joseph said, "it is my understanding that you have no family connections in the Maryland district. Is this correct?"

"Yes, it is," Andrew said.

"And you, John?" Joseph said.

"My family are all Old Order," John said.

Andrew did not have to look at John to know he was meeting Joseph's gaze.

"The lack of relatives erases any doubt about whether you can both obey the *mei-*

412

dung and visit members of the Conservative Amish Mennonites. You cannot serve both God and mammon."

"You must stop," Bishop Yoder said. "They are under the ban."

"Andrew, do you deny that you visited Marylanders with whom you have no family connection?"

"No," Andrew said.

"And you, John? Do you deny this?"

"No."

"Then you are confessing your sin to us. As ministers we believe you must stand before the congregation and confess your transgression. Clara, you will confess the sin of leading your fellow church members astray."

Andrew no longer resisted the urge to turn his head toward Clara, who was pale, and John, who was red in the face.

"With all due respect," John said, "I will do no such thing. Neither will I accept your false accusations of Clara."

"The lot fell to Mose Beachy," Andrew said. "Shouldn't he be here?"

"The lot fell to him to be bishop," Noah said. "God selected us as ministers and we will serve. Sometimes our duty is unpleasant."

Andrew doubted the Yoders felt any unpleasantness in their demand.

"You must stop," Bishop Yoder said again. "The Marylanders are all under the ban."

Andrew narrowed his eyes at Joseph. "Are you sure your father has recovered?"

John stood. "You know that most of the congregation believes the ban on the Marylanders should be set aside."

"But it has not been set aside," Noah said. "Perhaps your confessions will help others to take it more seriously for the sake of the entire church."

"You cannot single us out simply because you happened to meet us on a road driving south," John said.

"If you will not submit to the discipline of the church," Joseph said, "we will have to place you under the ban as well."

"Will you place two-thirds of the congregation under *meidung*?" Andrew stood now as well, taking Clara's hand and pulling her to her feet with him.

John took a step toward the door. "The congregation will not tolerate it."

Clara's eyes were wide and her lips pressed together, but she did not tremble, not with Andrew's hand wrapped around hers.

The door opened, and Mose Beachy stepped in — all three hundred pounds of him — and looked around the room.

"I was not aware there was a meeting of the ministers," he said. He closed the door behind him.

Clara breathed relief. Mose's large form shifted the balance in the room the way leaning to one side in a boat on the river threatened a capsizing.

"Our brothers propose to put us under a ban," John said.

"Only if you refuse to confess," Joseph countered. "I pray you will make the right choice."

"Threatening the ban is serious," Mose said. "Why doesn't someone tell me what happened. Andrew?"

Clara listened to Andrew relay the summons to see the bishop, only to discover Bishop Yoder in the chair behind the table. Mose paced around the room as he absorbed the details of the conversation.

"Joseph, please take your brother and your father and join your families. I'm sure they're waiting for you."

"We have not concluded our businesses," Joseph said.

"On the contrary," Mose said, "I'm quite sure you have. I did not ask to be bishop, but neither will I shirk my responsibility. You can be assured I will conclude the matter in an appropriate manner."

Noah took his father's elbow, and the Yoders shuffled out of the room.

Mose gestured to the chairs. "Please be comfortable while we talk."

They took seats.

"They should not have misled you about which bishop you would find when you came in the room," Mose said, "and they should have spoken to me about their intention."

"We were certain you would feel that way," Andrew said.

"Imagine my surprise when Wanda Eicher asked if I had finished meeting with you."

"We would have come to you," John said, "just as soon as we walked out that door."

"I have no doubt. It would have been the right thing to do."

"Thank you for understanding," Andrew said.

"Clara," Mose said, "you have done nothing wrong in visiting your relatives. I hope you enjoy many more visits with your aunt and your cousins."

"Thank you." Clara's shoulders lowered, but the hesitation she heard in Mose's voice kept her on guard.

Mose stroked his beard. "I am not going to ask you to confess to the congregation, and you will not be under a ban. But I will ask you not to see the Schrocks."

Clara gasped. "They've been my neighbors for many years."

"But they are not your family," Mose said. "And they only just left the church. It is not the same as the families who left a generation or more ago."

"They have not sinned," Andrew said. "Their only fault — and I do not believe it is a fault — is that they choose to worship somewhere else."

"It's a complicated question."

"Is it?" John said. "You're the bishop now. You can lead the church through change."

"I plan to seek counsel on that question from more experienced bishops outside our district," Mose said. "For now, I would like for the question of the Schrocks not to stir the pot."

"But we are not the only ones who will want to see them," Clara pointed out.

Mose nodded. "Surely you are correct. I will have other conversations if I need to. You are all good friends to me. For the peace of the community, I am asking for time."

Mose was the first to leave the room. Stunned, Clara trailed Andrew and John.

"We'll talk more," Andrew whispered.

"We'll take the car out."

Clara nodded. Her father approached, and Andrew paced away.

"Rhoda asked me to see if you were coming home," Hiram said. He glanced at the anteroom door. "Have you been speaking to the bishop?"

The story spilled out of Clara. Hiram shook his head and sighed.

"Your mother would be horrified to see what has happened all these years later. She voted against the *meidung.*"

"That's what Aunt Martha told me," Clara said. "But I thought it was a unanimous vote."

"In the way that a twisted arm is a healthy arm," Hiram said. "I was never in agreement, either, but I raised my hand. Your mother didn't. She told me later when I confessed that I was sorry I had."

"Oh *Daed.*"

"I'll tell you who else did not vote — Betty Stutzman. She was outside watching you nap in the grass when the vote was taken."

"John's grandmother? With me?"

"She was quite fond of you." He chuckled. "As if she didn't have enough *kinner* in her own family. How could we know that within a few weeks, Catherine and Betty would both be gone?"

"I was hoping things would be different if Mose was bishop."

"They might yet be," Hiram said. "*Gottes wille.* We cannot expect Mose can undo all these years in one month. He'll want what's best for the church."

Clara nodded. Her father was right. Mose had been bishop for less than a month, while the vote to uphold the ban was more than twenty years old, and the division of interpretation of the Bible another twenty years older than the ban.

But time was running out. Across the meetinghouse, John Stutzman picked up his youngest child and kissed her cheek. Clara wondered how many more Sundays she would witness John's care for his family.

CHAPTER 35

Andrew left the Model T on the shoulder of the main road eight days later while he walked the final yards and stepped onto the lane leading into the Kuhn farmstead. He and John had been fortunate last week to find Clara alone and sweep her away in the buggy with minimal fuss. Andrew had no doubt that rumors already circulated about the summons to see the bishop that took John and Andrew and Clara into the anteroom with the ministers. This time Hiram or Rhoda might object to an invitation for Clara to take a ride. Certainly they would object if they saw the automobile.

Rhoda came out of the front door and snapped dirt out of a rug. Four sharp jerks loosed gray plumes, rising and then falling. Mari, too young to join her siblings at school, held on to her mother's skirt. Andrew hovered at the top of the lane as Rhoda retreated into the house. Scanning the farmyard, Andrew saw no other activity and took a few steps toward the barn. The milk cows and horses were in the adjoining pasture.

Clara could be anywhere. Hiram, full of questions, could emerge from one of the outbuildings. Rhoda could come out with another rug. But Andrew wanted to see Clara. A flash of gray fabric in the loft window of the barn drew him closer. He slipped inside.

"Clara," he whispered.

A few seconds later, her face looked down at him from the hayloft. "What are you doing here?"

"Let's go for a ride," Andrew said.

She paused. "In the Model T?"

"We'll go visit John."

She was descending the ladder now, hay caught in the folds of her dress and trapped under the edge of her *kapp*. When she reached the floor and turned to meet his eyes, Andrew wished he could capture the beauty of that simple moment, like an *English* photograph or painting. It would not be a graven image to him, but a reminder of loveliness in simple things.

"The Model T is up on the road," Andrew said, when what he really wanted to say was, *May I kiss you right here?*

Clara did not even glance back toward the house as they walked side by side up the lane. This wasn't like Clara. What was Clara doing in the hayloft in the middle of the morning? Something had been amiss in the Kuhn household for months.

But he asked none of his questions. When Clara got in the car, her blue eyes brimmed with trust. She would go with him, wherever he drove, by whatever method of transportation.

"Is John all right?" Clara asked once they were well away from Kuhn land.

Andrew shrugged one shoulder. "I feel a particular kinship with him these days. I'd just like to see him."

Clara pressed her shoulders into the upholstered bench. The top was up on the automobile now, enclosing the rectangle in which they sat. Without it, the November chill would have bitten at their faces in the wind.

They found John easily enough in one of his fields, walking with a toolbox and inspecting fence posts.

"Any more word from the bishop?" John asked as he set down his toolbox and brushed dirt off his knees.

Andrew chuckled. "Which one?"

"The only one who matters now," John said.

"No, nothing," Andrew said. "I may try to have a word with him, to hear more what is in his mind."

"Mose Beachy is a good man."

"The auction is next week," Clara said. "Will your wife be showing a quilt again?"

John cleared his throat. "Under the circumstances, we think it would be better if we did not attend this year."

"What circumstances?" Clara said.

John used a hammer to nudge a split rail into its slot more securely, testing it with one hand. His hat brim blocked any view of his face.

"John," Andrew said. "Please speak your heart with us."

John straightened and looked at their faces again. "We've decided to join the Marylanders immediately. Mose will have our letter withdrawing our Old Order membership by tomorrow."

"But John!" Clara said.

Unself-conscious in John's presence, Andrew put an arm around Clara's shoulders. "I thought you might. You asked a lot of questions when we visited Maryland last week."

"I will not shun people who have done

nothing more than find another way to worship the same God," John said. "When Mose asked us not to visit the Schrocks, I knew the time had come for my family to leave as well."

"But Mose just wants time," Clara said. "In his heart he doesn't agree with the *meidung*."

"For twenty years most of the church has not agreed with the *meidung*," John said. "Yet it exists. If I cannot peacefully submit, then it is better for the congregation that I go."

Andrew tilted his head at the sentiment that echoed his own parents' choice.

"But your family is dear to all of us," Clara said.

"And you are dear to us," John said. "When Mose finally sorts things out, whether in one year or ten, we will see each other again."

"We'll still see you," Andrew said.

"No." John shook his head. "It is better if you respect Mose's wishes. We are not moving to Maryland, as the Schrocks did, but Mose will view us the same way he sees them — trouble to stir the pot."

Clara's shoulder trembled under Andrew's arm. His own tremble was inward.

They drove halfway home in silence.

"The Pennsylvania district will never change if our strongest families leave us," Clara said finally.

Andrew took a long pause. "I think that's the point. People should feel free to worship elsewhere if God leads."

"But what about the shunning? Freedom to leave is one thing, but we are pushing people we care about into a corner. They have to choose between worship or being part of the way we take care of each other."

"The Yoders, and those who agree with them, think shunning will bring people back."

"That might work in other places where there is only one Amish church," Clara said, slapping her hands on her thighs, "but around here it's easy to go to another building on Sunday morning and find another community waiting for you."

Andrew let another long pause hang before he spoke again. "We could do that, too. Either the Schrocks or the Stutzmans would be at whichever congregation we joined."

"And how many other friends would we leave behind?" Clara's words fell in a halting cadence. "And what about my brother and sisters? My *daed*?"

Andrew drove without speaking. Leaving

the Old Order district would cost Clara too much — and he would not go without her.

"The rope on the well frays more every day," Fannie told Elam.

"I know. You've told me half a dozen times."

The edge in his tone startled Fannie.

"Will you have time to replace it soon?" Fannie chose to ignore his mood and carried the last of the lunch dishes to the counter.

"I have to go to Grantsville for the rope."

"I'll go with you. Sadie would love it."

"No need."

Perhaps her own withdrawal colored her perception, but it seemed to Fannie that Elam's responses to ordinary conversation were growing terse. He remained playful with Sadie, and he'd had no trouble being hospitable and conversational when Clara and the others visited the previous weekend.

It's only me, Fannie thought.

Had he no idea of the enormous effort it took for her to remain upright? Of course he didn't. Fannie didn't tell him. She had his meals on the table at the appointed hours — for the most part — and the house remained tidy. It was the weeds in the vegetable garden that ran rampant all fall,

426

and the mending pile that doubled every time she looked at it, and the eggs left in the henhouse until it was too late, and the fruit that went soft before canning — all details Elam would pay no attention to in the face of a triumphant harvest and caring for the animals. She would have to do better and have something to show for her efforts, something Elam could see and appreciate.

"I know you're pleased with the harvest," she said, her spirit not nearly as bright as her voice. "Next year will be even better, I'm sure."

"I thought I would cut back next year."

"Cut back?"

Year after year Elam talked about seeding more acres even as he let some fields lie fallow. They still had at least ten tillable acres he had never touched. Cutting back made no sense.

"We can live on less."

"But I thought you wanted to expand the farm. You've always dreamed of buying more land someday."

Elam ran a finger back and forth along the edge of the kitchen table. "That was when I was planning for sons."

He might just as well have sliced through her with a harrow blade. Her throat instantly

427

threatened to cut off her air.

"Have you given up, then?" she whispered.

"Haven't you?" He did not seek her eyes.

The answer lodged in Fannie's throat, unformed.

"Sadie will marry and move to another man's farm," Elam said. "Without sons it will be hard to work more acres than we have now."

"We could hire someone. I could help."

"There will be no need."

Sons.

Sadie burst into the room with slate and chalk. "*Daed,* will you help me with my letters?"

"Of course." Elam scooted back his chair and took Sadie into his lap. "What are we going to spell?"

"How about *boppli*?"

"What sound do you hear when you say that word?" Elam asked.

Sadie sucked in her lips and then said, "Buh."

"And what letter makes that sound?"

Sadie thought hard. "B."

Elam nodded.

Next spring, during planting season, Sadie would turn six, and next fall she would go to school. Someone else would teach her to spell and read and make sums. Fannie had always imagined that by the time Sadie's first day of school came, two more children would fill the days. Now she wondered what it would be like to be home alone, Sadie at school and Elam in the fields.

By then her mother's new babe would be pulling up on the furniture, perhaps even beginning to toddle.

Elam patiently guided his daughter's hand as she formed the letters of her selected word. He always had time for Sadie. He did not want her in the fields, where in a few seconds she might come to harm with the animals or blades while he turned his attention to some needful task, but he welcomed her in the barn and was already teaching her to milk.

They finished the word.

Elam lifted Sadie off his lap. "Your *mamm* wants me to go to town and buy rope."

The words he chose stung. *Your* mamm *wants.* The rope needed to be replaced or they would have no water in the house. It had nothing to do with what Fannie wanted.

"I want to go with you!" Sadie abandoned her slate.

"We'll have a delightful time."

"Is *Mamm* coming?" Sadie looked at her mother.

Fannie caught the flicker of Elam's eyes

before he looked away.

"Your *mamm* has things to do," he said.

Fannie began scrubbing plates in the sink. Perhaps Elam observed more than she realized. Mentally she listed the tasks she could accomplish while Elam took Sadie to Grantsville. She stood on the porch and cheerfully answered Sadie's frantic good-bye waves with her own.

When the *clip-clop* of the horse's rhythm faded and the buggy was out of sight, Fannie hugged the solitude, striving to welcome it with aspirations of productivity.

Sons. Elam deserved a house full of sons to teach with patience and understanding. He had given up on sons, and with it the farm. On her.

A cow's soft *moo* alerted Fannie that Elam had fetched it from the pasture and taken it into the barn. She followed its call and scratched behind its ears to assure herself the animal was well. Elam had said nothing about why he had brought the animal in at midday. How many other decisions did he say nothing about?

Fannie could not fault Elam. She, too, felt the weight of effort to say more than was necessary.

She had come to the barn with no cloak. The brisk November day rushed through the open barn door, chilling her. Fannie reached for a horse blanket and wrapped it around her shoulders, keeping company with the cow for a few more minutes.

Then she opened the stall next to the cow, saw that Elam had freshened the straw, and sank down to her knees to pray.

She ached to pray.

She longed to pray.

But she could not pray.

She lay in the straw, wrapped in the blanket, and gave way to sleep.

CHAPTER 36

By Thursday, the news had sifted its way through the district. John Stutzman had delivered his letter to Bishop Beachy on Tuesday morning. The Yoder brothers pronounced the Stutzmans under the ban. The bishop, in office a scant five weeks, reluctantly agreed. Two churchwomen stopped by to spend a morning sewing with Rhoda on Wednesday, and every time Clara overheard a snatch of conversation, it had to do with the Schrocks and Stutzmans, who were now subjects of somber prayer for repentance.

Clara dragged through the days, finding chores to do. She cleaned the henhouse, put quilts in the buggy for the winter, and yanked overgrowth from the flower beds across the front of the house. For three days she did not leave the farm. Clara wanted to speak to no one, not even Andrew, while the Stutzman tempest brewed and settled.

When she did manage to escape her grief over John's decision for a few minutes, trepidation mounted over Martha approaching labor. Incessant activity between waking and sleeping was her only path to release. On Thursday afternoon, the children arrived home from school just as Clara had readied the buggy to go to Niverton for a few items, an errand for which Rhoda gave lukewarm agreement to its merit.

Hannah's eyes lit up. "Can I come with you?"

Clara's stomach sank. Rhoda would not agree.

Rhoda stepped outside to welcome Josiah and Hannah. Josiah acknowledged her greeting before going directly inside. Hannah, though, stood beside the buggy.

"I want to go with Clara. Please, *Mamm,* may I go with Clara?"

"You've only just arrived home from school," Rhoda said, taking Hannah's lunch bucket. "You have chores to do."

"I'll do them when I get back. I promise." Hannah stroked the horse's neck.

"There's no reason for you to go."

"I just want to," the girl said. "I never get to go with Clara anymore."

"You see Clara every day." Rhoda put a hand on her daughter's back to point her toward the house, but the child did not budge.

Hannah tilted her head back, eyes pleading. "Please, *Mamm*?"

Clara squatted in front of her sister to look her in the eye. "I'm sure your *mamm* has a snack waiting for you. She always does."

"I'm not hungry," Hannah muttered.

"Still, go freshen up."

Hannah dragged her feet through the dirt, leaving a set of tracks between the barn and the house.

Clara pivoted toward Rhoda. "What have I done that makes you think I deserve your shunning?"

"I don't know what you're talking about." Rhoda hung Hannah's lunch bucket over one arm and paced toward a clothesline.

Clara strode after her, close on her heels. "It's been almost six months. You won't let me help in the house. You won't let the children spend time with me. I don't even know how Hannah feels about Priscilla moving away."

"I have told her as much as she needs to know." Rhoda swiftly removed four clothespins and draped two of her husband's shirts over one shoulder.

"And what do you tell her about me?" Clara stayed only two steps beside Rhoda, her voice rising.

"She's my daughter."

"You used to tell me I was like your own daughter."

"You are." Rhoda removed two more pins, and a pair of Josiah's trousers dropped into her arms.

"And you were the mother I didn't have when I was Hannah's age." Clara's voice cracked. "So why? I only want to know why?"

"This is for your own good. I have to do what's best for all my children."

"Hannah is my sister." Words pent up for months, a river running too high, gushed unstoppable through Clara's lips. "Will I only be allowed to see her if I marry? Do you want me out of your house so badly? Or perhaps I have to wait for Hannah to be old enough to choose for herself. Is that what you have in mind?"

Rhoda abandoned the clothesline and finally confronted Clara's insistent eyes. "This is as good a time as any to tell you that I spoke to your *English* family."

"They're not *my* family," Clara said. "I only work for them a few hours a week."

"Yesterday I let them know you're not available to come any longer."

Clara's lips twisted in fury. "I am not a

child. I can decide for myself if I want to clean house for an *English* family."

"Well, it's done. He said he had in mind someone else to ask and wished you well in your marriage."

"Marriage! But I haven't said I was getting married."

"Cleaning other people's homes is as much as saying you intend *not* to marry and have your own home." Rhoda yanked two more garments off the line.

Clara swallowed hard. "When I was a little girl, you filled an empty place in me, and I will always be grateful. But this — whether I marry or where I work — is not for you to decide."

"I'm only helping you live in the way of our people." Rhoda looked around, her shoulders covered with clothing and her fists full of clothespins. "I should have brought a basket out."

"A basket! Are you more concerned with the laundry than with me?" Clara snatched one of Mari's tiny dresses from its pins and hurled it at Rhoda.

Hiram marched across the pasture and slipped through the fence into the farmyard. "Clara!"

She bit her tongue.

"You will not speak to Rhoda in this manner."

Clara forced herself to take a deep breath. "Did you know Rhoda thinks my work cleaning houses means I won't marry?"

Hiram looked from daughter to wife and back. "She has your best interest in mind."

"I'm a grown woman," Clara said.

"When you marry," Rhoda said, "you'll have a home with your husband. Until then we decide what's best."

"By shaming me? By depriving me of affection?" Clara refused to surrender to the hot tears pooling in her eyes.

"Mind your tone. Look!" Hiram gestured toward the house.

Clara saw three sets of young blue eyes looking out the front window.

"You are forgetting your place in the household," Hiram said.

"I seem to have no place in the household," Clara said, in control of her tone but still unable to filter her words.

"Think carefully about what you do and say." Hiram glared.

Clara clamped her lips closed, her face flaming. She climbed into the buggy and put the horse in motion. It was all too much. Rhoda excluding her for all these months. Fannie's melancholy. The Schrocks and the Stutzmans. The Yoders' determination to punish Andrew and her. Hannah's pleading eyes filling with disappointment over and over.

And now Clara had behaved like an impetuous ten-year-old. What example to her siblings was she now? She had just given Rhoda every reason to safeguard her impressionable children from their wild older sister's outbursts.

She could be married to Andrew within the month if she chose. He had a thriving farm and a lovely house that she could make her own. Rhoda might relax.

But Clara was uncertain she could ever forgive.

She would marry Andrew when she was ready — truly ready — and not because her stepmother held hostage three young children.

Andrew braced his feet, raised the sledgehammer, and slammed it down on a half-rotted fence post. The old wood splintered and crumbled. He stepped back, and Mose Beachy knelt in the dirt to toss aside the larger pieces and scoop rot out of the posthole. Andrew exchanged the hammer for a spade to widen the hole while Mose lifted a new post upright from the back of his wagon.

"Time matters," Andrew said.

"God's time matters," Mose countered.

"How many more families will we lose?" Andrew loaded the shovel three more times, tossing dirt and debris aside.

"As many as God chooses." Mose tipped the post into the hole and then straightened to look at Andrew.

"What if God is not choosing?" Andrew said. "What if people are simply becoming impatient?"

"Why did God make Abraham and Sarah wait so long before He fulfilled the promise?"

Andrew had often wondered. He had no answer.

"What about morale?" Andrew said. "If people realize you are going to enforce a ban that you don't believe in —"

"Who said I don't believe in it?" Mose wiggled the post snug into the bottom of the hole.

Andrew leaned on the handle of his shovel. "Do you?"

"A strong argument can be made for respecting tradition on the matter."

Andrew tilted his head as he considered Mose's response. Never before had he heard

Mose take this position. "Mose, what are you saying?"

"The question is not whether to remove the *meidung* for people who go to the Marylanders," Mose said. "The question is what is best for the district. What will bring peace and unity to the church?"

"I don't understand," Andrew said. "How can it bring peace and unity to the church to watch our families leave?"

"They will not all leave."

More would. Andrew was certain of that. He had not supposed Mose Beachy to be one to lead by waiting for naysayers to leave.

"I hope that given time, we will have some productive conversations," Mose said. "In due time we might yet move ahead together on the question. Does not belonging to the community carry greater weight than being right or wrong on a single doctrine?"

Andrew pushed his black felt hat back off his forehead.

Mose chuckled. "I can see you are not persuaded."

"No," Andrew admitted. "I'm not."

"If I am to be bishop, I must care for the entire flock."

"And the sheep who wander to Maryland?"

"They will find their belonging there, I

imagine. But if I lift the *meidung* with a simple announcement, then where will those who hold to it find their belonging?"

Andrew had not thought of that.

"The ninety-nine and the one lost sheep," Mose said. "Each one matters. No one is diminished."

Andrew moved dirt. "Would not those who hold to the *meidung* also submit to a new tradition?"

"Like owning automobiles?" Mose said.

Andrew's eyelids flipped up. "You know?"

"If I act too swiftly and in the extreme," Mose said, "the road to peace will become even more rocky."

Andrew lifted his hat and scratched the top of his head.

"I do not ask you to trust me," Mose said. "I ask you to trust God. All will be well in God's time. Now let's set this post before we lose the light."

Yonnie put his hands flat on the table and leaned across it, glaring into his coworker's face.

"You will see," Yonnie said. "The ban will hold."

The other young man laughed. "The ban has never held. Why should anyone take it seriously now?"

"I will pray for you," Yonnie said. "I will pray every night for the Holy Ghost to convict you."

"You seem to have taken that job on yourself."

Laughter spattered around them. Heat crawled up the back of Yonnie's neck as he set his jaw.

"What's going on in here?" Dale thundered into the workroom.

Distracted employees turned back to their tasks.

"Yonnie, please come to my office." Dale pivoted and marched out.

At a less brisk pace, Yonnie followed Dale, finding his employer behind the desk by the time he reached the office. Yonnie crossed his wrists in front of him as he spread his feet to a solid stance.

"The time has come," Dale said.

"The time?" Yonnie glanced at a clock.

Dale nodded slowly. "The time for you to find somewhere else to work."

Adrenaline broke free in Yonnie's core. His inquiries so far had led to no other employment possibilities, not even among his Yoder relatives.

"I'll count you out a month's pay to give you time to make other arrangements," Dale said.

One month. What would change in one month — during the winter when Yonnie could not even hope to find odd jobs on the farms?

"I was hoping you might settle down when Mose became bishop," Dale said.

"Settle down?"

"Become less . . . persuaded on certain matters. But since you can't set aside what you think about church doctrines or accept that others might disagree with good reason, it's time for you to go."

"They egg me on," Yonnie said. "They ask me for my thoughts and then laugh when I answer."

"I believe you," Dale said, surprising Yonnie. "But the dairy will still be more peaceful if you're not working here. I only held on this long because I heard you were asking around for work. I thought something would have turned up for you by now."

"Nothing has."

Nothing in the Amish shops. Nothing on the farms. Even at the height of the harvest, Yonnie had not found anyone who would let him run an Amish farm stand to sell to the *English.* If he had to lower himself to work for the *English* — Yonnie shook away the notion.

"Give me another chance," Yonnie said.

Dale sighed. "I don't trust you, Yonnie. Your chances are over."

Dale turned his chair and leaned down to open the small safe he kept under his desk. When he sat up he began counting bills on the desk. Yonnie was too stunned to keep track of how they totaled.

CHAPTER 37

Five days might have been five years. When her mother turned her back in the kitchen, Hannah lifted her blue eyes to Clara. When Clara opened her eyes at the close of a silent prayer before a meal with the family, she saw Hannah's wide orbs fixed on her. During family devotions, as their father read from the Bible and Hannah sat tucked in between her mother and Josiah, the sisters watched each other.

At church the past Sunday, Hannah had been the one to be brave. During the meal, she took her plate and sat down next to Clara before her mother settled at a table. Rhoda looked at the two of them, Clara avoiding her stepmother's eyes and Hannah staring into them with a dare.

I'm not moving, her posture said. *Don't try to make me.*

With Mari and Josiah, Rhoda moved to the next table, where she could watch Clara and Hannah.

It was something, Clara thought. In the safety of a hundred people having lunch together in the meetinghouse, she could at least converse with her sister.

Clara peppered Hannah with questions about school and her friends, all the while thinking how unfair it was to expect a six-year-old to understand the shift between her mother and her big sister, two people she loved and trusted. Hannah chattered, spilling overdue news of who was in her class this year and what she did when they went outside at lunchtime. Several times she said, "Priscilla used to . . ." or "I wish Priscilla could . . ." When they had finished eating, Hannah leaned against Clara, spreading an awkward embrace around her and whispering into her ear.

"I want it to be like before," Hannah said, wiggling her way into Clara's lap even though her parents would have said she was too old for that.

Clara welcomed her, inhaling the scrubbed scent of her hair, washed just last night, and snuggling the pliant form that squirmed to fit against Clara's.

But Hannah had gone too far. Rhoda approached with firm instructions for Hannah to stack dishes. Clara nudged the girl off her lap, but not before kissing one smooth cheek.

Now, on Tuesday morning, Clara watched all three of her young siblings make their best effort to sit still and appear attentive for the morning devotions before school.

After he dismissed the family with a blessing, Hiram asked Clara to stay behind. Her mind sifted her actions in the last few days, and she gripped the edges of her apron as if to lift it and catch whatever accusation would fall out.

"I was harsh," he said. "The sermon on Sunday convicted me that I must ask your forgiveness."

This was her old *daed,* the one who was quick to admit he was wrong when she was little and he was never certain of his parenting decisions.

"Please forgive me," he said. "You have not forgotten your place. You will always have a place here."

Clara's chest tightened, and she reminded herself to breathe out.

"I loved your mother very much," Hiram said.

Though Clara had only the whisper of memories of her mother, she had always known Hiram loved Catherine. Why else would he have been huddled in grief for most of Clara's childhood?

"Martha and Catherine were closer than any other two sisters I have ever known," Hiram said. "There was nothing complicated about the decision to let you grow up knowing your mother's family. I would never have kept you from them."

"I know, *Daed,*" Clara said. "I know there are some who think you should never have let me cross the border. I'm grateful you did."

He waved away the remark and stood up to put the family's Bible in its place on the shelf.

"Rhoda also has many qualities that make me cherish her," he said. "I have to think of her happiness."

"I know." Clara's gaze went to her lap.

"Your brother and sisters deserve to grow up in peace."

She felt his eyes on her and looked up into his face. "I know that, too."

Clara's heart closed around all the unanswered questions swirling in this conversation. *Do you think I am bad for the* kinner? *Don't you see Rhoda has her own form of* meidung?

"I'm going to muck stalls today." Hiram patted Clara's shoulder as he passed.

"I'll help," she said.

"There's no need for that."

"I want to."

"I can manage. You enjoy your day."

Oh Daed. Not you, too!

The sound of a racing buggy was not an easy one to ignore, even if Fannie was half asleep on the davenport on Tuesday afternoon.

"Who's coming?" Sadie popped up from the floor where she was playing with two faceless dolls and peered out the front window.

Fannie was on her feet as well. The pounding of the horse's hooves and the rattle of the hitch and buggy screamed urgency.

"It's the gray horse," Sadie announced.

Gray horse.

"*Onkel* Abe's horse?" Fannie crossed the room to open the front door.

Lizzie pulled hard on the reins and jumped out of the buggy.

"What is it?" Fannie's heart thudded.

"You'd better come," Lizzie said, breathless.

"*Mamm?*"

Lizzie nodded. "The babe is coming. It's been all day and still she labors."

"No one told me."

"She thought it would be better if we sent

word after the baby arrived. That was . . . before."

"Before what?" Sadie pulled on her mother's sleeve.

"Get your shoes and your cloak," Fannie snapped.

"Are we going to see *Grossmuder*?" Excitement put a squeal in Sadie's voice and widened her eyes.

"We'll find *Daed.*" Fannie glanced at Lizzie, who nodded. "You can stay with him."

"I want to see the baby!"

Sadie was rarely petulant, but Fannie took no risk. "You will stay with *Daed* and you will not complain. Get your shoes."

Fannie fastened a cloak around her neck and snatched up her daughter, shoes still in hand, and ran toward Lizzie's buggy.

"Where is Elam?" Lizzie started the horse moving.

"I'm not sure." Fannie was at least certain Elam had not left the farm, but they said so little to each other these days. She made her best guess. "Take the wide trail that goes to the north field."

Lizzie drove while Fannie shoved Sadie's feet into her shoes and fastened them. Only then did she see that her daughter's cloak had not made it into the buggy. Mid-

November was no time for a child to be out in a field without warmth. Fannie removed her own cloak and wrapped Sadie in it.

"There!" Sadie pointed. "There's *Daed.*"

Fannie expelled relief and gratitude for her daughter's sharp eyesight. Lizzie raced the wagon toward Elam.

"I have to go to my *mamm,*" Fannie said as she nudged Sadie out of the buggy.

"The baby's coming!" Sadie said.

Fannie fastened her eyes on Elam's. Their words may have dissipated over the weeks, but the understanding in his eyes had not. He knew she could not take a five-year-old into a difficult birth. As Lizzie started driving again, Fannie twisted in the buggy to see Elam rearrange the oversized cloak on the girl. Fannie shivered in the wintry air — and with a good dose of trepidation. The distance was only a mile and a half, but Fannie could think of a dozen things that could go wrong — a broken axle, the horse gone lame, a fallen tree blocking the road.

"How bad is it?" she asked.

Lizzie grimaced. "The midwife says the baby is not turned right. And it's taking a long time for a woman who has birthed five other children. When Martha started asking for you, the midwife said not to waste any time."

Fannie burst into the house while Lizzie tended to the buggy. Her father interrupted his pacing in the front room long enough to acknowledge her presence. Fannie touched his shoulder on her way past.

In the bedroom, on the same bed where Fannie was born nearly twenty-five years earlier, Martha writhed.

"She's so white," Fannie said to the midwife as she moved to the bed to clasp her mother's hand.

"Fannie," Martha whispered.

"I'm here."

"My precious daughter."

Fannie looked at the midwife, waiting for words of reassurance that the baby had turned or labor was progressing — something. But the midwife's face told nothing.

Fannie wanted Clara.

She went to the shelf where she knew her mother kept notepaper and pencils and scribbled a note. With a glance at her mother, Fannie strode into the front room. Two of her brothers had joined their father, and Lizzie was just coming in the front door.

"I need someone to take a message to Clara," Fannie said.

The boys looked at each other. Her father shook his head. He wouldn't leave now. None of them would.

452

"I'll go up to the main road," Lizzie said. "There will be somebody heading north."

"Give me the note," her father said. He turned it over and sketched a map, circling an *X* to mark the destination for its delivery.

Clara's eyes blurred as she read the note for the second time. An *English* boy brought it, shoving it awkwardly into her hand and mounting a sagging mare. Watching the animal's ponderous, slow progress back toward the road made Clara wonder just how long ago the boy took possession of Fannie's frantic scrawl on the Maryland side of the border.

Mamm in labor, it said. *Baby taking too long. Come.*

Clara put fingers to both temples. Her father had taken two horses to the blacksmith to be shoed. Rhoda had taken the buggy with a third into Springs before picking up the children from school on her way home. The fourth had a troublesome fetlock, and Hiram had told the family not to use it under any circumstance.

He could not have foreseen this circumstance, Clara thought. But she could not risk causing the horse to go permanently lame.

Please, God.

It would take at least ninety minutes to travel on foot to the Hostetler farm. If she ran most of the way, she might shave time, but running in thick shoes and long layered skirts under a woolen cloak would not make for good speed.

What choice did she have? Clara pulled the front door closed behind her, gripped her skirts to raise the hem, and established a stride at the maximum length her legs would permit. Anxiety fueled speed, and for the first mile she forced breaths.

In.

Out.

In.

Out.

Faster. Deeper.

Dread dredged her depths, burning her stomach and lungs.

Martha's last baby had been so long ago, and she had looked so unwell the last few weeks.

And the dream, with Martha grief stricken while a baby's cry faded away.

And Martha's sister had died birthing a baby at a much younger age. The absence of Clara's mother from her life stabbed her afresh. She had been too little to know what was happening to Catherine Kuhn, too little to know that the life flashed out of her mother's body, too little to know she missed her chance to say good-bye.

But Clara was not little now. She knew the danger Martha faced. Bending over and putting her hands on her knees, she paused to properly empty and refill her lungs several times.

Please, God. Please. Show me Your way in this.

Terrified that she was racing to say good-bye to her aunt, her mother's only sister, Clara resumed her trot for another half mile.

An automobile engine roared behind her, and the driver sounded the horn. Annoyed, Clara moved even farther to the side of the road. The horn sounded again.

"Clara!"

She stopped running again and spun around. "Andrew!"

He pulled up beside her, grinning. "Feel like a ride?"

"Maryland," she said, gasping. "Will you take me to my aunt's?"

His face sobered. "What's wrong?"

"I don't have time to explain. I know what Mose said, but I have to be there *now*. Will you take me?"

"Get in." Andrew leaned over to open the passenger side.

CHAPTER 38

The hours crawled into darkness.

In a narrow wooden chair with her knees pushed up against the side of the bed, Fannie held her mother's hand and folded her spine over her lap to press her forehead into the mattress. This was as close as Fannie had come to prayer in months.

"I'm so sorry, *Mamm,*" Fannie murmured. "So sorry. So ashamed. Will you ever be able to forgive me?"

"Love," Martha said between labored breaths. "Love bears all things."

Martha's face transformed as another contraction sliced through her. Her grip crushed Fannie's fingers. Fannie looked up at the midwife, who spread her hands on Martha's belly and nodded.

"It's better?" Fannie asked.

"The child is in position."

Fannie let out a long, slow breath.

Atlee Hostetler came into the room,

ashen. "It's never been this way before."

"Every birth is different," the midwife said.

"Why would God ask her to go through this?"

Fannie vacated her chair, making room for her father to sit beside his wife. He was never in the birthing room for the arrival of his other children. This time he shuffled in every hour or so when he seemed not to tolerate waiting in the front room, staying for a few minutes before withdrawing again. Even he felt the trepidation.

In the corner, next to the fireplace warming the room, Clara sat on a second narrow wooden chair. Fannie moved across the room and leaned against the wall beside Clara, whose face had no more color in it than Fannie's father's.

"I wasn't thinking," Fannie murmured. "I only knew I wanted you with me. I know how you feel about births. If you want to go —"

Clara shook her head. "You were right to send for me. I only wish I could do something to help. I hate how she is suffering."

"Even the midwife can think of nothing to do but wait," Fannie said.

"Then we shall wait," Clara said, "but I am praying with every breath."

They watched Atlee wipe Martha's face with a damp cloth, love still passing in their glances after more than a quarter of a century together.

"What if she doesn't survive?" Fannie's words rode a breath.

"We will pray that God brings her through her travail," Clara said.

But Clara sounded unconvinced. It was impossible that she was not thinking of her own mother's passing, Fannie realized.

"My father will not be able to manage a baby," Fannie said.

"Don't think of it!"

"I have to," Fannie whispered. "I'm her daughter. She would want me to take in the baby."

And in that moment, Fannie realized she would do so without hesitation. A helpless, motherless baby would suffer enough in the years ahead. She could give it a good start.

"At least . . . at least until he *could* manage," Fannie said. After all, the baby would not be hers. It was her sibling, not her offspring. Fannie would not try to replace the emptiness of her own womb with the fullness of her mother's. Her father would want to hold and rock his own child.

But Fannie would rouse to do whatever the child needed.

"Of course you would," Clara said. "And I would stay and do everything I could, just the way your mother did everything she could for me. But we must *pray,* Fannie. We must pray that this child will know your mother's love for many years."

Atlee kissed his wife's forehead and withdrew once again. Martha rested between contractions.

Fannie signaled the midwife, who joined the huddle in the corner.

"Tell me the truth," Fannie said.

"I don't know," the midwife said. "The labor is going into its second day, and your mother is very tired."

Fannie bore her gaze into the midwife's face. "Will she survive?"

Martha groaned.

Andrew had never met Atlee Hostetler before, but already he liked him. Nearing fifty, Atlee looked not like a sun-wrinkled, worn-out farmer, like many men Andrew knew, but like a bronzed, hard worker in robust health. The brown curls of his hair and beard showed no hint of going gray. This was Clara's *onkel,* the man who welcomed Clara into his home for weeks at a time during her childhood. Andrew studied Atlee's features, searching for some glimpse into the years before Clara Kuhn had flooded into Andrew's daily thoughts. This home, this farm, had always been a refuge for Clara. On another occasion, Atlee's eyes might have been a clearer window to Clara's history.

Atlee's face creased more deeply with each hour that Andrew observed him. Andrew had spent most of the evening on an amply stuffed davenport, while Atlee pulled a cushionless straight-back chair from the dining room — that could not have been comfortable beyond the first twenty minutes of his vigil — and positioned it in the corner of the front room nearest the bedroom. Atlee came and went from that chair, never seeking better comfort or a bit of nourishment. This was as close as Atlee could come to sharing Martha's suffering, Andrew supposed.

Atlee had sent his sons to bed hours ago. Andrew wondered whether any of them were sleeping. The oldest Hostetler son, Abe, had taken his little boy to an upstairs bedroom and stayed with him after extracting a promise from Lizzie to wake him the moment there was news. Lizzie floated between the kitchen and the front room with continuous pots of coffee and plates of food, first meats and cheese and later sweets. No one ate. Occasionally she went into the bedroom to minister to her mother-in-law in some small way.

Midnight came and went.

"Thirty-seven hours," Atlee murmured. "The others were not like this."

Andrew thought of the *meidung*. What if it were Mattie Schrock in travail and Caleb sitting stiffly in a chair? Or John Stutzman and his wife? If he was needed, Andrew would have come.

He stood up, crossed the room, picked up a dining room chair, and set it next to Atlee. He would not speak or make any pretense of understanding what Atlee felt, but he could sit beside him rather than in comfort across the room. Andrew listened to Atlee's breathing, shallow and jagged with nerves.

Lizzie came in from the kitchen with a fresh pot of coffee and filled the empty mug in Atlee's hands.

The scream that erupted from the bedroom jolted the three of them. Atlee sought a place to set down his jiggling mug, and Lizzie took it from him before he sloshed coffee all over himself.

Rapid footsteps closed the small distance between the bedroom and front room. When Clara appeared, the strain in her face lurched Andrew's heart rate up. At the same time, footsteps thudded down the stairs, and Abe appeared.

Lizzie set down the coffeepot. "I'm going back in."

Andrew stood, catching Clara's elbow. "What happened?"

"The midwife says the baby is coming soon now." Her breath came shallow and fast.

Was it still alive? Andrew left his question unspoken. He could only imagine its weight on Atlee, who stood to lose both wife and child.

Atlee rose abruptly. "I'm going to the barn. I have a cow that's been poorly."

They watched him go out the front door. Andrew looked from Clara to Abe, who seemed unperturbed at Atlee's withdrawal. Atlee had not left the house since Andrew and Clara arrived — and probably not for hours before that. A midnight visit to the barn confused Andrew.

"He's going to pray," Abe explained.

"He has claimed a sickly cow as long as I can remember," Clara said.

"Should someone be with him?" Andrew said.

Abe and Clara shook their heads.

"He is not alone. He will meet God in the barn," Abe said.

Andrew nodded. It would not be the first time God made Himself known among animals and hay.

"Am I weak for needing a break?" Clara said. "Martha has no relief."

"Lizzie went in," Abe said. "And Fannie is still there. My *mamm* will never be alone in this."

A wail came from upstairs.

"Is Thomas all right?" Clara asked.

"Probably just dreaming. I'll go back to him." Abe padded out of the room and up the stairs.

Fannie stumbled into the room, and Clara stepped over to embrace her.

"She's hardly talking." A sob disrupted Fannie's effort to speak. "She's exhausted. I don't know what to do."

The cousins clutched each other. No *mei-dung* could break the bond Andrew witnessed.

Fannie drew in an enormous breath. "I must go back."

"I'll be right there," Clara said. "Whatever happens, love surrounds *Aunti* Martha."

Fannie withdrew to the bedroom. Clara turned to Andrew.

"Are you all right?" he asked.

Clara blanched. "I can't help thinking about so many other births."

"They bring great joy."

"Most of the time," Clara conceded. "I was too young to come when Fannie's brothers were born, but I remember the celebrations still going on by the time I visited to see the new babies."

"Is the midwife worried?"

"She's not sure if she's hearing the baby's heart rate too slow or Martha's heart rate too fast."

Anguish passed through her face. Andrew gave no voice to the looming question. Shouldn't there be two heartbeats?

"Rhoda's first three babies came far too soon. No one would let me see them, but I know they were far enough along to look like babies."

"Don't dwell on that now," Andrew said.

"It's hard not to."

"This is not the same. This baby is ready to be born."

"When this is over," Clara said, "I have to tell you about Rhoda."

"And I'll be here to listen."

Clara could not bear the thought of watching Martha suffer. Neither could she wait outside the bedroom. A scream directed her choice. She jumped away from Andrew and pushed open the door to her aunt's anguish.

The midwife was on alert. Lizzie and Fannie were on either side of Martha, supporting her back for the final push.

"Here's the head," the midwife said. "Now the shoulders. Yes, here we go. One more big push."

Four women held a collective breath while the fifth bore down.

"A girl!" the midwife said.

Where was the cry? Clara was present when Sadie was born, and her cry filled the room immediately. Josiah, Hannah, Mari — she'd heard all their cries from down the hall. It was taking too long.

The midwife tied the cord and cut it in a well-practiced motion. "A blanket," she said.

Lizzie lurched into action, unfolding soft cotton.

"She's not breathing!" Martha reached out a hand.

The midwife turned the infant upside down. The tiny girl protested immediately. In five seconds Lizzie had her in a blanket.

"Let Clara hold her," Martha said, falling back against the pillows. "She is Catherine."

"Catherine!" Clara laid one arm across the other to cradle the child. The tiny one looked like an *English* doll, perfectly formed with long dark lashes sweeping against her cheeks. Tears filled Clara's eyes at the baby's perfection — and safe arrival. She raised a glimmering glance to her aunt. "I'm so glad you're both safe."

"After your mother died, Atlee and I always said we would name our next daughter for her." Martha laughed. "Then we produced a string of boys."

"You should hold her." Clara watched her aunt's beaming, exhausted face.

"Let me see her face," Martha said. "Then go show Atlee all is well."

Clara glanced at the midwife, who nodded as she awaited the afterbirth. All was indeed well. Seeking the fine line between holding the babe securely but gently, Clara inched up the side of the bed and turned little Catherine for her mother's inspection.

"If you ask me, she even looks like your mother." Martha cupped her new daughter's head. "That chin favors yours."

Clara smiled, uncertain that it was possible to detect a resemblance in a baby less than five minutes old. Nevertheless, it pleased her that Martha wanted this baby to look like her sister. Martha's damp hair was plastered against her skull, and perspiration stuck her nightgown to her skin. She hadn't slept in more than forty-eight hours.

And Clara had never seen her aunt look more satisfied, more grateful, more simply and radiantly lovely.

"Go," Martha said. "I want Atlee to see for himself, but I want to be cleaned up before he comes in here again."

"Should we clean up the baby first?" Clara asked.

"There's time for that later. Show Atlee."

Lizzie opened the door, and Clara walked through it with the baby. Abe was there with Andrew, and Atlee had returned from his prayer session in the barn.

Clara choked on the effort to speak. "A girl! And Martha is fine!"

The men gathered around to admire the newest Hostetler. Atlee put a broad hand under his daughter's back, but his gaze went to the bedroom door.

"She really is fine," Clara whispered. "She'll be ready for you soon."

Release sailed out of Atlee's lungs. "So this is our Catherine, at long last." He bent and gently kissed his daughter's face.

Clara blinked against the tears as her uncle began to drift toward the bedroom, whether or not his wife was ready. Andrew put an arm around Clara's shoulder, and they leaned their heads together to marvel at the new life. Clara decided Martha was right after all. The baby's chin was like hers.

Andrew stroked Catherine's cheek. "She

looks perfectly at home in your arms."

Clara was perfectly at home holding her, with Andrew's nearness stirring up a memory that was yet to be, when they would bend toward each other like this over their own child.

And they would have a child. She knew this now.

Fannie, Lizzie, and the midwife emerged from the bedroom.

"*Mamm* is already asleep," Fannie said. "*Daed* won't want to leave her now."

"We should take the baby back in," Clara said.

"There will be plenty of time for that," the midwife said. "Right now Martha needs to rest."

Lizzie moved across the room. "I'll make sure there's warm water in the kitchen to clean the new *boppli.*"

The midwife trailed after Lizzie. "The room must be warm before we unwrap her."

They disappeared into the kitchen.

"Here, Fannie," Clara said. "Hold your little sister."

Fannie shook her head. "I think I'll find an empty bed and rest for a while myself so I can be some help later."

Clara watched her cousin climb the stairs. Fannie had rallied for the birth. But this babe in arms, exquisitely beautiful, was no remedy for her melancholy.

CHAPTER 39

Morning was not far off. Exhaustion settled over the house for a few hours after the midwife left, but farm rhythms did not pause for the birth of a baby.

Though Fannie had slept in the bedroom of her girlhood, when she woke a scant four hours after pulling a quilt up to her neck, she was disoriented by the silence. Elam and Sadie were the morning noisemakers at her house. Fannie threw off the quilt and went down to the kitchen. With one hand Fannie pulled her shawl more snug, and with the other she shoved wood into the belly of the stove. This was not her farm, but Fannie knew well its demands.

Her father's footsteps in the hall betrayed his effort to be quiet. Fannie raised her eyebrows and closed the stove's door.

"They're sleeping," Atlee said. "Both of them at the same time."

Fannie gave a small smile. "All's well."

"Your *mamm* thought you might come back in during the night."

Fannie fixed her gaze on the bowl of eggs on the table, four different shades of shells. "I thought I could be more useful if I rested."

The rational part of Fannie's brain justified the truth that her sister's birth had irritated a festering wound, and Fannie had run from the sight of innocent Catherine.

"The cows don't stop for a baby," Atlee said, pulling his jacket off a hook and fastening it closed.

"The boys can milk," Fannie said, glad for the change of subject. "I'll get them up."

Atlee shook his head. "I'll want to do it."

He would be praying again, Fannie knew. This time prayers of gratitude, prayers for the future. If only she could borrow his unspoken words.

Satisfied that the fire in the stove was catching and would soon both warm the room and provide heat for breakfast, Fannie padded through the house. In the front room, Clara and Andrew startled her. Fannie's own withdrawal after the birth had been so swift that she did not consider that someone should offer them beds. Even Lizzie and Abe, whose farm was nearby, had stayed through the night. Andrew and Clara would not leave before daylight. Their heads tilted toward each other, shoulders meeting, each of them asleep under a quilt from the cedar chest under the window.

Clara would have known where to find more bedding, Fannie thought. Her cousin had chosen this closeness with Andrew. Envy stirred. Everything lay ahead of them. They had not yet decided to marry, but Fannie knew Clara well enough to be sure she would not rest so easily against a man she did not love. Though Fannie and Elam had not yet observed their seventh anniversary, their unmarried optimism was a far-off land already.

Careful not to wake them, Fannie slowly opened her parents' bedroom door and slipped in.

Her father had stoked the fire before he left for the barn. It snapped and crackled behind the grate, throwing heat and orange light into the corners of the room. Her mother was in a fresh nightdress and slumbered in fresh bedding with the baby on her chest. Atlee had tucked pillows on both sides of his wife, propping up the sleeping arms holding the baby.

Just in case, he would have said. He was a cautious man. A thoughtful man. A generous man.

Fannie used to think of Elam that way.

Little Catherine's mouth started to twitch. Was she hungry? Dreaming? Stretching against the tight bundling? Tiny sounds dribbled out of her mouth, not quite cries, not quite coos. If the household had been bustling at its usual volume, Fannie would not even have heard them.

Clara had tried to hand Catherine to her a few hours ago, and Fannie could not make her arms receive the child. Now she sucked in a series of small breaths.

This was her sister.

When she thought her mother might not survive, Fannie was willing to take this child home with her. In the face of fear, her heart was wide open. Why had it closed in the face of joy? She had not even touched Catherine's tiny hand.

Fannie wondered if her father was praying for her along with his new little daughter.

Pressing her lips together, Fannie moved toward the bed and lifted the baby from Martha's chest. She stepped toward the fire and opened the quilt to see her sister. The soft white cotton dress she wore was new. Martha had long ago given away the tiny clothing her other babies wore. Unbundled, Catherine began to kick her feet and thrash her arms. Her eyes opened, and though she seemed to look at her big sister, Fannie wondered what a baby really saw.

Sadie had been like this once. New and wondrous and vulnerable and delicate and tiny. Fannie had soaked up every sensation then, and if she had known she would not have another child, she would have pondered even more deeply in her heart.

Catherine yawned, her lips hardly bigger than a doll's, making the most perfect oval Fannie had ever seen. Fannie held her diminutive hand, stilling its aimless movement through the air and kissing the row of tender fingertips. Then she tucked the quilt back around the baby.

"Thank You," she whispered. A prayer. The first in a long time.

Fannie might never have another child, and she might never know what had closed her womb after Sadie's easy arrival.

Elam might never regain his ambition for the farm in the absence of sons or a larger family to provide for.

Fannie might — *would* — have aching moments when she did not understand why Catherine had come into the world and not her own child.

But Catherine had come. She was here in Fannie's arms, two sisters a generation apart while their mother slept.

If Fannie's only prayer was *Thank You,* it would be enough.

Martha stirred, her empty arms floundering briefly before her eyes found their focus.

"My girls," she said.

As tears filled Martha's eyes, they also spilled from Fannie's.

Clara's neck was oddly stiff, and a sharp pain shot into her shoulder and made her suck in air. She had begun her sleep with her head against the back of the davenport. When she felt Andrew's shoulder under her cheek later, she was too groggy to change positions. Now her head had slipped down to his chest. The heartbeat she heard was his.

Not too fast. Not too slow. Thumping steady and strong.

This was the first time Clara had heard Andrew's heartbeat, but it would not be the last. Andrew's heartbeat on one side of her and his arm wrapped around the other was where she wanted to live.

Cautiously, she straightened her neck to relieve the pressure of the awkward position.

Andrew murmured. "Is it morning?"

Clara glanced out the window. "Almost. The sun is just coming up."

"I love morning light," he said. "His mercies are new every morning."

Clara leaned away from him and took his hand. "Let's go see it. We've never seen the sunrise together."

Above them, Clara heard her cousins beginning to move around. Abe and Lizzie and Thomas had stayed the night, but they would need to get home to their own farm and waiting cows. Her youngest cousin was in his last year of school, and in his mother's eyes even the birth of his sister would be no excuse to be late. The other two knew a full day's labor awaited them. Clara wanted this moment with Andrew, just the two of them watching the mystery of spreading orange and pink hues give way to full light.

Outside, they leaned against a post on the porch, shoulder to shoulder.

"Thank you for bringing me," Clara said, unsure whether she had expressed her gratitude for his complicity in this unscheduled trip across the border.

"It was God's will," Andrew said. "Why else would I have been on the road to your farm at just the moment you needed a ride?"

Clara smiled, suspecting that he'd had other motives than purely putting himself at the disposal of God's will. Hadn't he said something about sneaking onto the farm to take her for a ride?

"I won't ever forget this night. Martha worked so hard! Fannie thought we would lose her, and the midwife didn't offer much reassurance. But Martha held on, and Catherine is safe."

"Many prayers answered," Andrew said.

"And Martha would do it again. I could see it in her face. Whatever it took, it was worth it. I always thought of joy as something to feel. Now I know it is something to hold."

Andrew angled himself toward Clara. "Would it be worth it to you?"

She met his eyes.

"I would be right there," he said. "Whatever it took, and whatever happened, we would face it together."

"I know," Clara said. "I know."

"The wedding season has only just started."

She nodded.

"We can have our banns read."

Clara nodded again, this time more dramatically. She wanted him to ask the question — again — so she could reward his patience with the answer he'd waited so long to hear.

"I can talk to Mose," he said. "Of course I should speak to your father first."

She breathed in through her nose and waited.

"Rhoda will come around, won't she?" Andrew said. "She'll help you get ready for the wedding, surely. It's what she wants, isn't it?"

Clara locked her eyes on his.

"It won't be perfect," he said. "We won't always understand God's will, especially in days of pain. But whatever it is, we will hold the joy together."

She moistened her lips and nodded.

"Clara Kuhn, are you saying that you're ready to marry me?"

"If you would ask a proper question," she said, "I would give a proper answer."

He smiled. "Clara Kuhn, will you become Clara Raber and let me love you for the rest of our lives?"

"Nothing would make me happier."

Clara leaned into his kiss, her lips tangling with his in a delicious moment that Andrew seemed keen to prolong. Clara offered no objection as she wrapped her arms around his waist and his hands took her face in his.

Atlee cleared his throat, and they jumped apart — but not very far.

"Somehow," Atlee said, "I suspect our Catherine's safe arrival will not be the only good news we celebrate today."

Clara laughed. How long had Atlee been standing there?

The sky shimmered with morning hope. Atlee went into the house, and Andrew and Clara remained on the porch to stare into future glory.

Inside a few minutes later, Clara went straight to the kitchen. Sausage sizzled in an iron skillet, and Fannie was cracking eggs three at a time into a bowl. The smell of biscuits in the oven made Clara suddenly ravenous.

"The baby is suckling," Fannie said. "They don't all latch on so well, but Catherine seems to know just what to do."

Fannie's tone surprised Clara, along with her industrious efforts to put breakfast on the table. Clara opened a cupboard and took out plates.

"We'll need ten plates," Fannie said. "I've sent one of the boys to fetch Elam and Sadie."

The contents of three more eggshells plopped into the bowl. Fannie turned around and dropped butter into a second skillet heating on the stove, the largest one Martha had. Clara peered into the bowl and saw at least twenty yolks.

"The *kaffi* should be ready," Fannie said.

Clara's hands moved to the shelf that held

coffee cups.

Fannie whisked the eggs together and glanced at the melting butter. "If you're willing to check the cellar, *Mamm* probably has some apples."

"I'll go right now," Clara said.

She stood at the back door and watched Fannie's cooking frenzy. Had hope settled on her cousin as well? Or was she merely forcing herself to do what a daughter ought to do? Clara watched Fannie's face for a few seconds. When she heard humming from Fannie's throat — a hymn of some sort but more joyous than the *Ausbund* hymns — Clara dared to believe that light had at last cleaved the darkness.

CHAPTER 40

Andrew only vaguely recognized the boy who turned up at his farm the next morning. His black trousers and suspenders over a white shirt, and the child-sized black felt hat, left no doubt that he belonged to the Pennsylvania Old Order district.

A Yoder, Andrew was fairly certain, but there were so many branches of the Yoder family tree. Andrew himself hung from one of them because of his mother's maternal grandmother, but he never thought of himself as a Yoder. Whatever his last name was, this boy might not be any more closely related to Joseph and Noah Yoder than Andrew was.

He was just a boy, nine or ten years old. What were they doing sending him to summon Andrew?

"Thank you for bringing the message." Andrew took two apples from the bushel on his front porch. "Maybe your horse would like this — and one for you."

The boy hesitated but took the apples. "They said I was to make sure you come immediately."

Indignation swirled. Where did they find the gall to suggest that one boy on a sagging sorrel could demand Andrew — or anyone — comply?

"You've done a fine job delivering the message." Andrew wished he could call the boy by name. "I suppose you're already late for school."

The boy polished his apple on his shirtsleeve. "My *mamm* teaches me at home."

That narrowed the possibilities considerably, since nearly all the Amish children attended the same Crossroads School Andrew had gone to. Still, Andrew would not be hurried.

"I have some things to tend to," Andrew said, "but I'll make sure they know you faithfully carried out their instruction."

The boy looked conflicted about what he was supposed to do, but Andrew stepped back into the house and closed the door between them. When he looked out the front window a few minutes later, the boy and his horse were gone. Andrew poured himself another cup of coffee and set out the clean shirt he would don later in the day to go speak to Hiram Kuhn. Then he picked up the list, begun the day before, of all the repairs he would make around the house before bringing Clara home to live there. Out in the barn, he made sure all the stalls had fresh hay. He walked along one side of the pasture to make sure none of the fence posts jiggled.

The delays did nothing to temper his ire. He muttered prayers for self-control and resisted the urge to take the Model T for spite. Over the last few weeks he had cleared a shed of tools and equipment no one had used since Andrew was a boy. He was nearly ready to bring the automobile home to his own property.

And he would, no matter what the Yoder brothers had to say about it.

He exhaled exasperation. He had Clara to think about.

Andrew arrived at the Yoder farm at his own readiness. It should not have surprised him that this was Yonnie's doing.

"We have a witness," Joseph Yoder said, "who has taken seriously his obligation to speak to us about his brothers and sisters who choose their own convenience over the good of the congregation."

Andrew could think of no one else, other

than the Yoders themselves, who fit this description. He had not noticed anyone on the road when he picked up Clara, but her distressed state had made everything fade away.

"A witness of what?" he said as he stood in Joseph's study before a thick German Bible open on the desk.

"You have made two transgressions," Joseph said. "You visited Marylanders with whom you have no family relationship, so there can be no doubt that this violates the *meidung*. Second, you drove an *English* automobile in the process."

"If you will excuse me," Andrew said, "I have a farm to run."

"I am sure you can take a few minutes from your busy day to repent," Noah said. "Our Lord is faithful and just to forgive us our sins."

"Please sit down," Joseph said. "Let us pray for you, that you might have a clean heart once again."

"I will not repent when I have not sinned."

"If we say we have no sin," Joseph said, "we deceive ourselves. We read this in 1 John."

"I didn't say I have *no* sin," Andrew said. "I only believe the actions you named are not sinful." He might have to repent if he lost his temper, but he would not repent for taking Clara to Maryland.

"Please." Noah gestured to a chair. "Come, let us reason together."

Andrew wondered if they intended to quote the entire Bible to him one verse at a time. He sat down, calculating whether they would dismiss him without a statement of repentance if in fact they could have a reasonable discussion.

"Yes," he said, "let us reason together. I will be happy to explain to you my conviction."

"You must repent," Noah said.

Andrew regretted sitting down. "And if I don't?"

"Then we will have no choice but to put you under the ban."

"The Marylanders will welcome me with open hearts."

Clara's face flashed across his mind. Would she agree to move to a new congregation and leave her family behind? And the wedding — she might not be agreeable to marrying outside their own district.

I am betrothed. Clara was aware of the silly grin on her face, but driving the Kuhn buggy alone on the road to Andrew's farm, she did not care. In a few weeks, Andrew's home would be her home. The shine of the events on the Hostetler farm had not worn off, and Clara prayed they never would. When she told Hiram the baby's name, his lips had parted and spread.

"My Catherine would have been embarrassed," he said, "but another Catherine to remind us of her . . ."

His voice trailed off, and emotion flushed through him. All these years later, with another wife and three more children, her father shared with her aunt the memory of the woman they loved.

Clara saved the news of her betrothal. Andrew had made her promise to wait until he spoke to Hiram, and Clara had made him promise not to wait very long. At home she let everyone think her light mood rose only from the baby's arrival.

Andrew was not on his farm. Thinking he might be at the Johnson place, Clara pulled the rig back out on the main road and found herself blocked by a sorrel who seemed to be resisting the reins.

"I'm sorry," the young rider said. "I only came back to make sure Mr. Raber went."

"Went where?" Clara asked, waiting for the boy to get control of the horse.

"Joseph Yoder's," he said. "They sent me this morning to find him. I don't want to be in trouble if he didn't actually go."

"I need to get by you, please," Clara said.

She zigzagged through the back roads to Mose Beachy's farm. He was a reasonable man, a kind man. And he was the bishop.

She raced onto his property. He could be anywhere on the farm, but Lucy would know where to send Clara. With the firmest knock of her life, Clara rapped on the front door.

Rather than Lucy, though, Mose answered the door.

"They have Andrew." Clara spat out the words.

The pleasant greeting in Mose's face soured. "Where?"

"At Joseph's."

Mose reached for his hat on a hook beside the door. "Lucy, I'm going out."

Clara lengthened her stride to keep up with Mose, who aimed for her buggy rather than take time to hitch up his own.

"I'll drive," he said, taking up the reins. "You tell me what this is about."

As they jostled along the road, Clara stumbled through an explanation.

The pressing message about Martha's labor.

No buggy to take from the Kuhn farm.

Andrew turning up on the road just then.

The automobile.

The urgency.

The fright.

"It's the only thing I can think of," she said, catching her breath. "It's either because he has the Model T or because he used it to drive me to Maryland."

"Andrew and I will have to talk further about the Model T," Mose said, "but I could not have made myself more clear with Joseph and Noah about having these confrontations about the *meidung* without speaking to me first."

As they traveled, Clara wished for the speed of Andrew's automobile. They would be at the Yoders' by now if they were in the Model T.

Finally, Mose turned into the farm's lane and they scrambled toward the house, where Joseph's wife did not dare deny the bishop entrance.

Joseph's study was dark and foreboding. Clara's heart battered against her ribs.

"I speak German, Pennsylvania Dutch, and English," Mose said with impressive calm. "If you will tell me your preference, I will make sure that I am communicating clearly."

Joseph glared. "Our brother is in need of repentance, and as ministers it is our calling to guide him to it."

"He has done nothing to repent of!" Clara cried.

The Yoders remained infuriatingly calm.

"He visited a Marylander family to whom he is not related, and he drove an *English* automobile to get there," Noah said.

"I was with him," Clara said. "Were you planning to send for me next?"

"You went to see your family," Noah said. "And while you rode in the automobile, you did not drive it and neither do you own it. You have done nothing wrong."

"But we were together the whole time. What he did, I did. What I did, he did. We made the choices together. He took me because I asked him to."

"Clara," Andrew said quietly.

"You did not sin, but Andrew did," Joseph pronounced.

It made no sense to Clara. She turned to Mose.

Mose repositioned a chair and indicated that Clara should sit in it. Trembling, she obeyed. Only an hour ago she had left home with a brimming heart and the expectation of a joyous day. She wanted Andrew to kiss her while they planned for him to visit the Kuhn farm that afternoon. When they spoke to Mose — together — it would be about publishing their banns, not about whether either of them harbored sin for which they ought to repent.

"Are you prepared to dismiss Andrew from this conversation?" Mose said, still standing.

"He has not yet repented," Noah pointed out. "We would like to pray for him and await the Holy Ghost's conviction."

Clara watched Andrew's face. Though stiff, his expression told little of what might already have transpired. How long had he been there? What had they threatened him with? His eyes met hers, and he shook his head slightly.

Clara sprang to her feet. "Are you trying to chase us to the Maryland district? Is that what you want? To be rid of us?"

"Clara." Mose and Andrew spoke at the same time.

She ignored them and scowled at the brothers. "Don't tell me this is for the good of the congregation. Accusations and threats are no way to hold the church together."

Noah gave a sharp clap. "Contain your impudence!"

Mose gestured to Andrew. "Please take Clara outside and wait for me there."

"Our meeting has not concluded," Joseph said.

"Andrew, please," Mose said.

Andrew took Clara's elbow, and together they let themselves out of the Yoder home. Clara squinted into the sunlight as she pushed out a series of short breaths. Silent, they waited a few minutes beside Clara's buggy. Andrew had brought only a horse. He glanced at the house every few seconds, as if willing the door to open and Mose to emerge.

"This was Yonnie," Andrew said. "I have to talk to him."

Clara laid a hand on his arm. "Not while you're angry."

He laid one hand on her cheek. "I will not speak in anger. I will do my best to speak the truth in love."

"Mose asked us to wait for him," Clara said.

"He's taking too long," Andrew said. "I'll explain to him later. Will you be all right getting your buggy home?"

"Mose rode with me," Clara said. "I have no choice but to wait for him."

Andrew leaned in and kissed her. "Come find me later, at the Johnson place. I'll tell you everything."

He swung himself astride his horse and galloped off the farmstead.

Behind Clara, Mose's voice boomed. "Andrew!"

Andrew paused long enough to look over his shoulder. But he did not turn around.

CHAPTER 41

If there were repercussions for defying Mose's request to wait outside the Yoder home, Andrew would face them later. Clara would understand, and Mose might scowl but he would listen — which was more than Andrew could say for the Yoders. He rode straight to the dairy, confident that if Yonnie had done the morning rounds he would be back by now.

"I let him go a week ago," Dale said when Andrew politely asked for a few minutes of Yonnie's time.

"Let him go?" Andrew echoed.

"We came to a parting of ways." Dale riffled papers on his desk. "And if you know him half as well as I think you do, you know why."

"Where is he working now?"

"I haven't heard that he is." Dale stood up. "If I run into him, I'll let him know you were looking for him."

493

Andrew nodded at Dale's empty assurance. The dairy owner was not likely to run into his former employee.

So where was Yonnie?

Andrew mounted his horse and puffed his cheeks.

Riding out to Yonnie's family farm carried the risk that he had not told his parents or siblings of his loss of employment. Andrew knew Yonnie not half as well as Dale suspected but twice as well. And Yonnie would get up and leave the farm on his normal schedule rather than concern his parents before he was ready with an announcement that would put them at ease.

Andrew let his horse enjoy a restful pace, riding with his hands crossed over the horn of the saddle while he tried to think as Yonnie would think. Once, when they were eleven, Yonnie let himself get talked into a prank with some boys that got them all suspended from school for three days. Andrew doubted Yonnie's parents knew to this day. Yonnie left the house in the morning with his brothers and sisters and stepped out of the group just before students entered the Crossroads School. In the afternoon he caught up with his siblings along the path home. Years later Yonnie admitted to Andrew that he spent those three days hiding in an abandoned outbuilding, afraid to be seen during school hours.

An abandoned outbuilding.

At the next turn, Andrew swung the horse down a less traveled road and coaxed a canter from the animal. He approached the old Johnson place with a mixture of gratitude that he'd thought of it and trepidation for what Yonnie might be doing there.

Andrew eased off the horse and left the faithful servant tied loosely to the low branch of a tree on the outer ring of the clearing around the structure, the ground now covered with the brown, wintry decay of unmowed summer weeds that would no doubt be back with a vengeance next year. He scanned the surroundings. The decrepit barn's door was closed as snugly as it ever was — which was hardly secure — but Andrew drew no conclusions from this. He scanned the clearing systematically before staring into the surrounding woods.

Seeing nothing, he called out. "Yonnie?"

Andrew was uncertain whether the roll of shadow revealed movement within the barn or a shift in sunlight through the trees. He moved closer and pushed the door open enough to slip inside, waiting for his eyes to adjust to the dim interior.

"Yonnie?"

This time Andrew heard the shuffle and turned his head toward the sound.

In the far corner, with the Model T between them, Yonnie hunched against a wall.

Alarm shot through Andrew. Yonnie held a two-foot length of cast-off pipe.

"What are you doing here, Yonnie?" Andrew moved slowly around the automobile, hesitant to cause Yonnie to move suddenly.

"It's out of the elements, at least," Yonnie said.

"You won't make things better by smashing the car." Andrew was fairly certain now he would be able to intercept Yonnie's efforts.

Yonnie laughed. "Is that what you think I'm here for?"

Andrew said nothing as he moved closer.

Yonnie raised the pipe.

"Don't, Yonnie," Andrew said.

"I'm not going to wreck the car." Yonnie tossed the pipe to one side, where it clattered against a wall. "You can sell the car and give the money to the poor."

Making no promise, Andrew stood in front of Yonnie now, examining the circles under his eyes. He touched the torn shoulder of Yonnie's coat. "What happened here?"

"An altercation with a tree." Yonnie brushed off Andrew's touch.

"An accident?"

"Of course it was an accident. Who runs into a tree on purpose?" Yonnie met Andrew's gaze. "Have you come from Joseph and Noah?"

Andrew planted his feet, prepared to prevent Yonnie from rushing past him and out the door until they had it out.

"Yonnie, why?" Andrew said softly. All through their boyhood he had shrugged off Yonnie's quirks, rarely losing his temper and usually finding amusement. Now he had Clara to think of, and he had promised not to speak in anger.

For a long moment, Yonnie looked over Andrew's shoulder at the opposite wall. "Because it was the right thing to do."

"Was it? Where do you find such unabated certainty?"

"In the teachings of the church. In the faith of our fathers."

"What about *our* faith?" Andrew said. "What about *your* faith?"

"Don't ask ridiculous questions." Yonnie's spine slackened, and he slid down the wall of the barn.

"Yonnie." Andrew reached out to touch his shoulder.

Sitting on the ground, Yonnie pulled his knees up, rested his arms on them, and hung his head.

Andrew had not meant to hold his breath, and now his lungs ached for relief.

"Are you going to marry Clara?" Yonnie mumbled.

"Yes. She has finally agreed to have me."

"I hope you'll be very happy."

"Thank you. I think we will be." Squatting in front of Yonnie, Andrew narrowed his eyes at the odd shift in conversation.

"You're not any older than I am," Yonnie said, "and you have a farm."

"With a mortgage," Andrew reminded Yonnie. His parents had left him to take over the farm, but it was not free and clear. He had also assumed the debt.

"All the same," Yonnie said, "you have something to offer a woman. Something to make her care for you."

Andrew twisted to sit beside Yonnie, their backs against the wall. "I'd like to think I have other qualities at least equally as appealing."

"I have nothing," Yonnie said. "No farm, not enough money to persuade the bank I'm a worthy risk, no one to drive home with after the Singings. No job."

Andrew grimaced. "I stopped by the dairy."

"Then you know," Yonnie said. "The

buggy I drive belongs to my father, along with everything else. I have a horse of my own that can barely keep up with a three-year-old child, and a few untillable acres on the edge of my father's farm. That's it."

Even if Andrew had not promised Clara to hold his temper with Yonnie, the urge to unleash it passed. Over the years, Andrew had seen Yonnie obstinate, gullible, fearful, and eager to please anyone he thought of as holding authority. Despondence had never colored Yonnie's features as it did now.

"It won't always be that way," Andrew said.

"What I have is the church," Yonnie said. "I have the promises that come with obedience. I can't let go of them."

"No one is asking you to," Andrew said, "only perhaps to be less . . . insistent on the forms obedience takes."

"The church must stay together." Yonnie hit the ground with the flat of his hand. "If we don't have that, we've lost everything."

Andrew ran his tongue over his teeth, resisting the urge to pursue a theological debate.

"You know," he said, "I'm alone on my farm. I could use another hand I could count on. Even over the winter there's a lot to do when it's just me."

"You've always managed."

"You should see the list of things I never get around to."

"Maybe if you spent less time with the Model T," Yonnie said.

Andrew swallowed his response. "I understand if you don't want to work for me."

"I didn't say that."

Andrew crossed his legs out in front of him. "I know you disapprove of the car, but I was putting it to good use when I took Clara to Maryland. She had a very good reason for getting there in a hurry, and I was glad to be able to help her." He still had not sorted out when Yonnie could have seen them and supposed he would never be sure.

"We have rules for a reason," Yonnie said.

Andrew counted to ten beneath his breath.

"I shouldn't have said that." Yonnie tilted his head back against the wall. "I'm envious. I'm angry. I'm lacking in love."

"Love casts out fear," Andrew said. "Love thinks the best. Love never fails."

"Let us keep our eyes on love." Yonnie sang softly from the old *Ausbund* hymn.

Andrew nodded.

The barn door opened, flooding the space with daylight. Clara stepped in.

"Oh," she said, when she spotted Yonnie.

Her eyes took in the scene.

"It's all right. We're all right." Andrew stood up. "Yonnie's going to work for me for a while."

Clara's eyes widened and bulged.

"At least I hope he is." Andrew offered a hand and pulled Yonnie to his feet.

Yonnie glanced at Clara, sheepish. "I understand you've finally decided to throw your lot in with my old friend."

The sound that Clara emitted was not quite a word.

Andrew stepped toward her. "Someone had to be the first to know. Why not my boyhood friend?"

He kissed her mouth. Later she could hear the whole story.

Nine days later, Clara sat in church, still stunned that the old friendship between Andrew and Yonnie had resurfaced. They sat beside each other in the first row of single men right behind the married men.

It bothered her that Yonnie was the one who knew their secret.

The skirmish with Noah and Joseph Yoder persuaded them to wait before speaking to Clara's father or Mose. Neither of them wanted news of their engagement tangled in speculation about their future in the church.

They had told each other this and agreed to wait.

Whatever Yonnie's attitude was now — and Clara was not sure she knew — the damage was done. Joseph and Noah had called Andrew to task, and with Mose's dissenting opinion, the ministers disagreed on what action the Bible required them to take. Neither Andrew nor Clara wanted their engagement lost in the swirl of the dark clouds. Andrew had waited two years for her to accept his proposal. They would wait a few more days or weeks.

Clara adjusted her shoulders, which had started to ache, and moved her eyes forward. Mose stood beside the preaching table, giving the main sermon.

" 'And let the peace of God rule in your hearts,' " Mose read, " 'o the which also ye are called in one body; and be ye thankful. Let the word of Christ dwell in you richly in all wisdom; teaching and admonishing one another in psalms and hymns and spiritual songs, singing with grace in your hearts to the Lord.' "

Mose looked up here, catching eyes around the room before he continued.

" 'And whatsoever ye do in word or deed, do all in the name of the Lord Jesus, giving thanks to God and the Father by him.' "

Mose put one finger on the page open on the table.

"This is what the apostle Paul wrote to the believers in Colossae, and his words are of equal guidance to us." He paced a couple of steps away from the preaching table and scanned the assembly. "I do not make light of the differences of opinion among us, even as we are called to be one body. I urge peace and unity above all else, just as Paul did two thousand years ago. On the matters which confound us — and I do not believe I must list them now — I seek the wisdom of bishops in other districts. I seek the word of Christ, that I might share it with you richly. Your part is to grant me patience and continue to live in love one toward the other. Then we will know the peace of God together."

Clara hoped Mose would agree to marry her and Andrew. These were the sort of humble words she wanted to attune her heart to on the day she committed to love Andrew for the rest of their lives.

Mose did not close the door on change. Neither did he swing it wide open. He would be a wise leader. Clara would be glad to see her children grow up under his teaching.

Her children. What an odd sensation it was

to permit herself to think those words
without fright.

CHAPTER 42

The bride in her new blue dress paled against the charm Andrew saw in Clara's face. Clara wore the same color, starched and unsoiled, with a sparkling white apron. Andrew wondered if she would stitch another new blue dress for their wedding or choose purple or a darker blue. On the last Thursday in November, Peter Troyer and his attendants sat in three chairs facing Ruth Kaufman and her attendants at the front of the church. Directly across from Clara, Andrew watched her eyes, turning over in his mind the question of how quickly Clara would want to marry.

Soon, he hoped.

They could marry here, in the Flag Run Meetinghouse, where her parents had wed.

Andrew heard little of the sermons, but there would always be another sermon. In a white *kapp,* Clara's head tilted slightly toward Mose Beachy as he preached, but her eyes seemed to look beyond him as if boring through the meetinghouse wall. Was she also thinking about their wedding?

When the wedding party began to shift position, Andrew realized Mose had made the statement that would transition the worship service into the wedding ceremony.

"If anyone here has objection, he now has opportunity to make it manifest." Mose paused and looked at the wedding couple. "I hear no objection. If you are still minded the same, you may now come forth in the name of the Lord."

The bride and groom held hands and stood before Mose. With earnest voices, they promised love and loyalty for the rest of their lives.

Andrew's gaze moved back to Clara, who now caught his eye.

Clara's lips turned up. Anyone else would think she smiled in gladness, hearing her friend pledge her future. Andrew knew that smile was meant for him.

"I don't want to wait," she told him as soon as the wedding was over. "Talk to my father."

"Today?" Andrew said. "Now?"

"He'll give us his blessing."

"You're sure?" Andrew glanced at Hiram Kuhn.

"Aren't you?" Clara said. "What are we waiting for?"

Andrew nodded. This was their congregation. They belonged here. Speculation had nothing to do with when or where they married.

"I want the Hostetlers to come," Clara said. "I can't imagine getting married without Fannie."

"We'll ask Mose."

Mose Beachy said I can have whomever I want to stand up for me.

Fannie read Clara's orderly handwriting on the crisp pale blue paper a week later.

And I want you. Please say you'll do it.

Fannie's eyes filled. Of course she would do it. After all, Clara had been her attendant when she married Elam. Fannie did not imagine an Old Order wedding was much different than a Conservative Amish Mennonite wedding.

We've decided not to wait any longer than we have to for the sake of planning and sewing the dresses. The banns will be read on Sunday, and we'll marry two days after Christmas. My daed and Rhoda seem relieved but pleased. Daed gave his blessing almost before Andrew finished asking for it. I'm sure they will come to see how dear Andrew is.

Hannah is the most excited, as I'm sure Sadie will be when you tell her.

A tear dropped on the page just as Elam came in the back door.

He paced to the stove and peered into the coffeepot.

"The *kaffi* should still be warm." Fannie wiped her eyes with the back of one hand.

Elam gestured at the letter in her hand. "Bad news?"

Fannie shook her head and smiled. "Just the opposite. Clara and Andrew have made their plans. She wants me for an attendant."

"Then you must do it," Elam said.

Fannie felt him watching her and looked up to meet his eyes. "Do you remember, Elam?"

"Remember what?"

"When we decided to marry? When we told our families? When everything was ahead of us like a ripe, abundant harvest? When God's will was a blessing so full that we could hardly stand it?"

Elam broke the gaze and poured the last of the coffee into a cup, the slosh of the liquid the only sound in the room.

"I remember," he finally said.

"We dreamed of so much," she said.

Their arms and hearts and minds were entwined in those days. Seven years later they orbited each other on elongated paths that spun each other out for long distances before drawing near again. In those days Elam would have caught her hand in the kitchen before reaching for the coffeepot. Now, wordless, he clinked a spoon in the sugar bowl. In the void between them, Fannie heard the granules slide off the spoon and drop into the lukewarm liquid.

"Elam," she whispered.

He hesitated but met her eyes again.

"Will we always be this lost?"

He stirred his coffee.

Elam was a good man, just as good as the day Fannie married him. He might yet get past his disappointment that God's will collided with his own dreams, just as Fannie might yet find relief from the ache that plagued her.

He put his spoon in the sink. "No. God willing, no."

Hope flickered in her chest. Fannie moved toward Elam and laid a hand on his arm. He did not pull away. His hand grazed hers on the way back to his coffee cup.

Sadie was spinning slow circles as she came in from the dining room.

"Have you told her?" Elam asked Fannie.

"Told me what?" Sadie steadied herself on a chair.

Fannie could see Sadie's eyes took a few seconds to come into focus. In fine weather Fannie sent Sadie outside for her determined dance with dizziness, but in early December the weather was unpredictable.

"I got a letter from Clara," Fannie said. "She's getting married."

Sadie's eyes widened. "To that man who came when baby Catherine was born?"

"That's right. Andrew."

Sadie drew in a long, excited breath. "I liked him!"

Fannie laughed. "Clara will be glad to hear that."

"Are we going to the wedding?"

"Yes."

"All of us?"

Fannie glanced at Elam.

"Yes," he said, "all of us."

"Did Clara send me a new story?"

"Not this time," Fannie said.

"I want to write her a letter," Sadie said. "I want to tell her that I'm very happy she's going to marry Andrew, but I still want her to send me stories."

"I think it would make Andrew very happy if she did."

"Good. Are we going to go see *Grossmuder* for supper?"

"My goodness, you're full of questions

510

today." Fannie slid Clara's letter back into its envelope.

"Well, are we?"

"We'd better," Fannie said, "because I promised to bring the biscuits and the green beans."

"I want to help make biscuits!" Sadie slid a chair across the linoleum to her favorite helping spot at the counter. "Can I give baby Catherine one of my dolls?"

"If you'd like to," Fannie said, "but she'll have to be a little older to play with it."

"I'll teach her to play."

Her daughter's wide-open heart was fresh every day. It pained Fannie to think how much of it she had missed in the months of her melancholy.

In the late afternoon they packed up the biscuits and the green beans and Sadie's favorite doll, and the three of them rode in the buggy to the Hostetler farm.

Sitting in the same rocker where she had held all her babies, Martha put a finger to her lips when they entered the house.

"Is she asleep?" Fannie whispered.

Martha nodded.

The bundle in Martha's arms seemed already to have doubled in size since the night of her frightening birth. Every time Fannie saw her tiny sister, the change in appearance astounded her. With a look warning Sadie not to wake the baby, Fannie scooped Catherine out of her mother's arms and inhaled the intoxicating new baby scent. These days Fannie's hips easily found the automatic sway that had soothed Sadie a lifetime ago. She planted a delicate kiss on Catherine's forehead.

Martha stood up and smoothed her apron. When she paused to stand beside Fannie and admire the sleeping infant, Fannie turned her head and kissed her mother's cheek as well.

How rich she was in love.

"Fannie is coming?" Rhoda blinked at Clara.

"I can't imagine getting married without her." Clara stacked her plate on top of Rhoda's and took them both to the sink. Hannah and Josiah were in school, and Mari was napping. Her father was gone all day with a couple of other farmers, already beginning to plan for spring. It had been only Rhoda and Clara for a simple quiet lunch. With only a few weeks until the wedding, nearly every conversation Clara had found its way to wedding details. Without acknowledgment or explanation, Rhoda had warmed to Clara once again.

"What about Wanda," Rhoda countered, "or Sarah? You have many friends who would love to be an attendant at your wedding."

"I asked Sarah," Clara said. "But Fannie — if I had to, I would change the date in order for her to be there. Bishop Beachy has given his approval."

Rhoda looked away, picking up a napkin to fold. "I would hate for there to be any awkwardness on your wedding day."

"Why should there be?" Clara said, though she wanted to say, *How could anything be more awkward than these last few months?*

Rhoda went to a drawer and pulled out a sheet of paper. "I've got a list. Maybe it will help you."

Clara took the paper, which had two columns. On the left was a list of tasks — the *Forgeher* to usher, waiters, *roasht* cooks, potato cooks, tablecloths, *hostlers* to care for the horses. On the right, names matched up with every effort required for a traditional Amish wedding.

"Many people will want to help," Rhoda said.

"You don't think they're worn out from all the other weddings this season?"

Rhoda put a hand against Clara's cheek, a gesture reminiscent of the first time she ever touched her new stepdaughter. "This is *your* wedding. Of course people will want to give you a lovely day. *I* want to give you a lovely day."

Under Rhoda's touch, Clara twitched, stifling a tremble before it roared up and ripped her open. In Rhoda's face, Clara saw the wide-set blue eyes and high cheekbones of her little sisters.

"I've only ever wanted what is best for you," Rhoda said. *"Alli mudder muss sariye fer ihre famiyle."*

Every mother has to take care of her family.

When Rhoda removed her touch, relief and regret warred in Clara.

"You were a good mother to me when I was young," Clara said.

"Did you think I stopped being a good mother?" Rhoda ran her hands down the front of her apron.

Clara let out her breath slowly as fragments of the last few months tumbled against each other in her mind. The times Rhoda politely said, "No thank you" or "Don't bother." The times Rhoda redirected her children away from their older sister. The rows of celery growing in the garden as if Rhoda were pushing Clara toward marriage whether or not she was ready. Weeks and weeks of feeling shunned in the home that had been hers before it was Rhoda's.

"I know you've found me hard," Rhoda said, "but it was for your own good."

These were the sort of words Yonnie would say, or the Yoder ministers. Shunning is for the person's good, to draw that person back to the church. But Clara had never left the church or her family.

Clara looked at the list in her hand. "Thank you for this. They are good suggestions."

"Your father and I are pleased with your choice of Andrew Raber."

Pleased or relieved? Clara wondered. If Rhoda thought Clara should marry and run her own household, did it matter who the groom was?

"We have much to do," Rhoda said.

Clara swallowed. Whatever Rhoda's motivations, she wanted to help and Clara needed help. Her wedding was just three weeks away.

"Hannah and Mari are very excited." Rhoda dampened a rag and wiped off the table.

"Sadie is, too." The words slipped past Clara's usual censors.

Rhoda turned to wring out the rag and hang it over the edge of the sink.

Clara pushed forward. "Hannah and Sadie have always wanted to meet each other. A day of celebration is the perfect time."

"Yes." Rhoda lifted the towel draped over a bowl of rising bread dough that had grown into a great white bubble.

"It will be all right," Clara said. "They're little girls with normal curiosity. Why should we teach them to fear or judge each other?"

"You're right," Rhoda said. "A wedding is a new beginning."

Clara's eyes sought Rhoda's, and they looked into each other. Clara saw uncertainty behind Rhoda's smile, but it was a sincere uncertainty. Rhoda's outward ways may have befuddled Clara — even wounded her — but the heart that had embraced a motherless child still lay within. Grief and gladness mingled in the smile Clara gave in return as she prayed for grace in this moment.

"I have something more than a list and celery," Rhoda said. "Come with me."

Clara followed Rhoda into her bedroom, where she opened the cedar chest at the foot of the bed and lifted a package wrapped in brown paper and tied in string.

"What is it?" Clara's curiosity was genuine. It looked like a bundle from the mercantile in Springs.

"Open it."

Clara laid the thick square package on the bed and pulled away the string. When she folded back the paper, a vibrant, piercing, rich purple burst out.

Clara gasped and plunged a hand into the folds. Smooth and soft, the fabric was perfectly dyed. The cotton may have come from the mercantile, but the color had not.

"You dyed this for me?" Clara said.

Rhoda nodded. "You always said you wanted to wear purple at your wedding."

"I still do."

"There's enough for three dresses."

"Mine and Fannie's and Sarah's."

"Actually," Rhoda said, "if we cut carefully, I think we can get two more dresses — smaller ones."

Clara looked up. "Sadie and Hannah."

"They won't be attendants, of course, but they'll think it's great fun to match your dress."

Clara drew in breath drenched in grace.

CHAPTER 43

Just because it was tradition did not mean Clara was obligated to be pleased.

She could have stayed home, in a room warmed by fire, while the rest of her family went to church. Instead she had chosen to ride with them to the Summit Mills Meetinghouse, where instead of going inside the building she transferred to Andrew's buggy — which would soon be her buggy as well — and wrapped herself in quilts to sit on the bench and stare at the meetinghouse.

From her chilly post in the line of look-alike buggies, Clara heard the hymns, slow and somber. The stolid, unchanging tempo was a reminder that although Clara felt in a hurry, no one in the meetinghouse would rush. The sermons and prayers were long stretches when no sound from the church service reached her ears. Instead, Clara listened to doves cooing and squirrels rustling through leafless trees and *English* automobile engines chugging past on the road beyond the clearing.

Clara supposed she would have to stop thinking of automobiles as belonging to the *English* if she was going to marry a man who owned one.

And that, after all, was the reason she was sitting outside rather than on the women's side of the congregation sneaking glances at Andrew across the aisle.

Today, at the end of the service, Mose would publish the news of their engagement. Tradition dictated that the bride-to-be not be present when this happened. The date would be announced for December 28, and Hiram would invite the congregation to attend the wedding.

A hymn started. *This should be the final hymn,* Clara reasoned, and then the various announcements would begin. She sat up straight and let a quilt fall away.

The door the men used to go in and out of the meetinghouse opened, and Andrew stepped out. Clara dropped out of the buggy.

"They're still singing," she said when Andrew reached her. "You'll miss the banns."

He took her hand and pulled. "You have to come inside."

519

"But the banns —"

"That's not the only announcement Mose is going to make. I think you'll want to hear with your own ears."

They paced back toward the meeting-house. Clara had sat outside all this time — nearly three hours — only to be present for her own engagement announcement after all.

"What's going on?" she said.

"I wish you had heard Mose's sermon," Andrew said. "When he said he had one further announcement to make at the close of the service, I knew you would want to be inside for it."

They reached the doors. Andrew kissed her cheek and left her at the women's door. When Clara saw him slip back into the service, she did the same. She found a corner in the back, though. Behind the last row, Wanda Eicher swayed with a child on her hip. Otherwise all eyes were fixed on Mose Beachy as he stood to speak again.

"I have the pleasure," he said, "of publishing the engagement of Clara Kuhn and Andrew Raber. The couple requests that we remember them in prayer, so we will want to do so."

Mose gestured to Hiram, who stood. "Rhoda and I invite the congregation to attend our daughter's wedding on December 28 at the Flag Run Meetinghouse."

Standing in the back, Clara saw heads tilt toward nearby worshippers and heard indistinguishable whispers buzzing like gossiping bees. It happened after every engagement was published. Some claimed to have suspected, while others were surprised at the particular pairing. Smiles broke out at the happy news.

Although Clara had whispered this way many times, it was an odd sensation to watch the reaction to her own engagement. Most brides did not have this view. Wanda caught her eye and smiled. Later, Clara knew, Wanda would pry details out of Clara — when had they decided to marry; why had they waited until the end of the season; had she known she would accept Andrew's proposal? Clara had heard countless versions of these questions over the years as she watched her friends marry. Now it would be her turn to answer them.

Mose Beachy cleared his throat, and the congregation settled.

"You have heard me preach this morning that the heart of God is love," he said, one hand on the closed Bible that sat on the preaching table. "My hope is that our congregation will continue to live in the heart of God and know His love for us and in turn offer God's love to those around us.

"After searching the Scriptures for a greater understanding of certain matters, and after consulting with the wisdom of bishops who lead other congregations, my decision is that we will no longer observe *meidung* toward our brothers and sisters who leave us to worship in another church."

The congregation sucked in a collective breath.

"I have confidence that this is the will of God for us," Mose continued. "On other matters, we will continue to discern God's will. When we discuss matters of modern convenience, we will seek to understand the blessings God may have in mind for us as well as the need to protect our community from falling into idolatry. Some of you also raise the question of a Sunday school for our children. We will continue to discuss whether it is appropriate for our young ones to learn the Word of God in this way. Whether or not we choose to organize a Sunday school, we will no longer consider our Marylander brethren as having transgressed because they have chosen this path.

"I will meet with gladness the opportunity to speak to any of you privately on these matters. For now, let us share our meal and our hearts with one another in true Christian fellowship."

Clara's gaze moved to Noah and Joseph Yoder, seated in front facing the congregation and scowling. Had they known Mose intended to make this announcement? Had they tried to dissuade him?

It did not matter. Mose had spoken, and his words rolled weight off shoulders up and down the benches. If the physical reactions Clara saw were any indication, most people welcomed both his removal of the *meidung* and his invitation to conversation.

Clara wished she had heard Mose's sermon. *The heart of God is love.*

The men began to file out. Clara slipped out the women's door and stood in the clearing to wait for Andrew. His automobile, her stories — in God's time there might yet be a place for them in their own church.

Andrew came and stood beside Clara, taking her hand in his while they received congratulations. She was glad to be marrying Andrew on the brink of a new season in the church. She was grateful to begin their life together by responding to a call to the heart of God. She squeezed Andrew's hand.

EPILOGUE

June 26, 1927

The crash that came from the upstairs bedroom made Clara blow out her breath and roll her eyes.

"Would you like me to go up?" Andrew raised both eyebrows.

"No," Clara said. "You'd better see how Little Mose is doing with the horse. I'm still not convinced he's strong enough to handle the hitch on his own."

"We have to let him try." Andrew took his black felt hat from the hook beside the back door and put it on his head. "One of these days he'll do it."

"He's only seven, Andrew. Were you hitching up the family buggy when you were seven?"

"I could let him try his hand at cranking the Model T instead." Andrew's eyes twinkled.

Clara smiled. The Model T had provided

a steady flow of fond memories over the years, and Andrew had proven himself a worthy mechanic in keeping it running as it aged. He even worked a few hours each week for Jurgen Hansen, whose garage had nearly doubled in business since Andrew first approached him for help.

"I don't think he's strong enough for that, either," Clara said. "Besides, we agreed long ago not to use the automobile for driving to church."

He kissed her cheek as another crash echoed through the house. "What could those girls be doing up there?"

"Oh, let's see," Clara mused. "Katie is sprawled on the bed without having brushed her hair because she's reading one of those *English* storybooks you brought home."

"You're the one who taught her to recognize a good story by keeping a scrapbook."

Clara ignored him. "And Rachel and Rebecca are quarreling over whose turn it is to stand on the stool to clean their teeth."

"Rachel will be pointing out that she's nearly a year older and Rebecca should respect her elders."

"And Rebecca will answer that Rachel takes too long on purpose and selfishness is a sin."

"So they've knocked each other off the

stool twice already."

"And Katie will claim she did nothing about it because she didn't hear anything." Andrew put a hand at the back of Clara's neck and leaned down to kiss her lips this time, letting his hat tumble to the floor.

He tasted of breakfast scrapple and blueberry jam, as he did every Sunday morning, and she welcomed the lingering kiss. Ten and a half years and four children later, she would not trade away a single day of their marriage. Now if only she could master getting four children ready for church on time.

She pulled back. "Let's not get distracted."

"It's not too late to change your mind about taking the Model T," Andrew said.

Clara slapped his shoulder. "Go make sure your only son hasn't injured himself." She had three sets of braids to tie and pin. Hopefully she would find a clean *kapp* for each of the girls. At the third crash, Clara pushed Andrew out the back door with the thought that he had the easier job. Perhaps it would be worth her while to teach him to braid. After all, her father had learned when he had no wife in the house.

Clara scurried up the back stairs of the rambling house. Despite her light step, the girls heard her coming and scrambled around to position themselves as beyond fault. Three-quarters of the way up the stairwell, Clara slowed to give her daughters time to put things right. She had no desire to catch them in the act of their transgressions. Daily life offered ample opportunity for that. Today she simply wanted to get them out the door looking suitably assembled. By the time she turned the corner into the upstairs hall, Katie was brushing her blond hair and Rachel and Rebecca were demonstrating admirable cooperation. Clara picked up a brush and began running it through the nearest head of brown hair. With the practice of tending to the girls' hair every day, she could very nearly braid with one hand now, the fingers of the other ready with pins.

Twenty minutes later, the Raber family was in the same buggy Andrew had used to drive her home from Singings or to meet her out under the night sky at the edge of her father's farm. They were about to outgrow this buggy, though Andrew did not know that yet. Clara would tell him soon about the new babe, but not in the midst of daily chaos. She would find an evening when the children were in bed and invite Andrew to stand in the yard and admire the handiwork of God the way they used to.

They rumbled out of the farmstead and

turned south toward the Flag Run Meeting-house in Niverton, a destination that brought some relief to Clara. On the Sundays when the congregation met in Summit Mills, the Rabers were challenged to get out of the house early enough to accomplish the additional distance in a timely way. Flag Run was comfortably close. No matter which meetinghouse the congregation used, lately Little Mose had been nagging to be allowed to sit with his father on the men's side of the aisle. Soon Clara would have to let him, though it pained her to think that her little boy was old enough for this.

A buggy rattled toward them, heading north.

"Who's that?" Clara said.

Beside her, Katie leaned forward in serious examination. "Yoders," she pronounced.

"Be kind," Clara said.

"All I said was that it was Yoders," Katie said. "I recognize the horse from school."

Behind his parents, Little Mose scrambled for a look, waving his hand fiercely. The other buggy passed them without greeting.

"They didn't wave back!" Little Mose said. "That's rude, isn't it, *Mamm*?"

Clara turned her head to look down the road. It did seem inhospitable, but a larger question loomed. "Where do you think they're going?" she murmured to Andrew.

He shrugged. "Bishop Beachy's announcement two weeks ago was more than clear. He wanted to be sure we are sufficiently accommodating the families who live south of Flag Run."

"What if they weren't there?" Clara said.

"They were," Katie said. "Ezra Yoder threw a lima bean at the back of my head during lunch. I remember."

Clara glanced at her daughter, who was four months past nine. While Katie liked to hear stories and was learning to read for herself, she had never been one to make them up. If she said Ezra Yoder's family had been in church, Clara believed her.

"I'm hungry," Rebecca said.

Though the child had eaten breakfast, Clara was prepared and handed her youngest a piece of strudel. It was better to permit a snack on the way to church than endure the mood that would ensue during the three-hour service if Rebecca grew hungry before the midday meal.

"There's another wagon." Little Mose leaned over Clara's shoulder and pointed. Enthused, he began waving again.

This time Andrew lifted his hand in greeting as well and even slowed the horse. "We'll find out what's going on."

But the rhythm of the oncoming buggy did not falter.

"The Troyers," Clara murmured.

"Yoders and Troyers," Andrew said, glancing at her. "The Troyers live just on the other side of Niverton. They would have driven right past the meetinghouse."

"Why aren't they coming to church?" Katie asked.

"We don't know," Andrew said, "and we will not speculate."

"What does *speculate* mean?" Little Mose asked.

"It means guessing when we don't know the answer," Andrew said. "And we're not going to do it. That's how rumors get started."

When the Raber buggy approached the Flag Run Meetinghouse, Clara scanned the buggies and horses. Andrew parked, and they assisted the children out of the buggy.

"Those two families are not the only ones missing," Clara said softly to Andrew.

Hannah and Mari waved at Clara from across the clearing and made their way toward her. Tall and sure of herself, Hannah was past sixteen now — closer to seventeen. She had been going to Singings for a year. Josiah attended as well. If the next ten years passed as quickly as the last ten, Clara would be as reluctant to admit that her own daughter had become a young woman as she was to recognize this truth about her sister.

At thirteen, Mari's interest was simply to collect her nieces and nephew before turning back toward the meetinghouse. Hannah lingered.

"You probably heard," Hannah said.

"Heard what?" Clara reached into the buggy for the loaves of bread she had baked for the meal later.

Hannah gestured toward the diminished row of buggies. "Where everyone is."

"We heard nothing," Andrew said.

"They're at Summit Mills," Hannah said. "The Yoder ministers are meeting there."

"But Mose Beachy announced Flag Run," Clara said.

"I know. But one of the Yoders came by two days ago and told *Daed* they would be at Summit Mills and he should join them."

Clara's breath drew in quickly. "What did *Daed* say?"

"That they misread him," Hannah said. "He would having nothing to do with disrespecting Bishop Beachy."

"Of course he wouldn't," Clara said.

Andrew unhitched the horse and gave it freedom to nuzzle the ground and swish its tail for the next few hours. Clara caught his eye.

"We'll talk to him," Andrew said.

Hannah fell into step with Clara.

"Does everyone know about the other church service?" Clara said.

"They only talked to *Daed* because they thought he might come with them." Hannah tilted her head to one side. "You should have heard him telling them how the time was long overdue to make things right. I didn't understand what he meant."

"It's a long story," Clara said.

"I guess the Old Order and the Beachy Amish won't be together anymore," Hannah said.

"Beachy Amish?" Andrew cocked his head.

"We'll have to call ourselves something, won't we?"

Clara looked into her sister's face, wondering when she had grown so perceptive.

"I'd better go find my *mamm,*" Hannah said. "Are you going to sit with us today?"

Clara nodded. "If you can stand to have my wiggly little ones take turns in your lap."

"I'll save you a place." Hannah slipped into the building.

Clara turned to Andrew before he would

leave to take his place among the men lining up.

"This is not what you and I wanted," she said. "We hoped for change, but not this. Not two churches. Mose has always preached unity and peace. Now the Yoders are leading a split?"

Andrew breathed in long and slow through his nose. "They will say *Gottes wille.*"

"Is it?" Clara challenged. "Is it God's will for the congregation to divide after so many have worked to keep it together?"

"God's ways are not our ways," Andrew said. "God is our peace. Mose will want us to affirm that above all else. It takes a century for God to make a sturdy oak."

He squeezed her hand and left her then.

Clara turned in a slow circle that allowed her to take in the entire clearing where the meetinghouse had stood for decades. The fallen log she had loved to climb on when she was as young as her children were now had long ago rotted at the center and been cleared away. Two others had been felled in its place and hosted her children's play on Sunday afternoons. Rather than going inside, Clara now paced to the log and sat.

Beachy Amish. Mose was certain to dislike the appellation, wanting neither credit nor blame for the division that seemed inevitable.

Clara placed a hand over her thickening womb.

Perhaps this child would know a church of unity.

Perhaps this child would know the church received her gifts, whatever they were.

Perhaps this child would know peace.

Clara prayed it would be so.

AUTHOR'S NOTE

This Amish Turns of Time series brings to life turning points in Amish history. For this story, my research turned up interesting tidbits, such as writings and Bible interpretation that undergirded the position represented by the Yoder ministers, as well as information about Moses Beachy's cautious leadership toward change that seemed inevitable.

I have taken some liberties with the time frame. While the prologue, set in 1895, and the epilogue, set in 1927, rise from historical events that mark turning points in the prolonged controversy at the heart of the story, I condensed Moses Beachy's leadership. My hope was to faithfully represent his heart for peace and unity in the congregation, while showing the arc of his leadership within a few months rather than the eleven years between his becoming bishop and announcing the end of shunning those who left to join another church. I also took some license with the circumstances of age and illness that led to Bishop Yoder's resignation.

Most of my characters are fictitious, though some are based on true people. John Stutzman is based on a man named John Yoder, who in the early 1920s refused to shun. By this time, Mose Beachy was being less cautious, and his statement that he would not put John Yoder under the ban caused increased friction with his fellow ministers, Joseph and Noah Yoder. Within months, the Yoder brothers did what Beachy had resisted doing for years and led a break-off group. Since he never intended to lead a split, Beachy was not fond of having the branch bear his name. Within two years, the Beachy Amish allowed automobiles, electricity, and telephones, decisions that distinguished them from the Old Order Amish who, even nearly a century later, remain far more selective in adopting modern technology.

The Old Order and the Beachy Amish continued to share the meetinghouses in Flag Run and Summit Mills on alternate Sundays until 1953, when the Beachy Amish constructed a more modern building.

ACKNOWLEDGMENTS

I am grateful for Annie Tipton at the Shiloh Run imprint of Barbour Publishing for receiving my original proposal for this series positively and shepherding it through to publication. JoAnne Simmons, coming alongside me in the details of the manuscript, is incredibly smooth to work with. My agent, Rachelle Gardner, rallies to the sometimes obscure things I like to write about. I was especially enthused about writing Amish stories firmly rooted in historical events, and having companions on the journey made it that much easier.

In the writing of this book, I was especially grateful for people I've never met but who have taken great care to preserve pieces of Amish history and make them available for me to find easily in the age of the Internet. *The Historian,* a publication of the Casselman River Area Amish and Mennonite Historians out of Grantsville, Maryland, yielded several rich, specific articles: "History of the Amish Mennonites in the Forks of Garrett County, Maryland" (October 2001) and "Church History in the Summit Mills Area" (January 1998), both by David I. Miller, and "The Preachers' Tables" by Joanna Miller (January 2004). The September 1986 issue of *Mennonite Life* gave me "Memories of an Amish Childhood — Interviews with Alvin J. Beachy" by Robert S. Kreider. Alvin was the son of Bishop Moses Beachy and his wife, Lucy.

The Small Archives Collections of the Mennonite Church in Goshen, Indiana, turned up an interview with Henry Yoder from June 2000 (transcribed by Dennis Stoesz) recounting his understanding of the events that led to the split between the Old Order and Beachy Amish. Henry was the grandson of Moses and Caroline Yoder.

ABOUT THE AUTHOR

Olivia Newport's novels twist through time to find where faith and passions meet. Her husband and two twentysomething children provide welcome distraction from the people stomping through her head on their way into her books. She chases joy in stunning Colorado at the foot of the Rockies, where daylilies grow as tall as she is.

The employees of Thorndike Press hope you have enjoyed this Large Print book. All our Thorndike, Wheeler, and Kennebec Large Print titles are designed for easy reading, and all our books are made to last. Other Thorndike Press Large Print books are available at your library, through selected bookstores, or directly from us.

For information about titles, please call:
  (800) 223-1244

or visit our Web site at:
  http://gale.cengage.com/thorndike

To share your comments, please write:
Publisher
Thorndike Press
10 Water St., Suite 310
Waterville, ME 04901